# ROOSEVELT
# THE STORY OF A FRIENDSHIP

# THE WRITINGS OF OWEN WISTER

THEODORE ROOSEVELT IN RIDING COSTUME

From the painting by P. Laszlo in the living room at Sagamore Hill

OWEN WISTER

# ROOSEVELT

## THE STORY OF A
## FRIENDSHIP

1880 - 1919

NEW YORK

THE MACMILLAN COMPANY
MCMXXX

# ILLUSTRATIONS

## PROLOGUE: TO EDITH CAROW ROOSEVELT

Here is your book; a page of old acquaintance; Harvard, as he and I knew it, Boston, as it used to be; by-gone events that stirred us all in their day; much of my by-gone self, and all that I saw and thought of him you wedded. Bricks need straw, two must go to make a friendship; I am the straw here. You will be reminded of friends who, like those quiet dead in the play, will wake and be themselves again while your thoughts visit them. But he you oftenest think of sits every day alive among the immortally remembered.

1

# I.

When you become a freshman, you become pretty nearly nobody. It is a long drop from the exalted state of the last year at your preparatory school. There, as you passed by, you heard your name on the lips of little boys saying to boys still smaller and newer:

"That is so-and-so. Strokes the first crew Halcyon;" or, "Half-back on the Old Hundred." But now as you pass by not a whisper is raised, your glory is departed, your turn at the bottom of the ladder is come again as it came in your first year at school, and you wander about obscurely and anonymously.

I wandered so in Harvard during the Autumn of 1878. I had never been anything so great as half-back or stroke, but I had supposed myself to be something; here I knew that I was nothing; and here to me at the bottom of the ladder, the names of those at the top, upper-class men, juniors and seniors, the great ones, began to grow familiar before ever I had seen their faces. Their fame was in the air. There was Foxy Bancroft. He was captain of the crew. He had beaten Yale. In those days Harvard used to beat Yale. And there was Stowe. And Nat Brigham. Another giant. On the Glee Club, too. Had a tenor voice. You ought to hear him sing "In the sunny Rhineland." And there was Bob Bacon. An oarsman, and the best looking man in Harvard. His brother Billy was better looking still. Class of '77, you know. I nodded my head. I didn't know in the least. I came from Philadelphia. And then there was Teddy Roosevelt. He was '80. Same class as Bob Bacon. There he goes now. See him? That fellow with whiskers and glasses. But I missed him.

3

## II.

Shortly before I was nineteen, and shortly before Theodore Roosevelt was twenty-one, I had my first sight of him. He was in vigorous action. What he did, proved to be so true an illustration of the boy being father of the man, that twenty-two years later, on September 14, 1901, when I was called upon at a moment's notice by the editor of *The Saturday Evening Post* to dictate something about our recent Vice President, who had suddenly become President in Buffalo, I cast about how best to begin. That first vision of him rose in memory, and made the beginning for me.

It was in the old gymnasium that used to rise like a gas tank from the pie-slice of ground between three streets on the yard side of Memorial Hall. The Harvard Athletic Association was holding its spring meeting. Roosevelt, '80, was entered for the light weight sparring at 135 pounds. Up in the gallery to watch him was a group of his Boston friends, Saltonstalls, Lees, Alice Lee, whom he was to marry not long after his graduation: pretty girls in nice furs, with their best young men. Through Papanti's Dancing Class I had already met some of them; I had begun to find my way about Harvard and Boston, and was no longer quite the lost dog I had been six months before.

The bout between Roosevelt and W. W. Coolidge, '79, at 133¼ pounds, was won by Roosevelt, who, according to the *Harvard Advocate* of March 28, "displayed more coolness and skill than his opponent." Ladies' hands applauded delicately from the gallery, and we freshmen looked on from the inconspicuous floor.

But this did not give Roosevelt the championship. Mr. C. S. Hanks, '79, entered at 133½ pounds, had won the first bout over his antagonist, and was consequently paired with Roosevelt for the final bout. *The Harvard Advocate* has to say of this . . . "a spirited contest followed, in which Mr. Hanks succeeded in getting the best of his opponent by his quickness and power of endurance." But we freshmen on the floor and those girls in the gallery witnessed more than a spirited contest; owing to an innocent mistake of Mr. Hanks, we saw that prophetic flash of The Roosevelt that was to come.

Time was called on a round, Roosevelt dropped his guard, and Hanks landed a heavy blow on his nose, which spurted blood. Loud hoots and hisses from gallery and floor were set up, whereat Roosevelt's arm was instantly flung out to command silence, while his alert and slender figure stood quiet.

"It's all right," he assured us eagerly, his arm still in the air to hold the silence; then, pointing to the time-keeper, "he didn't hear him," he explained, in the same conversational but arresting tone. With bleeding nose he walked up to Hanks and shook hands with him.

That was March 22, 1879, when he was twenty, and of slight build. Not many who were there to see are here to remember the boy as he looked that day in the old Harvard gymnasium; but will not many who came to know the man at forty or fifty, heavy in build, and much changed in aspect, recognize him completely in that spontaneous outbreak? In 1912, he is shot close to the heart on his way to make a speech, nobody can stop him, he speaks for an hour and a half, and then goes to the doctors. In 1913, he wins a libel suit for ten thousand dollars against an editor who had published the favorite falsehood about his drinking. He waives the damages. Defendant in a libel suit brought by a political enemy during the Great War, and with a jury containing Germans, he denounces the sinking of the *Lusitania* which happened during the trial, regardless of how this may affect the verdict. At the Convention of 1912, approached by the emissary of thirty disgusted Taft delegates with an offer that would put the Republican nomination in the hollow of his hand, he sends the emissary back, explosively. "This is a crooked convention," he exclaims, "and I don't touch it with a forty rod pole." In 1917, upon our entering the Great War, he offers to raise a division himself, and go over to fight. Cannot many who knew the man, match these instances with a score of others?

"A strange figure for our time," said a distinguished French-man to me in 1929; "an apparition from other days; chival-rous; of the crusades; simple in spirit; yet with a note of the modern."

It is still said that he was spectacular and sought the lime-light. He was his own limelight, and could not help it: a crea-ture charged with such a voltage as his, became the central presence at once, whether he stepped on a platform or entered a room — and in a room the other presences were likely to feel crowded, and sometimes displeased.

Did he perceive this at Harvard? Certainly he knew it later. During those years when his dangerous doctrines of initiative, referendum, and recall, had very naturally estranged and an-tagonized many of his friends and followers, and before the splendor of his patriotism between 1915 and 1918 had won their hearts back to him, he said to me one day:

"When I walked in to the meeting of the Harvard Overseers last Monday, I felt like a bull-dog who had strayed into a sym-posium of perfectly clean—white—Persian—cats."

Some of the very finest cats never grew to like him. The cause lay deeper than politics. Indeed, they knew well enough that though he had sometimes upset the stock market, he had made stable the true value of their property — had probably warded off a social revolution. What they could not forgive were his free and easy departures from the code of their college-bred, colonial order, which was chill and genteel, especially in New England. He was one of them, but he would not behave like one.

"What an inveterate actor he is!" said a Beacon Street cat to me, after an Overseers meeting. "Did you see him pretending he couldn't remember the name of the proposed degree, and how he whirled round to you to prompt him?"

When Harvard gave him his LL.D. in June, 1902, Woodbury Kane and I, deputy marshals on that Commencement, were de-tailed to be Roosevelt's special escort. Kane had distinguished himself as Captain in The Rough Riders. While we were fol-

lowing the President from some function to some other, I said
to Kane:

"When we were in college, you didn't used to like him much.
How do you feel now?"

And Kane replied:

"If he and I were crossing Brooklyn Bridge and he ordered
me to jump over, I'd do it without asking why."

"What are you fellows dangling behind for?" said the President.  "Come alongside."  He made a peremptory motion, and
as we ran forward, I had time to murmur:

"Unconditional surrender?"

"Absolutely, old man."

Kane was sparing of words, more sparing of praise, his talk
was chiefly trifling banter, and this sweeping phrase about the
Brooklyn Bridge, so utterly uncharacteristic of him, meant a
revolution in him regarding Theodore Roosevelt.  No association with Roosevelt in time of peace, nothing short of war, no
experience milder than sweat, blood, grime, discipline, and gun
powder, could have so revoked Kane's college distaste for
Roosevelt.

Kane was born ironic and fastidious, alive to all the infirmities
of democracy.  The serious part of his character was buried
deep and seldom brought into play; he mostly neglected his
better self.  He was light in touch, bored by boisterous, eager,
enthusiastic people with a purpose, unwilling to read books,
seldom willing to scrawl a letter.  His personal charm was the
greatest I have known in any man — it was so pervasive that
even his silence was agreeable; it was in his voice, his looks, his
manner, in the easy grace with which he wore anything from a
football sweater to a white waistcoat: many men at college had
clothes as good as his, but he was always better dressed than
anybody.  Through sheer indifference he tolerated many
people, but liked very few, and Roosevelt had not been one of
these.  He frequented yachts, Newport, and the Knickerbocker
Club.  Yet this child of sophistication, when war stripped his
character to the bone, proved of the tempered steel, fought with

the same natural ease that he dressed; and in his brief gallant adventure as Captain of the Rough Riders, his college prejudice gave way and he capitulated totally to the great qualities of his Colonel.

Upon this Harvard Commencement, twenty years after our own, we talked it all over, late into the night and early into the morning—everything: our Beck Hall spread on Class Day; Mrs. Jack Gardner and the other smart folks of Boston, New York, and Philadelphia, who had been there to drink our champagne and bid us Godspeed. We talked of the Dickey theatricals, the Pudding theatricals, the Club, freshman year—and of that sparring match between Hanks and Roosevelt in the old gymnasium; the bloody nose, the hoots and hisses, the instant gesture, and the instant righting of the wrong that was being done to his adversary. . . .

Seventeen years passed: The Presidency, the Northern Securities, The Coal Strike Commission, the Panama Canal, the African journey, the South American journey, the libel suits, the Milwaukee shooting, the Bull Moose party, the Great War: all gone into yesterday's eternal silence. Woodbury Kane was long dead; and one January morning came the news that never again were we to see the face of Roosevelt or hear his voice. And the next morning came a cartoon, a great cartoon. Once again, and for ever, it was that Roosevelt of the Harvard gymnasium. He is in cowboy dress, on his horse headed for the Great Divide; but he is turning back for a last look at us, smiling, waving his hat. On his horse: the figure from other days; the Apparition, the crusader, bidding us farewell.

### III.

The next time I saw him, I had become a sophomore. It was in October, 1879, and in my own room. Even so, I did not meet him.

The "games" were being conducted in my room. These made part in a tortured week preliminary to one's initiation into the

ROOSEVELT, THE HARVARD SENIOR, 1880

Dickey. The Dickey in 1879 was a survival of an earlier, younger Harvard. It was a secret body within a larger, more respectable society, the Institute of 1770. Some fifty out of each class were elected in batches of ten. About May, each sophomore class would choose ten freshmen to carry on, and these, when college re-opened in September, carried on by electing a second ten; those twenty chose a third ten, and so on. By the end of October, the number of the elect was usually complete, and the gates of hope closed.

It was a time of suspense, wondering, whispering, yearning. On election nights, many a sophomore lay sleepless in his dark bed, listening. Was that roving midnight chorus, whose progress he could mark in the distance, going to approach and stop beneath his window with its jaunty serenade announcing he was "in," and so send thrills of triumph and joy through his young body, or was he destined only to hear it wander and pause beneath luckier windows, and die away? To be left out of the Dickey meant that your social future at Harvard was likely to be in the back seats. What could be more alien to democratic theory? What more inevitable in human life? Injustice was done; yet, looking back over the fifty years since, it is astonishing that more injustice was not done. Some wrong ones we took in, some right ones we left out—but not many of either sort.

The week of bedevilment following the happy serenade bore its analogy to the practice of hazing elsewhere. You had a mentor. You had a book. The mentor guided and advised you to a certain extent. He was often some intimate friend who had become a member of the Dickey ahead of you. You were given by somebody, or various somebodies piling it on at their whim, a name, a string of epithets and sentences, which you must fluently recite whenever ordered to do so by any member of the Dickey. According to the imagination and taste of those who had devised this name for you, it descended from the level of sheer fantastic nonsense and frank satire about your character, to very rough stuff.

Here Roosevelt appears for a moment, not in connection with me, but with my classmate and lifelong friend, Frederick Mather Stone. Stone had been chosen one of the glorious first ten from our class, and during his week of running for the Dickey, he ran upon Roosevelt, who demanded his name. It was particularly filthy.

"You don't want to say all that nastiness?" inquired Roosevelt.

Stone did not.

"Very well. The next man that asks for your name, Stone, you answer 'Rocks, by God.' That's name enough. Tell him I said so."

Roosevelt's mind was a great deal cleaner than the modern lip-stick girl's.

When in later years Stone came to marry a lady for whom Roosevelt had a warm regard, he said to her:

"Susy, who is this man Stone?"

"Rocks, by God," she replied at once; and by that word he knew that Stone was good enough for her. And "Rocks" proved a baptism for life. Roosevelt the Junior fixed it on Stone the freshman, because he hated witless indecency, which most of us did not; and while most of us often swore, he swore very rarely, then, or at any time in his life.

I have said that at the beginning of our bedeviled week we were given a mentor, a name, and a book. It was in this book that were written down all the services we were to perform for the benefit or entertainment of those above us, for instance: Call Mr. Woodbury Kane at 7.30 every morning with *Boston Daily Advertiser,* and bottle of soda. Wake Mr. W. Y. Peters every morning at 7.35 with Ethiopian song and dance. Wear your coat backside before and use a yellow shoe-string for a necktie. If any one asks you what it is, reply "Chest protector, you dam' fool."

And so forth and so forth. Hence our quaint figures were to be seen dashing between Beck Hall and Holworthy, and all over the yard, upon our errands in the early morning, with eyes nervously averted from any acquaintance we happened to meet. But if we unknowingly met any member of the Dickey and failed to touch our hats to him, he might very well stop us, inquire the reason for our unpardonable lapse, and punish it with a Black Mark inscribed in our little book. Ten of these (or was it eight?) condemned us to a second week of running.

Sometimes an upper classman who had given you a Black Mark showed mercy. As I hurried up the stairs of Weld one morning to wake somebody, a man coming down stopped me.

"You have omitted to touch your hat. Why is this?" He was smiling pleasantly.

"I—I didn't know you, sir."

"You don't know my name?"

"No sir, I'm afraid I don't."

"Hadn't you better take a Black Mark?"

"Yes sir." And I began lugubriously to write it down.

"How many have you?"

"Six, sir. This makes seven."

He smiled more delightfully than ever. "In that case you can take it off. My name is Richard Sprague. Be sure to know me next time." And he went his way down stairs. I began to love him that moment. A great many besides me loved Dick Sprague, '81. And just as these acts of mercy in hours of stress couldn't die from our gratitude, so acts of needless oppression lived in our resentment—live still. Running for the Dickey left black marks and white marks indelible in our memory.

Our nights of running were consecrated to the games, when for the space of an hour or two we had to be the sport of the upper classmen. They put us through whatever feats of nonsense mental or physical came into their fantastic heads, and it was to my room that Roosevelt came with some other seniors on the evening that the games were being held in my room.

"Let nobody commit a nuisance," he immediately said: and I don't think I ever heard him say anything broader; and in comparison to what you might hear at the games, it was very mild indeed.   I forget if he ordered us to perform anything in particular, or if he merely looked on for a while.   But him I remember, and not who the others were who came in with him, though before very long I became acquainted with all seniors who belonged to the Dickey.   That is the point: he stood out.

They all went away pretty soon from our circus, and my tribulations were over on the following Wednesday.   With the rest of my group of neophytes, I passed through the final mysteries and ordeals, and at length stood unblindfolded, blinking, damp, embarrassed, deliriously happy, with friends gripping my hands.

Bless the old merry brutal ribald orgiastic natural wholesome Dickey!   Bless the handful of wild oats we sowed there together so joyously!   What friendships sprang from them! How few it harmed, how many it moulded for their good! What a company of leading citizens all over the land once clinked glasses in those festive rooms!   It opened hearts to each other, its rough and tumble, straight out of the eighteenth century, knit sophomores, juniors, seniors, graduates, into a Harvard texture closer than any modern mechanisms or rotarian methods can compass.   Its day belongs not to these wholesale times of mass production—but I wish I might stop and write a whole chapter about us: our initiation nights, the graveyard, the blindfolding, the river, the corpse, the coffin, the blanket, the branding, the inquisition of Pater Primus, the Awful Sliderias, and our theatricals.   How one December night after a rehearsal of *Ivanhoe,* Isaac of York and Rebecca and Rowena and everybody threw all the scenery out of the old rooms in the mill and watched it sway and plane safely fifty feet to earth and there be caught by the Templars and Saxons of the chorus and hurried through the silent Cambridge streets to our new rooms because the class of '81 had not paid its rent for the previous year and the class of '82 had no intention of assuming this debt, and the landlord would have attached all our chattels had he caught us moving in the daytime.   When next he came to visit his property, he found complete vacancy, and "Good bye from '82" burned into his wall with a gas cigar lighter.

Did Roosevelt attend our *Ivanhoe* just before Christmas, 1879, or did he think he could spend his time better upon his *Naval History of the War of 1812?*    I should hardly have seen him from my seat.    My seat was at the piano, left of stage, with my back mostly to the crowd, and I was a very nervous young sophomore that night.    I hadn't been able to eat any dinner. After the utterly unexpected roar of enthusiasm that burst over the room at the end of our opening chorus of cooks and scullions getting dinner ready for Cedric the Saxon—they made us sing it again; its music was the bell chorus from *Les Cloches de Corneville,* the words were mine:

> Beaf Steak,
> Onions, pickles,
> Black cake,
> Sauce that tickles
> Belly ache,
> Wine that trickles
> Softly down your inside—
> Goose fat,
> Cream and ices,
> All that
> Very nice is,
> For this
> Pleasant crisis
> We've supplied.

After this was encored my anxious nerves felt better.    But still I attended strictly to my business while our wonderful group of singers and actors—Elliot Pendleton, Harry Gillig, Evert Wendell, Gus Tuckerman, Jimmy Bowen, Guy Waring, Clint Edgerly—song upon song and act after act, carried *Ivanhoe* to a success that broke all records and became a legend. We were—though we didn't know it then—lively atoms in the great comic English-speaking tradition of *The Beggar's Opera,* and *Bombastes Furioso,* and *The Critic,* and Fielding, and Shakespeare; Ellis Island had not yet diluted Harvard and imported Broadway into the college-spirit of our shows.    Next day, the fame of *Ivanhoe* was all over Boston, and spread to New York.    We gave it in both cities, together with our mid-winter show, *Der Freischütz,* to the private performance of which in the Dickey rooms Roosevelt came—and was made furious by some lines of mine.

My office covered a good deal.    These burlesques which we picked out from Lacey's *Acting Edition of British Drama* (if that was its right name) contained, besides their dialogue in rhymed couplets full of inexcusable puns, sundry songs and choruses written to melodies in vogue at the time in England, but unknown in America, and out of date in both countries. For these words I had to find tunes up to date and popular, often re-casting the words, often adding lines when those in the text were insufficient for the length of the tune I had selected, and not seldom interpolating musical numbers to give our fine singers more chance.    I trained privately the soloists and the chorus, accompanied the rehearsals and the performances.    For *Freis-chütz* we had fifty-nine rehearsals, total or partial, and sang some Gounod, Rubinstein, and Wagner, besides Sullivan, Offen-bach and Lecoq.    To fit a tune from *La belle Hélène,* I was obliged to extend the words in the text:

> Each lucid ray
> Has gone away,
> And so we'd better part.
> Just like, by Jove,
> The cove who drove
> His doggy Tilbury cart.

Tilbury cart was my clue.    Roosevelt was conspicuous as the only man at Harvard who had a dog cart.    So I continued:

> Awful tart,
> And awful smart,
> With waxed mustache and hair in curls:
> Brand new hat,
> Likewise cravat,
> To call upon the dear little girls.

HASTY PUDDING THEATRICALS—THE LADY OF THE LAKE. OWEN WISTER WITH BANJO

When the curtain fell on the act, the usual riot of cheers and calls arose amid the cigar smoke and the beer. After the third and final curtain, more riot and cheers. All the principals had to come before the curtain and bow, and so did the musical manager. He was not in the least aware that an incensed senior was back there in the noise and smoke. He learned it next morning. Teddy Roosevelt was reported very angry. Said that some personalities were not permissible.

"Who says he said so?"

"Oh, it's got around. He said it was bad taste."

"Waxed mustache and hair in curls bad taste? His mustache isn't waxed. How very sensitive!"

"It's calling on the girls. He's rumored engaged."

"Well he hasn't announced it to the Dickey, has he? He's crazy."

He was not crazy, he was merely in that heady state which overtakes the strenuous lover at times, and has been the subject of some of the best literature; and so he jumped to the conclusion that our quite unconscious hit was deliberate.

He was now half through his senior year, and I half through my sophomore. This was Winter, 1880, in June he would graduate. We had been eighteen months in the same college, twice in the same room, and had not yet exchanged a word. There seemed no particular reason or likelihood that we should ever so much as shake hands; the Harvard world was large, and we lived in different parts of it:—large, I say; but will it seem so when I note that the treasurer of the University Foot Ball Club during my freshman year, Herman S. LeRoy, reported total receipts for that year as amounting to thirteen hundred and ninety dollars, eighty-seven cents, of which the Yale game furnished three hundred and forty dollars and twenty-four cents?

Within a month I was seeing Theodore Roosevelt familiarly. Out of the clear sky I was taken into a Club of less than twenty, among whom I found him. The time I wasted there was better spent than the hours over my books. Whenever we who are of it happen to meet in Vienna, Peking, London, anywhere the wide world over, we convene in its name. Two of us encountered between Richmond and Washington one day in 1863, when one took the other prisoner, and they found out who they were.

"Well," declared the Southerner, "it's the only decent thing in the North."

Almost every day Roosevelt and I met there when he was twenty-one, I nineteen. It was literature in the main, and liking the same things and hating many of the same things, which brought the senior to take cordial notice of the sophomore. He scolded me for my tepid opinion of Longfellow. He knew Longfellow to be a much better poet than it was then—or is now—the fashion to think him. But the sophomore, earlier in his life, had been obliged to commit painfully to memory "The shades of night were falling fast," and "It was the schooner Hesperus"; and he couldn't get over it, his heart was hardened against the man who wrote them. The senior urged him to read the Norse poems, which he did, but remained unconverted for long years after he had ceased to be a sophomore.

Senior and sophomore set small store upon most *literary* literature, perfectly nice, well behaved prose and verse, that read as if Alfred Tennyson or Charles Lamb had been diluted with warm water and stirred round in a tea cup by a teaspoon. But Roosevelt was not ready — never became ready — to go as far the Tom Jones way as I went, even in that day. At his Dakota ranch not long after these college discussions, he read Tolstoi's fiction, fully appreciated its greatness, but disapproved of its author's moral standpoint because he recorded without censuring certain actions of his characters. I had already reached, without definitely formulating them, four convictions: that the whole of life is fiction's field, that nothing is wrong that hurts nobody, that within the ever shifting limits of good taste anything can be told, and that the writer should leave moralizing to the reader.

Roosevelt never had the chance to approve or condemn certain plain talk in my Western tales published in Harper's magazine; this talk never "got by" the blue pencil of my warm friend and backer and greatest editor, Henry Mills Alden, liberal as he was for those genteel times; but it was in consequence of Roosevelt's immediate and unchanged objection to the facts about what Balaam did to Pedro in *The Virginian*, which Mr. Alden had allowed to go into print, that I suppressed the details in the later version of that story, when it became a chapter in the book.

Who were the authors then, what was *Then* like, anyhow, while this senior and sophomore were comparing likes and dislikes, and becoming Teddy and Dan to each other; and the horse cars, the old Cambridge cars, rumbled beneath the window? The bells on the horses tinkled as they went clopping by with the car, they got to Bowdoin Square, Boston, in forty-five minutes, a pair of them in the months of dust and mud, four of them in the months of slush and snow. Straw was strewed thick over the floor of the car during the cold season to keep your feet warm, many citizens spat in the straw, which was seldom changed; who had heard of germs, or Pasteur? You couldn't have your appendix out then, you didn't know the word, you got something they called peritonitis, or inflammation of the bowels, and usually died. The Yale Game had yielded three hundred and forty dollars and twenty-four cents, the presidential election had been stolen from Tilden, Rutherford B. Hayes and his temperance wife Lucy were in the White House. Poor Hayes used to come to Philadelphia, go escorted by a leading lawyer from the train to the Union League Club, and safe inside fling his arm round his escort's shoulder and say, "for God's sake, Patterson, give me a drink!" William M. Evarts said that water flowed like champagne in the White House. He had recently defended the Rev. Henry Ward Beecher, named as co-respondent by a husband in his congregation. Henry James was writing in his early manner; Howells, one timid eye on Mrs. Grundy, was trying to see life steadily and see it whole with the other. You got off the horse car at Charles Street if you were going to dine in good society, you continued to Bowdoin Square if you were going to sup in bad; and until you were a junior you weren't asked to parties. Pinafore had recently blazed its trail of tune and laughter all over our map, pretty and witty comic operas from Paris and Vienna drew crowded houses, not a musical show had yet been concocted by the Broadway Jew for the American moron, clean cut muscular light music hadn't yet rotted into the fleshy pulp of jazz.  You could see Booth in *Hamlet*, Sarah Bernhardt in *Froufrou*, Modjeska in *Camille*, Janauschek in *Bleak House*, Lotta in *The Little Marchioness*, and fall in love with Adelaide Neilson as Imogen and Juliet. Tom-and-Jerry was a drink that went to the right spot during a sleigh ride.  Long John Silver was soon to become our favorite villain, Mulvaney had not yet risen out of India to warm our hearts, the great grey genius of *War and Peace* and *Anna Karenina* had not yet loomed up as the highest peak in fiction. Phillips Brooks was preaching big broad Christianity in Trinity Church, Father Hall was preaching incense in the Church of the Advent, there was no such thing as Massachusetts Avenue, Hereford Street was the very outpost of habitation, genteel travelers put up at the Revere House and the Tremont House; eight separate parochial railroads ran out of Boston from eight different terminal hovels, a ninth was to be added to them soon. The Boston and Albany and the Boston and Providence, with the help of connections, did gradually get you to New York, and produced fair imitations of express trains three or four times a day.  The Old Colony took you to Newport and cranberry bogs on a single track.  The Eastern took you on a single track to Beverly Farms, and there were those who said that both it and the Boston and Maine would deliver you in Portland if you were hardy and patient; but nobody except the Exeter and Andover boys was quite sure about the Boston and Maine, whose cars looked as if Druids patronized them.  The Fitchburg went nowhere in particular, except to Ralph Waldo Emerson, whom I was asked to go and see, and like a young fool did not.  The Boston and Lowell trundled you part way to St. Paul's School, but had to be helped out by a local New Hampshire company; the railroad that started for somewhere from the foot of Summer Street kept changing its name, and was seldom mentioned; and two wild little railroads, the Nashua, Acton, and Boston, and the Boston, Clinton, and Fitchburg, jumped about somewhere in the brush, and never got to Boston by themselves at all.   You could meet Dr. Holmes in Boston Common, if you were lucky; Longfellow came along Brattle Street at times—they called him Old Poems—Memorial Hall stood for the Last Word in architecture, there was no music in *Lohengrin,* except that wedding march; at least five people in Boston said that they understood *Sordello,* at least thirty others said nobody could understand *Sordello,* and that compared with Tennyson, its author couldn't write poetry anyhow.   Student quarrels could still arise hotly over the relative merits of Dickens and Thackeray, Stubby Child taught you Chaucer in curly hair, Soapy Goodwin taught you Greek with a wagging beard, Pa Lane taught you Latin with a merry eye and a sharp tongue, Charles Norton opened the world of letters and beauty for you over good claret, Jimmy Mills Pierce had you to dine on the best food in Cambridge, William James was just beginning.   Over in the chemical room in Boylston Hall, Jopey Cook would tilt an open bottle with a hand shaken by palsy over a half filled test tube, saying: "Gentlemen, if I were to pour two drops from this bottle into the test tube, this building would be instantly reduced to powder.   Gentlemen, I will now pour one drop"— and the stink of it would go right across the hall, where Jakey Paine was analyzing Beethoven's sonatas in Music 3.   I cannot hear the first theme of that early sonata in F minor without the prompt reflex action of bracing my smelling apparatus against phosphuretted hydrogen.   Jakey warned us against Wagner, and a New York critic had spoken of the "Oriental jungle" of *Carmen* (new to us in 1879) while another said he had found "some pretty gypsy music" in it.   Dry monopole, frappé, was delicious on Saturday nights.   Rum and ginger ale was just right for Sunday mornings, shandy gaff quenched thirst at almost any hour, and Chambertin was already among my first and enduring loves.

And all the while, some pleasant doors in Boston, and round

about in Milton, Brookline, and Chestnut Hill, stood open to the sophomore, had opened to him directly he came to Harvard. They that lived in the houses had books, and pictures, and horses, and wine; were gentlefolk, not restless or ostentatious with their riches; hospitable, not mere entertainers; had spent Winters in Rome, crossed the Alps by *diligence,* or in private carriage, heard Rachel at the Théâtre Français, spoke of Grisi and Mario, lost brothers and sons in the Civil War. They had passed through that fiery furnace, had seen slavery ended, Lincoln assassinated; their spirits had been deepened by adversity instead of shallowed by prosperity. English they were by their colonial names, by their decent standards, by their stable characters;—and not one of them had forgiven England for what her spokesmen said and did against our Union when our Union was fighting for its life, and on the edge of losing it.

That was the epoch and that the Boston and Cambridge which surrounded the senior and sophomore while they discussed Longfellow, or *The Ring and the Book,* and the horse cars rumbled beneath the window, and Prexy Eliot like a flagstaff in motion was going after the millions which were to make Harvard College a University.

Our discussions rose, certainly once, to a pitch which brought the door into the next room, where more silent ones were sitting, shut to upon us with a slam of withering emphasis. No doubt about it, Roosevelt, eyeglasses and whiskers and an armful of note-books clamped between elbows and ribs, would enter that atmosphere too breezily, would hold forth too fluently, for the taste of Woodbury Kane and his like. Kane got over it in the Rough Riders, but some of the others, not having the Rough Riders or any such experience to change their minds, did not get over it. The other side of it was, that here was the Roosevelt of twenty-one, perceiving the enthusiasms of a younger man, drawing them out, hospitable to what the younger man had to say, giving the younger man, in short, the full sunshine of his attention, just as he was going to give it all the rest of his life to any enthusiasm, any promise, any achievement in any worthy activity of the human body, mind, or spirit, which he could understand and encourage.

During those months of our first acquaintance, a fit of conscience impelled me to tell him one day that I was the author of those offending lines in *Der Freischütz*. He looked puzzled. I grew embarrassed. So far as I knew, his engagement was not yet announced, and no business of mine. It seemed best just to go on and repeat the lines to him:

> Awful tart
> And awful smart . . .

He had totally forgotten the whole thing, and was much amused at me. Years later, when I was meditating a more important confession, and put the matter to him, he exclaimed:

"Never indulge yourself on the sinner's stool. If you did any harm, that won't undo it, you'll merely rake it up. The sinner's stool is often the only available publicity spot for the otherwise wholly obscure egotist."

## IV.

What happened to me was of little profit to me or anyone until 1885, when my health very fortunately forsook me.

In June, 1882, I had graduated with highest honors in music, and a *summa cum laude* degree. Our class, like all classes then, had been forced to learn stuff that was utterly worthless in Wall Street and little good for turning even a dishonest penny anywhere. The New Youth had not yet asked Higher Education, What did Homer do for Moses, or, How much did Cicero help Jacob to put it over on Esau? Higher Education was satisfied to turn out, year after year, an absurd product known as the college-bred man; a youth whom it had brought face to face with subjects utterly behind the times, such as the age of Pericles, and ancient Rome, and the great intellects of mankind, and the hoarded experience of our race; a type happily obsolete. To-day our education, from top to bottom, makes everything safe for democracy.   Jakey Paine had corrected my canons and fugues, and assured me that I was competent to become a composer of operas and symphonic poems.   This had been the only thing I wanted to do since I had discovered, as a boy at St. Paul's School, that I could make tunes and devise harmonies.   This did not at all appeal to my father, who insisted upon an authoritative European judgment before he would give his consent to such a choice of career.

In Wagner's house at Bayreuth, that first summer of *Parsifal,* I played to Liszt my proudest composition, *Merlin and Vivien.* He jumped up in the middle and stood behind me muttering approval, and now and then he stopped me and put his hands over my shoulders onto the keys, struck a bar or two, and said:

"I should do that here if I were you."

And he wrote his old friend, my grandmother, Fanny Kemble, that I had *"un talent prononcé"* for music.

Following this, I went to Paris.   There, after a winter's study with Ernest Guiraud of the Conservatoire, a monkey wrench was thrown into my aspirations most unwittingly by Major Henry Higginson, himself a thwarted musician in his youth. He told my father that he would like to have me start in the office of Lee, Higginson & Co.   One night in 1883 Guiraud drove all over Paris with me, repeating again and again, *"N'abandonnes pas la musique!"*

I was brought back to State Street.   There, however, business had meanwhile slumped.   Atchison was very sick; Lee Higginson & Co. couldn't take on young men just then; and so, until they could, I went below stairs into the Union Safe Deposit Vaults, pioneer of its kind in America, and sat on a high hard stool computing interest at $2\frac{1}{2}$ per cent on the daily balances of our depositors, and helping to make up the pass books each month.

During this period The Tavern Club was organized by a group of painters, writers, musicians, doctors, and other good company, with Howells as our first president.   Henry Irving was our first guest of honor.   He came to supper after the play

and stayed till six next morning. I sang him a lot of songs, and
went down at nine to my hard high stool at 40 State Street
with quite a head. During this period certain Harvard under-
graduates, sitting where Roosevelt and I had sat as senior and
sophomore, became my intimate playmates. Winthrop Chanler would come at the end of office hours in the Vaults to take
me for a drive. Amos French was another constant playmate.
Our dinners and doings I shall not forget. No friends of my
youth surpassed, and very few others ever equaled, the wit and
humor of that pair of gay seniors, as they had become before the
end of my thirteen months in the Union Safe Deposit Vaults.
During this period also I came to know Howells well.

It was my first novel that began this friendship and led me
to call him mentor in later days. On my disciplinary stool, I
planned the novel, asked my cousin Langdon Mitchell to do
parts of it, and he did them—a very important chapter while
our hero was a boy at a High Church School, and some further
chapters where a painting master was concerned, and the hero's
virtuous and unsuccessful love affair, and part of his virtuous
and successful love affair, leaving him in the arms of the wrong
wife for him, who was certain to understand nothing about
what he cared for most. He was born to be a painter; and his
father and the general American idea forced him into business.
*A Wise Man's Son* was the novel's name. And then, good, kind
Howells read the entire manuscript—a matter of some two hundred thousand words.

"So much young man never seems to have got into a book before," was the opinion that he gave of *A Wise Man's Son;* and
it convinced him that the clerk in the Union Safe Deposit Vaults
could write novels if he chose. The clerk wondered. He had
merely written his own story and put a bitter-sweet ending to it.
Did this necessarily show that he was by nature an author?
Howells had no doubts; he had felt a good many pulses in his
time, he said. And then, after many encouraging words, he
became an adviser to the clerk, who was just twenty-four. He
urged that *A Wise Man's Son* be never shown to a publisher;

some publisher might accept it, and the clerk would regret such a book when he was older. Were it a translation from the Russian, said Howells, there would be no objection to such a book; coming from a young American, it was certain to shock the public gravely; it was full of hard swearing, hard drinking, too much knowledge of good and evil, and a whole fig tree would not cover the Widow Taylor. Put it by. In time to come, it would furnish the young American with a mine of material.

No publisher has ever seen that novel. That was in 1884; it was perhaps a dozen years later that Howells asked me, was I not going to do something with it?

About that time, angry murmurs concerning Roosevelt were stirring in Beacon Street. What had happened to him thus far since his graduation is of general knowledge except, perhaps, that he finished his *Naval History of the War of 1812* mostly standing on one leg at the bookcases in his New York house, the other leg crossed behind, toe touching the floor, heedless of dinner engagements and the flight of time. A slide drew out from the bookcase. On this he had open the leading authorities on navigation, of which he knew nothing. He knew that when a ship's course was one way, with the wind another, the ship had to sail at angles, and this was called tacking or beating. By exhaustive study and drawing of models, he pertinaciously got it all right, whatever of it came into the naval engagements he was writing about.

His wife used to look in at his oblivious back, and exclaim in a plaintive drawl:

"We're dining out in twenty minutes, and Teedy's drawing little ships!"

Then there would be a scurry, and he would cut himself shaving, and it wouldn't stop bleeding, and they would have to surround him and take measures to save his collar from getting stained.

In 1884, cartoons of him as the slim young reformer, assemblyman at Albany, were familiarizing the public with his appearance. They were not very good likenesses; the cartoonists had not yet found the formula for him—the eye-glasses, the teeth, and the belligerent jaw. Whiskers were gone. I don't know who put a stop to them. He was still Teddy. By the time I began to see him often again, he had become Theodore. I don't know who put a stop to Teddy. Very soon in his married life he had become father and widower. And now Boston was displeased with him.

The Republicans had nominated Blaine, the Democrats, Cleveland. The Republicans had made a mistake. They tried to repair it by asking Cleveland, what was he going to do about his mistress and her child?

"Tell the truth," he said.

Important leaders soon deserted the Republican party. George William Curtis, Free Soiler and abolitionist, went over to the enemy with his oracle *Harper's Weekly,* and his deadly sharp-shooter, Thomas Nast. If the shots that Nast's cartoons fired at Blaine, notably the "Tattooed Man," had not mortally wounded him before the appearance of the Rev. Burchard, the Rev. Burchard certainly did for him at a reception held in his honor one night at the Fifth Avenue Hotel. In an address of welcome, the Rev. Burchard greeted Blaine as our champion against—

"Rum, Romanism, and Rebellion."

Two days later, an item in a funny column reported that a man had handed the conductor on a Western train a hundred dollar bill, asking to ride as far as that would take him, and giving his name as Burchard. Cleveland was elected.

He was the first president for whom I ever voted. That campaign was hot with rancor. To many Republicans it was unthinkable that any Republican should vote *against* the party that had saved the Union, and *for* the party that attempted to destroy it. Families split over it, and friends fell out. Blaine's son, Emmons, came one day into the Somerset Club from New York, and joined a group of us, never doubting we were with him. It was an embarrassing, painful scene: we, his old college-mates, fond of him, sorry for him, striving in vain to turn the

subject which he forced on us—and his face as the truth broke
on him at last.    I have seen worse campaigns since, more personal, more distressing, but that one was bitter enough, and
grew worse as it progressed and more deserters went over to
Cleveland.    Mugwumps they were called, and voters were
warned that the Democrats would smother in their cradle our
infant industries, which at that time were about the size of
Goliath.    And down in the dim Union Safe Deposit Vaults one
morning, I heard the voice of the originator of that pioneer institution, my chief, and the devoted friend of three generations
of my family, Henry Lee, growling these words at his desk in the
private office:

"As for Cabot Lodge, nobody's surprised at *him;* but you can
tell that young whipper-snapper in New York from me that his
independence was the only thing in him we cared for, and if he
has gone back on that, we don't care to hear anything more
about him."

I doubt if that message was delivered to Theodore Roosevelt
by his father-in-law, to whom it was given.    George Lee was
Henry Lee's cousin, and affectionately known as "snub-mana-
ger" by all the clerks and cashiers in the Vaults; and Alice, now
dead, had been his daughter.    It was in this fashion that these
Lee cousins of the older generation not infrequently spoke to
and of each other, and of most of the important citizens of Boston, who were generally apt also to be their cousins.    Henry
Lee had a vast store of scandalous genealogical anecdote; and
to have him take you round an ancient churchyard after a
funeral and demolish the characters of his collateral ancestors
and the ancestors of his friends in every grave you came to, was
worth all the histories of Salem and Massachusetts Bay put together.

He was as proud as Lucifer of his state, and his town, and
Harvard; served all of them loyally, wouldn't have exchanged a
single Yankee ancestor for ten of the very best from New York
or South Carolina; and one day when I was with him, he said to
a kinsman, while quizzical humor wrinkled his face:

"Waldo, don't you wish Massachusetts was the only State in the Union?"

"You really mean that, you know!" I said.

"Do I, Dan; do I? Well if this be treason, make the most of it!"

Henry Lee was one of those fine Americans with colonial traditions who knew how to be rich.

So Cleveland was elected that Autumn of 1884; one of our best Presidents; too good for his party, as Roosevelt was too good for his; as our best presidents are apt to be. Roosevelt disappeared into the West. Particularly in the eyes of all Boston Mugwumps was he found wanting: in spite of having married into one of their best families, he had been unfaithful to what they expected of him, had not left his party and come out for Cleveland. Instead, he had listened to Cabot Lodge, one of themselves, but his evil genius; they were done with that young Theodore Roosevelt from New York.

"He has one idea, and a great many teeth," said Martin Brimmer, whose house was on Beacon Hill, five minutes from Henry Lee's.

If Roosevelt had met me then, he would have assured me that he was politically dead. He assured me of this several times in later years.

Still there was no place for me at Lee Higginson & Co., still I sat on the high-legged stool computing interest on daily balances at 2½ per cent, dining at the Tavern Club, or in the happy company of Winthrop Chanler and Amos French and the genial boys out at Cambridge. There was no prospect of the Vaults ending. I wrote a letter to my father. I would go to the Harvard Law School, since American respectability accepted lawyers, no matter how bad, which I was likely to be, and rejected composers, even if they were good, which I might possibly be. This letter I showed Henry Higginson during a week end with him at Manchester, and begged his advice.

He smiled his most whimsical smile. "It's probably the

best way out.   Don't be too rough on your father.   Good parents have a bad time."

In Philadelphia I sat nibbling at Blackstone in the law office of Francis Rawle until the Law School should begin a new year in the Autumn; and now my health very opportunely broke down.   I was ordered by Dr. Weir Mitchell to a ranch of some friends in Wyoming.   Early in July, 1885, I went there.   This accidental sight of the cattle-country settled my career.

### V.

In the Autumn of 1891, I returned from my fifth summer in search of health and big game in Wyoming, and wrote two stories about that country and its people.   True, I was now a Harvard LL.B. and A.M., and member of the Philadelphia bar; true, I had begged and got leave from Francis Rawle to argue a case for the plaintiff before the Circuit Court, brought for infringement of trade-mark, which the office had lost on demurrer in Common Pleas; and I had won it.   True, though we lost it on appeal from Common Pleas to the Supreme Court, where I argued it again on the same lines as in the Circuit Court, my brief led Judge Mitchell to write a dissenting opinion, based upon the line I had taken, and that opinion changed the law as to equitable trade mark in our state; and true also, that Francis Rawle saw symptoms of a lawyer in me: all true: but I couldn't get Wyoming out of my head.

Never before had I been able to sustain a diary, no matter how thrilling my experiences; and among others, certainly the experience of Bayreuth and *Parsifal* and Liszt had been thrilling.   But upon every Western expedition I had kept a full, faithful, realistic diary: details about pack horses, camps in the mountains, camps in the sage-brush, nights in town, cards with cavalry officers, meals with cowpunchers, round-ups, scenery, the Yellowstone Park, trout fishing, hunting with Indians, shooting antelope, white tail deer, black tail deer, elk, bear, mountain sheep—and missing these same animals.   I don't know why I

AT THE MAMMOTH HOT SPRINGS, 1887.   GEORGE NORMAN, OWEN WISTER
AT THE RIGHT

wrote it all down so carefully, I had no purpose in doing so, or any suspicion that it was driving Wyoming into my blood and marrow, and fixing it there.

And so one Autumn evening of 1891, fresh from Wyoming and its wild glories, I sat in the club dining with a man as enamoured of the West as I was. This was Walter Furness, son of the great editor of Shakespeare, Horace Howard Furness, my kinsman and mentor. I was lucky in my mentors. From oysters to coffee we compared experiences. Why wasn't some Kipling saving the sage-brush for American literature, before the sage-brush and all that it signified went the way of the California forty-niner, went the way of the Mississippi steam-boat, went the way of everything? Roosevelt had seen the sage-brush true, had felt its poetry; and also Remington, who illustrated his articles so well. But what was fiction doing, fiction, the only thing that has always outlived fact? Must it be perpetual tea-cups? Was Alkali Ike in the comic papers the one figure which the jejune American imagination, always at full-cock to banter or to brag, could discern in that epic which was being lived at a gallop out in the sage-brush? To hell with tea-cups and the great American laugh! we two said, as we sat dining at the club. The claret had been excellent.

"Walter, I'm going to try it myself!" I exclaimed to Walter Furness. "I'm going to start this minute."

"Go to it. You ought to have started long ago."

I wished him good night, he wished me good luck. I went up to the library; and by midnight or so, a good slice of *Hank's Woman* was down in the rough. I followed it soon with *How Lin McLean Went East*. Lin was my camp companion in *Hank's Women*. In the revised version, I put the Virginian in Lin's place, having made the Virginian's acquaintance in *Balaam and Pedro*, and *Em'ly*, which were the next stories written; and finding that to get all which was to be out of *Hank's Woman*, I needed a "Greek chorus" of an intelligence more subtle than Lin's. A check came for those first two stories from Alden, the first editor who saw them, and I wondered if I should ever know the joy of being illustrated by Frederic Remington.   I had also a sneaking suspicion that suits in equitable trade-mark, and all suits whatever, might be over; that if any one in future should come knocking at my door, he was less likely to be a litigant than an editor.   And some years later, George Horace Lorimer, aged twenty-nine, the new editor of the *Saturday Evening Post,* did come, bearing a letter of introduction from his predecessor.

Francis Rawle was as proud of the check from Messrs. Harper and Brothers as I was; he kept me in his office, where I worked at fiction for twenty-five years, and at law nevermore.

*Hank's Woman* came out.   Friends in Philadelphia said, "I haven't read your story."   Friends in New York didn't know I had written one.   Friends in Boston said, "What a horrible place the West must be!"

It was Theodore Roosevelt who hailed me the next time we met with:

"Bully for you!   I'm *particularly* grateful for 'his—twink-ling—white—tailless—rear.' "   He spaced his words for emphasis, as was his way so often, and he went up into that falsetto which always denoted emphasis of one sort or another.

So there I was again in the full sunshine of his attention; and this was the exact moment when our old college acquaintance began to ripen toward the intimacy that it became.

Not many golden strokes of fortune equal the friendship of a great man.   I owe it entirely to the failure of my health, and the fact that to both of us at nearly the same time came the same experience—we went West.   He saw Dakota, I saw Wyoming. After Commencement, 1880, until that lunch with the Cabot Lodges in Washington, when he started off at once about *Hank's Woman,* we had occasionally met on just the pleasant old familiar Harvard basis; now I signified something more to him— or might.   He hoped I might.   He hoped I would do what he had been looking for somebody to do in the way of interpreting that West through works of imagination.   He scrutinized and questioned me eagerly at that lunch.   Truly, I was on fire with delight as we compared impressions.   I told him how every

word he had written for the *Century Magazine* about his ranch
life at Medora had absorbed me, and how few of our immediate
friends could possibly know how good those articles were; he
had been the pioneer in taking the cowboy seriously, and I loved
what he said about that bold horseman of the plains.   Did I?
Did I, indeed? he exclaimed; and seemed as pleased as if what I
thought was of importance.

"And I showed Remington your 'twinkling white tailless
rear,'" he continued; "for in one of my articles, he had drawn
an antelope with a tail; and I told him that no antelope I had
ever met so far had a tail."

*How Lin McLean Went East* came out.   Alden had kept it
for his Christmas number.   I was hunting White Goat in the
mountains above the Methow river in Washington at the time.
I travelled out to the railroad at Coulee City through the snow,
three days in a freight wagon.   The wagon was to bring in
Winter supplies for the trading store.   The first day, we passed
the cabin of Cheval.   Cheval was all the name he had any
longer.   He had been in the employment of that eccentric French
marquis, whose ranch was neighbor to Roosevelt's.   He had
known Roosevelt.   When he found that I knew him, he talked
with great enthusiasm, and wanted me to stop there for the
night.   This was impossible, I had to get on, or the chances
were that I should be snowed in.   Then I must take his coat,
mine was not enough for this weather; and he ran and got it—
a thick fur coat.   But, I objected, it was three days to the railroad, and no one could say how many days back it would be,
and how could he or I be sure that he would ever see the coat
again?   Never mind.   I was a friend of Roosevelt.   I had to
take the coat, or offend Cheval.   Without it, I think I might
have frozen.   The snow had come with a vengeance before the
freight wagon got back a great many weeks later.

The life of Roosevelt as he spent it at his ranch near Medora,
and the impression which he made upon those who saw him and
worked with him there, Hermann Hagedorn has recorded in his
admirable book, *Roosevelt in the Bad Lands*.   The following

innocently profane words add a touch to the same picture; they were by one who saw him then.

"It was about '83, in the Bad Lands about eight miles south of Medora . . . at a rounding up camp. It was in the morning and we were sitting around . . . near the rope corral where the horses were gathered; there were about seven wagons there. They were lassoing the horses to start out for the round up. Linc Gates threw his rope over a mighty fine sorrel horse. The horse he got nervous and jumped over the corral. The corral went down, and as the horse stepped out, Linc got caught by the foot in a twist of the rope. There were about fifty people . . . and I was sitting not far from Roosevelt. He was a light little feller in them days. The thing all happened in a minute, so quick by God, that I didn't have no time to think what to do. 'Twas all over, by God, before I thought what I ought to do. Why hell, I had ought to have been quick enough to shoot the horse! But by God, Teddy was on his horse most before the thing started and that noose with sixty feet of rope behind it went over that horse's head same as if it was glove! By God, I never seen anything like it. It was the quickest thing I had ever seen. And when he come back I said to him: 'What would you have done if you had missed that horse?' And he said: 'Why, I'd have shot the horse, of course.' Hell, of course that was the thing to do, but by God it was so quick I didn't have time to think of it.

"I'm here to tell you that Teddy Roosevelt was the best roper that ever hit that country. I never seen a man that could rope a horse like he did. By God, I believe he was the best roper that ever was."

Forty years after, by Henry's Lake in Idaho, the boy who had seen it in his 'teens, could see it still and tell it so as a man of fifty-eight. What wonder that Cheval, who saw like doings near Medora, should force his fur coat upon Roosevelt's friend? What wonder that Rough Riders from the West should flock to follow Roosevelt to Cuba, and were ready to follow him to France?

It was in the Northern Pacific train between Spokane and St. Paul, that I got my first tidings of *Lin McLean*. Harper's was out, and on the news stands; and a fellow traveller in the Pullman handed me the magazine and recommended my own story to me.  I did not tell him my name, the coincidence was likely to prove too strong for him, and I had no wish to have my identity doubted.  It doesn't always do to tell strangers who you are.  At Ogden in 1911, when I registered at the hotel there, the clerk informed me that I was dead, that it had been in all the papers.  What is a man's word against the papers?

When I got home, Philadelphians were saying, "It isn't as good as Bret Harte."  They were right; but ah, Philadelphia! New York and Boston friends made no comparisons in the very welcome letters which they wrote; and this time, Roosevelt went into his highest falsetto as he shook my hand and quoted from my story with perfect accuracy a passage concerning Honey Wiggin after he had won a pinto from a Mexican by good card playing:

" 'The new owner, being a man of the world, and agile on his feet, was only slightly stabbed that evening as he walked to the dance-hall at the edge of the town.  The Mexican was buried on the next day but one.' "

According to his wont when quoting words that pleased him, he delivered every syllable as if it were a morsel of food particularly to his taste.  "And—I—don't—*think*—you'll—peter— out," he added, spacing his words, and measuring me with his eye.

Cleveland was in his second term, then, and too good for his party.  At their worst, the Democrats are no worse for the country than are the Republicans at their worst; but the Republicans at their best are better than the Democrats at theirs. In the early nineties, the Democrats were having their silver insanity.  Had Grover Cleveland not stood as a rock of sanity against it, American credit would have collapsed.  He staved this off; and the amiable McKinley, who wobbled in any direction that the wobbling seemed good, inherited a situation in which his earnest effort to wobble failed, and a gold plank was forced into the Republican platform at the St. Louis convention.

*Balaam and Pedro,* as I have said, brought a vigorous protest from Roosevelt. Soon after it appeared, the Boone and Crockett Club held its annual dinner in New York, and he came up from Washington to attend it. I sat but two or three away from him, and half through the meal he turned and spoke of the story; beginning with words in its favor:—but, he asked, how had I ever come to write the sickening details of Pedro's tragedy? His cousin, West Roosevelt, had thrown the magazine down, and declared that he would never read a word of mine again. But the thing had actually happened, I replied; I had seen it with my own eyes, and it was not an isolated case, but typical of a certain streak of cruelty which belonged to that life. Quite true, he asserted; he knew that; but life every day offered degrees of repulsiveness which were utterly inadmissible in Art, where violent extremes and excrescences had no place. I stood up for myself; I had seen it, I insisted. What if I had? he asked. That didn't justify repeating it in fiction. Still I stood up for myself. The incident had made a deep impression on me, to strike it out would weaken the story. And I reminded him that we had never liked tea-cup tales. He twisted his mouth and puckered his brow, and looked as if he was going to purr; and intensity came out all over his face. And he let me have it:

"I'm perfectly aware, Dan, that Zola has many admirers because he says things out loud that great writers from Greece down to the present have mostly passed over in silence. I think that *conscientious descriptions of the unspeakable* do not constitute an interpretation of life, but merely disgust all readers not afflicted with the hysteria of bad taste. There's nothing masculine in being revolting. Your details really weaken the effect of your story, because they distract the attention from the story as a *whole*, to the details as an offensive and shocking *part*. When you come to publishing it in a volume, throw a veil over what Balaam did to Pedro, leave that to the reader's imagination, and you will greatly strengthen your effect."

Before I agreed with him about *Balaam and Pedro*, nine years had passed by.

## VI.

The following is the earliest of his letters that I can find. He was compiling and editing with George Bird Grinnell, a book of big game articles by members of the Boone and Crockett club, written from their personal experiences. I had been wandering in Texas and elsewhere, out of recent touch with the post office.

UNITED STATES
CIVIL SERVICE COMMISSION
Washington, D. C.

April 4, 1893.

DEAR DAN:

To my delight I received your letter today. You will probably get all of mine in a batch on Saturday, and will know that it is not too late. I could give you till the first of May, but I would much prefer to have the manuscript here by the 20th of this month. I have been very anxious to have you write the white goat piece for us. I have so far five first class articles for the Club Book, by Chanler, Rogers, Grinnell, Col. Williams and Col. Pickett. I have three or four others with which I am less contented, and I have the promise of four more, which will be very good indeed, if they are written as they ought to be. In any event I think I can say the success of the volume is assured. Winty's article was very short, but he has the real literary gift, and his piece is in some ways the best I have had yet. In literary style there will be but one that will surpass it, and that is yours. I should like to make yours quite a prominent feature, one of the three or four most prominent, so don't give me less than five thousand words; anywhere between that and ten thousand will do. The longest piece I have accepted so far has been twelve thousand. It was by Grinnell about the buffalo. The shortest has been Winty's elk hunt piece, which had about two thousand words. Make yours between five and ten thousand, and nearer the larger figure than the smaller. I have had some fearful work with two or three would-be contributors. Unfortunately reading and writing do *not* come by nature, and even a man of considerable experience may put that experience into wholly impossible form.

Yours truly,

THEODORE ROOSEVELT.

The following note was written in his own hand, and carries on the subject of the Boone and Crockett volume:

April 22, 1893.

. . . . . . . . . . . .

The goat article is, of course, admirable; equally of course it needs no editing.   It is interesting in every way—from the "Hurry up Eds" to the actual hunting: I am going to take it over for the Lodges to read.   We shall have 12 articles in the book; 8 of them first class; and but one or two on a level with yours in interest and literary merit.

Will you be at the cabin for the opening on the 15th?

. . . . . . . . . . . . . . . . . . . . . . .

The cabin was the exhibit of the Boone and Crockett Club on the Wooded Island at the World's Fair in Chicago.

April 20, 1894.

DEAR DAN:

I was much pleased to get your note, and I am delighted that you like my article on Americanism.

Now, my good Sir, don't you think there is just a wee bit of affectation in telling me to note what you say about the Indian matter if I "happen" to read your piece in the June Harper? You know perfectly well that I greedily read all your western articles, and that I can quite sincerely say that they rank with Bret Harte's and Kipling's pieces.   I have long been praying to have somebody arise and write articles of that kind and I am delighted that it should be a friend of mine who has arisen.   I am glad you stirred up Barringer, and I hope he will keep the mark.

I am also sincerely pleased at your liking the very parts of the Wilderness Hunter which I took most pride in myself.   I wanted to make the book a plea for manliness and simplicity and delight in a vigorous outdoor life; as well as to try to sketch the feeling that the wilderness, with its great rivers, great mountains, great forests, and great prairies, leaves on one.   The slaughter of the game, though necessary in order to give a needed touch of salt to the affair, is subsidiary after all.

Yours ever,

. . . . . . . . . . . . . . . . . . . . . . .

May 26, 1894.

. . . . . . . . . . . .

Of all the pieces you have written I think your June Harper article the best.   You have treated the story in first-class form. When will you get out these stories in a volume?   I want to ask the permission of the Atlantic Monthly to review them.   I really think you have done for the plainsmen and mountainmen, the soldiers, frontiersmen and Indians what nobody else but Bret Harte and Kipling could have done, and neither of them have sufficient knowledge to enable them to do it even had they wished.

Good bye, and good luck.

. . . . . . . . . . . . . . . . . . . . . .

The story to which he refers is *Little Big Horn Medicine*, which became later the first in my first collection, *Red Men and White*.   These sketches were appearing each month in Harper's, and not one of them ever failed to bring a comment from him.

UNITED STATES
CIVIL SERVICE COMMISSION
Washington, D. C.

August 27, 1894.

DEAR OWEN:

I do not know but that I agree with you about Specimen Jones; though I like the continuation in "The General's Bluff" as much, almost, as I did the account of his first acquaintance with his young friend.   I am amused at your having changed the name of Willis to Kinney.   Your hero was a good deal like my friend I am sorry to say.   We are going to have a first class second volume of the Boon & Crockett book.   I have good articles from William A. Chanler about his big game hunt in Africa, and from Lieut. Allen about his wolf coursing experience in Russia last year.   I do wish you would write Barringer and stir him up about giving me an article he promised about a dog sledding trip. I am very anxious to have it but do not seem able to get it.   Do you know I am not sure but that I like your Little Big Horn Medicine better than all.   Have you seen a story by another Harvard man, John Fox, that has been running in the Century, called "A Cumberland Vendetta"?   I think it very well done, and have written to him.   I would awfully like to have you visit us some time.   When are you coming east?   I am just going to spend a month on my ranch.   I wish I could manage to have you and me meet Fox.

Faithfully yours,

THEODORE ROOSEVELT.

The change from Willis to Kinney in *Little Big Horn Medicine* was due to Roosevelt's telling me, on my sketching that story to him one day, that he knew a real Willis in Dakota, who would have done just what my imaginary Willis did on the Little Big Horn as the white agent of evil in the young Indian chief's downfall.

Feb. 27, 1895.

DEAR THEODORE:

Once again I must write you how much I like what you have written.   This time it's American ideals. . . .   I have the happiness to hold a firm belief in the American.   I think that material prosperity has been too much for him in these days and that he needs—do you remember Thackeray's Fairy Blackstick?—"A little misfortune" to bring him back to his good sense and fundamentally fine standards. . . .   Were I asked what our first 100 years had demonstrated I should be obliged to say an already ancient truth, about silk purses &c.—but apparently we must all burn our own fingers in experience. . . . Waite was downed in Colorado and I think his tribe will have brief prosperity.   Well—this is only a word and good night to you. . . .

My reference to Waite was to a sort of political mad dog who ran a brief career in Colorado, and was known as the "blood to the bridles" governor.   He disliked people who had money; and this made him very popular with those who hadn't, until a day came when various enterprises in Colorado needed money and found it difficult to borrow any.   Waite was soon extinct.

Roosevelt writes next:

February 27, 1895.

. . . . . . . . . .

If you didn't yourself continually write things you would save me from the necessity of seeming so flat as to say a good

word about something you have written whenever you have alluded to anything that I have done; but even at the risk of ap-
parent sycophancy, I must say that I think your last account
of the proceedings of the left wing of Price's Army in Idaho was
one of the best things you have written yet.   Indeed personally
I liked it best of all, but I suppose this was because of my own
interest in the politics of Montana at the time when it was just
out of the sway of the combined persimmon and shamrock.   I
saw one ardent Republican at Thompsons Falls who had brought
about a riot by posting up "No Irishmen or Missourians need
apply."

I am glad you liked the Forum article.   It was written at a
white-heat of indignation after the strike.   Funnily enough, the
immediate suggestion as to writing it came from a paper by you
on the Pennsylvania National Guard in Harpers Weekly.

I wish you were going to be on here in Washington.   There is
much I should like to talk over with you.   I am an optimist, but
I hope I am a reasonably intelligent one.   I recognize that all
the time there are numerous evil forces at work, and that in
places and at times they outweigh the forces that tend for good.
Hitherto, on the whole, the good have come out ahead, and I
think that they will in the future; but I am not so sure that I can
afford to look at the coming years with levity.

What fools they are at Harvard to try to abolish football.

A little later he writes:

March 30, 1895.

I hope you received my telegram.   Kipling will come Friday
next to my house, 1215 Nineteenth Street, Washington.   You
must not fail me, as this is especially gotten up for you, and I
have invited Austin Wadsworth.   I have also invited Remington.   Can't you write him a line to tell him to come?

Monday evening.

DEAR THEODORE:

Housed with a contemptible cold which I caught yesterday
being too fashionable, I console myself by telling you what an

awfully delightful evening you provided for me. . . . My re-
grets are all because of not seeing more of everybody.   You had
such a roomful of people I should like to have heard at length,
that the memory is a little like having dreamt one saw them.
The appearance of your colleague Procter I loved and—good
heavens this is a half sheet.   Forgive it.   I can't go and coldly
copy my overflowing sentiments over again—I should have delighted to hear him talk of the days when he was twenty.
There's a charm about the mere twinkle in a certain sort of
Southern eye that goes with their pronunciation and makes you
glad the war is all long over. . . .   Rockhill should be treated
with cork screws.   With Page and Hay I did manage to have
talk—and I'm glad I stayed against my instinct of altruism and
kept you awake a little longer.   I hope it wasn't too long.   You
were blinking pitifully.   You brought it on yourself, Theodore.
. . .   The next day certainly made the visit a reality so far as
Kipling was concerned.   He was no dream and I saw him for
three extremely pleasant hours.   We sat and talked in the
smoking room most of the way to Philadelphia. . . .   He
doesn't like the name I've (so far) chosen for the first volume of
stories: *Tales from the Sage-brush;* and he gave me one which
for the moment I liked better: *Various Citizens.*   But now I
don't—Can you invent one for me?—Harper has the 8 now—
the book to come out about Christmas time. . . .   So give me
*the* name Theodore. . . .   Before I go to New Mexico I shall
try to run down to Washington. . . .   Thank you once more
for last Friday.

But I had to find the name for that first volume: *Red men and
White*.

"The papers" in the first sentence of the next letter, are several numbers of *Arthur McEwen's Letter,* a short-lived weekly,
a paper of protest in San Francisco, and some specimens of
"Prattle", a column which Ambrose Bierce wrote regularly for
the San Francisco *Examiner*.

April 6, 1895.

I send herewith the papers.   I was really greatly struck by
them.   In a certain way Ambrose Bierce and Arthur McEwen

complement each other. Bierce is altogether too pessimistic, and has too great a contempt for the "greasy multitude"; while McEwen errs on the other side, and has a slight leaning toward Populism, or at least toward the excusing deeds of semi-anarchy. But what I was especially struck by was the very real literary merit shown in the articles of the one and in the newspaper of the other. I certainly know nothing in the East that can quite be compared with them. If only the New York Nation had a little of McEwen's originality, clear insight and good literary judgment, it would be very well for our cultivated classes in the East. I am very glad to have had a chance to see these two papers.

By the way, I was a good deal interested in the account of your methods of work. Of course imaginative work is something very different from writing like mine, which is largely a simple record of facts. I wish I could make my writings touch a higher plane, but I don't well see how I can, and I am not sure that I could do much by devoting more time to them. I go over them a good deal and recast, supply, or omit, sentences and even paragraphs; but I don't make the reconstruction complete in the way that you do. John Fox tells me he does it too. I am not perfectly certain as to whether I have done well in trying to write history while engaged as actively as I am in my work as Civil Service Commissioner. It was all right to bring out the Wilderness Hunter, for that was of course mere narrative; though personally I like it better than anything I have done. The Winning of the West, however, was a more ambitious attempt. I am a little shaky as to how I ought to have done; still, it would not have been written at all if I had not tackled it in odd moments, and I am going to bring out the fourth volume anyhow and see the result.

I enclose together with the papers two cuttings containing the story about which I wrote you. Of course it is full of all the innumerable sins naturally committed by a tyro who has been a cow puncher and is a railway mail clerk, and it doesn't sustain the interest; but I do think that in the first part, the two columns in the first cutting, the description of the town, and the people who come to the dance, and the dialogue of the men playing poker, are all very good.

I am exceedingly pleased to have caught a glimpse of you, and am delighted that you came on. I thought we had a very pleasant dinner. Kipling was as nice as possible.

. . . . . . . . . . . . . . . . . . . . . . .

He must soon have sent me something of his own, asking for comments; I cannot remember what it was. He writes from Washington, April 16, 1895:

DEAR DAN:

You are very good to have taken the trouble to read through the piece. Your judgment is exactly my own upon it, but I wished to have that of some one who was more of a professional literary cuss than I was.

I am really pleased at the fact that you like my historic style, for yours is an opinion I greatly value. I am having a horrid time trying to write my fourth volume.

I am delighted that you should have made such friends with Kipling. . . .

His reference is to his fourth volume of *The Winning of the West*.

What facts about him do these letters of the nineties, while he was a member of the Civil Service Commission, disclose? How do they count as brush strokes in his portrait? Let us pause and consider. We know that, politically, nothing during that early period of his official life was nearer to his heart than Civil Service Reform. Although the close of his letter, dated February 27, 1895, may imply a recognition of such omens as Governor Waite, to whom my letter of the same date refers, the threat of class-war had not as yet struck him as a peril against which to make ready, and with which to deal with all his might. It is also well known that he shirked his duties as a Civil Service Commissioner just as little as he shirked every task he undertook, that he carried it through to the full limit of his intelligence and strength. What else did he find time for during those nineties? When you count it up, you are puzzled to see how he contrives to put it all in. He found time to read, and write me about everything I was publishing; to read the story by John Fox Jr., write to him, and meditate a meeting of the three of us; to bring Kipling and me together; to edit a volume of the Boone and Crockett Club; to concern himself with the exhibit of that

Club at the World's Fair, and to write, beside a number of occasional articles, a long volume of History.   Where did he glean the hours and minutes for all this?

While he was in the White House, and we were walking one day, he muttered, with his head bent thoughtfully, as if thinking aloud—he often did this—

"I wish I knew how Washington managed to go his work."

Washington, in my opinion, would have wondered just as much how Roosevelt managed.   But, in a way, the explanation is not obscure.   Certain men have the power to organize and concentrate themselves wholly upon a given matter, in an instant, leaving nothing of themselves out; and then, when this is despatched, drop it as if it had never existed, and go on to the next matter.   This does not mean that they are not carrying a multitude of other matters in their heads, turning these over, studying them, getting ready for conclusions that some day will seem to leap out like improvisations, it means merely that they are men with a capacity of the first rank.   While they are giving you their attention, you feel that you are the only thing to which they have to attend.   It is the mark, as I say, of very superior men.   Several times in the White House, Roosevelt made me stay while he received a caller on business.   We might have been talking about Harvard, or cliff swallows, or cliff dwellers, or anything whatever: directly the conversation with the caller opened, Roosevelt had at his fingers' ends the points of the business in hand.   Somehow, somewhere, he had found the time to go over the papers connected with it, grasped what was essential, and now asked questions and made comments that went to the root of the affair, all so clearly and simply that it seemed as if you could have done it yourself.

Further familiar letters he wrote from Washington, or while on brief visits to New York during those early nineties, show that he was able to take frequent exercise with Cabot Lodge on horseback, that he and Mrs. Roosevelt gave entertainments and went to them, and that when the hot weather drove her and their children to Sagamore Hill, he kept bachelor's hall with Cecil Spring Rice, then attaché at the British Embassy, and later to become British Ambassador to Washington.   And so, besides his hard work at the office, he rode constantly, read constantly, wrote constantly, and took great pleasure in society, when society was to his mind; but it had to be to his mind; you may say that he was quite as exacting in his standards about the qualifications of a dinner guest as he was about the qualifications of any office seeker.

"Springy and I (he writes from bachelor's hall) are having great fun together; he is *so* gentle and pallid and polite."

A month later:

"Springy and I have been having very pleasant times together.   He is a good fellow; and really cultivated; in the evenings he reads Homer and Dante in the originals!   I wish I could.   At times he has a most querulous feeling toward America; he oughtn't to be a diplomat; he is too serious."

To any one who recalls the British Embassy between 1914 and 1918, this comment will count as a prophecy.

"Cabot (he is writing of Lodge) is very gloomy at present; desoeuvré, and convinced that his career is a failure and his work useless.   The old boy will get over it all right. . . .   At last the little runt of a President has approved the Indian rules."
"On Friday evening (he had been in New York) Reed, Cabot and I made speeches at The Federal Club dinner."   (I omit an accurate but too vivacious characterization of Chauncy Depew.) "We then adjourned to Chase's studio to see Carmencita dance. . . . There we met . . . about half the four hundred, who were unintelligently interested in Reed and confusedly anxious to know *first* him, and then who he was."

The four hundred are now the four thousand, but remain in other respects what he thought of them.   During the Great War, one of them was surprised that the President should need a private secretary, when he already had the Secretary of State to take care of his correspondence.

"It is pleasant to meet people (Roosevelt writes about Washington) from whom one really gets something; people from all over the Union, with different pasts and varying interests, trained, able, powerful, men, though often narrow minded enough."

Roosevelt seldom approached anyone as a member of a class, but almost invariably as an *individual:* had he, for an evening's let-up from work, been offered the conversation either of the dull wife of the biggest Newport millionaire, or that of an acute and observant boot-black, it is the latter he would unhesitatingly have chosen. This, too, lay at the root of that resentment which he aroused in sundry important social bosoms. When you are a member of fashion, but otherwise a vacuum, you recoil from intelligence—and, when you are intelligent and likewise a member of fashion, you recoil from vacuity. Roosevelt recoiled from absolutely nothing or nobody, when his patriotic duty was involved; but the following passages from his letters, while of the Civil Service Commission and in his early and middle thirties, show plainly what he felt about being bored during his hours off.

"We had asked Count A—who, thank Heaven, could not come. I am surprised such a gourmand should wish to . . . our teas are so perfectly simple. . . . The company is generally good."
"L M and L J turned up . . . they are not exciting. . . . Young M took dinner with us, too. . . . He is honest and manly — but oh, how dreadfully commonplace and middle class British dull. . . . I never can like, and never will like, to be intimate with that enormous proportion of sentient beings who are respectable but dull. . . . I will work with them, or for them; but for pleasure and instruction I go elsewhere."
"Now to our horror X Y and Z have turned up and we are at our wits end to know what to do with them. They are all nice people, but so utterly hopeless at a small dinner where the rest of the company count for anything."

"The X'es make an excellent couple, well-bred, good looking, well dressed, good tempered, good manners, good morals, and *no* intelligence."

"The most entertaining dinner from a spectacular standpoint to which we went was one at Senator B's. . . . He looks like Judas, but unlike that gentleman has no capacity for remorse. There were thirty guests. . . . I took in Mrs. ——— , who told me she thought the Washington monument 'common'; I told her that an Indiana lady of my acquaintance, thought the same of the Pantheon, but, being tactful, she was careful to avoid saying so. This opening seemed unpromising; however, we got on famously afterwards; and she promptly asked us to dinner, which we even more promptly declined. Friday we dined with the X'es. The two other secretaries . . . were there; their manners and I suppose their morals are good, but looking at them from the standpoint of pure intellect I should never be surprised to see them develop tails and swing from a bough."

This letter is dated February 12, 1894, when he was thirty-five. In the spring of 1907, when he was forty-eight, thirteen years more of experience with men and women of every station, as head of the New York Police Department, as Assistant Secretary of the Navy, as Lieutenant Colonel of The Rough Riders, as Governor of New York, and as President of the United States, had by no means softened his views. He and Mrs. Roosevelt with a few intimate friends were having coffee after lunch on the piazza which is off the blue room. The company was talking lazily about this and that, while they enjoyed the fine weather. . . . Mrs. Grant La Farge had carried on an idea of Prosper Mérimée's into the question of putting this idea into personal practice.

"I have always wondered," she said, "that if one had the magic finger, and by touching any one they would drop dead, and one wanted to remove all the knaves, and the people who hurt others by their lives, and who were against decency and freedom and kindness—how many people, what percentage of the world, one would have to touch. Would forty per cent do?"

This was an engaging notion to discuss; it set every one to

offering his or her own estimate of the proportion of knaves alive at any given moment who should be removed. Some one increased the figures of Mrs. La Farge to sixty per cent. And then Roosevelt astonished them all.

"Not sixty per cent," he said; "eighty."

Mrs. La Farge protested at such an estimate of the human race. The discussion grew more lively, until Roosevelt said:

"You must include the fools;" and the discussion waxed livelier than ever.

"It would need the wisdom of a god."

"How about the children of criminals and idiots?"

"Do you believe those statistics about the Jukes family?"

"Very hard to steer clear of race prejudice."

"Well—I'm very glad I haven't the magic power! I'd be certain to use it.'

These remarks, with others, were dropped by the company.

"Of course," said Roosevelt, "any one who used the power, would undoubtedly deprive the world of some valuable individuals—but so does a plague, or a famine. A great many useful people would be helped. A plague could easily remove every person present without the slightest discrimination."

This sally ended the serious part of the talk; they drifted into wondering which of them would be spared, and they called the exempt twenty per cent the "new four hundred."

Very soon after this scene at the White House on the piazza outside the blue room, Mrs. La Farge repeated the whole of it to me. No more than she, was I prepared for such a sweeping census of undesirable citizens, although by that time (I was forty-six) it had long been clear to me that most of the trouble in this world is made by the well intentioned. But in the cordial warmth that poured from Roosevelt, I had always been ashamed to confess my views. He was the one man I have known who never cast a shadow, but only sunlight. Even his angers and his denunciations, which could be truly blasting when he turned on his full voltage, were not thunder from black clouds, they were a tropic blaze of heat.

"He is systematic, methodical and cold in the discipline of his private life (I am translating from the French), in the ordering of his work, in the regulating of his intelligence, in a sort of strong and sane healthiness of his genius. He is simple, all of a piece, a model of loyalty to his friends, in sympathy with every one of talent, inexhaustible in his encouragement of beginners . . . he belongs to that sturdy race of thinkers and men of action, with whom action and thought make one."

This is not Roosevelt, but how near it comes to describing him! It is Fromentin, writing about Rubens. Having walked and sat in the Dresden gallery, the Louvre, the Prado, and at Antwerp and Vienna and Venice, and Florence, where great portraits hang, it is not Van Dyck, nor Titian, Rembrandt, Hals, Holbein, nor even Velasquez, it is Rubens I should have chosen as the right man to perceive and interpret more of Roosevelt than any one who did paint him has been able to put on canvas.

How to reconcile his eighty per cent of undesirables with his buoyant hopeful outlook, set me thinking then, and has often set me thinking since. I never thought to ask him about that talk on the White House piazza until many years later, at Sagamore Hill, in October, 1918. Then it came back to me; I wondered if I remembered it right, or if possibly Mrs. La Farge had not completely reported it, or if I had misunderstood her— and so I spoke to him. Did he recall a certain talk at the White House with Florence La Farge and a few others about the proportion of people who were a detriment to the general welfare at any given moment, and his putting it at eighty per cent because he included the fools.

"Perfectly!" he exclaimed. "And that's what I think still."

I now return to his letter of April 16, 1895, in which he refers to *The Winning of the West*. It was his last as Civil Service Commissioner. Very soon, he was President of the Board of Police Commissioners in New York; and from there wrote several notes about reviewing *Red Men and White*, parts of these are quoted in the preface to the uniform edition of that volume. One of his notes, dated Nov. 19, 1895, from the Police

Department, 300 Mulberry Street, concludes with a reflection that is evidently an outcome of his new office:

"The thing that strikes me as the most astonishing at present is the ferocious indignation of us Americans with the very men whom we ourselves refuse to turn out of public office; we criticize crimes but we refuse to hold criminals responsible."

In November, 1895, *Red Men and White* came out, and by December 26, he has written his review, and adds:

"On Saturday January fourth Prof. Lounsbury of Yale, whose Fenimore Cooper is the best bit of literary biography I know, is to dine with me.  I have asked Brander Matthews; don't you think you can come too?  I wish you would.  At 689 Madison Avenue.  I'll get Winty if you'll come."

"Winty' is the Winthrop Chanler of my Safe Deposit Vault days.  He was now married to a lady as clever and charming in her own distinguished way as he was in his.  They often spent their winters in Washington during those years, and formed a part of the most brilliant and agreeable society that I have known in America.  Mrs. Chanler, a niece of Julia Ward Howe, had grown up in Rome.  Italian, French, German, and good music, were languages as much hers as her own, and she drew around her all the most interesting and entertaining people in Washington—of whom there were a good many, and highly civilized.

Here is a letter from Chanler.  The essay to which he refers is now added to the preface of *Red Men and White*.

CLIFFE LAWN<br>
NEWPORT,

Sept. 14th, 1895.

OMAR DEAR DANIEL:

The "Evolution of the Cowpuncher" is the best thing (with the exception of my new man-child) the Porcelian has produced in years.  You *did* hit it right that time and I rejoice with you, as you rejoice with me, on our joint production.  I have jawed over it with Theodore Roosevelt and many others—some who don't care a damn about Cowpunchers, and some who do, and all like it.

Come to us whenever you can, my boy. We shall be here till after the 15th of Oct. The 14th is my birthday and there will be entertainment galore. But on or before that date at any time and always you are welcome as you know.

My blessed wife sends you her love and greeting and echoes my sentiments. . . .

It was on one of my week ends with the Chanlers in Washington, that Winthrop and I took the elevator to the top of the Monument, but decided to walk down. As we were descending step after step, deafening echoes from the sight-seers in the heavily clanking elevator drowned our talk and split the air. Whereupon Chanler described us and our situation:

"Inhabitants hurrying down the Tower of Babel. Hurrying down to get the dictionary."

I don't know that he went to meet Professor Lounsbury at Roosevelt's dinner on January 4, 1896. I could not. That Winter began by administering to me a full dose of misfortune. When I returned from Europe, where the doctor had sent me, there was Chanler on the dock at Hoboken to meet me and take me to Tuxedo for the night, but first to lunch down town with Roosevelt and Cabot Lodge.

William Jennings Bryan had come to the fore. His demand for "free silver," and his genius for uttering emotional sound, had hypnotized a huge legion of followers. That he should be the Messiah of millions of American voters, struck me as a very dark omen for our democracy. And at lunch I asked them all —Roosevelt, Cabot Lodge and Chanler—if the country had sunk to the possibility of such a wind-bag becoming our President. They thought not, they thought McKinley would win; and all of us, of course, were going to vote for him. Not many years later, Roosevelt said that McKinley had a chocolate éclair backbone. But this did not hinder any of us from voting for him a second time; even with a backbone of that nature, a republican was better than free silver, even though free silver should possess the backbone of an ichthyosaurus.

"How long do you give the government at Washington to last?" I asked Roosevelt and Lodge as we sat lunching.

Those two students and writers—and makers—of history, well versed in the causes which have led to the downfall of the empires, kingdoms and republics that have had their day and gone into the night, were both silent for a moment; then one of them said:

"About fifty years."

Which of the two set this limit, I do not recall; I remember only that the other did not contradict him.

After that lunch, Roosevelt took me to Mulberry Street, and there described some of his activities as President of the Board of Police Commissioners in the City of New York; his midnight rambles and excursions, and how some of his ways gave serious offense in high quarters.

He was putting on weight and impressiveness with the passing of years, and the jaw was acquiring a grimness which his experience of life made inevitable; and beneath the laughter and the courage of his blue eyes, a wistfulness had begun to lurk which I had never seen in college; but the warmth, the eagerness, the boisterous boyish recounting of some anecdote, the explosive expression of some opinion about a person, or a thing, or a state of things—these were unchanged, and even to the end still bubbled up unchanged.

A certain Dr. Marvin Palmer, who had his day as a local celebrity, walked into Roosevelt's office in Mulberry Street, seeking an appointment as police surgeon. Dr. Palmer was generally to be seen of an evening, seated in a sort of park known as the Palm Garden over on Ninth Avenue, with a very large dog seated beside him. The doctor would smoke and blow each puff into the nose of his expectant dog, who inhaled it with thorough appreciation.

He bore to Roosevelt a letter of recommendation from one of the powers in high quarters, Mr. Crofts, surveyor of the port.

Mr. Crofts wrote that Dr. Palmer was perfectly qualified for the position of police surgeon; that as the Board was bi-partisan, a republican appointment would be timely, and that he "hoped and expected" Dr. Palmer would receive the appointment.

"I entirely agree," said Roosevelt, finishing the letter, "that a republican appointment would be timely.  And I am quite sure, Dr. Palmer, that you are qualified for the position."

He stopped; and the applicant felt that he was now a police surgeon, with a salary of 3,500 dollars a year.

"And here's the way you can get the position," continued Roosevelt, heartily.

"How?"

"Stand first on the Civil Service list."

Dr. Palmer said nothing.  He wheeled round to the door into the hall.  Then, with the door conveniently close, he turned.

"You can go to hell," said he; and shut the door quickly, for he did not wish to be caught by the neck and thrown down stairs.

Such were the proceedings of Roosevelt in Mulberry Street; and little imagination is needed to picture the feelings of the higher powers.   On that day in his Mulberry street office, 1896, Roosevelt assured me that he was politically dead.

The Spanish War was two years off; with his Governorship of New York as the direct consequence of the Rough Riders; with Senator Platt kicking him out of his way from the Governorship upstairs into the Vice Presidency to be politically dead henceforth; and with that bullet at Buffalo lurking quietly in the locker of Fate.

## VII.

The campaign preceding McKinley's election did not quite equal in bitterness and recrimination the days of 1884, when the issue was Cleveland or Blaine.  The issue in 1896 was in its essence very much graver: the issue was the economic honor and stability of the United States in the eyes and credit of the world. Nothing comparable to that had faced us since 1860, when it had been Union or Disunion, complicated with the momentous question of slavery. But this silver issue did not split the party which since 1860 had stood for Union, it bound it all the more tightly together. The number of silver Republicans was negligible, while the number of gold Democrats, though larger, raised within that party no additional discord to that which Cleveland in his stand for gold had already created. So here was a more serious question, evoking less violent recriminations.

Bryan was a true politician, a sham statesman, offering quack remedies with the persuasion that appeals to ignorance; but he was the voice of a growing protest against a growing abuse—the interlocking directorates between Big Business and Government. "Sixteen-to-one" held a magic more popular with multitudes than the appeal to reason, and the evils of a debased currency. To explain that sixteen-to-one would mean repudiation of our debts to foreign creditors, a loss of honor and prestige as a trustworthy nation, did not strike every voter as disastrous. Damaged credit and damaged honor were a weak answer to sixteen-to-one in many quarters of the Mississippi Valley.

The intelligence of this part of the country, like the rural centre in any country, was bound to suffer from its geographical position. No frontier had ever compelled it to think of foreign invasion as a possibility, no sea coast had ever brought ships and merchandise and foreign exchange and arbitrage and all such matters to its doors. As late as 1916, I tried to convince a man from the Mississippi Valley, who sat in a Pullman smoking compartment, that our state of unpreparedness was very dangerous. He was quite evidently in some sort of successful business where he lived, but what he said was, that it would give him pleasure to hear that New York had been bombarded; it would do those people in Wall Street good. That such an event was sure eventually to cause him and his town and state the gravest inconvenience, was something that I could not make conceivable to him.   He thought of the Mississippi Valley as related to nothing but itself; as late as 1916 his was the typical brain of one dimension.   That brain was even more so in 1896, and the McKinley-Bryan campaign was a season of great suspense.

Something that Roosevelt wrote during this period led me to reproach him for his will-to-optimism, and ask him how he could be so sweepingly buoyant in the face of a quantity of symptoms of which he was perfectly aware, and some of which we had discussed.   In his reply, he admitted that everything was not altogether so "couleur de rose" as he had implied.   That is the only phrase I recall; the letter, to my grief, has disappeared, as have several others which were of great interest.

William McKinley was elected in November, 1896, and Reason gave a long sigh of relief.   William Jennings Bryan, amiable, persuasive, important for many years after that, continued to pour out his unsubstantial eloquence, and it was during the Great War, that it reached its highest peak when he declared that if we were invaded, a million men would spring to arms before sun set, and Roosevelt inquired, to what arms would they spring?   This was answered in 1918, when we sprang to the arms which the Allies lent us in France.

These next two letters were written while Roosevelt was Assistant Secretary of the Navy, and concern my second Western book, *Lin McLean*.   At the close of the second letter, he tells me, evidently in answer to my having mentioned our difference of opinion about *Balaam and Pedro*, that he continues to disagree with me.

NAVY DEPARTMENT
Washington, D. C.

December 10, 1897.

. . . . . . . . . . . . . . . . . . .

Nothing could please me better than to see a volume of your stories; and, unlike your former volume, there will be some of these which will be new to me, because I have been so busy recently that I haven't read anything of any kind or sort. Aren't you going to get on here soon? The Lodges and I would be very glad to see you. Winty Chanler is coming here in a few days. Why can't you come on with him?

. . . . . . . . . . . . . . . . . . .

P.S. This was written the minute your volume came. I have just opened it at the last page. I like the poem so much, especially the final stanza—the immense silence and loneliness brooding over the plains, and the puncher, utterly indifferent to the gloom and awe, and gayly defiant of whatever fate has in store for him.

NAVY DEPARTMENT
Washington, D. C.

December 13, 1897.

. . . . . . . . . . . . . . . . . .

I have now read all your book, and taken it over to the Lodges. There was only one article I had not read. Need I say, what I am sure you would know without saying, how much I like it? There are a couple of points which I shall criticise when we meet, but they touch what I have already spoken to you about. I like not only the individual sketches, but the book as a whole. Yes, it is well summed up in the closing poem; and that's what I like about it. It has the broad humanity that comes when we deal with any men of strong and simple nature, with any kind of strenuous endeavor; and then it is a historic document for one phase of the life of endeavor in our race's history which is as evanescent as it is fascinating. There is more than Lin McLean in the book. There are Shorty and Chalkeye and Dollar Bill. There is the foreman, and why he was foreman: there is Honey Wiggin, and how he benefited by being a man of the world. There are the pine-clad mountains, and the endless plains of lilac-gray sagebrush, and the cotton woods that fringe the dwindling rivers. Of course all appeals to me with peculiar strength.

No, I have never changed about the eye incident. It should be done in the same way as Stevenson did the incident of the torture of the squirrel.

I am very glad that "A Virginian" is to appear in book form. It will include the "Emily"-hen, will it not?

. . . . . . . . . . . . . . . . . . . . . . .

Presently, bad news began to come from Cuba; and the advance agent of prosperity, as President McKinley was termed, had step by step to face the unfamiliar possibility of a war. Roosevelt as Assistant Secretary of the Navy, was, it was said, an uneasy thorn in the side of the Administration.   New words crept from Cuba into the daily dictionary of the American people—such as protocol, trocha, concentrados; and the cartoonists made us familiar with the appearance of General Weyler.   Spanish rule was creating havoc, distress and revolution in Cuba, and General Weyler was the instrument which Spain employed to reduce the Cubans to order.   In spite of his drastic measures, news of which came to occupy the general attention, Cuba got worse.   Protesting American voices were raised and grew louder, and more numerous.

War is little to the liking of both the British and American people; but the presence of hostile neighbors across twenty miles of salt water, has compelled the British for many centuries to take war into account as one of the evils at times necessary for self preservation.   Very naturally, the three thousand miles of salt water which have stood between us and possible invaders, have helped us to leave war out of our reckoning.   The case of Cuba aroused us for several reasons: the chief one being that the noise was just at our doors; we might have ignored cruelty and oppression, had they been further off; as it was, we began to feel it to be our duty in the name of liberty and humanity to help the weak little neighbor, and also to abate the nuisance.   Still, we hesitated, until the accident to our battleship the *Maine,* which had been sent to Havana harbor, settled our doubts.   The popular belief that the *Maine* had been blown up through Spanish agency may have been an error; probably it was; investigation pointed that way.   But we declared war on Spain almost in a flash after that.   "Remember the *Maine*" was the phrase that carried our national emotion.

On the day we declared war, I was married.   From her girlhood, my wife, Mary Channing Wister, had devoted herself to bettering in every way that she could the lot of needy and unfortunate children in Philadelphia. She conducted an Evening Home for boy waifs, where they could find both shelter and occupation more wholesome than the street. Their numbers increased as time went on. To give them something systematic and entertaining to think about, she taught them the operas of Sullivan and Gilbert. She picked the soloists and chorus, simplified the music, trained the singers, conducted the rehearsals, and carried through successful performances before an audience of friends and acquaintances. These watched her seated at the piano, playing with one hand, leading with the other in critical moments, and inspiring her devoted waifs to give spirited impersonations of Sir Joseph Porter, Little Buttercup, and the other personages of those tuneful and diverting compositions. The minds of several politicians began to consider with favorable interest this young woman, her sympathy, authority, and constructive power; and at the age of twenty-seven she was appointed very much the youngest member of the Board of Education. She was found to be a reformer whose high ideals never went beyond reasonable and practical accomplishment, who never tried for the impossible; and her power of persuasion was able to bring round to her way of thinking many who had been used to very different ways of thinking. It was her speech in 1897 before city councils that changed their adverse minds and won an appropriation for introducing music into the public schools. That she did not care for the credit of any wise suggestion that she made, but only that it should be carried out, was something they had seldom met before. As she matured, her usefulness and zeal increased, she became president of the Civic Club, and her name was known not only all through her State, but in many other States, from which people came to ask her advice in going about matters of public welfare in their own community. When she was forty-three, death removed her from the world, and the flags on Philadelphia public schools flew at half mast. She left six children. Fifteen years after her death, a memorial tablet to her was unveiled by one of her daughters in the new school building that bears her name.

There is but one piece of spiritual good fortune that surpasses having had the friendship of a great man, and that is to have had a perfect marriage.

All this is far away and long ago, doubly far and long, as it looks across the gulf of the Great War.  In those other days, it was much more uncommon than it is now for women to bestir themselves in matters of the public welfare; and to do so in Philadelphia was to step rather conspicuously outside of established convention—the things that "a lady could do."  It took a number of years for my wife to dispel the cold surprise with which her course was regarded here and there; but she did this in the end by keeping quietly and steadily on, avoiding notoriety, and never falling into those unwise extremes which are so often characteristic of people who mean well.

When Roosevelt discovered what sort of person she was who had been willing to have me for a husband, I think that his good opinion of me increased considerably.  It was some time before they met.  He had resigned as Assistant Secretary of the Navy, and plunged into the adventure of the Rough Riders.

A quick whirl of history blew round the United States between April and the end of that Summer of 1898.  Various European ambassadors met at the Austrian embassy in Washington to compose a threatening note to the United States, designed to give us the warning, Hands off Spain.  Their unfriendly plan was foiled by the English Ambassador, under whose roof they met the second day, and out of whose door they went discomfited.

I have told this tale at length elsewhere.  It is a tale which the Irish haters of England—mayors of New York and Chicago, and others—never tell.  Any more than they tell what the English admiral said to the German admiral before Dewey's fight in Manila Bay.  Any more than they tell what the Englishman in Egypt did about the coaling of the Spanish fleet that was going to sail for Manila through the Suez Canal.

In Manila Bay, Dewey said, "If you are ready, Gridley, you may fire."  Captain Clark sailed the *Oregon* round Cape Horn and came in time for the battle off Cuba. In Cuba the Rough Riders rode into history on San Juan Hill. McKinley did few better things than when he saw the stuff that Dr. Leonard Wood was made of, and, to the undying resentment of West Point, promoted him.

We lost but few lives in battle during that brief war, compared to the young men who died in swarms from foul conditions in camp. Nevertheless, that brief war opened a new chapter for us. The whirl of history put us among the world's great nations, which other great nations had never till then held us to be. We remain even to-day more ready to proclaim the glory of this, than to accept its responsibilities.

After disgusting Europe by our victory, we displeased her still more by our generosity. We did not annex Cuba. We liberated her, cleaned the yellow fever out of her, and came away, with the understanding that she must get on properly by herself. This, with one or two other conspicuous acts of a like nature, has made Europe peculiarly sensitive to our shortcomings; and to-day, since the future seems to be ours and the past hers, she is more sensitive than ever.

## VIII.

Out of that brief war, the Rough Riders also rode into the heart of the American People. Roosevelt had to be Governor of New York, greatly to the annoyance of Senator Platt; there was no resisting the demand for his nomination by the Republican party.

About this time I was evidently writing a tale for *Harper's,* entitled *The Game and the Nation,* which was designed to become subsequently a chapter in *The Virginian,* the general plan of which had been definitely formed since 1896. *Lin McLean* had followed *Red Men and White,* and I was now at work sometimes on *The Virginian* and at other times upon tales which were independent of that scheme. I had asked for some local Western information from the Governor of New York. He answered:

STATE OF NEW YORK
EXECUTIVE CHAMBER
Albany

March 16th, 1899.

DEAR DAN:

I have yours of the 15th inst.   I do wish I could see you.
I am really anxious to.   The stage coach times from the Black
Hills North to the Northern Pacific had a spasmodic existence.
From the end of 1883 to sometime in 1885 one ran to Medora.
After that time one ran to Dickinson.   The latter was the more
successful route, as it was all the way on an open prairie; whereas
the Medora route went part of the way through the Bad Lands.
It was a pretty wild country at the time the Medora line was
flourishing—the buffalo not yet gone, and an occasional scrap
with Indians of a mild sort.

Always yours ——

The day following, I wrote him some bad news of a Western
companion of mine of whom I had grown very fond, and who
had got into trouble.   He answered:

March 18th, 1899.

. . . . . . . . . . . . . . . . . .

I have yours of the 17th inst.   It makes one melancholy to
think how one's heroes get theatrical and noisy.   It is worse
when they die.   One of the men in my regiment, Darnell, the
bronco buster, a very brave and quiet man while with me, has
just been shot in Arizona, and my friends write me that it was
simply a case of his growing tough because he had been a Rough
Rider, and swelling about and doing the theatrical act, until
as Lt. Green remarked to me (with the magnificent vagueness
of the Southwesterner in dealing with such matters), "they
up and shot him."

By the way, I must say that I was very agreeably disappointed
in the southwesterners in my regiment.   I must have gotten
an unusually high class, for they were excellent men.   A great
many of them ran for office when they got home.   The Arizona
ones were all beaten.   The New Mexicans were generally
elected.   The present Speaker of the House and President of
the Senate in New Mexico were both members of my regiment
—game men and good fellows.

Remember me warmly to Mrs. Wister. I think that was a delightful, although odd way of spending the first summer.

. . . . . . . . . . . . . . . . . . . . . . .

This letter was of course type-written like its predecessor. But scrawled across the top of it in his own handwriting, evidently after it was laid on his desk to sign, are these further details about the journey from the Black Hills to Medora:

In going up from Deadwood to the N. P. you would have to pass through the following brands of cattle at the time you write—the E 6, the Lazy S, the Hash Knife, the O X, and the Three Sevens, besides smaller outfits. Also the W bar; the Bar open A, &c.

It was characteristic both of his astonishing memory and of his attentive friendship, that amid his crowded and heavy duties as Governor of New York, his mind should go back to what I had asked him in my first letter, and what he had answered; should perceive that he had not told me everything he knew which might be of use in the story I was writing, and proceed to furnish me with those details about the cattle brands. His remark about our odd way of spending the first Summer, refers to my having told him that my wife and I had left civilization after a wedding journey in South Carolina, and gone camping in the mountains of Washington, where I had shot white goat in 1892, and had been the guests of my class-mate Guy Waring, impersonator of Richard Coeur de Lion in the Dickey *Ivanhoe,* and now frontier trader in the valley of the Methow.

During the next twelve-month, Mr. Charles C. Harrison, Provost of the University of Pennsylvania, called me to help him in a matter of forest conservation; and out of this grew the correspondence which opens with Roosevelt's prompt reply to my appeal to him. His replies were invariably prompt.

March 26th, 1900.

. . . . . . . . . . . . . . . . . .

I have your telegram of the 26th.
Like the tantula (*sic*) I have troubles of my own even about

the Adirondack forests.    But of course I will do anything that
I can.    What is it I can do?    Why don't you write at once to
Lodge?    Something ought to be done and it ought to be done
by men in Washington. . . .

"Tantula" of course is a type-writer's error, which escaped
the eye of the Governor of New York when he was looking over
and signing his huge pile of dictated letters.    He had dictated
"tarantula", and it was a reference to an incident in the Santiago
campaign.    The chaplain of the Rough Riders, the Rev.
Church, got up one morning and was about to put his foot into
his boot, when a fine specimen of this sub-tropical spider
jumped out.    He killed it promptly, remarking, "Even a tarantula has troubles of its own."

UNITED STATES SENATE<br>
Washington, D. C.

March 28, 1900.

My dear Wister:
Over a month ago my attention was called to the matter of
the Calaveras trees.    I did what I could on my side toward
preserving them, and at the same time action was taken in the
House with the result that on March 3rd a resolution passed the
House authorizing the Secretary of the Interior to open negotiations for, and if possible, procure a bond upon the lands occupied by the trees with sufficient adjacent lands for their preservation, management and control.    This resolution then
passed the Senate, was signed by the President and is now a law,
so that the trees are safe.    I send you a copy of the resolution
as it passed and became law, and I trust that this will ease
your mind.
I will certainly give your message to Mrs. Lodge.

Very sincerely yours,

H. C. Lodge.

But Mr. Harrison assured me that there was something un-
disclosed, evidently unknown to Cabot Lodge; and I wrote
Roosevelt again.

April 4, 1900.

. . . . . . . . . . . . . . . . . .

All right.   Write me exactly what you want me to do and
I will do it.   Any button that I can touch I will touch.   This is
the third day before the adjournment of the Legislature, and
I eat, drink, sleep and think appointments and legislation—
machine men and mugwumps all in a conglomerate.   Now you
must tell me what you want me to do and I will do it right
away. . . .

Two days later he sent me a copy of his letter to the Secretary
of the Interior.

April 6th, 1900.

HON. ETHAN A. HITCHCOCK,
    Secretary of the Interior,
        Washington, D. C.

MY DEAR MR. HITCHCOCK:

Will you let me intrude for one moment to speak about something that I know is close to your heart also.   I do hope that
you will do everything, from straining the Constitution down
and up, to save the big trees at Calaveras.   We are all looking
to you to help us out in this.   I have been able to get started
here a scheme for saving the Hudson River Palisades, and
though I am up to my ears in the work of the closing hours of the
legislative session, I must just take a moment to beg you to do
what I know you will do anyway, and that is, save the Calaveras
trees if it is within the bounds of possibility. . . .

The reply to this he sent me on April 12.

April 11, 1900.

DEPARTMENT OF THE INTERIOR
Washington

HIS EXCELLENCY,
    GOVERNOR THEODORE ROOSEVELT,
        Albany, N. Y.

MY DEAR GOVERNOR:

I duly received, and thank you, for yours of April 6th regarding the preservation of the Calaveras trees, and need hardly
assure you that nothing shall be lacking, on my part, to save

the same, for the same reasons that you were inspired to save the Hudson River Palisades.

Underlying the proposition to save the Calaveras trees, however, there is one of the biggest and most iniquitous jobs that has turned up this session, which is saying a good deal, and which will be exposed in due time.

The scheme is to make Congress believe that the two groves had actually been purchased for a hundred thousand dollars, and that the trees thereon, large and small, would be cut up into lumber, unless the Government pay such a price for the property as the supposed buyer chose to demand, whereas the facts are that the owner of the trees has evidently entered into a conspiracy by which a deed for the sum named has been put in escrow in a California Bank Funding Congressional action, which, if successful, would enable the combine to divide the proceeds of millions upon millions of feet of lumber at at least two dollars and a half *per thousand* for property which costs them forty-four dollars and thirty-five cents an acre!

I may say to you in strict confidence that I am preparing a Bill and report asking Congress to give me authority to condemn the property under a proper appraisement, but it will not do to let this be known at present, as I am not quite ready with my report and Bill.

"For ways that are dark and tricks that are mean, the heathen Chinee is" *not* the only one that is peculiar. . . .

I treated the above as Roosevelt requested in the following:

April 12th, 1900.

. . . . . . . . . . . . . . . . . .

Treat the inclosed as purely confidential.

You remember how in Italy they sometimes bring birds around in front of houses where kind hearted people live and torture them unless they are ransomed? . . .

Again he refers to the matter, writing from Oyster Bay, May 16:

. . . I have just received the paper cover of your book and shall expect to find the book itself at Albany when I return. I shall enjoy it I know, for I enjoy everything that you ever write.

By the way, I tried to prod them up on the big tree business when I was in Washington. . . .

Amid the multitude of matters which occupied him daily, this had not slipped his mind. The singularly minute and tenacious quality of his brain may be very fairly compared with that of George Washington, whom he resembled in but few other points, except his muscular patriotism. In reading the fourteen volumes of Washington's letters which have been so admirably edited by Mr. Worthington Ford, one's amazement at Washington's capacity to be dealing with the life and death of his country without losing track for a single moment of household and plantation matters at Mount Vernon, never wears out. In the midst of such a time as Valley Forge, with starving troops to deal with, with desertions, lack of clothes, lack of powder and shot, and with a legislature mostly of imbeciles to lean on, Washington carries the whole load on his shoulders, and yet finds intervals to write about this and that slave, or to say that claret is enough hospitality in the way of wine for strangers who call without any claim; and that the madeira is to be kept for visitors who are personal friends. In a wholly different era, and with wholly different and less desperate, but more complex problems, Roosevelt's mind acted in the same fashion; the large questions, the misdeeds of insurance companies for instance, did not engulf the little ones, the little ones did not divert his attention from the large; he attended to both. In short, the brains of Washington and Roosevelt had a tremendous grip. This similarity between them has been obscured by their widely unlike temperaments; Washington stately, silent, patient, passionate; Roosevelt bounding through existence, vivacious, humorous, impatient, trenchant, scattering hearty words and hard blows wherever he came.

He said to me once in the room where he worked at Sagamore Hill, sitting at the desk near the telephone, and spacing his words in that way of his for emphasis:

"I have—only—a second rate brain—but—I think—I—have—a—capacity—for action."

I repeated this to Lord Bryce in London, a few years after Roosevelt's death.

Lord Bryce shook his head. "He didn't do himself justice there, you know. He had a brain that could always go straight to the pith of any matter. That is a mental power of the first rank. And that is what it's for you to bring out when you write about him, which you should."

Need it be brought out by any one to-day? That power to go to the pith of any matter manifested itself in various ways, and quite often. His very phrases were compact instances of it: *Speak softly and carry a big stick; race suicide*. These, with many like them, are still remembered after a quarter of a century, because they hit the truth at a blow. Some of the papers found *race suicide* amusing, and ridiculed it.

"But my dear Dan," he remarked, "they seem unable to see that it's simply a question of the multiplication table. If all our nice friends in Beacon Street, and Newport, and Fifth Avenue, and Philadelphia, have one child, or no child at all, while all the Finnegans, Hooligans, Antonios, Mandelbaums and Rabinskis have eight, or nine, or ten—it's simply a question of the multiplication table. How are you going to get away from it?"

And on that subject, another day, he read me a letter in the morning mail. When I recall what his morning mail looked like, my own, rather alarming at times, dwindles to microscopic proportions.

The letter came from a good woman in the Middle West. She mentioned the income upon which her husband and she could depend, and that it would support no more children than were already born of their union. But that if he could provide them the additional sum required, they would have another child as soon as possible.

Lord Bryce on that same day in London, 1921, with the proofs of part of his final book on the table, also said very slowly, thinking of the book:

"A political career brings out the basest qualities in human nature."

"That is a very sad remark," I said.

"I fear that it's true, though."

"But there have been some pretty noble exceptions."

"Very few."

"What would our friend have had to say to that?"

"Ah, but Roosevelt wouldn't always look at a thing, you know!"

There Lord Bryce put his finger on the secret of the wistfulness that lurks so deep behind the gaiety and the battle which shone in Roosevelt's eyes for every one to see.

Stand, some day, if you have the opportunity, in front of the Lee of Fareham portrait which hangs in the great living room that his friend Grant La Farge built for him at Sagamore Hill. Study the eyes very carefully. Energy in repose is expressed by the vigorous, seated figure. He wears riding breeches, holds a crop across his knees, and he is looking straight at you. It is the Roosevelt who has been a Rough Rider, and has gone on to greater things, and is by no means finished with them. He is in the noon of his strength. But there, in the eyes, is that something else which the painter had caught, and which John Sargent catches also in the portrait which hangs in the White House.

Emerson and Walt Whitman are both said to have lacked an adequate vision of evil; and to this is ascribed what some people have thought was a serious defect in their philosophy. Roosevelt was quite aware of evil, vividly so; he had come face to face with every stage of it, from its crude forms in the West, up through its complexities in New York night life, to its final sophistications in the world of politics. He could write me from Mulberry Street that America criticized crimes but refused to hold criminals responsible. That is an accurate generalization about one of the sinister threats to our national health. Yet he would frequently publish an article giving us so clean a bill of health, that it impelled me to protest; upon which he would write back and admit he was afraid we weren't quite so well as all that. And it pained him to hear evil about some one of whom he had too hastily thought well.

He had come back from one of his Western trips about 1905,

and was speaking with the warmest enthusiasm about a man he had met during his journey. I ought to know him, he said; and told me of some good achievement by this man. I had known him once, I answered. And I told him of something which the man had done, not under stress, but by some clever calculation, which was analogous to cheating at cards.

"Don't take my word for it," I said. And I named others whom he might ask; for I wasn't sure that he mightn't be thinking of appointing this man to some office.

And while I was talking, he looked at me fixedly, and the pain came into his face more and more.

"Really!" he exclaimed in a subdued tone when I was finished. "Really!" he repeated. And the wistfulness blurred his eyes— that misty perplexity and pain, which Sargent has caught so well. This look was the sign of frequent conflict between what he knew, and his wish not to know it, his determination to grasp his optimism tight, lest it escape him in the many darknesses that rose around him all along his way. Vigor, humor, animal spirits were a great help.

On May 26, 1900, he writes from Oyster Bay. He is still Governor of New York, but the end of that is drawing near.

. . . . . . . . . . .

Just a word to say how much I like the *Jimmyjohn Boss* and your other stories. But then I always do like your stories. I particularly prize having the book with the inscription from you. . . .

This was my third Western volume. It included all the sketches written between *Hank's Woman* in 1891, and *Padre Ignacio* written in 1899, which had not gone into *Red Men and White* or *Lin McLean*, or were not designed to become chapters in *The Virginian*. It brought one of Winthrop Chanler's characteristic letters, so racy, so graced with style; the sort of stuff English literature abounds in, and American literature will produce when our civilization attains maturity.

U. S. M. S. "St. Paul."

May 23d, 1900.

OMAR DEAR DANIEL: (This was Chanler's customary bad pun: Oh my dear, Omar dear, because I sometimes wrote verse)

I lied like a foul fulsome beast when I wrote you that I had read your new pup—I hadn't done no such a thing. I read the cover. Then I ran through the Jimmy John Boss with only half an eye and over the Kinsman of Red Cloud and so slept till morn. Since, I have read your bookie through and likes it all. I like all you have to say about Sharon in "20 minutes" and the "choice." I like the Jimmy John boy, though a *leetle* over drawn, but full of plums. Specially the old pedlar "that's what"—I don't like Nap. Shave tail. It is not the real thing, and doesn't ring true, not a line of it, but the two buck chiefs pulling over the tepee with a lariat and finding the dead man inside saves it.

Last of all I read P. Ignacio. My Missus will like that. It is the only one she will like because she is hampered by a foreign bringing up and a total distaste for the West acquired in an exile at the Maillard ranch.

That is a nice story and a new departure. Keep it up. Lin McLean et al. can't live forever.

Goodbye. Love to your real nice wife.

Yours

WINT

The *Game and the Nation,* now a part of *The Virginian,* was in *Harper's* at the time, and brought comments from another American socially seasoned by inheritance. John Jay Chapman's letters usually teemed with abuse and dripped with cultivation. Chanler was his brother-in-law.

JOHN JAY CHAPMAN
ATTORNEY & COUNSELLOR AT LAW
56 Wall Street
New York

May 16, 1900.

DEAR DAN:

Your story in the current Harpers is A 1.

I read it with all my prejudice against you. Against the

West.   Against Harpers Magazine, and against short stories—in full blast.

It is frightfully well done.   It is cooked up and genre.   I call anything genre which asks you to humor it more or less.   But it has a quality that is common to real life and great fiction—that the words said by the characters and the real thing that is happening in them, run two separate courses.

Yours aff

JJC

On June 11, 1900, the Governor of New York writes from Albany:

. . . I have just received your two letters.

The hitch about West as far as I am concerned is that I simply can't recommend a man I do not know in a State in which I have no earthly concern.   If I were Secretary of the Interior your recommendation would have the very greatest weight with me, but Warren would not pay the slightest attention to a letter from me on such a matter and would probably regard it as an impertinence.   I hate not to do anything you ask.

I do hope I shall see you at Philadelphia.   Use this letter to get admission to me at once anywhere I am. . . .

His final sentence refers to the approaching convention of the Republican party, where McKinley will be nominated for a second term, and the Governor of New York will be caught in the net skilfully woven for him by the Boss of New York, Senator Platt, whose schemes have been sorely hindered by the Governor.

Those Sunday morning breakfasts which the Governor has been taking with Mr. Platt, have disturbed Mr. Platt's digestion even more seriously than they have scandalized the parlor pets of Virtue.   The voice of these pets has been raised in horror that Roosevelt should be breaking bread with the Devil. The New York *Evening Post,* and the *Nation,* which, with Godkin as editor, began as a paper with a brain behind it, and high independent ideals, had, through its incessant bitterness about evil and its too faint praise of good, degenerated into a common scold, a paper without a country.   *The Nation* was virtually a

IN AMBUSH FOR THE ROUGH RIDER
From the New York World

weekly version of *The Evening Post*.   It was the chief organ of the pets.   Roosevelt was held up as Our Great Disappointment, gone over to the Enemy.   He gave his account of those breakfasts to me now and then at the time; since then, he has spoken of them in his own writings, and there is no need for me to explain the perverted interpretation that was put upon them by the *Evening Post* school of reformers.   In a word, Roosevelt *laid his cards on Platt's breakfast table* for Platt to fall in with his plans, or fight them: mostly Platt had to fall in.   But here I certainly will point out one inadvertence on the part of these critics in 1900.   If breakfasting with the Devil was satisfactory to the Devil, if he got what he wanted out of Roosevelt at those meals, why did the Devil get rid of Roosevelt as quick as ever he could?   Why kick a useful tool upstairs into the Vice Presidency?   The pets were silent on this point.

Roosevelt's reference to West in his letter, was to a friend of mine who wished, if I remember—to be a forest warden. George West was a dear friend, a companion in many of my long camping trips up Wind River and over the Divide to Jackson's Hole.   A personal experience he told me in 1887 suggested the tale *How Lin McLean Went East.*

The Republican convention at Philadelphia came off.   For some time before it, the air had been skillfully filled with the suggestion that the Governor of New York would make a "good running mate" for McKinley, would be of great aid in killing the sixteen-to-one snake, which was scotched, but by no means dead.   Bryan had almost a strangle-hold in the Middle West.

I was easily able to "get admission" to the Governor of New York.   The Philadelphia Club was not five minutes from his room in a hotel.   It may well be that he lived other hours of his life more distracting, but this one I saw.   As I came in, he sprang at me from the circle of reporters that surrounded him, hailed me with a kind of shout, tried to say something, was caught by the elbow, asked a new question, turned to the questioner, turned to me, waved a hopeless arm, dropped a word

about hoping for a chance later, that I saw what this was like;—
and was again amid the eddy of reporters.

The room was not large, the weather was not cool, and a
human mass of people with pencils surged and wedged round
him without ceasing.  Sweat glistened on everybody.  I stood
back for a while by the door, watching, and listening to fragments of questions and replies.

"My work at Albany I regard as important for the public
good, and—"

A voice would cut in on words like this he was hammering out,
each word struck with a blow of emphasis.

"No.   I can be of more use in my present—"

Another interruption.  Another attempted answer.  Roosevelt whirling from one questioner to another, meeting, parrying.
Somebody rushing in with later news.  Platt's net closing on
him.

"I will say that my own personal wish—"

Turmoil, interruptions; suppose the American people demand?   Does he prefer to help his party, or his State?   Pencils poised like hawks.

"You may say—"

And so forth.   Fights were as wine in his nostrils; but not
this fight, if it can be called one.   No joy was in his face as they
badgered and harried him; he wanted those breakfasts to go on.
But Platt did not.   So Platt's net closed on the Governor, and
the Republican ticket nominated at Philadelphia was McKinley
and Roosevelt.

And what had the parlor pets of Virtue to say then?

"Why did he go to Philadelphia if he didn't intend to be Vice
President from the first?"

Senator Platt was well satisfied: a good time for him coming
with no more Sunday breakfasts.   So far as he was concerned,
Roosevelt was politically dead.

I do not remember whether Roosevelt told me that he was
politically dead when I went to Sagamore Hill during July.   He
had written on the 9th, " . . . Can you not get down here for a

night sometime this summer?    I should like to talk with you over many things. . . ."

That is what always happened: we talked over many things—so many, and often with such a rush, that what I had selected in my head to ask him was generally swept out of my head; in time I took to making a list.    The list would contain political, historical, literary, and personal questions—sometimes about birds. I knew just a little about birds.    I had tried twice to tame young sparrow hawks.    Did he think it could be done?    Or, did he know if there was any difference between the English and American barn swallow?    Or did he know anything new that was characteristically American in fiction?    Once he had answered this by recommending *Tales of Soldiers and Civilians,* by Ambrose Bierce.    I think he sent me the book.    It is a book which should be more famous than it is.    I will go so far as to say that I think some of the tales surpass the very best of Edgar Allan Poe's.

The only clear thing which I recall of this visit in July, 1900, is that about sunset, as we were walking toward the house across the lawn at the back, young voices came to us from an open window in the second story, and he stopped.

"That is Mrs. Roosevelt with the children and their religious teaching," said he.

One question I asked him he was never able to answer, it had puzzled him often: When and why did the American rule of the road change from the English?    It was the sort of trifle in the history of manners and customs which had a particular appeal to him.

On the 14th, he says—"I was glad to read West's letter which I return herewith.    Remember I am to see you somehow this summer. . . ."

After that visit, I was in California and in Oregon, correcting proofs and collecting facts.    I completed my facts about the Modoc War and Captain Jack and the massacre of General Canby, which had taken me from Arizona to Portland in distance, and two years in time.    When participators and witnesses found I had struck the real trail, they became frank. I talked with every accessible army officer surviving, and was ready to begin a tale based upon that war and the Battle of the Lava Beds, when I suddenly discovered that the villain of the piece had been the father of a lady who had shown me every hospitality. That ended it. To change my villain was utterly impossible, owing to the facts of the case. So that book was never written; and I doubt if the true story of the Modoc War will ever be told, which is a pity; it would make a dark and thrilling page of our frontier history, it would place the blame for that tragedy where it belongs, not where report and tradition have rested it. In Oregon I went over the ground of The Bannock Campaign with an old army scout, J. W. Redington. My stories in *Red Men and White* had set him to writing to me; he had participated in some of the incidents I described. This led to a long friendship. As to the Bannock War, I heard his memories of it, and saw Malheur Lake, and after leaving Redington, and making full notes and drawings of the lay of the land, these also went on the shelf along with the notes which army officers had given me about the Bannocks and Buffalo Horn, their evil medicine man, and Chief E-egante. That tragic tale, to Redington's disappointment with me, never has been, and never will be, written; and it also would make a thrilling page in our frontier history. I shall digress here, and tell one incident which I told Roosevelt, and which very naturally fascinated him. It was related to me by my friend and his, F. A. Edwards of the 2nd Cavalry, when I was staying with him at San Carlos, Arizona, a post now long abandoned.

In Idaho, where Edwards had been stationed just previous to the outbreak of the Bannocks, he had made friends with E-egante. E-egante was an extremely handsome chief, tall and royal in bearing, and friendly to the white man. It was his habit to ride into the post frequently and when he came, he always paid a visit to Edwards. He could speak English fairly well. During one of these visits, a great storm set in, and then the dark. The Indian, who would have put his tepee at the disposal of the white man in a moment, had the situation been reversed, said:

"E-egante will sleep here."

This was something Edwards could not have at all; he answered that his quarters contained but one bed.

The chief indicated a sort of sofa, covered with Indian blankets.

"That will be good," he said.

But again Edwards offered some objection.

Still in perfect good faith, the Indian stretched his arm towards the bear rug in front of the fire.

"E-egante will sleep there."

When he was met by the third objection, the truth broke upon his completely trusting and naïf understanding. He drew himself to his full height, threw his blanket over his shoulders, and without a word departed into the storm and darkness.

He continued to visit the post as before, and as before, whenever he rode in, he paid a visit to Edwards: but on these visits he was now always accompanied by an interpreter: through this interpreter the visit was ceremoniously conducted, E-egante stating in his own language what he wished to say, and the interpreter translating it to Edwards. The chief never again addressed a direct word to Edwards.

To Captain Frank Edwards I owe countless events and details of that old frontier military life, and endless hospitality at the old frontier posts where I was his guest. He passed me on to military friends all over the West, and so, being passed from one officer to another, I became the guest of Major McGregor, southwest and northwest, of Captain John Pitcher, Captain George Anderson, Captain Markley, Colonel Arnold, Captain Boutelle, Captain Fowler, Colonel Kent, General Forsythe, and others. Through all of these hospitable officers I learned a great deal at first hand, and saw a great deal; and it would have filled a dozen more volumes of American romance than I have been able to write. To none of these army friends with whom I passed so many interesting and delightful hours from the

Canadian to the Mexican border, was I ever able to make any return better than my grateful appreciation—and inscribed copies of my scribbling, save to Frank Edwards.

When Roosevelt became President, Edwards wrote me asking my advice as to the tact of his requesting the appointment of military attaché to some European embassy.  He had passed a quarter of a century in the wilderness, fighting Indians, or vegetating at horrible posts like San Carlos.  Having no political pull, he had never got any relief or change from this life. He had seen younger men with political pull able to get away from military duty with their regiments, and pass idle weeks and months, and sometimes years, in Washington, or elsewhere, on details procured for them by influence.  Didn't I think it was time he had something?  Should he write Roosevelt?  I answered, "you wait."  I kept Edwards in mind, and one day in the summer of 1902 at Sagamore Hill, I opened the subject.

"Frank Edwards!" exclaimed the President.  "I should think so!  A capital officer and a capital fellow.  What does he want?"  And when I told him, he immediately made a note of it.  "Thank you, Dan, for telling me that.  I might never have thought of it.  Edwards shall have something the very first chance that comes along."  When the chance came, Edwards was appointed military attaché at Rome.

STATE OF NEW YORK
EXECUTIVE CHAMBER
Albany

December 22, 1900.

. . . I have your note of recent date.  No, I never got that note from Mrs. Wister.  I am awfully sorry.  Will you give her my regards and say I beg her pardon.  I wish I could accept but it is absolutely out of the question.  I cannot undertake another speech of any kind or sort at present.

I am rather amused at that magazine having said that I was going to write.  It asked me to write on the ground that you and Remington were going to. . . .

And nine days later, New Year's Eve:

. . . It was a great surprise to me to receive your sketch of Grant.   I am so glad you wrote it.   I am sure I shall like it, for I doubt if you have in America a more consistent admirer of your writings.

With warm regards to Mrs. Wister and wishing you both a Happy New Year. . . .

UNITED STATES SENATE
Washington, D. C.

Personal.

January 29, 1901.

MY DEAR WISTER:

I read last night your Life of Grant and I want to congratulate you upon it with the utmost sincerity.   It seems to me most beautifully and admirably done, and I appreciate the difficulties of dealing with such a career in so contracted a space.   You have given a most vivid picture of the man and brought out in high relief his greatness.   It is an artistic triumph to paint such a picture on so small a canvas.   We may differ, and men may always differ, about Grant's rank purely as a soldier; I should rate him much higher than you do, and I remember well John Ropes admitting to me at the time of Grant's death, when I wrote a long sketch of him for one of our newspapers, that the Vicksburg campaign was quite equal to the campaign of Ulm. But you have shown that upon which I think we all ought to agree, although it is too often over-looked, that he was a great man with a grasp of the central principle, with a simplicity and purity of purpose and a magnanimity which are very splendid things to number among our national possessions.   Such a brief sketch as yours, in order to succeed, had to have the qualities of the lyric in its compactness, concentration and force.   I think you have attained to this in a very high degree.

Now, I am going to complete my criticism by finding fault, not with anything relating to Grant, but as to two statements of yours which are merely incidental to the narrative.

You speak of the issues of the greenbacks as if it were both a crime and a blunder, and although I am probably quite as hostile to an irredeemable currency as you, I think you are mistaken on this point.   The issue of the greenbacks was not to borrow money.   As a forced loan the amount was trivial compared with what we borrowed by bonds.   The object of the greenbacks was to give us a circulating medium.   You know nothing of the time by personal experience, and I was only a child, but I still remember the days when we had no currency except postage stamps and tokens of various sorts issued by shop keepers.   If we had not supplied ourselves with a currency the war could not have been carried on.   A circulating medium was essential, and the issue of greenbacks was one of the great measures which saved the Union.   Since the invention of paper credit, if you will stop to consider the question for a moment, you will find that every great, protracted war has been carried on upon an irredeemable, paper currency.   We fought, and won, our revolution on paper money of the most debased kind.   England suspended specie payments and fought the Napoleonic Wars on irredeemable paper.   Waterloo had gone into the past four years when the Bullion Commission reported (1819).   It was not until two or three years later that England resumed specie payments.   France fought the great battles of her Revolution against banded Europe upon the assignats.   There is no need to multiply examples.   The thing is inevitable if the war is sufficiently great and sufficiently protracted.   Moreover, there is no more wrong in borrowing money in this way and supplying a circulating medium than there is in borrowing money to build a house.   If the paper is subsequently repudiated that is in the highest degree dishonest, but we have redeemed the greenbacks in gold, just as we have paid all other debts in gold.

The other point is this: You say Sheridan, if he had had an opportunity, might have surpassed all the other men, and ranked with Charles of Sweden and Condé.   I agree with you that he might have surpassed the other men, but why say that he might have equalled Charles of Sweden and Condé.   There is not one of the men you mention on that page who is not far greater as a soldier than either the Swedish King or the French Prince. Charles the 12th was a brilliant adventurer; he inherited a great tradition and the best army in Europe.   He won some battles, and lost some.   He had a meteoric career, displayed great courage and much incapacity in his last fight, and went down under defeat.   He had no staying powers whatever.   He belongs in the same class as Montrose, whom Gardiner, with the love of the perverse, which characterizes the modern antiquarian historian, has tried to set above Cromwell.   I should think that in military talent, Charles might rank with Forrest, who was, in his line, a very remarkable man.   As for Condé, if you take from him his royal blood, the adjective "great" and half a mile of pictures at Versailles, not a great deal remains.   It is true that he won Rocroi and a number of very brilliant actions.   He was a gallant gentleman, with a certain showy talent, but he never got anywhere and the wars of the Fronde were as ineffective as any fighting that I know.   He was distinctly inferior to Turenne and to his own pupil Luxembourg.   The fact is that great soldiers divide themselves into two classes.   We have Alexander, Napoleon and Hannibal the greatest of them all, towering geniuses who stand in a class by themselves.   Then there are the very great soldiers of history who are all in a distinctly lower class, but who differ among themselves in degree but not in kind.   The English speaking race has never produced a soldier of the Caesar or Napoleon type, and I do not believe ever will, but we have produced a number of very great soldiers of a type peculiar to the race.   Among these are Cromwell and Marlborough and Wellington; Washington, Lee, Stonewall Jackson, Grant, Sherman, Sheridan and Thomas.   Men's opinions may vary as to the amount of talent in each of these men. I think myself that they all stand about equal as to their greatness and capacity.   There are some continental soldiers who would rank with them, but certainly neither Charles 12th nor Condé.

I think to say that Sheridan might have reached the rank of Charles and Condé is very much as if we were to say that Washington, if he had had the opportunity, might have reached the rank of Bolivar.

I am afraid you will think my discussion of these two points not only long and tedious but that it outweighs what I have said about your book generally, but I assure you that I should not have trespassed on your time so much if the book had not deeply interested me and aroused in me very great admiration.   I can, I think, almost forgive Charles and Condé for your single line in regard to Wolseley's criticism of our war  when you say that he had not then suppressed the Boers.   That is quite perfect. I can only say, in conclusion, "do it some more."

With kindest regards,

Sincerely yours,

H. C. LODGE.

VICE PRESIDENT'S CHAMBER

Washington

March 11th, 1901.

. . . I have now read through your book again, most carefully. . . . It seems to me that you have written the very best short biography which has ever been written of any prominent American.    Indeed, I cannot now recall any volume of the same size as yours about any man of Grant's standing which comes as high.    Now, other things being equal, the best short book is always better than the best long book; for while it is very easy to write a second-rate short account of a great man, it is the most difficult of all historical tasks to write the best possible short account of a great man.    This you have done.    Your book is a masterpiece of eloquent condensation, without the slightest sacrifice of historical perspective.    It is noble in manner and noble in matter.    In it you sketch in sharpest outline the silent soldier who will stand forever as one of those few men—few in any nation—who must be called great even when judged by world standards.    I thank you for having written such a book. . . .

Oyster Bay, N. Y. March 20, 1901.

. . . Are you coming this way soon?    I want very much to see you.

Cabot (Lodge) told me what he had written to you about Condé and the 'Swedish Madman'.    In a way I do not agree with his estimate of Sheridan as compared with these two men. But I was sorry you thought it necessary to couple his name with theirs at all, for they seem to be entirely different types of commanders.    Condé at Rocroi won one of the great battles of history, performing a greater single feat than ever Sheridan did and quite in the Sheridan style.    On the other hand, Condé afterwards sank below the Sheridan level.    As for Charles (of Sweden) he really was an Alexander *manqué*.    His wonderful brilliancy and stupendous folly make it exceedingly difficult to compare any other commander with him. . . .

Oyster Bay, N. Y. April 4th, 1901.

. . . I do not know precisely what point Lodge made about Condé and Charles 12th in connection with Sheridan, but from curiosity I have been looking up their careers and I want to say, in the first place, that I appreciate better than I did why you selected them for comparison with Sheridan; and in the next place, that I feel they will loom larger in the history of the military art.    I think the comparison to be made or implied in connection with them is very partial, but each belonged to the dash-

ing order of generals— to the type that strikes quick and hard
and always strives to get the drop on the adversary.   I think
that Sheridan at the end was a greater general than either
Condé or the Swede was at the end, for Sheridan grew, while an
astounding thing about each of the others is that he was at his
best in the beginning and fell off afterwards.   But I do not think
that Sheridan's best was ever equal to the best of either the
Swede or the Frenchman. . . .

By the following letter I appear to have written him con-
gratulations on the news that he was to receive a degree from
Yale; and to have added that he was too young for LL.D.'s yet,
and ought to wait till he had silver hairs.   And I evidently expressed my admiration for Frank Norris, whose *McTeague* remains still vivid in my memory—more vivid than his *Octopus*,
or any other of his novels; though in *Moran of the Lady Letty*,
written before Norris had fallen under the misleading spell of
Zola, he drew an unforgettable woman.

Oyster Bay, N. Y. July 20th, 1901.
   . . . I am immensely amused over the first part of your note
of the 19th.   If LL.D.'s were only to be granted to old men,
well and good.   But they are not only so granted.   I took the
greatest pleasure in voting one for Rhodes.   He has won it.
But these honors are chiefly a matter of rather small vanity, and
I only mentioned it because of the contrast between Yale, Columbia, and Princeton on the one hand and Harvard on the other.
At Yale this year I understand that Seth Low, Whitelaw Reid,
Bishop Potter and Archbishop Ireland are to be among my
companions in getting the LL.D.   Unless I mistake, it has been
given by Harvard to Leonard Wood and also to General Miles—
which last is preposterous.   It was eminently proper to give it
to Wood, although he is neither a scholar nor gray haired.
   Your coming here started me to re-reading your pieces.   I
want to reiterate my judgment that the Pilgrim on the Gila,
Specimen Jones and the Second Missouri Compromise are
among the very best.   I think they have a really very high
value as historical documents which also possess an immense
human interest.   When you speak of the teachings of the Mormon bishop as having no resemblance to the Gospels but being

right in the line of Deuteronomy, you set forth a great truth as
to the whole Mormon Church.    I shall always believe that
Brigham Young was quite as big a man as Mahomet.    But the
age and the place were very unfavorable.

When I see Hitchcock I shall try to get you the insides of that
Big Tree intrigue.

Now, about that book by Frank Norris, *The Octopus*.    I read
it with interest.    He has a good idea and he has some power, but
he left me with the impression that his over-statement was so
utterly preposterous as to deprive his work of all value.    A good
part of it reads like the ravings which Altgeld and Bryan regard
as denunciation of wrong.    I do not know California at all, but
I have seen a good deal of all the western States between the
Mississippi and the western sides of the Rocky Mountains.
I know positively that as regards all those states—the Dakotas,
Montana, Wyoming, Idaho, Colorado and New Mexico—the
facts alleged in the *Octopus* are a wild travesty of the truth.
It is just exactly as if in writing about the tyranny and corruption
of Tammany Hall I should solemnly revive the stories of Mediaeval times and picture Mr. Croker as bathing in the blood of
hundreds of babies taken from the tenement houses, or of having Jacob Schiff tortured in the Tombs until he handed over a
couple of million dollars.    The overstatement would be so preposterous that I would have rendered myself powerless to call
attention to the real and gross iniquity.

Of course the conditions in California may have been wholly
different from those in every other western State, but if so,
Norris should have been most careful to show that what he
wrote was absolutely limited by State lines and had no application to life in the west as a whole.    What I am inclined to think
is that conditions were worse in California than elsewhere, and
that a writer of great power and vigor who was also gifted with
self restraint and with truthfulness could make out of them a
great tragedy, which would not, like Norris's book, be con-
temptuously tossed aside by any serious man who knew western
conditions, as so very hysterical and exaggerated as to be without any real value.

More and more I have grown to have a horror of the reformer
who is half charlatan and half fanatic, and ruins his own cause
by overstatement.    If Norris's book is taken to apply to all the
west, as it certainly would be taken by any ordinary man who
reads it, then it stands on an exact level with some of the publica-

tions of the W. C. T. U. in which the Spanish War, our troubles in the Philippines, and civic dishonesty and social disorder, are all held to spring from the fact that Sherry is drunk at the White House. . . .

What I am inclined to think is that conditions were worse in California than elsewhere.

In that surmise, Roosevelt was entirely right—unless my own sufferings on the Southern Pacific railway were exceptional; and unless what my friends in San Francisco had to say of the sufferings of California in general in the huge grasp of the Southern Pacific were very much overstated; and I don't think they were.   I did not hear these complaints once, I heard them season after season during those years of the early nineties when I was constantly, and for weeks together, in San Francisco. Unless you came by sea you could not get into or out of California, except by the Southern Pacific, until the much later arrival of the Sante Fé.   Every passenger over land, every head of stock, every grown fruit or vegetable, every manufactured article, had to travel over the rails built and controlled by C. P. Huntington and his small group of associates, who also controlled the legislature.   Consequently, the rates that shippers had to pay, with the arbitrary discriminations against which they had no redress, did constitute a very oppressive tyranny indeed. And, as Roosevelt suggests, a great tragedy could have been created out of all this by the right man—an American Dickens, with more restraint than Dickens.   Norris based his main situation on a notorious incident—the Mussel Slough:—but the fortune of being intelligently criticized never befell this very highly endowed writer, he was surrounded by mere admirers, and his book did not rise to the level to which his rare talent might have lifted it.   *The Octopus* presents no proportionate recognition of the fact that the courage, the vision, and the ability of C. P. Huntington created the original railroad, the Central Pacific, pushed it across the barrier of the Sierra Nevada, and linked California with the rest of the country.   This put the State on the map of reality instead of the map of romance; it touched commerce and transportation to life. The man who does this for any community is an enormous benefactor to that community, no matter how much he may afterwards abuse his power, which C. P. Huntington undoubtedly did.

In this connection, I beheld with my own eyes in December, 1893, a Southern Pacific drama, not a great tragedy, but a high comedy, enacted at the foot of Market Street, San Francisco.

From that point the Southern Pacific ferry ran to Oakland. The fare to Oakland was twenty-five cents. The citizens using the ferry back and forth each day, found this price excessive; and right under the Southern Pacific's nose next door, a little independent ferry started business, and charged—I think—fifteen cents to go over to Oakland. I heard much rejoicing expressed at this: now they would show the Southern Pacific what you got for being a hog. The Southern Pacific made no observation; it merely put its fare to ten cents (if those were the figures; the point is, it merely made its fare lower than that of the little independent ferry). This was a wage on which the little ferry could not do business and live. But what did the intelligent business men traveling between San Francisco and Oakland do? They bitterly upbraided the new ferry for being dearer than the Southern Pacific, to whose ferry they all promptly returned. The little ferry struggled feebly a few days, and starved to death. Then the Southern Pacific put its fare back to twenty-five cents.

To conclude this brief historical summary: In time C. P. Huntington, a giant type of peddler, was gathered to his fathers, and a civilized man of higher constructive genius took hold of the Southern Pacific—E. H. Harriman. The personality of the head of any corporation, no matter how extensive, permeates it from top to bottom. Almost in the twinkling of an eye, train service improved, employees ceased to be indifferent and brutal, and the Southern Pacific was transformed. It was firmly established by now, and ready to get out of politics. Therefore, when Hiram Johnson got it out, the credit which this brought him among those who were not behind the scenes, very greatly exceeded the amount of struggle that he had to make. Upon the wave of this credit he rode very far for a number of years; and in 1919, when I was last among the Californians, I learned from many who gave instances to prove it, that the political machine which Hiram Johnson had substituted for that of the Southern Pacific, was quite as unscrupulous in method, and gave that state less for its money.

## IX.

Soon after his letter of July 20, Roosevelt must have gone to the Adirondacks; it was the last, unless some are missing, that I ever received from him as Vice President. On September 14 he was President of the United States. No need to recall in detail here the crime at Buffalo; the messenger hastening with his news into the woods; Roosevelt hastening out of camp to the railroad, and to Buffalo; the few days of suspense; the nervous stock market—still not quite itself again since the "corner" in Northern Pacific in May—and then, after suspense, certainty; and with it, many financiers aghast. Their feelings about Roosevelt differed not much from their feelings about dangerous anarchists. He was quick to announce to the country from Buffalo that he would disturb nothing of his predecessor's policy. The stock market recovered.

I had sent a telegram to Buffalo. To receive an answer at such a time, astonished me, accustomed though I was to his marvelous promptness. He did not telegraph, he wrote, and with his own hand. It covered, if I remember, but one page, or at the very most two, of rather small note paper, and this, also, I can no longer find. But one striking phrase in it has stuck in memory, almost word for word:

"I can't know that I have the ability, but I do know that I have the will, to carry out the task that has fallen to me."

And so the next occasion that I saw him was in the White House. For the second time it was a question of forests in the West. I was anxious to show the Secretary of the Interior on a map of Wyoming a part of the country at the head of Wind River along the Continental Divide which I was anxious should be protected by being made part of the national forest reserve. I wanted a note from him to Mr. Hitchcock. He asked me to come down. I had never been to the White House before. I sat in the hall upstairs, waiting till he could see me; and around me a set of typewriters were clicking, and a set of clerks buzzing, and ink pots, and waste baskets; I seem also to remember spittoons; and a great ugly door with a window of frosted glass cut this upper hall in two. It was a nasty place to be the First House in the Land. Presently I was summoned, and he came to the door of the room we were to sit in, and this had not been invaded by the apparatus of administration. But I was so excited, that nothing of the room's appearance made any impression; I can recover no distinct picture, except that the windows overlooked grounds at the back, and that after I had begun to explain about Wind River, Alice rushed in from somewhere to say how d'ye do, and rushed out. I went on explaining about Wind River, and Alice rushed in, got something, and rushed out. Just as I approached the end of my explanation, she flew in again.

"Alice," said her father, "the next time you come, I'll throw you out of the window." So I finished; and he wrote me a line, with which I went to Mr. Hitchcock.

"Why don't you look after Alice more?" a friend once asked Roosevelt. "Listen," he said. "I can be President of the United States—or—I can attend to Alice."

Some of the successive families in that house may have resembled each other; none, I am perfectly sure, ever bore the slightest likeness to the Roosevelt family; nor for that matter, could the guests of the other families even remotely have approached in their variety and their contrast the company drawn thither by Theodore Roosevelt's incessant lookout for merit in any worthy walk, and his instant impulse to give merit his emphatic recognition and encouragement. Bat Masterson would be coming to lunch. If you were to be there, Roosevelt would manage to tell you of Bat's formidable pistol and his use of it in discouraging murderers in the alkali.   If Seth Bullock were invited, you would hear in advance about his friendship and admiration for Seth Bullock in the Lawless Band Lands.   Or it would be John Fox Jr., and we would get him to sing us the folk-songs of his favorite mountains.   Or it would be a geologist, an ornithologist, a Danish authority on tropical diseases, a German who had written a remarkable work about crustaceans, or somebody who had got farther south, or farther north, or farther up Mount Evarest, than anybody else.   Or it would be some Balkan historian who had brought letters, and there were indications that he would turn out a distressing bore; but you were not to worry, he would put the Balkan next himself and do his best, and you were to sit between Alice and Daisy Chanler. And Florence La Farge was coming to dinner.   Would you like to sit between her and Mrs. Cowles?   You should do so, if it didn't disarrange Mrs. Roosevelt's plans.   His solicitude that all should go well with you never lost sight of you at any meal on any day, and the reservoir of his interest in what the geologist had done, what the Danish authority was doing, the precise trail which had been taken by the mountain climber, or those historic details which Jusserand the French Ambassador had collected about Shakespeare in France—this reservoir never ran dry.   How he managed accurately to know and competently to discuss the work of his guests, belongs to that lightning power of grasping and retaining anything to which he gave his attention that marked his mind.   In the train going to Washington one afternoon, I finished a book just published which I felt sure would interest him.   When he came into my bedroom for a talk about half-past five, which it was his habit to do, I put the book in his hand, *The New South*.   He turned the leaves over, decided to read it, and took it away.   Next morning at breakfast, he reviewed the whole volume and discussed its main points; thought very well of it, on the whole.   Now, he had left my room after six, we had a large dinner party, and additional guests after it until bed-time about eleven.   Bed-time was seldom late in the White House.   Somewhere between six one evening and eight-thirty next morning, beside his dressing and his dinner and his guests and his sleep, he had read a volume of three-hundred-and-odd pages, and missed nothing of significance that it contained.

To see him conduct a lunch with Bat Masterson from the alkali, and a clergyman from Vermont, and a philanthropist from the Philippines, and a bi-metalist from Aberdeen, and a leading lady in Newport society, and Lord Bryce, and everybody's wife or husband, if they had one, all seated around the table, and each brought into the talk for his particular contribution, was something never to forget.   Year after year, I witnessed Roosevelt's astonishing vitality animate a meal just as vigorously as it had been animating his hours of work over the Northern Securities, or the Coal Strike, or the Panama Canal, or whatever was at the moment demanding his attention.

He could never have made these holiday intervals, these hours off, what they so brilliantly and successfully were—the high water mark of American Society—had it not been for Mrs. Roosevelt, whose part in them was as important and extraordinary as his own.   She was the perfection of "Invisible Government."   When I think of her at that table, I still wonder, How did she banish every sign of strain?   For all responsibility or preoccupation that she showed, she might have been merely one of the guests.   She chatted, she listened, she drew her neighbors out, yet never stepped once beyond the magic circle of her discretion—and she caused the neighbors to remain discreet: I doubt if any one ever said to her more than once what they should not.   In private, she could indeed express herself, and at times saw people more accurately than he did.

Was he ever wholly aware of what she did for him?   Is any husband wholly aware of a devoted and tactful wife until he has lost her?

And yet, on one dumbfounding occasion, when the three of us were alone, moved to it by I don't know what, he suddenly got on his legs and began to address me as if I were a convention.

"Dan," he apostrophized, "of course you have often noticed the amazing smoothness with which Mrs. Roosevelt runs this exceedingly complicated establishment. You may also be aware that this never diverts her mind from attending to every one of our children as capably as if she had nothing else on her mind. But I doubt if you realize——"

At this point, Mrs. Roosevelt, serene in her chair, intervened.

"Theodore, you're talking just like an obituary."

"Why *Ee*-die!" he exclaimed in dismay; and sat meekly down. So to this day I have never learned what qualities of hers he doubted if I realized.

There was another time. I had been at the White House for part of a week with him alone. Mrs. Roosevelt was making a journey, I forget where. At breakfast each morning he would inquire, whom should I like him to ask to dinner? It was Robert Bacon on one of these evenings; and despite the protests of the President, Bacon and I were of the opinion that our country offered no traditional and accepted career, such as England offered, to the college-bred gentleman; that, save in wartime, there was no *market* for the Woodbury Kanes. The Woodbury Kanes of England entered the open doors of political service to their country, and had been the builders of the British Empire. Here, the doors were shut in their face, and had to be broken open with such persistence and force, and with methods so disgusting to most decent men, that they either chose careers where business was on the watch for ability and gave it every chance, or turned to idleness and were, like Woodbury Kane, simply wasted. We had all known Kane, admired him, and lamented him. I had started the subject, Roosevelt had disagreed with me, Bacon had thought and felt as I did; and so our dinner was spent in a very brisk and interesting discussion. By the following evening Mrs. Roosevelt had returned from her journey, and he, she and I sat at dinner.

"Why, Theodore," she said, "did you actually go and have champagne, in spite of what the doctor says?"

"Of course I had," he answered. "Bob Bacon came and Dan was here, and of course I gave them champagne."

"But you know the doctor says that it doesn't agree with you at all, and that you mustn't drink it. You could have given them anything else you wanted."

"Why *Ee*-die! I didn't want anything else. And I drank about one glass and a half!"

Mrs. Roosevelt smiled and shook her head. "He doesn't wish you to have any."

I do not know how the ridiculous rumor that Roosevelt was intemperate ever gained currency, and was kept alive for so long. I can only surmise that the exuberance of manner, into which he could explode on almost any occasion when he was extremely diverted, or suddenly surprised by enthusiasm, gave it some show of likelihood among people who knew nothing about him, and whose minds were unequal to the effort of thinking. Any man doing Roosevelt's daily official work, besides wrestling for exercise, walking fellow pedestrians weary, riding fat majors and colonels to bruised pulp (he rode a hundred miles at one stretch with Amos W. Barber, Governor of Wyoming, and seasoned to the saddle, finishing fresh himself with Barber exhausted), hitting bear and elk accurately in the Rocky Mountains, lions in Africa, able to rough it anywhere, is not the kind of person who habitually drinks too much. And yet the tale was repeated to me again and again, and I was asked what I knew about it. I was apt to reply that congenital imbecility was the only excuse for such a belief about such a man. But sometimes I took the trouble to go into it a little more than that. Even at Harvard, at our Club dinners—very festive occasions for both the old and the young—Roosevelt not only drank sparingly of his wine—we never had whisky or gin, nothing but the best French wines we could procure—he refused to drink more than his moderate custom, even when urged by enthusiasts to do so. In the White House days I cannot say how many times we came in from a walk and he asked me if I would like some whisky. Then, while we stood at the sideboard, I drank alone. He never took any. He did not particularly like the taste of strong spirits, and I imagine used them as stimulants on rare occasions when he was fatigued and obliged to exert himself, and at very few other times.

And so I was, on the whole, beginning with Harvard and coming down to whatever contemporaneous day it happened to be, in a fairly good position to express a fairly trustworthy opinion. Sometimes it gave me considerable pleasure to express this opinion—as when, for example, a lady in Philadelphia said that she had seen the President in a deplorable condition at a recent reception at the White House.

"Give her my compliments," I said to the friend who reported this to me; "I didn't notice her presence at that reception, and I didn't notice anything wrong with the President when I said good night to him."

I suppose that it will always be a trump card for politicians and the meaner sort of any man's enemies, to weave stories like this around his reputation, elusive anecdotes and instances, that are difficult to run to earth and kill. Roosevelt waited in silence for years, until one day that Michigan newspaper, *Iron Ore,* printed the accusation in a form which the law could seize upon and a plaintiff could bring a valid suit. The whole contemptible scandal came to its dramatic collapse in the court room at the close of the trial in Marquette, when Roosevelt jumped up, asked and got leave to address the court, waived the ten thousand dollars damages which the judge was about to instruct the jury to award in case they found for the plaintiff, said that all he wished was once for all in his lifetime to clear his good name before the world, was in consequence awarded six cents damages to save him the legal costs, and went off to the train, followed by the affectionate cheers of the American people.

It is to be said in any intimate account of the Roosevelts in the White House, such as I am attempting to give, that the necessity of forcing himself to be the common denominator so constantly for a set of social fractions that otherwise had none whatever, gave the President gradually the habit of holding forth at times when it wasn't necessary.  But if he did hold forth, who minded?  What he had to say was apt to be so humorous, or picturesque, or vital, that one forgot the hour of day or night.

The family lunches were entirely different from the mixed lunches; with the family, and anybody she counted as a member of it, Mrs. Roosevelt allowed her participation to be far more active, and conversation was apt to be general; she, the little boys, and Ethel, and their father, all talking, while Alice and I exchanged frivolities.

Once when I had said something or other, she exclaimed, "That's a bromide, anyhow!"

"It's not," I declared; "it's a glorious sulphide."

The President caught these words.  "What's all that?  Sulphide, bromide, what do you mean?"

We pitied him that he had missed this charming and useful invention of Gelett Burgess, which had been part of our dictionary for a number of years: and we repaired his ignorance, and give him examples; suppose you met a man aboard ship and found after several days that he knew your Aunt in Rio Janeiro very well, and you said, How small the world is!—that would be a bromide.  But when Heine saw Alfred de Musset on the boulevard, and said, There goes a young man with a great future behind him—that was a sulphide.

The President tilted his head down at his plate, and it must have been half a minute before he muttered thoughtfully:

"All the same, I have to use bromides in my business."

I repeat that I don't believe the White House ever had a family in the least like the Roosevelts living in it.  One day some people were coming to lunch, and I strayed a little ahead of time into the red room, where I found John Hay waiting.  We stood talking as we looked out of the window with our backs toward the door into the hall.  A slight sound from that direction caused us to turn; and for a moment one could not be sure what it was. There we saw three forms in single file bent at right angles from the waist with arms stretched out on a level and hands flat open. These came in and crouched towards us keeping this Oriental attitude. When they got close they stood upright. It was Roosevelt, and behind him Alice, and behind her a young foreign diplomat in uniform; and the President said:

"We consider that this is the correct attitude in which to approach and salute the Secretary of State and a distinguished author."

Just as it was well nigh imperative for Lincoln to tell jokes and read Artemus Ward to his cabinet, and so for a while to drop and forget the heavy load of his cares, it was excellent and wholesome for Roosevelt to shake off the Northern Securities, or the Coal Strike Commission, and behave like a school boy let loose on the playground. It can hardly be repeated too often that in Roosevelt's nature from his beginning to his end there lived what Shakespeare calls the "boy eternal."

His talk at table in the presence of a dozen people, about conspicuous persons not present, and about acute situations in public affairs, was often wholly comic and perfectly reckless. He was at his ease, among friends; office seekers and senators were done with for a while. He came from his morning's work, and he threw it off in this way like a horse who rolls over and kicks his legs in the air when the saddle has been taken off after a hard ride. He flashed out characterizations of congressmen or governors, or anybody, that the conventional politician might possibly have whispered into the ear of a confidential adherent, after exacting an oath of secrecy. You can't imagine a person like McKinley uttering such remarks without first shutting all the doors and windows, and then getting under the table.

"Any sparks from the buzz saw to-day?" asked Winthrop Chanler at one of these meals.

Roosevelt's face gleamed and corrugated with amusement. "Sparks from the buzz saw," he repeated in the sort of murmuring purr that he would fall into when suddenly and highly diverted; "sparks from the buzz saw."

During the first Autumn of his in the White House, I do not recall any visit to him definitely, except the one that I made in order to get him to tell the Secretary of the Interior that whatever I had to say about Wind River could be trusted.   Very likely I made no other, and I should not have ventured to invite myself at that time.   Those early months were full of new pressures and preoccupations for him, and I had *The Virginian* to complete and get ready for publication in the spring.   The existing and already published episodes made about half of the book, the rest, although planned, had to be shaped and written. It was not in the White House but in Charleston, South Carolina, that I next saw much of him.

## X.

We had found ourselves enchanted with Charleston, my wife and I, when we went there directly from our wedding in April, 1898.   At that time we had prolonged our stay considerably before going to ride on horseback among the mountains of North Carolina.   We had hoped for a chance to return there ever since, and now the chance came.   Charleston was to hold an exhibition, and my wife was appointed to represent Pennsylvania in an official capacity appropriate to her.   In the Autumn of 1901, I went to Charleston in search of a house for us and our three young children; and soon after the first of the New Year, we all arrived to spend the Winter and most of the Spring.

The town which had fired on Fort Sumter looked forward with warm enthusiasm to Roosevelt's coming there.   It had invited him to come and speak at the Exposition, he had accepted. Since the Civil War, no President had paid Charleston a visit. That this one was not a Democrat did not count much; he was the youngest President in our history—forty-three when his office began, only forty-four now, and this was interesting; more interesting still to these Southerners was his character.   His whole career, his outright and downright ways, his picturesque unmistakableness in speech and in action, all this was greatly to their liking.   They set out to do their very best for him.   The various stages of his welcome were carefully planned by the

Committee in charge of this—dinner at the Charleston Hotel, presentation of a sword to Major Jenkins, of the Rough Riders, by his former Lieutenant-Colonel, visit to the Exposition and Ladies lunch there, visit to the Summerville, boat excursion to view harbor and Forts Sumter and Moultrie, and so forth; and every one was eager to be gracious and cordial to the heroic Lieutenant-Colonel, now President, and a gentleman in whose veins flowed Southern blood.

Behind the ceremony of the sword, was the stunning praise which Roosevelt had written in his account of the Rough Riders about the courage of Major Jenkins. When it was known that the President had accepted the invitation to visit Charleston and speak at the Exposition, this led the South Carolina legislature to make an appropriation for a sword, which the President would be asked to present to the gallant officer who had served under him in the Spanish War.

The prevailing and spontaneous cordiality in Charleston had been anything but chilled by an affair that had happened in Washington during the Autumn, and that was still quite fresh in Charleston's memory. Senator Tillman, from South Carolina, had been invited to dine at the White House, and had accepted the invitation. Before the appointed day, Senator Tillman, in the Senate, fell upon his brother senator from South Carolina with both fists, and they had what is sometimes termed a little difference. It made a wide stir. Thereupon a suggestion quietly reached Senator Tillman that he withdraw his acceptance to dine at the White House. He did not take this suggestion. In consequence the White House withdrew its invitation. This made a very wide stir indeed. A distinguished foreigner was involved in this, rather oddly, as shall presently appear.

The Tillman incident had highly pleased Charleston. He was from the "up country," rustic, forcible, honest, anything but urbane, hostile by birth to the civilized Charlestonians, and he seldom had lost a chance to let them know it. But there was another aspect of the matter. Directly the President's projected visit to Charleston was known, threatening letters began to arrive. Threats never stopped him from anything that he intended to do, they merely made him intend to do it more—but those who were near him felt anxious. This anxiety was shared, I think, in Charleston, although I cannot recall that anybody there spoke a word of it to me; but the Committee of Arrangements was peculiarly strict in making known its decision that the President was to enter no private house whatever.

He came. He won their hearts by his good easy manner, his ready tongue, his vivacity; won them not politically, be it well understood; that most solid part of the Solid South would never vote for him, or for any Republican; he knew this; but personally he won their hearts—and lost them all in the twinkling of an eye. But not then. That came later. While he was there, he was *persona gratissima* to Charleston. This came to us from every side, and we were rather mixed in and up with a good part of it. In his speech he had one sentence, not of local or occasional application, but as permanent in the truth it expressed as any which lies at the foundation of sane government anywhere: "You can not create prosperity," were his words (or words to this effect) "by law. Sustained thrift, industry, application, intelligence, are the only things that ever do, or ever will, create prosperity. *But you can very easily destroy prosperity by law.*"

That was an example of the sort of bromide which Roosevelt meant when he told Alice and me that he had to use bromides in his business: but he could put old truths home in his own vivid fashion which made whatever he said striking.

Some bad moments of anxiety came to those who knew about the threatening letters, while they waited at the Exposition grounds for the ceremony of presenting the sword, and watched the thick uncontrolled crowd pressing and encroaching:—some bad moments, and then a long breath of relief. Just as it looked as if the Committee had lost its grip on precautions, marines appeared, led by Captain Leonard, cutting through the confusion, shoving the trespassers back, and order was restored and maintained. At the sight of Captain Leonard's one arm, Roosevelt's extraordinary memory flashed into action. During the troubles in China, Leonard had jumped into a river where a soldier—a brother officer, if I remember—was going under, and saved his life; but somehow got an infected arm, and lost it. The President spoke a few words to him about that, beginning by hailing him by name; and Captain Leonard was a proud and happy man.

And now, back come Senator Tillman and the White House dinner again, together with the distinguished foreigner: they have as direct a bearing upon the sword, and upon the strict orders that the President was to enter no private house in Charleston, as, let us say the inaction of Charles Evans Hughes in 1908 as to his becoming Roosevelt's successor had upon the chapter of catastrophes which began to befall the Republican party in 1910, and the whole country in 1912.

Benjamin Ryan Tillman's relations with his brother Senator from South Carolina, John L. McLaurin, had been growing worse and worse for some time before the day when what he said caused McLaurin to retort that he was a liar. This promptly produced the physical encounter between the Senators. Up in the visitor's gallery was Prince Henry, of Prussia, travelling *incognito,* as it is called in diplomacy, not a guest of the nation, a personal guest at the White House. He had come to represent his brother the Kaiser, whose new yacht, built in the United States, the Kaiser had asked Alice Roosevelt to christen. The dinner to which Tillman had been invited and uninvited was given in honor of Prince Henry, who had witnessed the brief fight in the Senate.

Now if Charleston had been pleased by that rebuke to the up-country Senator, the up-country was so little pleased that it set out to spoil the plan of the sword. Tillman had a nephew of the same name, and the nephew was Lieutenant-Governor of South Carolina. He gave out that there would be no sword and no presentation. Upon this, Mr. Gonzales, the editor of the *Columbia State,* and compiler of certain volumes of negro folk-lore in the "gullah" dialect as admirable as anything of the sort I have met, started a popular subscription through the columns of his paper, inviting everybody to contribute one cent. In this he was joined by other papers. It was successful. The sword was procured. Hugh S. Thompson, a former Governor of the State, and a former colleague with Roosevelt on the Civil Service Commission, represented the legion of contributors. He presented the sword to Roosevelt, who then presented it with a few words to Major Jenkins, who replied while my mind wandered back to the White House dinner, and I reflected that now every vibration arising from that incident was finished. Long afterwards I discovered my mistake.

At those Exposition grounds, when the procession was forming to march I forget where, a comical incident passed before my eyes. The director of the procession was a Mr. Hemphill, at that time editor of the Charleston *News and Courier*. He seemed very much aware of his responsibility, and read out his directions in a voice of perfect importance. He was telling us all what positions we should take, and he began (I think) with where the President of the United States was to stand. The President misunderstood him, apparently, and took a few obedient steps.

"Not there," said Mr. Hemphill, peremptorily; "there." And he pointed.

"I will go wherever I ought," murmured Roosevelt with an inflection of meekness that wholly upset my gravity, and caused some heads to turn in surprise at me.

During these crowded Charleston hours, somewhere, I went back to our old disagreement about *Balaam and Pedro*. I told him that I was drawing near the end of *The Virginian*, working every day at it, sometimes nine hours; that the book was to be published in the Spring. Did he still insist that I ought to suppress those details which had so shocked him nine years ago?

"Speak now," I said, "or forever after hold your peace."

"I shall never change my mind about that," he said. "I beg you won't keep that passage. It will deform the book."

I went to my desk and re-wrote the page, and recorded the fact in my dedication of the novel to him.

Of Charleston at the time when Roosevelt came there early in this twentieth century, the ancient Charleston of fine traditions and fierce prejudices, something still was left. Though its prosperity lay shattered and its wharves and warehouses gaped with silence, more mellow beauty hung over the town, its houses, tiled roofs, gardens, grave yards, streets, and unexpected nooks, than ever I have seen elsewhere, even in New Orleans, where an enchanted fragment of the past also lurks, unpoisoned, unmocked by the present, waiting its curtain down. Amid this visible fragrance of time, enclosed by walls and roses, there dwelt in much quiet, with entire absence of show and aversion to show, a group of ladies. Their dress was a sort of seclusion in itself. Elderly they were; their voices, their manner, their ease and simplicity, which was the reverse of rustic and came from something within them that many educated generations had seasoned and transmitted, would have prevented their feeling at a loss, no matter in what company they found themselves. As girls they had known the crest of the wave, and next its darkest gulf, they had looked upon the Civil War, lost their men folk down to brothers in their teens during those four years, and were still sitting in the shadow of that, because it was the final eclipse of their sun. They referred to it hardly more than they would have imparted family secrets. Being of the true metal, the uses of adversity had merely tempered them still more. They were very few in number. One of their qualities was to wear their poverty lightly, more naturally than many wear their riches; and in their hospitality to be as spontaneous with their scantiness as they would have been with their plenty. They opened their doors to kindred no matter how remote. They opened their hearts, never hastily, but when they had become sure. They shut firmly out certain things that are more than welcome today, such as publicity in the social columns, and conversations about the stock market and such other matters, which they deemed proper in a men's office, and out of place in the drawing room.

Upon the point of social publicity, I recall that it made its

first appearance in the winter of the Exposition, 1902; and that
the female editor of that column apologized for the innovation
by saying that the time had come for Charleston to follow the
lead of the age.   Upon this same point I held a most characteristic talk with one of the elderly ladies who, knowing who I was,
introduced herself to me at the Women's Exchange, early in my
stay.

"I am So-and-so's aunt," she said.   "And how do you like
our Exposition?"

"Extremely.   There's only one thing."

"And what is that?"

"So few of your beautiful portraits by Romney and Gains-
borough and Reynolds that I see in your houses seem to
have been lent to the picture gallery in the Fine Arts Building."

"I will explain that to you.   We in Charleston are very old-
fashioned, and we do not care to expose our private ancestors to
the public gaze."

When Charleston accepted any stranger within its gates, I
doubt if one of its fashions of so doing could be, for the very
charm and delicacy of its grace, matched anywhere in the world.
My wife and I had arrived there from the north late one night
to spend our honeymoon.   By breakfast time next morning, a
bowl of fresh garden flowers was brought to us with a card and
the greetings of a lady we had never yet seen.   She, with certain
other friends of my family, was aware of our coming beforehand.   The bowl was of rare china; and had not my mother
given me instructions what to do in case such a welcome met us,
I should have been obliged either to reason it out in embarrassed
suspense, or else to ask the lady who kept our boarding house
for guidance.   The proper conduct in a case like this was to
acknowledge the compliment at once, and to keep the bowl until
the flowers were faded, and then return it with a suitable message.
With an ancestress by the name of Mary Middleton buried in
the churchyard of St. Michael's at Charleston, I fell heir to the
roses in that bowl and to the open doors of very distant cousins

and *their* cousins, as my mother and aunt had done before
me.

Those of their generation that were still living revealed the
constancy in kinship and friendship which was so deeply marked
in old Charleston people.    Some of them had relations in Europe.
After the Civil War, many Southerners left the United States
never to return, and were to be found established in various
cities—London, Paris, Florence, Rome.    And so it befell that
at the age of twelve, in Rome, I made the acquaintance of an
exile from old Charleston, so handsome, so stately, so truly a
presence, a personage, that thing we no longer produce, a great
lady, that I can remember her still.    Her father's story draws
an important side of Charleston character as it still persisted,
even as late as the visit of Roosevelt.    Should you ever find
yourself in St. Michael's churchyard, read his long and beautifully worded epitaph.    His name was Pettigrew, and he was a
judge.    When South Carolina seceded from the Union, he stood
almost alone in his dissent, and although he lived in this wild-
est storm centre of slavery and secession, he not only never
changed his mind, but so greatly was he esteemed and revered
for his integrity, that he never lost the regard of his fellow
citizens; and when he came to die, they surrounded his memory
with the feeling and the admiration which may be read in that
epitaph.

He had another daughter; and through a word she once
dropped to William Makepeace Thackeray, another trait in
Charleston character is drawn.    When the author of *Vanity
Fair* was presented to her, he somewhat oddly and unwisely
remarked that he was delighted to make her acquaintance,
for he had heard that she was the fastest woman in South
Carolina.

"Oh, you mustn't believe everything you hear," said she.    "I
heard that you were a gentleman."

Now that happened quite a number of years before ever I
saw Charleston; forty at least, I should think, if not fifty; but
had they forgotten it?    Not at all.    In this proud little place,

once so busy and important, now a lost echo of what had once
been, it was cherished as a legend; and during my first seven
days there I fancy that it was quite seven times repeated to me
by ladies and gentlemen who, at the time when Thackeray visited
Charleston, were either very young indeed, or else not yet born.

Metamorphosed as to its particulars, but the same in its
underlying principle, this passage-at-arms between the great
author and the great lady served as a valuable brush stroke
in the portrait of the place and its people which I was to attempt
several years later, although no such ambition dawned upon
me when I first learned it from such a series of informants in
1898, nor even during my second and much longer sojourn in
the winter and spring of 1902.   In those months it may well be
that this portrait, not yet contemplated, was nevertheless taking
on not so much shape as color, all unknown to me, as I pegged
away at *The Virginian,* or marvelled at Charleston during
Roosevelt's vertiginous visit, or wandered and meditated and
looked across the dreamy, empty rivers to their dreamy, empty
shores and the grey-veiled live-oaks that were all of a piece
with the wistful silence.

All of a piece.   That is exactly what Charleston had remained,
exactly what New York had not.   Here was a city, not a village, though much smaller than many villages.   Such places
as Worcester or Springfield had revealed to me that a village
can swell and swell, yet always be a village.   Charleston now
revealed to me that you can shrink and shrink, yet always remain a city, a centre, a capital in prestige.   Full of echoes this
little, coherent, self-respecting place was also full of life; retaining its native identity, its English-thinking, English-feeling,
English-believing authenticity; holding on tight to George
Washington and the true American tradition, even though loyal
to its lost cause.   What an oasis in our great American desert of
mongrel din and haste.   To be behind the times, yet intensely
vital; to keep itself whole and never break into a litter of fragments that didn't match and so lose its personality as New York
had done.

What a lady had once said to Thackeray was still vivid and ready for telling to a stranger; a stranger with what Charleston held to be the right to walk in was received at once; a stranger with wrong credentials could no more cross its social frontier than a traveller without a passport and proper visas can enter a European country today.

The forefathers of Charleston and their families had been painted in London by English masters of the eighteenth century, their sons and grandsons had studied law in the Inner Temple, their daughters had danced in the great world, a Charleston boy had attempted to help Lafayette escape from his Austrian prison, and the mark of the great world was still set upon this civilization, plain to see.   Yet it bore this stamp of the past without losing grip on life; sidetracked as the town had been since 1865, in its deep old roots it possessed the secret of persistence.

In *Lady Baltimore,* my portrait of Charleston, the emphasis is laid upon the passing elders more than upon the coming youth, for the sake of a precious thing that was never to return. Roosevelt quarrelled with it, as will be seen, falling heavily on my praise of the South at the expense of the North.   I agreed and made changes.   As much as he I was Union, never anything else.   Any *idée fixe,* like the Southern view of a State, must perish when it begins to hinder growth.

"After all," said Mrs. St. Julien Ravenel to me (she was one of the elders), "it is much better for us that the Union won. Had we split off, by now we should be split into several republics."

Roosevelt's three whirling days in Charleston gave him no chance to see and know the place.   He brought there his historic knowledge, his Union patriotism, and his general passion for social justice.   He took just that away.   Friendship with people like Mrs. Ravenel would have tempered his severity. Even I wrung from him next year a tremendous concession. That was at the White House after we had met at Harvard and at Newport where he stood godfather to Winthrop Chanler's small son.   I possess a collection of perfectly good grandmothers; but the one who lies beneath the spire of St. Michael's has a special value for me.

While we were still down there, I evidently wrote him in the interest of a friend, a citizen of the town.

WHITE HOUSE
Washington
March 21, 1902.

. . . I have your note of the 18th instant.   It is never any-thing but a pleasure to hear from you.   Give your friend a let-ter from you to file with his application for whatever post it is he seeks.   I hope we can see you both on your way back to the north. . . .

April 5, 1902.

. . . I am sincerely grateful to you.

Now be sure to bring Frost up and then I shall try to have both of you and him dine with me. . . .

Frank Frost, of Charleston, and a Harvard friend, member of that same small club when I had first known Roosevelt, had en-listed as a private in the Spanish War, because he could not get a commission, and was not easy in his conscience at the indiffer-ence to the Spanish War which his fellow citizens were showing. This I had seen happen in 1898, when my wife and I had paid Charleston our first visit.   I had wished Roosevelt to know this about Frost, because its gallant patriotism was certain to appeal to Roosevelt particularly.   That explains the first sentence in his letter above.

In May, 1902, *The Virginian* was published.

WHITE HOUSE
Washington
June 7, 1902.

. . . I did not think it would be possible for you to combine those short stories into a novel without loss of charm and power. Yet I think you have greatly increased both their charm and their power as you have made the combination.   It is a remark-able novel.   If I were not President, and therefore unable to be quoted, I should like nothing better than to write a review of it. I have read it all through with absorbed interest and have found myself looking forward to taking up the book again all through the time I have been at work. I do not know when I have read in any book, new or old, a better chapter than Superstition Trail. . . .

Did I like his invariable attention, and the praise that he so often and so warmly gave to my scribblings? I should think so! It far surpassed my hopes, and used to surprise me more even than I am surprised nowadays when somebody in a newspaper discovers that *The Virginian* is not the only book for which I am responsible. It had the luck to be a "best seller" for six months, was dramatized, heartily damned by the New York critics, ran for a while in non-American Broadway, for ten years on the road, is still played in stock after twenty-seven years, and has been three times filmed, and once translated. It made money, actual money;—an agreeable experience, wholly new for its author. A critic of to-day has lately pronounced it "overlong, tedious, and by turns too saccharine or too melodramatic." That it was not found so in 1902, proves merely that taste is never stationary, but perpetually changes, and that almost no fiction can long survive its own epoch. Yet it is possible that the critic who has found it so inferior a performance may be a trifle in advance of his own age: between May 1, 1928 and May 1, 1929, thirty-three thousand nine hundred and eighty-six copies of *The Virginian* were sold.

## XI.

We stayed at the White House, my wife and I, from January 8 to January 12, 1903. It filled me with a certain pride to reflect that I was the fourth generation of my family that had stayed there. My great-great aunt, Miss Isabel Mease, went there when Dolly Madison presided over it; my grandfather Pierce Butler when General Pierce was President; my mother during the same administration; and now here were we, the

guests of Colonel and Mrs. Roosevelt.   None of us had ever
been invited for political reasons, but merely because of personal friendship; which seemed a better sort of welcome.

Our train from Philadelphia, due at 6.10, was forty minutes
late.   Dinner was at 7.30.   Everybody was dressing, of course,
when we arrived at seven and were shown to our rooms, breathless with suspense—but our trunks were there, dispatched two
trains ahead of ours.   We descended out of breath and were
still more so on being shown to the dining room where the company was already seated, and upon our entrance, rose.

Soup was not yet served, we had missed being on time as nar-
rowly as that; and in my embarrassment I said:

"Mr. President, don't arrest me, arrest the Pennsylvania
Railroad!"

Mrs. Roosevelt was gracious and consoling; she had not
known of our arrival or they would not have sat down.   Various shiftings of places were caused by our coming, but the company was not large.   It was all easy and informal and gay, as
Roosevelt most liked to have it and did have it whenever political or diplomatic guests did not spoil it by their imperfect understanding of what agreeable society means.

I recall a dinner at the White House subsequently, where
Judge Oliver Wendell Holmes and Mrs. Holmes were, and we
all knew each other very well; in the midst of the excellent talk
and laughter, the President in sheer joy suddenly put both his
hands on the table, bowed over them and exclaimed:

"Oh, *aren't* we having a good time!"

One or two Presidents as great as he have been hosts of the
White House before him; but none as familiar with Europe,
with History, with very nearly every important subject in the
world, and as delightful in dealing with any of them.

This particular dinner of Thursday, January 8, 1903, was my
first meal there since the whole place had been done over beneath the guiding taste of Mrs. Roosevelt.   He knew how a
room ought to look, but less minutely how to make it look so.
In matters of dress, he was apt to wear anything that befitted

the occasion, dinner party or walk in the woods, without much thrashing the matter out with his tailor—and somebody like Woodbury Kane or Winthrop Chanler should have chosen his cravats for him.   Her exquisite and very personal simplicity of dress was attained as all art is attained, by gift united to cunning thought.

It was a changed White House indeed since they had come to live there.   Inkpots, waste baskets, frosted glass doors, clicking typewriters, the whole back-stairs of office running, removed from the front stairs where it had been suffered to encroach, and put decently out of sight.   Very handsome admirable dining room, new furnished; simple, dignified new wainscoting of natural wood; and round about, the solemn heads of moose and elk.   All the rest of the house in keeping; a sense of quiet throughout, instead of the ugly sights and sounds of business rattling away just outside bedroom doors.   No display, everything simple—but dignified—as the President's house ought to be.

As to the food itself, there was never a piling on of courses, it was always good—and simple, with sherry and white wine, but not champagne, unless by exception.

On this evening, as usual, he allowed us but a short time for our cigars; we soon followed the ladies upstairs into the room where they and the ladies of the President's cabinet were to assemble before the Diplomatic Reception.   A member of the Cabinet and his wife were already there, and soon came John Hay with his daughter, and Attorney Philander Knox with Mrs. Knox, and the room gradually filled.

Miss Isabel Hagner, Mrs. Roosevelt's private secretary, a lady for whom we had a warm regard, took great pains that my wife should meet every one, and so did the wife of the member of the Cabinet as soon as she was introduced to her.   Tucking her under her kind and motherly wing, she took her up to her husband and said:

"Poppa, here's Mrs. Wooster."   Then, smiling to my wife, she added: "I can remember the name by the sauce."

John Hay I knew already, and had an interesting little talk
with him before the President rejoined us to form the procession.
He confided to me that it was an awful experience to have letters
which you had written when you were an obscure and incautious
youth turn up after you had become mature and a shining mark.
A *barrelful* of letters like this had been mercifully discovered
by a good friend of his at an autograph dealer's in New York.
They dated back to his early twenties in the days when he was
still an irresponsible bachelor, and they had been addressed to
an intimate chum, long dead.

"Good Lord!" I said. "Good Lord!" And my brain went
scrambling distractedly back into my past, and the sort of letters I exchanged with fellow sophomores. But I returned to
the present quickly. "Never mind," I continued. "When the
Duke of Wellington received word from a woman to whom he
had once made himself as acceptable as a young man can, that
perhaps he would like to have the letters he had written her
back for a reasonable consideration, or should she publish them?
he answered—you remember what he answered?"

" 'Publish and be damned,' " quoted John Hay. "Yes, but
this is chaste America."

"Chaste be blowed," I said. "Don't you know how they behave in all the rural districts?"

"One must never jolt hypocrisy," said John Hay, "personal
or national. But the friend who found my letters bought the
whole barrel and sent them to me. In the hands of a reporter
who knew his business they would have made three columns of
good scandal.—But you don't learn," he continued with a sigh.
"Every day I still write notes filled with indiscretions, and I
can't help it."

So do many men, I fancy. Were a venomous and lop-sided
selection of my intimate letters to college mates, cowboys, army
friends, and my occasionally furious letters to other people to
be made, and published upon my death, I might well cut a sorry
figure.

Then I remembered a pleasant thing. I told John Hay that

when I was ten, and in Europe with my parents, some one had
sent them a newspaper cutting with *Little Breeches,* just appeared; and that I could still hear my father's laugh as he read
aloud to my mother:

> I want a chaw of tobaccer,
> And that's what's the matter with me.

Presently the President appeared again, the procession was
formed, and we marched down to the blue room.    For the next
two hours, we were there.    The diplomats, followed by the
great American People, passed, making their exceedingly various kinds of bow, or shaking the President's hand.    The diplomats of course were very "correct;" and the presence of uni-
forms and decorations among the company, brightened the
monotony of the general aspect.    As for the hand shaking business, the President showed me a patent plan of his whereby he
saved his knuckles from being crushed to pulp.    I can't describe it accurately any more, but the main principle of it was
that the other party to the hand-shake found him (or her) self
wafted onward along the line without either being precisely
aware of what had occurred, or at all feeling that somewhere
there had been a lack.

With whom was the hand-shaking started?    By whom will it
be stopped?    High time to stop it and many other needless
burdens that wear our Presidents out.

The President and Mrs. Roosevelt stood side by side at the
head of the room, roped off from us guests.    I do not see how the
natural welcome of a hostess and the dignity of a great position
could be more perfectly blended and expressed.    She also looked
very well; not tired, which seemed wonderful, considering the
exactions that she had to meet every day.    Next her and her
husband the cabinet ladies were lined up, and behind them stood
John Hay, which I thought must be pretty slow for him; he took
about as much part as one of the candlesticks.    Next the President, stood a Secret Service man, a truly ambrosial creature with
shining clusters of yellow hair, a yellow mustache, a man's fine

figure, and an eye that must certainly have turned the heads of many distracted females. The President told me that he was a mountaineer from West Virginia. Cabot Lodge said while I was looking at him and commenting on his impressive appearance:

"Yes; and it's not pleasant to reflect that as he stands there, his hand is on his revolver from start to finish."

And so for two hours the American People with each name announced passed in at the door to the President's left, and across the space roped off, and out at the door to the right, and into the big ballroom, the East Room; and the sight of them coming and going was more than Niagara. Women, men, children, some solemn and awkward, some composed and easy, some smiling; in every sort of dress, with every sort of hair, brushed or dishevelled—and all of them showing somehow that emotion was possessing them as they greeted their President. The Star Spangled Banner was waving in their hearts.

One of the people addressed Mrs. Roosevelt as well as her husband, saying:

"Good evening, Mrs. President."

She told me that it was the first time this had been said to her.

Nothing of any mark occurred on this occasion; but upon another, a very short stout lady came along, and gave her name to the usher, who was rather tall. He looked puzzled, bent down to her, and she repeated it. He stood up, hesitated, and once more bent down as she met it by standing on her toes and once again giving her name. He stood straight, and with a forlorn expression and a failing voice announced:

"Mrs. Rooster."

"Mrs. *Brewster*," shrieked the lady.

My wife stood against the rope with the other ladies, watching the American People during most of the ceremony; while I came and went, circulating about, meeting many whom I knew, and being most kindly presented to people whom they thought I should like to meet by Mrs. Cowles, or Miss Hagner, or Miss

Bessie Kean, an old friend, whose brother was Senator from New Jersey.

At this Diplomatic Reception in the White House, Sir Michael Herbert, the British Ambassador, dropped amiable words on my being presented to him, and so did his wife.   I had known him in Paris during the Winter of 1882–83, along with Gerard Lowther, and Villiers, and other young attachés of the British Embassy, where I had dined now and then with Lord Lyons.   I had also seen them, Lowther especially, at the very pleasant dinners and dances of the small English speaking colony.   I alluded to those old days.

"Yes," said Sir Michael Herbert.   "I—ah—confess not to remember you *then*.   But now that you've written *The Virginian* I'm really awfully glad to have seen you."

So I assured him that there wasn't the slightest reason he should have remembered a boy just out of Harvard who was merely dining and dancing about in Paris twenty years ago. Sir Michael Herbert was astonishingly unchanged in his youthful and handsome appearance.

The room was full of old friends and acquaintances: Bob Bacon of Harvard '80, Teddy Baylies of '79 and his wife, General Young whom I had seen last in the Yellowstone Park, General Bates, Paymaster, with whom I had gone through the Yosemite, and a new acquaintance, destined to write the greatest American Biography so far—Senator Beveridge; an engaging, vital, eager, charming creature; but too young for his years at that time.   His flattery was a trifle obtuse, though quite sincere, as was his unbridled admiration of the President.   The President told me that he had begun by overwhelming him with visits in the evening, when he would have nothing to say of any value whatever.   He would generally begin:

"Understand, sir, it is not for my good that I come here to-night, but for yours."

And then once:

"It's time now, sir, for you to govern by psychic suggestion. That is how I won my Indiana campaign; psychic suggestion."

In those days Beveridge was like that, a trifle "fresh."   But he had the quality that endeared, and made you remember him, and be always glad to see him.   As we sat together a few years ago at a dinner given by Nicholas Murray Butler to the American Academy of Arts and Letters, Beveridge was deep in his *Lincoln,* and made the meal delightful by his enthusiasm and his account of the interesting documents he had unearthed, pamphlets, newspapers, ephemeral at the time, but of the highest value now as revealing the spirit of that time.   My last sight of him, when he came to receive the Roosevelt Memorial Medal for his *Marshall,* was a very sad one.   As he spoke, we wondered at the absence of that quality which had made his speeches so arresting; we did not know that he was a dying man; we knew it all too soon.

The presence of nobody at that Diplomatic Reception thrilled me so much as that of "Mr. Dooley."   As soon as I learned that he was there, I went in search of him, and directly he was pointed out I waited for no introduction, I rushed up and introduced myself.   His charming wife was with him, and we fell to talking with much energy.   His company was as brilliant as his writing, every accessible word of which I believe I had read. Everybody read it, everybody quoted it, everybody waited for the next.   I had been piously brought up on James Russell Lowell's Biglow Papers, and to-day they strike me as on the whole very much the best thing that Lowell ever did.   Dooley goes beside them.   I can think of no other humorous and searching comment of American politics and public doings at any epoch which compares with them, unless it be Will Rogers.

We had the good fortune to sit at supper with him.   After the great crowd was gone, about eleven, certain invited guests went up to the hall above, and then sat at little tables and were refreshed with much needed bouillon; and champagne, and ice cream.   My wife and I came wandering along the hall, and were hailed by Cabot Lodge and Mrs. Rhinelander Jones, and Dooley—perhaps I should give him his baptismal name—by Finley Peter Dunne.   They called to us to come and sit at their

table, which we were glad enough to do.   It was not long before
we saw the President approaching, stopping at each table to
see that his guests were comfortable; and so he gradually made
his way to us.   He checked our rising with a quick gesture, as
he often did, and then placing his hand on Dooley's shoulder, he
addressed us in a strong Irish accent:

"I haven't time f'r to tell ye th' wurruk Tiddy did in ar-rmin'
an' equippin' himself, how he fed himself, how he steadied himself in battles an' encouraged himself with a few well-chosen
wurruds whin' th' sky was darkest.   Ye'll have to take a squint
into th' book ye'ersilf to l'arn thim things."

"I won't do it," said Mr. Hennessy.   "I think Tiddy Rosen-
felt is all r-right an' if he wants to blow his hor-rn lave him do it."

"Thrue f'r ye," said Mr. Dooley. . . .   "But if I was him I'd
call th' book 'Alone in Cubia.' "

His recitation was longer than I have quoted; and all the time
that he was delivering it with the most vigorous gusto and a
countenance beaming with mirth and appreciation, his hand lay
on the shoulder of the man who had written it, Finley Peter
Dunne.   It was one of Dooley's most brilliant satires, written
when the President's story of the Rough Riders had been published after the Spanish War, and while he was Governor of
New York.   It was an example of the President's astonishing
power to retain what he read.   All of us had read it when it
appeared, and recognized it, though none could have repeated a
word of it by heart.

"By George, that was bully!" said the President to Dunne.
"I did enjoy that!"   And he laughed with the rest of us.

Dunne did not laugh.   His face had gone purple while the
President was reciting, but at the end he had recovered.

"Do you know, Mr. President," said he very gravely, "the
appearance of your cabinet is a great disappointment to me.
*I don't believe one of them has ever killed a man.*"

The President, as I have said, won the heart of Charleston at
once, and immediately lost it.   The cause of this was his appointing a negro to the office of Collector of the Port.   It fin-

ished him with those high spirited, sorely bruised people.  Nobody who realized to the full how deep the bruise had gone, could have supposed that they would see with composure any negro whatever, no matter how honest and worthy, holding office among them.  Dr. Crum was such a person, this was freely admitted—but he was a colored man!  The President had come to Charleston, had been made welcome, had uttered all sorts of friendly and enthusiastic words, had reminded them that he was part Southern himself—and had then gone away and insulted not only the whole city, but the whole South!  That is how they put it.  My wife and I heard them often enough, and were able to understand it through living among them.  It was the deep bruise; and the President, meaning well but not aware how sore it was still, had pressed it.  It was not the Civil War, it was what came after the Civil War, it was Reconstruction that was the real, lasting bruise.  War makes everybody slightly insane, upsets normal equilibrium; so that the same man, in peace time just a usual man, may be turned by the slumbering immensity within him waking up and taking control—may be turned by this into a hero, a saint, an angel, at one moment, and the next into a fiend.  Congress, the North, passed some amendments to the Constitution, sent politicians down into the South to re-establish order and Government, under these amendments, and sent troops and guns down to put through by force, if necessary, what these politicians did.  Many of them were dirty scoundrels, who under the mask of giving political equality to the negro, ran a riot of tyranny and corruption.  The South, prostrate already by war, was ground still deeper by dirty scoundrels protected by guns.  It is a dreadful story of stupidity, incompetence, dishonesty, and every sort of violence.  In about fifteen years, sanity came back to the North; fanatics are always incurable; but Washington took in (for a moment) the fact that our Federal Government can not make any of these United States do what they are determined not to do; and that the white South would never submit to being ruled by the black South, no matter how many laws were passed.  President Hayes took the soldiers away, Reconstruction fell to pieces, and the Constitutional Amendments died slowly in silence, and joined the collection of legal corpses which lie unburied all over this Union.

But the bruise had come to stay; and Theodore Roosevelt in his zeal to do the negro justice, did not see this quite adequately. This point I ventured to bring up—I didn't often tell him when I disagreed with what he had done, and I didn't often disagree. When I was silent, it was either because I felt that he must know more about it than I did, or because he hated so to have you not think as he did, if he cared for you.  This was the charming natural boy that lived in him; he could become absolutely plaintive as he pleaded and argued for his own view.

It began at the first breakfast in the White House the morning after the Diplomatic Reception, and he brought it up again at every succeeding breakfast.

Mrs. Roosevelt remained in her room, regulating her household in seclusion, and the young ladies did not come down; only Ethel and Archie were there, and they not every morning.  The President put my wife on one side of him and me on the other. And so it began, that Friday breakfast, January 9, 1903.  I can think of nothing more characteristic of him than this whole discussion.

"I don't think you ought to have appointed Dr. Crum," I said.

"You don't?"  He stared at me astonished.

"No."

He turned briskly to my wife, sure of a very different opinion. He knew the good works to which she was addicted, he knew that Dr. William Ellery Channing was her great-grandfather, that her background was crowded with New England worthies from the beginning, that she visited the Hampton school for negroes near Old Point Comfort, and greatly admired its organizer, General Armstrong.  Very naturally he turned to her from my unexpected heresy.  Then he discovered that she was a heretic too.

"Why, Mrs. Wister!   Mrs. Wister!"

He looked in bewilderment from one to the other of us.   We remained mild but firm.

"Why goodness me!" he broke out.   "Why don't you see— why you *must* see that I can't close the door of hope upon a whole race!"

He went into it then, volubly and vigorously, not at all the plaintive school boy any more, but the mature and earnest Roosevelt, ably presenting his reasons—the political reasons and the moral reasons.   He would favor no man who was unworthy, once he knew that he was unworthy.   He had taken the greatest pains in this case.   He was perfectly aware of the Charleston prejudice.   He particularly wished to avoid it.   He had especially chosen the office of Collector of the Port, because a person holding that position would not be brought into contact with many Charleston people in the discharge of his duties.   He must recognize and support the party of which he was the head; but he must recognize much more his wider obligation as President of the whole people and not merely some of the people, he could not rule out any class as a class: and he wound up as he had begun by repeating that he could not close the door of hope upon a whole race.

"But you didn't open it when you appointed Dr. Crum," I said, "you shut it a little tighter."

There was no use in another appeal to my wife; he saw that we were of one mind about this, and he continued, addressing us both; my saying that he had merely shut the door a little tighter, set him off on another tack: Lee had surrendered in 1865; that was almost forty years ago; the evil policy of Reconstruction had ceased twenty-five years ago; there was not the slightest warrant any longer for this attitude of a certain class in the white South; if an American citizen was worthy of an office, it should make no matter to grown up people with pretensions to reason whether the man's ancestors had come from England or Africa.

"Perhaps it shouldn't," I said; "but it does.   If your act theoretically ought to do good to the colored race, but actually does them harm by rousing new animosity, it's a condition you have to reckon with, not a theory."

Time had come for the President to go to work, there was no more of this at that breakfast; but next morning after pouring out our coffee for us, and eating his grapefruit and chirping away like some cheerful vigorous bird about various things, he unexpectedly exclaimed with one of his comic outbursts of despair:

"But here the negroes are; not by their wish but our compulsion; and I can not shirk the duty. . . ."

This re-opened the entire discussion of the previous morning. Everything was said over again on both sides, nothing new was added, because there was nothing new to add.   The school boy couldn't bear to have us—my wife especially—disagree with him; he pleaded and argued for the rest of the meal.   And so it was on the final morning; he went over all the ground again, and we again gave him the answer.   It was a condition, not a theory; he had done harm, not good.

And then, at the very last moment, the school boy gave it up. Our visit was ended, he would not see us at the next breakfast. As we stand at the breakfast room door, saying goodbye, he suddenly spread out both arms and clenched his fists.

"Well," he said, his jaw struggling over what was coming, "if I had it to do over again, I—don't—*think*—I'd—do it."

Many years later, one of that Charleston group whose hearts he had lost, a man prominent in the public concerns of the town, said (so I am told) that he did not see how Roosevelt could have well done anything else but appoint Dr. Crum to that office. The Republican organization had presented to him a series of names which he had rejected one after the other as being for this reason or that undesirable, and to reject every one whom the party recommended would have been very nearly, if not quite, impossible; he had at length selected the person likely to give most service and least offense.

But what remains with me of all this, is not so much its political bearings, delicate and difficult as these were; it is he that remains, his pleading, his persistence in trying to bring you over to his view of an incident that was closed; his youthful, unsophisticated, obvious worry that two people who were of no political value to him, but important to him only in his friendship, should stick to their adverse opinion, no matter what he said — and then, that last morning, the surrender, wrenched out of him in his completest school-boy manner.

He had made another surrender a few months earlier, and also in consequence of what an intimate friend said to him; but this time it was not a concession of mind about something that was over, it was a change of policy in regard to something that was briskly going on.

It was going on in the State of Delaware.   In Delaware, certain leading families, more persistently than in any other State, unless perhaps in South Carolina, have been to the fore, generation after generation, taking a hand in public affairs, with that instinct of responsibility to their country which comes only from continuity and inheritance.   From one of these families, the Bayards, came Florence La Farge.   Had she been a man, she would have been a statesman; had she been born in these times that have declared against discrimination of sex in politics, she would have been a leader.   And because of this, and of her being a close friend of Roosevelt's, they sent for her to come from New York to Delaware and help them, if she could, out of their trouble.

These troubles may be symbolized by the name Addicks.   He can be accurately described by a phrase invented later for other people by Roosevelt; he was a malefactor of great wealth, displeasingly linked with a concern known as the Bay State Gas company.   The whole story is too long to tell here: enough that his tie with Delaware was obscure and recent, that Delaware outside of Wilmington was poor, and that he decided he would become a United States Senator by the simple process of buying Delaware.   Through sales of ploughs, bicycles, shot guns, axes, and other farming tools and necessities at nominal price to small rural shop keepers, he had secured a number of votes in the preceding legislature (legislatures elected Senators then), and had money ready to buy more in the present legislature. It looked dark. A split just then in the Republican party did not make it any less so. So Florence La Farge came down to Wilmington, and was told all the details. Payne, the Postmaster General, and Mark Hanna, Republican leader in the Senate, a man of great ability, inventor of the interlocking directorate between Big Business and Government, were behind Addicks. But if only Roosevelt could be faced with the whole truth about Addicks, and then drop a public word against him, these big guns, together with lesser ones, would be spiked. If Roosevelt declined on party grounds to declare war on his own people and so make enemies of any policies, such as conservation, that he might need their support in, at least there was a chance of defeating Addicks if the President would go so far as to agree not to back him. Furnished with all points, the lady went on from Wilmington to Washington next morning.

She was to lunch at the White House by the President's invitation. He knew what her errand was, she had written him that she wished to talk to him about Delaware. Mrs. Roosevelt had asked her to stay the night, but she could not, she must get back to New York; she had just the brief, one chance of lunch and perhaps a short while after it, to succeed or fail, to sink or swim.

Arriving early, she sat upstairs for half an hour with Mrs. Roosevelt, who asked her no questions. Perhaps she didn't know; and perhaps—which is far more likely—she maintained, even with an intimate friend, that perfect discretion and detachment as to everything of a political sort that came into her husband's life. However this may have been, at the end of that half hour, Mrs. La Farge went down to lunch with her heart beating like a trip-hammer.

It was a small party, and in the breakfast room: Alice, another lady, a scientific man, and the editor of the *Brooklyn Eagle,* made seven with the President, Mrs. Roosevelt and the keyed-up emissary from Delaware. She had plenty of time to become more keyed-up, and also to conclude that her battle was to come off later; not one syllable about Delaware was uttered by the President. He talked with the editor about this measure and that, possible measures, needed measures, the men who were back of them, how to handle both measures and men; and then he went in to troubles in South America. Close to the end of the meal, he turned suddenly to Mrs. La Farge.

"Now, Florence, let us hear what you have to say about Delaware."

He was not the intimate friend, not Theodore at all just then, he was the President, and rather formidable. Quite plainly he was prepared, documented and armed, and not by any Bayards or Duponts from Wilmington, but from quite other quarters. Mrs. La Farge had a moment of dismay, but it passed.

"No, Mr. President, please, this is too important to talk about generally. Delaware is fighting for its honour as no South American Republic ever fought, and I want you to help. You must give me a real interview."

This was exactly what he had wanted to get out of; he had played for position, and lost. She had won.

"Very well, I'll come back to the library in half an hour."

As she rose, "you're fighting in a good cause, Mrs. La Farge," said McKelway, the editor; "don't give it up." She was grateful for that word.

She went up to the library with Mrs. Roosevelt. When the President arrived, she gave him the situation: the buying the farmers, the unsavoury background, the steadily rotting vote, the undermining split-off from Dupont, the regular Republican nominee, to Addicks. Would the President not speak a word, make a sign against this man who was trying to climb by means of dollars instead of character?

"Impossible. See Payne. I'll have you talk to him. He'll explain the party's need for Addicks."

"I don't want to see Payne. I'm not concerned with party needs, I'm concerned for the honour of the Senate of the United States. That is more important than party needs—and you are the man who knows that better than any one else."

This was a home shot; but he wasn't down yet.

"Payne and Hanna are set on Addicks. Payne and Hanna are leading spokesmen of the party of which I am the head. It is utterly out of the question that I should disregard them to such a degree as you ask. Moreover, they have promised to help me in several much needed bills, if I will help them get a large majority in the Senate. What will they do if I fail to perform my side of it? What you're asking for is a dead-lock. Don't you know that dead-locks get nobody anywhere at all, and meanwhile the country needs my bills?"

"I'm not asking for a dead-lock. I'm asking you not to support for the Senate of the United States exactly the kind of man you have always opposed and denounced."

"Addicks is the chosen candidate of the leading spokesmen of the Republican party," said Roosevelt—and now he boiled over to his undoing, "I'm here," he surged on, "to carry the Republican party forward, not to throw monkey wrenches into its machinery. Delaware is in a state of revolution. I'll not tolerate a state of South American revolution anywhere in this country, if I have the means to stop it."

"No, Mr. President. If Delaware was like the South American republics, it would indeed be in a state of revolution, with bloodshed and violence. It is only because the decent citizens there, the people of your own sort and class, are Americans with self-restraint, and not Latins with none, that Delaware in spite of its feeling has not broken out into bloodshed."

That was the shot which got him. He looked at Mrs. La Farge with a new expression, and for a moment was at a loss what to say. In that moment, she proceeded swiftly:

"I don't ask you to defeat your own bills, and I know they might easily be defeated. But you can't support Addicks. Promise me that anyhow. Promise that you won't come out for him, that you won't help him in any way. Do what you did with Platt again and again when you were Governor. Tell Payne that you cannot accept or back Addicks, tell him to find some one else acceptable to him, whom you can back."

The President was now thinking rapidly.

"If Payne persuaded Addicks," he asked Mrs. La Farge, "if he persuaded him to retire, would the Democrats let Dupont come in at once as a decent substitute and to finish the Addicks affair?"   (Only two years of the term were left.)

Mrs. La Farge went to the telephone, called up Wilmington, got an important Democratic leader, and put the President's question to him squarely.   He answered that he could not promise to hold his men, but that in these circumstances he himself would vote for Dupont.

When she came back from the telephone and reported this to the President, he had thought his way through.

"I don't believe," said he, "in the President interfering in the affairs of the states.   It is not his business and I won't do that. I won't interfere one way or another."

"And you won't let Payne speak for you or commit you in any way whatever?"

"Certainly not."

"Thank you, Mr. President.   Good bye."

"Good bye, Florence."

She returned to New York.   Dupont was elected Senator; Addicks, after having floated thus conspicuously on the surface for a while, sank beneath it again.   Some time after all this, when Mrs. La Farge was at the White House as a friend and not as an emissary, the case of Delaware came up incidentally in the general conversation, and the President turned to her.

"I owe that to you, Florence," said he.   "You got me out of a bad hole that time."

Other holes lay ahead for him to fall into, and he did.   The wonder is not that a person who went ahead at such a rate should fall into holes; the wonder is that he did not fall into more.

## XII.

In Europe, chiefly in France, after the seventeenth century down to my personal adventures, an institution known as the *salon* played a leading part. Its influence — political, intellectual, social — pervaded the times, and is recorded in many familiar memoirs. A *salon* was somebody's drawing room, the somebody usually being a woman with or without an important husband, but always herself ably equipped to draw the important about her. Charm was her magnet, seconded by tact, wit, worldly wisdom, brains, sometimes by imperfect virtue, and often by skill in flattering the illustrious. Beneath her social magic generals, poets, statesmen, smiled and expanded. I never saw a *salon* as a going concern, but I saw Madame Mohl. That day in 1883, in her drawing room on the left bank of the Seine, Madame Mohl talked to my mother and me about Renan, talked rather maliciously of the great man's small vanities. She was eighty, she had known other times, other manners, she was in solitude amid the new times; she could talk maliciously or otherwise about Victor Hugo, Stendhal, Berlioz, Sainte-Beuve, Mérimée, Lamartine, Thiers, Guizot, Taine, de Musset, Heine Chopin, George Sand—about any one you can think of since 1830, whom you would like to have met yourself: all had come to her.

Distinguished civilized men and charming civilized women came as a habit to the White House while Roosevelt was there. For that once in our history, we had an American *salon*. It was not a woman, as in France, it was a man who drew them together; but even such a man as this could not have done it without Mrs. Roosevelt. His clever and delightful sisters, Mrs. Cowles and Mrs. Robinson, helped. It was a combination such as Washington had never seen before, and is unlikely to see soon again. Anybody from anywhere in the world, no matter how eminent, or how hard to please, could dine at the White House from 1902 to 1909 without having to make their private allowances for Democracy. Ever since Thomas Jefferson, by way of asserting American simplicity, sat in dressing gown and shabby slippers to receive the minister of a foreign power who arrived in the prescribed attire of his country to present his credentials, Jefferson has had among our statesmen his imitators in this kind of simplicity. Within the last decade, one of these arrived in Washington from the Middle West, broadcasting the fact that he had never owned a dress suit. It was presently noticed that he had acquired one. The day is certain to come (though I shall not see it) when our whole Democracy will really feel at ease, and none of us will offer bad manners as a proof that we are just as good as anybody. At the place and time for it, Roosevelt wore cow-boy clothes, and he put on his white waistcoat and swallow tail when the occasion called for them; and he was at home in whatever he happened to be wearing. Both he and Mrs. Roosevelt took themselves as naturally as they did their responsibilities, whether social or political. That is why the zest and pleasure with which they made their guests welcome at the White House marked their hospitality as an epoch.

In one point my parallel between the French *salon* and the social White House obviously ceases: the hostess in France held herself in the background, stimulating the good talk lightly and imperceptibly; in the White House the host used to dash his opinions and challenges across the company much in the same manner that he served tennis balls in the court. During seven years it was my extraordinary good fortune often to be there when Roosevelt gathered round him both his Familiars and his Unfamiliars. You could never tell what the Unfamiliars were going to turn out, but you shared the President's dread of them. They were perforce a part of his or any President's job, they had to be "entertained," they arrived with credentials of many varieties, political, educational, philanthropic, scientific, and more often than not they stood for something—a tropical Commonwealth, a seat of learning in Nish, a medical mission to the hook-worm belt, the street railways in Kansas City, votes for women, the war against cigarettes—and they ranged from Ambassadors and Captains of Industry to the lowest strata of male and female enthusiasts.

Roosevelt would come hurrying in from his forenoon of work, and say, perhaps:

"Dan, Emily Tuckerman is expecting you to lunch at their house at one-thirty.   I begged her to save you from the people who are coming here."

Or he would say:

"I don't know what lunch is going to be like to-day, and we've all got just to bear it together.   I've put you at Mrs. Roosevelt's left with my sister Corinne next, and then Winty Chanler. There's a celebrated engineer coming from Chiasso, who is the leading authority on boring tunnels, and I'm afraid he's going to tell us all about it; and an equally celebrated economist from Leeds, who wishes me to urge the British Empire to adopt the decimal system."

After remarks like this, made with a comic twist of expression and a plaintive touch of his falsetto, our demeanor would be tremulous as we stood in the stately room, striving to keep a serious face while the eminent strangers began to arrive.   Perhaps Chanler's voice would whisper from behind, "Bet you the bearded guy's the tunnel borer.   He's going to bore us all."

Ceremonious introductions with careful bows and well-worn syllables of greeting followed, and presently we filed decorously into lunch.   There we Familiars would speak but little and behave with reserve, while Roosevelt, with a celebrity on each side, plunged deep into tunnels and the decimal system, and no social unity was possible.

And once the celebrity had started upon his specialty, Roosevelt's inexhaustible curiosity about all well presented subjects carried him along.   He would talk first as if a decimal and then as if a tunnel was the only thing in the world he had ever loved; he would refer to the Thames and Severn tunnels; and the incurable British dread of a Channel tunnel, and to the monetary system in China, or the currency experiments of Frederick the II of Hohenstaufen.   Sometimes for unity he tried to bring us into the conversation.

"Winty," he would call across the table, "you certainly must have been through the Saint Gothard tunnel.   Signor Castellomaggiore says it could have been put through at precisely five-sixteenths of what it cost.

"How very interesting, Mr. President! And what did it cost? I went through too rapidly to calculate." Chanler was versed in that kind of mischief.

"Yez. Five-sixteents," Signor Castellomaggiore would utter in a foreign accent, and with a cold eye for a moment on Chanler. Then he returned with determination to the President, who had worked at top speed all morning, and would have so liked to play for an hour. When the celebrities were safely gone, perhaps he would burst out: "Winty, how dared you! You nearly upset me."

Sometimes an Unfamiliar would prove a delightful surprise, and this possibility did leaven our dread with a pinch of hope; but *salons* are not made so, they depend on the preponderating presence of Familiars, and it was when none but Familiars assembled that Roosevelt let himself go, that the whole company let itself go, that it became sheer luxury to listen to these distinguished and brilliant men turning their minds loose to play. Most of them came straight from taking an official hand in the day's national or international doings; meeting here in a sort of free masonry, they dropped their caution; nobody was going to quote anything outside; therefore much inside was laid bare, and Secretary Root's "shop," or Secretary Taft's, or Senator Lodge's, became thrilling and alive, and sparkled with frequent "comic relief." Nor was "shop" by any means all: it might be Henry Irving and what he acted best, or Wilbur Wright and the new portent of the aeroplane, or Paderewski's concert, or jiu-jitzu which the President was practising with a Japanese instructor, or the German Kaiser and Venezuela, or the new conductor of the Boston Symphony Orchestra, or the sliding scale of honesty in a Central American Government, or Tillman beating the face of a brother Senator, or the scene of Mrs. Minor Morris leaving the Executive Office, or which of Walter Scott's novels was the greatest, or how much of Mark Twain was likely to live. Whatever it happened to be, it was skillfully tossed

about in general conversation, every one at his best through
Roosevelt's stimulating presence; it was never a collection of
mere tête-à-têtes, like today's dinner parties, exchanging puny
personal items.   This, too, was a special point in the White
House *salon:* the women, civilized and cultivated as they were
—Mrs. Holmes, Mrs. La Farge, Mrs. Lodge, Emily Tuckerman, Mrs. Cameron, Mrs. Chanler, for instance—did not take
the lead; it was the men who set the pace; but the ladies kept up
with them handsomely: and knew how to listen, as well as how
to reply.

## XIII.

Who were the Familiars of Roosevelt's Golden Age?   Some,
like him, are gone; some are still here; and when I close my eyes,
my memory can see them all.

In many great rooms of the Old World, faces of the Past look
down at one from the walls.   Certain of these in their lives won
such renown as to outlive Death.   For them, as he pauses before their portraits, the versed pilgrim need not consult his
printed catalogue, or resort for help to his guide book; he knows
something about Bonaparte, Francis the First, Erasmus, Lo-
renzo de Medici.   Upon the mortal aspect of others, no longer
known even by their names, about whom neither catalogue nor
guide book has a word to say, the hand of Titian, or Van Dyck,
or Velasquez, has conferred a voiceless immortality, and in their
revealing features the pilgrim can read intellect, generosity, heroism, faith, pain, passion, cruelty, pride, resignation—whatever
qualities were most exercized by the souls that once moulded
these countenances.   Still others baffle our guesses, are close
lipped as we watch them, conceal everything except that they
are concealing.

What should the discerning pilgrim to the White House read
in those faces of the Roosevelt Familiars, did they look down
upon him from the walls of the dining-room, where their talk once
flashed, and where their laughter once rang?

Here is evidently a great aristocrat. A soldier? Possibly; some hint of it. A dreamer? Probably; much hint of it. An intellect? Certainly; no equal to it in the whole gallery. Austerity is present; and Imagination. Irony is not absent. A face shining with some noble, life-long aspiration. A lonely man? Not on the surface; rather tolerant and social. An eye equally able to be stern and understanding.

It is Holmes the Judge. The Law his mistress since the Civil War. A captain in that. Three times wounded in those four years. Hurt in health for a while. Bearing in his soul for ever the mark—which all of his generation that had souls bore for ever—of our Union's four-years wrestle with death. Law student, attorney-at-law, teacher at the Harvard Law School, Chief Justice of Massachusetts, Associate Justice of the Supreme Court, writing opinions in his ninetieth year. The most illustrious and beloved figure ever in that Court; a great personage in its history.

He was lean as a race horse when I first knew him; and had just finished making a cup with red wine for his three guests, informally asked to supper on the South Shore. The ice tinkled in the pitcher as he brought it in. Art had gone into this, as into all else that he does. Throughout the evening it was my part to be seen and not heard, for I was the youngest there. Two brilliant listeners—handsome ladies both—set his talk going; and I was captured by it then as I have been captured by it since, through fifty years, often when he had no better listener than I. His talk would always bubble and sparkle from him, a stream of seriousness and laughter, imagination and philosophy, in which enthusiasm was undying; and the style of a master in English marked his improvisations, just as it marks his considered writing. In this, however, he naturally restricts his informalities to such expressions as "a dirty business"—his characterization in a dissenting opinion of prohibition agents tapping private telephone wires to catch citizens buying wine; while in his speech, he whimsically drops not infrequently into slang.

For example, he stood at his hall door in Washington to assure a departing friend that a welcome would always wait him.

"Don't forget that wittles is served regular," he said.

Certain ladies in those Boston days used to transport me beyond laughter by assuring me with concern that certain other Boston ladies "were spoiling Wendell Holmes."

"I hope they are," I sometimes answered. Even in a Boston spinster, there is a smack of the eternal feminine.

In those Boston days we had many walks; and by the time I was at the Harvard Law School, I would come in to spend Saturdays and Sundays at his house in Chestnut Street. And we students would entice him out to dine with us in Cambridge. There, over our champagne, he would loaf and invite his soul with beguiling expatiations.

Once on a walk, he stopped and turned to me with solemnity. "Young fello', think of it. I am forty-five to-day." The thought of it awed him.

On another walk, as we were passing the Parker House, I suggested that he come in and have a drink with me. There was something not remote from embarrassment in the disclosing of his strict code which he then made, putting it a little like an apology.

"Come up to my house," he said. "Before I went on the Bench, I didn't mind—but—you can understand I think—I don't somehow cotton to the notion of our Judges hobnobbing in hotel bars and saloons. The Bench should stand aloof from indiscriminate familiarities."

An aristocrat in morals as in mind, with a fortunate touch of both Puck and Ariel. During those same years, the horrified ladies of Boston appealed to him for a judgment on the new French author, Zola.

"Improving, but dull," he said.

He held "realism" to be a timely tonic for thin blood and happy endings. He was as impatient as Henry James with the genteel Victorian demand that a novel must be as comfortable as woolen stockings and as pretty as a Christmas card. But

*Photo by Brown Bros.*

OLIVER WENDELL HOLMES

with the absence in Henry James and his disciples of all muscular action, he was equally impatient. "Fifty years of polite conversation and nothing doing," he styled it to me one day in 1929. He liked to make and he liked to use the paradox and the homely analogy. He was the first to quote me this observation, which had delighted him:

"No generalization is wholly true—not even this one." He had a way of putting his thoughts so unusually that they stuck: "It's only when you mix your metaphors *badly* that it's wrong." "You can strike illuminating flashes by the juxtaposition of the unrelated." "Things that are 'just as good as' things ain't." In his book, *The Common Law,* to illustrate the early historic legal meaning of vengeance, he says:

"Vengeance imports a feeling of blame, and an opinion . . . that a wrong has been done. It can hardly go very far beyond the case of a harm intentionally inflicted: even a dog distinguishes between being stumbled over and being kicked."

That work, meditated by a man in his thirties actually published when he was but forty, seems to hold the essence of him complete, his attitude towards law, and his attitude toward life then and ever since. It has become a text-book in the Law Schools of the world. He says on the first page, that the life of the law has not been logic, it has been experience, that the law embodies the story of a nation's development through many centuries, and cannot be dealt with as if it contained only the axioms and corollaries of a book of mathematics. In addressing some young students a few years later, he tells them that in this Universe, "every fact leads to every other by the path of the air," and that as thinkers their business "is to make plainer the way from some thing to the whole of things." But he warns them "that to think great thoughts you must be heroes as well as idealists. Only when you have worked alone . . . and in hope and despair have trusted to your own unshaken will—then only will you have achieved . . . the isolated joy of the thinker, who knows that a hundred years after he is dead and forgotten, men who never heard of him will be moving to the measure of his thought."

"By the path of the air," "moving to the measure of his thought,"—it is by the eloquence of both intellect and of passion that Holmes strikes forth these phrases, glowing not merely with the perfection of their art, but with their embodied truth. By the path of the air Galileo went from the swinging lamp at Pisa to the rotation of our planet, and to-day both astronomy and physics move to the measure of his thought.

Naturally, none but a master can drop safely from formal language to phrases like "dirty business," and none but an aristocrat in mind and taste can move at his ease in any company, either of words or of men. Naturally, also, with Holmes, every fact leads to every other, and so all that he has read, thought, or done, ministers to his judicial being. His holiday habit of reading aloud with his wife some great author entire, is immanent throughout his legal opinions. He said to me of Wordsworth once, that several times in the middle of a Wordsworth desert of dullness, that they would be on the point of giving it up, when "the old boy would give a wiggle that connected you with the eternal," and they would keep on; "and in the end it pays," he added. He insisted often that you must humor any great man of a past era, you must "fall in with his stride;" and that the very heart of all criticism was to be able to look discerningly at a thing out of fashion. How did he account, I asked him in later years, for the continual translations of a light poet like Horace? "Because Horace," he answered, "sums up with unsurpassed felicity the philosophy of the man-about-town. Each great wave in thought, or science, or art, is left behind by successors. But the club man, the sceptical worldling, with his decencies and indecencies, had much the same standards and horizons in Rome as he has in New York. His point of view is constant. Therefore, whether he is dining out in sandals and a purple tunic, or in patent leathers and a boiled shirt, Horace is up to date with him." Holmes used to declare that in their division of the Earth's Kingdom, Artist and Philosopher break pretty even; he was ready to allow the priests of Beauty 49 per cent, and 51 to the Thinkers. A good glimpse of Holmes is to be had in the collection of addresses, of which he speaks as "these chance utterances of faith and doubt." In very truth they proclaim the great American Creed.

Before looking at the legal aspect of Holmes one or two of his letters will afford a glimpse of him both as Artist and Philosopher. The following was written in 1910:

". . . Very little literature this winter. But I have had one great experience—Dante—I know no Italian, but I found that with a translation and one's knowledge of Latin &c. one could read the original very easily. One of my favorite parodoxes is that everything is dead in 25 (or 50) years. The author no longer says to you what he meant to say. If he is original his new truths have been developed and become familiar in improved form—his errors exploded. If he is not a philosopher but an artist, the emotional emphasis has changed. But for all that a great man is discernible as great. And the great bottom feelings don't change even if the objects of them do. I found the intensity of Dante's Spiritual rapture so thrilling and absorbing that I could think of little else, and the song of his words is divine. Shakespeare will say a few words now and then that seem the beginning of the road to paradise ('In Belmont lives a Lady' &c.) But Dante does it every 20 lines, and he carries you there too. It is not merely the Italian. When I read the answer to him of the troubadour Arnaud, 'Jeu sui Arnaut, que plor et vai chantan', I had to rush out of Doors and walk it off. He weeps for he is still in purgatory, but he is a poet and a troubadour and he goes singing through his tears. Talk about a green thought in a green shade. D's paradise is white on white on white—like a dish of certain tulips in the spring. However I must leave a little room for Rabelais. . . . I read the last two books. What temperament, what gusto. Everything beginning to hum—like culture in Chicago.—And what a seed book, how many germs of Swift, Stern, perhaps even Thackeray. You see I am reading now for the day of Judgment, so as not to dead ("flunk" is the word Holmes might use today) if I am called up on some book that every gentleman is expected to have read. . . ."

Nineteen years later, Holmes writes of a book I had sent him and begged him to report on, warning him that it was not at all the sort of book his father would have written, but predicting solid renown for its gifted author:

". . . There is something quite remarkable about the author. . . . It is singular. An account of eating and drinking with a lot of fornication accompanied by conversations on the lowest level, with some slight intelligence but no ideas, and nothing else—and yet it seems a slice of life, and you are not bored with details of an ordinary day.

"It reminds me of a reflection that I often make on how large a part of the time and thoughts of even the best of us are taken up by animal wants. These lads so far as appears don't think of anything else. And I sometimes say that if a man contributes neither thought nor beauty to life—as is the case with the majority—I would let Malthus loose on him. But then this lad could write this book, which must be a work of art. It can't be accident and naiveté. So let him survive—but as you prophesied he would, let him leave his garbage."

In the letter of 1910, Judge Holmes had signed himself, "Your aged friend. (I shall be 70 at my next birthday!)"; and on that occasion he had talked about Dante and Rabelais; this time it was about Ernest Hemingway.

Because Mr. Justice Holmes and Mr. Justice Brandeis sometimes take the same view in a given case, the lay intelligence has supposed them to be of one kind; you will hear them classed together not infrequently. This superficial blunder may be likened to finding an identity between Shakespeare and the Old Testament, because Shylock hails Portia as "A Daniel come to judgment." I doubt if any gulf exists more impassable than the one which divides the fundamental processes of a Holmes from those of a Brandeis:—"East is East and West is West, and never the twain shall meet." Holmes descends from the English Common Law, evolved by the genius of a people who have built themselves the greatest nation in a thousand years; Brandeis, from a noble and ancient race which has radiated sublimity in several forms across the centuries, but has failed in all centuries to make a stable nation of itself. *Liberty defined and assured by Law* is a principle as alien to the psychology of that race as it is native with Holmes and his ancestors. His mission is the Law and to declare what it is; never to assert or to further any humanitarian or political bent. The law is a rule for him to observe, not a tool to carry out his preferences; and those who try to label him *radical* miss him as wholly as if they tried to label him *conservative*. He sits within the impersonal circle which should surround every member of the Supreme Court who intends to keep it what it was created to be; his own pen might have written the following:

"Nothing is to be more dreaded than maxims of law and reasons of state blended together by judicial authority. Among all the terrible instruments of arbitrary power, decisions of Courts, whetted and guided and impelled by considerations of policy, cut with the keenest edge, and inflict the deepest and most deadly wounds."

These words have been ascribed to James Wilson, one of the earliest members of the Supreme Court. Their warning has for the most part been heeded.

To know his opinions is to know that Mr. Justice Brandeis would never have laid down a doctrine so impersonal, because he does not sit immovably within the impersonal circle: humanitarian aspects of a case, individual hardships, push him out of it. I will give one illustration of this tendency.

In 1879, the owners of some coal land sold the surface, upon the buyers agreeing to waive any damage to them through the sinking of the surface caused by future mining of the coal. Forty-three years later, a state law forbade mining which disturbed the surface near a dwelling house. The coal owners gave notice to the surface owner of their intention to mine beneath his house. He invoked the law to stop them. The opinion of the Court, delivered by Mr. Justice Holmes, held they could not be stopped: the surface owner was bound by the

agreement under which the surface was bought, the coal owners
were protected by two Amendments to the Constitution.

Mr. Justice Brandeis dissented, invoking the Police Power.
This can prevent a man using his property so as to create a
public nuisance.    To his mind the fact that damage to the
surface owner was now imminent, set the surface owner free
from the agreement to waive such damage; his mind also dis-
missed the hardship to the owners of the coal; and the Constitution, which forbids the impairing of the obligations of a
contract, and the taking of property without compensation after
due process of law, did not embarrass his reasoning that no
property was taken here because the owners still had their coal
in the ground.

"Every restriction," he argued, "upon the use of property imposed in the exercise of the police power deprives the owner of
some right theretofore enjoyed, and is, in that sense, an abridg-
ment by the State of rights in property without making compensation.    But restriction imposed to protect the public health,
safety, or morals from dangers threatened is not a taking.    The
restriction here in question is *merely the prohibition of a noxious
use.*"

I italicize this characterization of the ordinary mining of coal,
because it is the exact moment when the reasoning becomes most
characteristic of Mr. Justice Brandeis: "noxious use" begs the
question in so light a whisper as to be almost inaudible.

The difference of this mental process from the reasoning of
Mr. Justice Holmes is worth the study of any who have thought
these two master minds alike.

"As applied to this case," says Mr. Justice Holmes, "the
Statute is admitted to destroy previously existing rights of property and contract.    The question is whether the police power
can be stretched so far.

"Government could hardly go on if to some extent values incident to property could not be diminished without paying for
every such change in the general law. . . .    One fact for consideration . . . is the extent of the diminution.    So the question
depends upon the particular facts. . . .

"This is the case of a single private house. . . . A source of damage to such a house is not a public nuisance. . . . On the other hand the extent of the taking is great. It purports to abolish what is recognized in Pennsylvania as an estate in land. . . . As said in a Pennsylvania case, 'for practical purposes, the right to coal consists in the right to mine it.' . . . It is our opinion that the act cannot be sustained as an exercise of the police power, so far as it affects the mining of coal under streets or cities where the right to mine such coal has been reserved. . . . To make it commercially impracticable . . . has very nearly the same effect for constitutional purposes as appropriating or destroying it. . . . The protection of private property in the Fifth Amendment presupposes it is wanted for public use, but provides it shall not be taken for such use without compensation. . . . When this seemingly absolute protection is found to be qualified by the police power, the natural tendency of human nature is to extend the qualification more and more *until at last private property disappears. But that cannot be accomplished in this way under the Constitution of the United States.*"

Again I italicize to mark the deep essential gulf between two brilliant intellects. For the one, if your wish is to do away with private property, do it through the Constitution. For the other, if this stands in your way, wrap it gently in a web of words and lift it into the Police Power. With the one, a Commonwealth stands secure; with the other, it crumbles to-day just as it crumbled in ancient days despite the sublime genius of its Oriental race.

"We are in danger of forgetting," says Mr. Justice Holmes in the next to the last paragraph of his opinion in this case (Pennsylvania Coal Company v. Mahon, U. S. 260, 393), "that a strong public desire to improve the public condition is not enough to warrant achieving the desire by a shorter cut than the Constitutional way of paying for the change."

That there are no short cuts to anything except perdition, is a legal concept beyond an Oriental mind, when humanitarian considerations, such as a hardship done to a poor man by a rich company, tempt it to alleviate an individual at the expense of a principle. Holmes has quite recently defined the duty of a judge to uphold the law apart from incidental policy:

"We agree to all the generalities about not supplying criminal laws with what they omit, but there is no canon against using common sense in construing laws as saying what they obviously mean."

It was in 1886 that Mr. Justice Holmes told those students, about to set forth on the Great Adventure, that every fact leads to every other by the path of the air; and later in the same address, and in a sentence of English which also has the wings upon which he can soar as none other, that "no man has earned the right to intellectual ambition until he has learned to lay his course by a star which he has never seen—to dig by the divining rod for springs which he may never reach." This is a more lofty phrasing of what he must have said to me many times in those old days—that to live the Great Adventure you must for ever be chasing a butterfly. Such spirits keep up their quest to the end:—and Holmes in his chosen pursuit has seized and given us thought after thought, made lustrous by its verbal incarnation.

"The common law is not a brooding omnipresence in the sky but the articulate voice of some sovereign or quasi-sovereign that can be identified. . . ."
"A word is not a crystal, transparent and unchanged, it is the skin of a living thought and may vary greatly in color and content according to the circumstances and the time in which it is used."

Room is here for but three sentences of Holmes in a case where theatre ticket scalpers objected to a new State law that interfered with their business, as being unconstitutional under the Fourteenth Amendment.

"—Police power often is used in a wide sense to apologize for the general power of the legislature to make a part of the community uncomfortable by a change. . . . *I am far from*

*saying I think this particular law a wise and rational provision.
That is not my affair."*

He could hardly chalk a cleaner circle round a judge's official
domain.

In the following passages from his dissenting opinion in a very
famous case, he washes his hands, with a gesture resembling
defiance, of every consideration tending to blur the boundaries
of the domain.

"Great cases like hard cases make bad laws.   For great cases
are called great, not by reason of their real importance in shap-
ing the law of the future, but because of some accident of immediate overwhelming interest which appeals to the feelings and
distorts the judgment.   These immediate interests exercise a
kind of hydraulic pressure which makes what previously was
clear seem doubtful, and before which even well settled principles of law will bend.   What we have to do in this case is to
find the meaning of some not very difficult words . . . with
the same natural interpretation that one would be sure of if the
same question arose upon an indictment for a similar act which
excited no public attention. . . .

"I am happy to know that only a minority of my brethren
adopt an interpretation of the law which in my opinion would
. . . disintegrate society so far as it could into individual atoms.
I should regard calling such a law a regulation of commerce as
a mere pretence.   It would be an attempt to reconstruct society.   *I am not concerned with the wisdom of such an attempt,*
but I believe that Congress was not intrusted with the power
to make it. . . ."

That part of the American world which is mentally equipped
to think soberly about the enormous issues raised by this case
(Northern Securities Company v. United States, 193 U. S. 197)
holds with Mr. Justice Holmes, dissents like him from the decision of the majority of the Supreme Court, thinks it was a mischievous meddling with economically wholesome tendencies in
our national growth.

Certainly it was a meddling, certainly outside considerations
blurred the chalk line Holmes draws, just as Judge Wilson, or a

contemporary, drew it in 1790 in the words I have quoted from him.    Well settled principles of law *were* bent in this case.    The "not very difficult words" of a law forbidding and punishing by fine and imprisonment combinations in restraint of trade, were distorted by "hydraulic pressure" turned on by Roosevelt; and Roosevelt was angered by the dissenting opinion of the judge whom he had recently appointed to the Supreme Court.    As he saw it, a menace hung over the United States so dangerous and so imminent, that it must be averted, if possible, even by a short cut like this suit to divorce two railroads who had been united by a marriage they had every reason, even the Supreme Court's authority in a previous case, to believe was a legal union.

The growing power of money had charged popular opinion with a force that already had devastatingly exploded in spots, just as the gathering force in the clouds detonates at length in the lightning.    Lest the social fulminations should cease to be local and become universal, Roosevelt took his first step, followed duly by several others, to dissipate what he believed (and rightly, as I think) to be a threat to the nation at large, by reassuring popular opinion.

I think the hydraulic pressure pushed the majority of the Supreme Court over the border of that domain so vehemently defined by Judge Wilson, into the adjacent territory which Mr. Justice Brandeis thinks it no trespass for a judge to enter; while Mr. Justice Holmes, true to form, sat tight.    There can be no legal refutation of his reasoning; but I cannot be sure, nor can he, nor can any man, that, had he been personally struck by the lightning in the air as I had been, he might not (consistently with his willingness to recognize hydraulic pressure when something bad is going to happen before there is any time to deliberate and take measures about it) have departed from his customary attitude here.

"Can you understand," I asked him twenty-seven years later, "how I'm able absolutely to agree with you in the Northern Securities, and at the same time be very glad that Roosevelt won that suit?"

"Perfectly," he said.

"And," I continued, "once that object lesson had been put across, to divorce the Union and Southern Pacific was a needless step."

He thought so too, naturally; he had declined to break up the merger of the other two railroads.

When I take up the letter Roosevelt wrote me after his election in 1904, I shall go fully into the national menace which brought on the Northern Securities case.

My portrait of Holmes is not quite finished. It is the most important I shall attempt to paint, because Holmes is altogether the most important figure among the Roosevelt Familiars. What the others were doing then was better known, what he was doing was caviar to the general; but what he has done is of such a quality, that, to quote again from his address to the law students, "a hundred years after he is dead and forgotten men who never heard of him will be moving to the measure of his thought."

Here is the complete passage from his dissenting opinion, where the Court decided in favor of Dry Agents tapping the private wires of citizens in order to catch them dealing with bootleggers.

"We have to choose, and . . . I think it a less evil that some criminals should escape than that the Government should play an ignoble part." (As he hadn't thought the Bench should hobnob in hotel bars, he didn't think the Government should eavesdrop: a question of decency and dignity.)

"For those who agree with me, no distinction can be taken between the Government as prosecutor and the Government as judge. If the existing code does not permit district attorneys to have a hand in such dirty business it does not permit the judge to allow such iniquities to succeed."

Until 1916, carrying the mail by the railroads was voluntary; in 1916, Congress made it obligatory, for reasonable pay. In 1921, some railroads complained to the Interstate Commerce Commission—the designated tribunal—that the pay was too small.   It required a long looking into before deciding.   Meanwhile underpayment went on.   The Government claimed that to take care of this, the roads should have made a separate protest.   This did not appeal to the common sense of the Court. In delivering its opinion, Holmes said in part:

"Obviously Congress intended the Commission to settle the whole business, not to leave a straggling residuum to look out for itself. . . .   No reason can have existed for leaving the additional annoyance . . . of a suit for compensation during the time of the proceedings. . . .   We put our decision . . . on the reasonable implication of an authority to change the rates from the day when the application was filed . . . and the fact that unless the Commission has the power assumed, *a part of the railroad's constitutional rights will be left in the air."*

Note again the essential difference between this attitude and that of Mr. Justice Brandeis, for whom in the coal mining case constitutional rights must be left in the air if somebody's house is in danger of being undermined.

I shall wind up with a couple of somewhat more extended illustrations of Holmes' mind.   Both concern matters directly human, and much less directly technical, than what I have hitherto presented.

In Buck v. Bell, 274 U. S. 200, the Virginia law providing for the sexual sterilization of insane persons or imbecile persons in State institutions was upheld as constitutional.   Holmes delivered the opinion of the Court, and had this to say (page 207):

"The attack is not upon the procedure but upon the substantive law.   It seems to be contended that in no circumstances could such an order be justified.   It certainly is contended that the order cannot be justified upon the existing grounds.   The judgment finds the facts that have been recited and that Carrie Buck 'is the probable potential parent of socially inadequate offspring, likewise afflicted, that she may be sexually sterilized without detriment to her general health and that her welfare and that of society will be promoted by her sterilization,' and thereupon makes the order.   In view of the general declarations of the legislature and the specific findings of the Court, obviously we cannot say as matter of law that the grounds do not exist, and if they exist they justify the result.   We have seen more than once that the public welfare may call upon the best citizens for their lives.   It would be strange if it could not call upon those who already sap the strength of the State for these lesser sacrifices, often not felt to be such by those concerned, in order to prevent our being swamped with incompetence.   It is better for all the world, if instead of waiting to execute degenerate offspring for crime, or to let them starve for their imbecility, society can prevent those who are manifestly unfit from continuing their kind.   The principle that sustains compulsory vaccination is broad enough to cover cutting the Fallopian tubes. *Jacobson v. Massachusetts*, 197 U. S. 11.   Three generations of imbeciles are enough."

In May, 1929, I went down to see Judge Holmes in Washington.   As usual, we talked of many things, and as not unusual, he came to what had been most recently engaging his mind. This was a dissenting opinion.   Certain sentences in it came from that sprite-like mischief in him which had spoken out when he told the Boston ladies that Zola's novels were "improving but dull;" and when he came to these passages, his beguiling and musical voice gave a chuckle.   Before he began to read aloud, he remarked:

"This is designed to occasion discomfort in certain quarters."

United States vs. Schwimmer.   The facts appear plainly in the opinion.

"The applicant seems to be a woman of superior character and intelligence, obviously more than ordinarily desirable as a citizen of the United States.   It is agreed that she is qualified for citizenship except so far as the view set forth in a statement of facts 'may show that the applicant is not attached to the principles of the Constitution of the United States and well disposed to the good order and happiness of the same, and except in so far as the same may show that she cannot take the oath of allegiance without a mental reservation.'   The views referred to are an extreme opinion in favor of pacifism and a statement that she would not bear arms to defend the Constitution.   So far as the adequacy of her oath is concerned I hardly can see how that is affected by the statement, inasmuch as she is a woman over fifty years of age, and would not be allowed to bear arms if she wanted to.    And as to the opinion the whole examination of the applicant shows that she holds none of the now-dreaded creeds but thoroughly believes in organized government and prefers that of the United States to any other in the world.    Surely it cannot show lack of attachment to the principles of the Constitution that she thinks that it can be improved.    I suppose that most intelligent people think that it might be.    Her particular improvement looking to the abolition of war seems to me not materially different in its bearing on this case from a wish to establish cabinet government as in England, or a single house, or one term of seven years for the President. To touch a more burning question, only a judge mad with partisanship would exclude because the applicant thought that the Eighteenth Amendment should be repealed.

Of course the fear is that if a war came the applicant would exert activities such as were dealt with in SCHENCK V UNITED STATES, 249, U. S. 47.    But that seems to me unfounded.    Her position and motives are wholly different from those of Schenck. She is an optimist and states in strong and, I do not doubt, sincere words her belief that war will disappear and that the impending destiny of mankind is to unite in peaceful leagues.    I do not share that optimism nor do I think that a philosophic view of the world would regard war as absurd.    But most people who have known it regard it with horror, as a last resort, and even if not yet ready for cosmopolitan efforts, would welcome any practicable combinations that would increase the power on the side of peace.    The notion that the applicant's optimistic anticipations would make her a worse citizen is sufficiently answered by her examination which seems to me a better argument for her admission than any that I can offer.    Some of her answers might excite popular prejudice, but if there is any principle of the Constitution that more imperatively calls for attachment than any other it is the principle of free thought— not free thought for those who agree with us but freedom for the thought that we hate.    I think that we should adhere to that principle with regard to admission into, as well as to life within this country.    And recurring to the opinion that bars this applicant's way, I would suggest that the Quakers have done their share to make the country what it is, that many citizens agree with the applicant's belief and that I had not supposed hitherto that we regretted our inability to expel them because they believe more than some of us do in the teachings of the Sermon on the Mount."

This was written, be it well understood, by a man whose next birthday would make him eighty-nine.   An aristocrat in thought and conduct; an artist; a widely illumined intelligence; driven onward from within, rather than by externals.   Titian alone would have been adequate to record on canvas both his beauty and his philosophy.

No master so aptly as Frans Hals could have brought out the significance of the next face in the White House gallery of Roosevelt's Familiars.   At the time his brush was busied over the portraits of those worthies we look at in the Liechtenstein collection, or at Haarlem, and The Hague, the stream of wealth which had poured during three hundred fat years into the pockets of the contented and capable Netherlanders through the Hanseatic League, had run dry.   But the ease of living it had brought them from generation to generation, got into the broad, untroubled features of their descendants; and as these gaze out upon you from their frames, you feel certain—whether or not you know who they were and what they did—that nothing which befell them in the way of adversity got under their skins for long enough to disturb their massive *bonhomie*.   If this unruffled and unfurrowed personage—for a personage he plainly is—could be taken from the White House, dressed in the rich fashion of the seventeenth century, and hung somewhere among the great Dutch or Flemish portraits of admirals, syndics, and burgomasters, he would pass perfectly as a member of that large family.   If he has been at the wars, they have not marked him; his expression hints nothing of pain, or of stress, or of ruthless steps taken in battle, nothing of the flinty determination of a Grant, or the serene sadness of a Foch; it suggests a man of action as little as a contemplative philosopher; what it principally conveys is good will on the verge of smiling—and after this, perhaps, equanimity.   A kind of jovial serenity seems articulate in the broad sweep of his mustache and the benevolence that sparkles in his blue eye. He does not look as if he could be any man's enemy long, and he entirely looks as if he could be a warm and constant friend. Aggressiveness of no sort is indicated, nor anything of the abstract, but rather those gifts of balance, common sense, looking at a thing all round, which make for taking life easily. And he might be imagined to say, "Though we are justices and doctors and churchmen, Master Page, we have some salt of our youth in us."

Once a shrewd physiognomist—a well known figure whose name you would know if I could remember it—was shown the likeness of a person unknown to him, and after close scrutiny said: "He is either a great cook or a great critic." It was Sainte-Beuve! What guess would such an acute observer make as to the man whose face I have been trying to present in words? He has not been a doctor or a churchman, but he has been a governor, a president, and a judge.

When William Howard Taft sat at that White House table, the genial glow around even that board seemed heightened. Tolerant outlook, jocular comment, a readiness to listen and to enjoy—these were his particular contributions.

"What would you do," he was asked by a somewhat puzzled friend who was having him to lunch with a foreign Prime Minister honoring the United States with a brief visit, "if I sat him, instead of you, at my right?"

"I'd go right home!" chuckled the Chief Justice of our Supreme Court—and sat, of course, where his host put him. What were precedence and Washington etiquette to him upon such an occasion? The point was to be pleasant and help things to go.

Not many months before this, when a great loneliness and darkness fell upon a colleague on the bench, it was the Chief Justice who stretched both hands to him, lost no chance of any kind to take burdens from him and lift him along. Are there many still alive who remember a certain illustrated edition of *A Christmas Carol* by Dickens, in which the Spirit of Christmas

Present is pictured?    The Spirit sits high amid all the happy
emblems of the season—it was then a holiday of chimes, and
peace, and good will, and holly, and plum pudding, and punch,
and children's games, and theatricals in the parlor, and parents
romping with their children.    I often think of our Chief Justice
as the very man to come down from the bench and play the part
of the Spirit of Christmas Present; and then after play, to go
back and leaven with his broad and balancing serenity the Court
over which he presided so admirably.

Perhaps the bitter time through which he was destined to pass
so soon after those cordial and laughing hours at the White
House merely mellowed him in the end.    Through no desire of
his own, he was summoned to sit in a seat that did not fit him
and was fairly pushed into it, willingly in the end, because
others wished it; later, when he was again living in his native element, perhaps he was able to count that evil time as a part of that
average of the rough and the smooth which no life ever dodges.
We who knew and loved the White House concert of Familiars,
and saw the discord which followed it, still bear, I think, the
scars of our distress.

Long years after it was all over, and Roosevelt was dead, I
wrote the Chief Justice for leave to tell an anecdote for which
he was authority, and for his correction, if I had it wrong.
Part of his answer runs:

"What Dr. Thayer of Baltimore has said to you is quite true.
You are a friend of Mr. Roosevelt, I knew, and therefore would
use the story in a way that would not bring any criticism . . .
for I would not wish to circulate it and have any such result. . . ."

Does not this draw a spirit that one would like to resemble?

Henry Adams should have been painted by El Greco.    This
will immediately suggest his appearance to those who have seen
the portraits by that strange master assembled in what is called
his house in Toledo.    He seems to me hardly ever to have
painted a face without giving it the quality of the aristocratic

and the element of the inscrutable.    Henry Adams often looked
at you in a way that made you feel, not only that you did not
know what he was thinking, but that he was probably not going
to tell you.    He had the disdainful intellect of his family, and it
was brilliant with rich experience of people and of books.    Two
of his own will certainly have to be read by any one who wishes
to ascend to the highest level of American literature, where the
pages of Emerson and Poe and Whitman and Hawthorne are
to be found with Huckleberry Finn.

In his youth he had seen the great world of London during
our Civil War, and has described that time and society for us
with the hand of a master.    As secretary to his father, our
Minister to the Court of St. James, he was serving his country
during those terrific years, while the future Judge Holmes was
serving it in battles at the front.    Both men were moulded by
that fiercest crisis we have known—none of the other Familiars
had come to sufficient maturity then; and this experience, taken
with their straight New England tradition, classed them together in a way, and in a way set them apart from the others.
The others knew the Civil War well enough through their books,
but they had been too young to learn it by living it.    Beyond
this, and their intellectual approach to the Cosmos, these two
Bostonians had little in common.    Neither man was easy to
please; but I think of Holmes as mostly keeping the doors of
his sympathy open, and of Adams as mostly keeping them shut.

"If the country had put him on a pedestal," said Holmes to
me once, "I think Henry Adams with his gifts could have rendered distinguished public service."

"What was the matter with Henry Adams?" I asked.

"He wanted it handed to him on a silver plate," said Holmes.

Now Holmes had gone after "it" tooth and nail; and hence
began as a student of law and ended an associate Justice of the
Supreme Court of the United States; while Adams ended sitting
bitter and hostile in his beautiful house in Lafayette Square,
having written a long and wonderful book to explain himself to
posterity.

*From a drawing by John Briggs Potter*

HENRY ADAMS

This is not all of him, it is the worst of him.   His talk was informed and pointed, he knew an extraordinary number of things very well—better than almost anybody you were likely to see in America—to be with him, dine with him, was a luxury and an excitement.   He fascinated not only beautiful and particular ladies, but clever and aspiring young men as well.   For some of these his influence was not quite wholesome; not only your patriotism, but your faith in life, had to be pretty well grown up to withstand the doses of distilled and vitriolic mockery which Henry Adams could administer.   There was but one antidote—to recognize that they were not the whole truth.   He was known as "Uncle Henry" to his circle of worshippers, and their affection for him is the touchstone of his secret: affection dwelt somewhere deep inside him, hard to reach, shielded beneath irony, perversity, and cynicism, hiding possibly because it had been hurt, but constant and true, once you got to it.

That last day, when the Roosevelts, husband and wife, were going out of the White House, and all was ended, he came over. They had drawn this difficult man to them, had made him one of the Familiars by what they were, nobody was to take their place for him.   He could easily have quoted—perhaps in his heart he was quoting—Sir Bevidere to Arthur:

> "But now the whole Round Table is dissolved
> Which was an image of the mighty world . . .
> And the days darken round me, and the years,
> Among new men, strange faces, other minds."

Henry Adams spoke to them simply.
"I shall miss you very much."
He shook their hands and went away.   The sound of his voice in those six words was never forgotten by Mrs. Roosevelt.

Henry Adams was slender in frame, delicate and distinguished in countenance, he wore a beard, and his eye had a permanent and piercing alertness.   For his own diversion it was his way at times to say what he partly meant, but to say it in excess of his meaning, and then watch for what you were going to do about it.

At a dinner with the Winthrop Chanlers, where both he and John La Farge were, and the company was small enough for general talk forth and back across the table, something had brought in a reference to Goethe. At once Henry Adams opened an attack upon him. Goethe was overrated. The Germans had imposed him upon an uncritical world. Voltaire was a keener and higher intellect. To be sure, Goethe had written some good lyric verse. But a mind of the first rank didn't keep on trying so many literary experiments. Goethe was a constant imitator—now of the Greeks, now of the Orientals. The first part of *Wilhelm Meister* was a hodge podge, the second part was unreadable.

Every now and then Mrs. Chanler would break in upon this with exclamations and protests. These were what Henry Adams wanted, and they made him worse. The truth was, Goethe was merely an amateur.

At this point I spoke:

"But don't you think there are traces of cleverness in *Faust?*"

Henry Adams looked at me.

"That's the way to stop him!" said John La Farge. These two friends had sailed the Pacific together, met Stevenson on his island, knew each other well.

In 1880, a novel entitled *Democracy* set everybody talking. It was a very skilful, penetrating, and acid piece of irony, levelled at our political methods in Washington. The thrusts were delivered by a hand evidently well practised with the rapier. Some thought they recognized Senator Blaine in the central figure, and others were sure that certain ladies in Washington society had suggested other characters; but who had written it? One heard that only four persons were in the secret, and not one would ever tell. Guesses concentrated upon Clarence King, John Hay, and Henry Adams, all close friends, as any one knows who has read *The Education of Henry Adams*. From certain passages about women's clothes in the book, too well executed for a man, there were those who were sure it must be Henry Adams, and that his wife had helped him in those passages.

Henry James was one in the secret.   Years and years later at his house in Rye, I told him I had become certain that Adams was the author of *Democracy*, and Henry James told me that I was right.

In one of his letters to me, Roosevelt speaks with disapproval of *Democracy*, and from the way his sentence reads, I wonder if he did not half suspect who its author was.   It is certain that he must have read a good many of Henry Adams's brilliant pages —and particularly the work on a critical time in American history.   Besides this, there was Adams himself, a neighbor across the square, a well esteemed Familiar, and how the President could know him and like him so well, and not discern the author of *Democracy* by the flavor of his style and the tenor of his blighting scepticism when he commented on American politics, I do not see.   Of course, he could not like such a novel, because through that medium its author put his finger unerringly upon some of the darkest spots in our political system, which Roosevelt did not wish to see, in spite of the contradictory fact that his whole career was a crusade against these very evils.   While he acknowledged that this that and the other were all wrong, and went at them to make them right, he disliked pessimistic *generalizations* because they made his will-to-optimism feel uncomfortable.   And in this his instinct was perfectly sound: a man can not be a leader unless he is an optimist.

One day Henry Adams put into my hand a copy of that first edition of *The Education of Henry Adams* which he had printed privately—privately because the public was not worthy of it!— and requested me to take it home and call his attention to any faults which I might observe.   That was a fine trap to lay for one—and also a piece of his pose.   Beside him, I was an utter ignoramus.   So I was just mischievous enough to write in regard to his simile of a wrinkled *Tannhaüser* returning to a wrinkled Venus at the Wartburg, that I had always understood that Elizabeth had lived in the Wartburg and Venus in another establishment with quite another name.   Also, that when he spoke of the old familiar custom, when society in Washington had been small, of seeing one's friends off to New York at the Pennsylvania Station, wasn't it at that period the Baltimore and Potomac Station?   He answered very good humoredly.   He had liked a small book I had written about George Washington, and had written me out of the clear sky about it, begging me to go on in that line.

"Well, how are you and what are you doing?" he asked when I went to see him one day in 1912.

"I'm damaged goods," I told him.   (Since I had last seen him, I had passed six months in bed and two years in getting about again.)

"Oh, I'm damaged goods too!" he laughed.   "But that shouldn't stop you."

"It's not going to.   I gave *out*, but I didn't give *in*."

"And what do you think of the state of things in this country?"   The Republican convention had been held some months before, and that campaign, which no one who knew and cared for the Golden Age will ever get over, was growing more and more venomous each day.

I shook my head and said nothing.

"Our old friend over there," continued Henry Adams, with a wave towards the White House, where we had spent such unforgetable hours in the days of the Roosevelts, "did his best. But whose best could save us?"

"Oh, well, I don't feel as black as all that about it!"

"You don't?   With that saturnalia going on up there?" And he waved in the direction of the Capitol.

Again I shook my head.

He continued to look at me with his most gimlet-like expression.   Then, suddenly, his countenance softened.   His eyes grew warm, he got out of his chair, came over and laid his hand on my arm, and in a voice quite changed said:

"Keep the faith!"

I am not sure what he meant; but he had wholly dropped his pose, and was for the moment a different Henry Adams, perhaps the real Henry Adams, the one who said good bye to those two Roosevelts so briefly and with such suppressed feeling.

The next—and the last—sight I had of him was at Tyringham in the Berkshires, when the days were darker than the darkest in 1912, and the Great War was on.  He was ill, but indefatigably using his intelligence.  His researches for his book about Mont St. Michel and Chartres had roused his curiosity about some ancient melodies—the music sung in *Langue d'oc* and *Langue d'oil* by the troubadors and trouvères.  He had procured the notes, and a lady played them for us while Henry Adams sat listening and observing with his watchful eyes, and now and then commenting or explaining.  A strange, tragic man; a remarkable and illuminating intellect; not easily pleased; a true and steadfast friend.

Copley, and only Copley, is the right man to have painted Henry Cabot Lodge.  Many of Lodge's kin and townsfolk did sit for him in their departed day, but this is not the reason; Copley would not be at all the right man for Holmes or Adams, whose kin and townsfolk he also painted.  In those old portraits hanging in Harvard and Beacon Street, sire or dame, young or ripe, godly or ungodly, it is unmitigated Boston that you see recorded; the eye of a robust, stiff-necked race of seventeenth and eighteenth century dissenters, with its plain living, high thinking, dauntless intolerance, bleak bad manners, suppression of feeling, tenacity in its stern beliefs, and its cantankerousness, stares down at you with cold disapproval.  No Italian or Flemish master outdid Copley in catching the inner meaning of his contemporaries and setting it down.  Boston in its fullest measure had produced both Holmes and Adams; but so much other than this got into them as they grew, that the Copley type is marked in neither; while Cabot Lodge remained unmitigated Boston to the end.  Nothing outside of it ever really got into him deep.  In his memoirs his affection clings to it; indeed, they exclude what's outside it too much, show that despite all he had seen, read, thought, lived, achieved in an epoch teeming with a world of things Copley's people never dreamed of, all this had merely orchestrated him more brilliantly, so to speak, without changing his weave.

When my town celebrated Benjamin Franklin's 200th anniversary, two unmitigated Boston words were spoken by illustrious guests from there. President Eliot was at pains to remind us in his address that Franklin's life had not been, in every particular, edifying. And Cabot Lodge told us plainly that Franklin was born in Boston. It brought a smile from Dr. Weir Mitchell, who said, that for a scholar of such historic erudition as Senator Lodge, this statement was a surprise: it was generally known that Benjamin Franklin had been born in Philadelphia at the age of seventeen.

The cartoonists have not been fair to Cabot Lodge. They reduced to its lowest terms their formula for Roosevelt—teeth, glasses, and sombrero—but it was generally good natured; their formula for Lodge was generally malignant, suggesting him by a forehead and a beard about to close the rest of his face in, as a valise shuts up its contents. His politics had often made them angry, but so had Roosevelt's. They could be savage about Roosevelt; they were mean about Lodge. It was his Bostonism that gave them their line—and his mastery of the sneer. Neither could be gainsaid; both put him in wrong with many who knew only this much about him, never knew the warm and generous side of him, cared nothing for his public value as a seasoned, educated intelligence—very uncommon among our Senators—could merely comprehend and resent his continuously narrow views and his too frequently sharp and sarcastic tongue. From Lodge's political views Roosevelt not seldom differed without this touching their warm personal relations. The friendship between them had begun soon after Roosevelt left Harvard, and among his Familiars Lodge was the earliest by many years, and on a footing quite apart.

It is too true that Lodge brought upon himself, by his dangerous gift of sarcasm, the bitter blame of those who thought that our "war to end war" had ended it, that we had made "the world safe for Democracy," and that our keeping out of the League of

*Photo by Brown Bros.*

HENRY CABOT LODGE

Nations had broken that pretty toy. You will hear it still, and it's possible that History may perpetuate this falsehood, as it has perpetuated many another:—They say that nothing but Lodge's personal hatred of Woodrow Wilson kept us out of the League.

I never squander my time arguing with either Deserving Democrats, as Bryan called them, or Deserving Republicans: both are equally impervious; but in writing of Cabot Lodge, I am vindicating him by recording the exact and demonstrable truth about that business: it was no feeling against Wilson, *it was to prevent the United States from registering a promise to take on foreign quarrels,* that Lodge, with his followers, not forgetting some twenty-eight Senators of Wilson's party, insisted upon certain reservations in the Covenant; and the American people as a whole were behind him, as the years have proved since. Lodge, with Root, Taft, and other Republicans were strong for a league to enforce international peace in 1916, two years before Wilson would accept the idea. Wilson had brought the Covenant home from Paris, and ordered the Senate to sign it as it stood, as if they were a set of Princeton freshmen. Lodge was willing to sign, once his protecting reservations were accepted. Wilson would not hear of opposition, would not brook the slightest change in his handiwork. When both England and France, speaking through Lord Grey and André Tardieu, readily accepted every one of the changes, the temper this threw Wilson into, reveals what the matter was. With our allies perfectly content with the Lodge reservations, what and who stood in the way? When it comes to a show down, it is the isolated figure of Woodrow Wilson that blocks the road between us and the League of Nations.

On that April day in 1917, when Woodrow Wilson went to the Capitol and asked Congress to declare war on Germany, the very instant he had finished, Cabot Lodge jumped up and exclaimed that the Republican party would stand solid behind the President. This is awkward for Deserving Democrats. More awkward still is what followed later in the month, when the President brought in his Conscription Bill, and Congress debated and voted upon it.    For the reader who would follow the details of this debate and vote, momentous for the United States, and even more momentous for Europe, the *Congressional Record*, Volume 55, parts 1, 2, and 3, tell the story at length. Cabot Lodge stood faithful to his pledge; what did the Democrats do?

On April 25 (part 2, page 1120, vol. 55 of the *Congressional Record*), Champ Clark of Missouri said:

"I protest with all my heart and mind and soul against having the slur of being a conscript placed upon the men of Missouri. In the estimation of Missourians *there is precious little difference between a conscript and a convict*."    (Italics mine.)

On May 16, the House voted upon the bill, technically known as the Selective Draft Measure.    Against it were 140 Democrats and 37 Republicans; for it were 149 Republicans and 42 Democrats.

In the Senate, which voted the next day, the showing is not so clear on its face, and must be analyzed from the ratio between the two parties there—54 Democrats to 42 Republicans: yeas, Democrats 34, Republicans 31; nays, Democrats 5, Republicans 3.    Thus nearly five-sevenths of the Republican Senators, and not quite one third of the Democrats, supported the measure; while against it were two more Democrats than Republicans.    Cabot Lodge voted for it, true to his pledge, and to his patriotism.

It was necessary to go somewhat explicitly into this, in order to give a valid reply to the statement that private antagonism to Wilson was what dictated Lodge's public acts; it merely acidified his words.    Some of his policies I thought unworthy of the best that was in him, but Lodge's patriotism was above reproach. So far, his own caste in Boston, like the cartoonists in the country at large, have dwelt chiefly upon his shortcomings.    Among his other enlightened deeds, authors owe him their present protection.    Before he brought about the copyright bill, pirated foreign works could, and did, undersell the books written by

Americans, and foreign authors got nothing for their books pirated and printed here.   Lodge brought home to our half-civilized Congress that whether it's a book or a horse, stealing is stealing.

Cabot Lodge had his pet prejudices.   England was one of these.   He disliked the English through thick and thin.   It would crop out anywhere.   In his letter of January 29, 1901, after calling me to task for a comparison I had made between General Sheridan and two great European captains, he says, "I can, I think, almost forgive Charles and Condé for your single line in regard to Wolseley's criticism of our war."   This single line was a sharp one, and at an Englishman's expense; therefore it pleased Lodge.   Whatever lay behind his hostility, I never understood it; and upon the one occasion when I challenged it, his answer may be styled cryptic.   During the Great War, after we were in, I had written a piece for a magazine about the voices to be heard in the street, and even in some houses, asking the truly idiotic question, What has England done in the War?   I told them plainly with facts and figures, what England had done. This article I expanded into a book entitled *A Straight Deal,* or *The Ancient Grudge.*   I thought better feeling between English-speaking nations was desirable for the peace of the world. I therefore told the true story of our relations and clashes with England from 1776 down through the Spanish War in 1898. Many of these had been suppressed or distorted in our school histories, and the complete picture had never been fairly attempted by any one, either in England or America.   I thought I had got my facts right; but I thought also that nobody could check them up better than Cabot Lodge.   I asked him to read what I had written, and he did.   He found no inaccuracies, and no pertinent omissions.   No man could be more generous with what he had to give, and Lodge gave me the benefit of his ample historic knowledge.   It was one night at his house in Washington.

"Then you think," I said, "that I've got it about right?"
"Yes."

"Then will you tell me, please, why you keep on hating England so?"

"Oh, they're so stupid!"

That was all.

Some of them are.   There's no doubt of that.   *Blackwood's Magazine,* year after year, affords as pretty a case of that sort of anti-American British stupidity, as Borah of Idaho affords of anti-British American stupidity—the sort on either side the water which makes for bad feeling.   The bright spot in such cases is, that death sometimes changes the policy both of the periodicals and the individuals.

Cabot Lodge, either in public or in private, was not much like what the cartoonists made of him.   On the platform, before an audience, he held himself straight, his presence carried dignity, and authority was in his voice.   Grace, and the flavor of digested knowledge, and wide contact with the civilized world, made what he had to say very well said, without in the least weakening its force.   Sitting at home, among his countless books, with a cigar, after dinner, he could be perfectly delightful. Like Holmes, like Adams, he lived much in the intellect.   What had happened to mankind in the way of far off things and battles long ago, and all the consequences to the great peoples of the world, to their faiths, their feuds, and their enthusiasms, was something he never ceased to think on; nor did he stop at history.   Much poetry was at his service for quoting.   There was enough of the artist in him to be moved by beauty to the verge of tears.   He read me that page in Homer one night where Odysseus returns from Troy and his wanderings to his home in Ithaca, and no one there knows who he is, except his old dog Argos.   At the end, he half flung the book down upon his knee, and exclaimed:

"The whole thing is the most beautiful story in the world!"

He could easily, as well as Holmes or Adams, have made his name as a writer, which he had begun to do.   He left an excellent literary beginning for the life of action, which Voltaire places very properly above the life of the thinker—that is, if you wish to take the Cash and let the Credit go: it is the Present that belongs to the man of action. But this by no means put an end to his intimacy with good books. Old books and new, he kept them near him, nourished his mind with them year in and year out; and if you half remembered some quotation which you wished to use and could not lay your hand on, there was no likelier man than Cabot Lodge to tell you where to find it.

I think of him as sitting in his office at the Senate, books of reference and official papers around him, breaking off in his dictation to his secretary, rising with a cordial smile of welcome to a friend who has looked in at the door: not an intimation in his manner or his words that he is busy and must not be interrupted. I think of him, too, in his great quiet room at home in Massachusetts Avenue, in the hours that grow serene toward midnight, seated with one long leg crossed over the other and slightly swinging as he talks, or reads from the diary where he records what he is witnessing of curious or important events, or else from some favorite book he has pulled down from the crowded shelves which make his background. Whether at the Senate, or on his horse, or in his easy chair after dinner, always in the careful dress of the occasion.

And so Cabot Lodge came and passed, a rare, memorable figure, always more sharply censured and always less heartily praised than he deserved; and he would have told you that better than the best of him was his wife. When he lost that radiant companion, counsellor, and guide, he went on as well as he could alone, he did not virtually cease as Henry Adams did when he was left in the same way; but he was never the same man afterward.

What guesses about his next Familiar would a stranger make? Here is a head proper for John Sargent, a study that would call forth Sargent's very best. Evidently some one who has carried through in spite of obstacles many enterprises of importance. By what means chiefly? Plainly not in the way Roosevelt's countenance suggests how he did the same thing—by kicking the obstacles over without too much attention to what else

might topple in the process.    Not that way, in spite of the power
and the determination in this face.    This man would keep force
to the very last, when every thing else had failed.    Knowledge
of men, especially of their weaknesses, seems indicated.    A
dreamer?    Decidedly not.    Nor a soldier.    Nor a man of letters—too much action is stamped all over this countenance.
Not so much a great intellect as a great intelligence.    Immense
resourcefulness and acuteness in that almost fiery look.    Something—is it humor, or caution, or the spirit which denies?—
something, qualifies the fieriness.    A person of solitude and the
woods?    Never.    A city face; somebody constantly dealing
with men and circumstances, rather than with ideas, guided by
externals more than from within.    Very striking.    Not easily
forgotten.    Are those eyes watching a star, or an opportunity?

Elihu Root will undoubtedly bring up in Heaven, but not, I
fancy, until after a decent stay in Purgatory.    When he comes
there, it will make Purgatory much pleasanter for me.    I was
never in any company with him that he did not add to its agree-
ableness, nor ever present at any discussion that he did not throw
valuable light upon it, some suggestion, some warning, that went
to the heart of the matter and pointed to the right course.    Any
one who has read Roosevelt's published letters, is aware of the
enthusiastic admiration of Root's powers as a statesman which
Roosevelt held; and any one who knows what Root has accomplished as a statesman, will be as sure as Roosevelt was that he
would have made an illustrious President, as faithful to his duty
and as capable to perform it as he had been in every position of
responsibility he had undertaken.

When it was necessary, he could be quick and formidable in
action.    Perhaps fearlessness is at the bottom of every instant
decision a man makes.    The Republican convention of 1912
had a temporary chairman, a sort of fluttering moth of a man,
about as up to ruling those roaring waves as a cork would have
been.    His hammering for order brought it no more than the
ticking of a watch.    When Root, duly elected chairman, took
the seat of the moth, the stroke he gave the desk instantly

ELIHU ROOT

silenced the din—except in the case of one noisy delegate from Pennsylvania.   Root looked at him, rose, left the platform, walked along the aisle to where this delegate sat, and told him that if he did not stop his noise, he would have him put out. Nothing more was necessary.

Elihu Root was one of the distinguished guests who came to Philadelphia for the celebration of Benjamin Franklin's 200th Anniversary.   He was at that time in Roosevelt's cabinet, and Roosevelt had written of him, "I am extremely fond of him and prize his companionship as well as his advice . . . no minister of foreign affairs in any other country at this moment in any way compares with him. . . ."   During the Franklin celebration, Root had stayed with Dr. Weir Mitchell, and had heard Dr. Mitchell's retort to Cabot Lodge, which I have narrated above.   In his "bread-and-butter" letter to Mrs. Weir Mitchell from the State Department, some of his unveiled opinions are to be read, as well as his relish of Dr. Mitchell's joke:

"You do not know the real pleasure I had in the visit. . . . It was a veritable oasis in the political desert through which I pursue my daily task.   In the desert, congressional cacti are always sticking their thorns into my legs, and foreign serpents hissing in my path, and lost Americans demanding that water be drawn from rocks; but with you everyone was interested in such delightful things and so sane and kindly.   I never before realized how wise Franklin was when he had a chance to choose a birthplace for himself.   There are, I suppose, inflexible and disagreeable characters not much affected by their surroundings. Thank heaven I am not one of them and that my surroundings have included 1524 Walnut Street. . . ."

In that charming letter is the Elihu Root I saw at the White House table, breaking bread with the man who had written, "I am extremely fond of him and prize his companionship;" affected by those surroundings—just the same kind which he found at Dr. Mitchell's house in the Philadelphia of that day; every one "interested in such delightful things and so sane and kindly."   His happy reference to Franklin and Mr. Mitchell's retort to Cabot Lodge, is as perfect an illustration of Root at play as the Republican convention of 1912 is an illustration of Root at work.

Some men become venerable, and some men do not, no matter what age they attain.   Dr. Weir Mitchell became venerable, even majestic, without at all becoming feeble.   Some of Elihu Root's predecessors as leaders of the New York bar grew to be venerable—Evarts did, and James Carter; in Root, something boy-like and engaging, that I often saw sparkle in his eye and hover on his lips as if he were about to laugh or to utter some pithy whimsicality, will prevent his ever seeming venerable to me.   Once, when the President was busy over something, Mrs. Roosevelt took Root and me to see De Wolf Hopper in some comic opera.   Much of it was horse play, and all of it was fantastic nonsense—and Root, Secretary of State, perhaps our greatest, might have been fifteen, and home for the Christmas holidays, the way he laughed all through the piece.

He was often like that at the White House: serious and penetrating, yet with the hint of humor in ambush; listening closely and rather dangerously to what you were saying—if it was a statement or a generalization—ready to pick precisely the right hole in it, while his luminous eye was fixed upon you, and that quaint rumple of hair strayed a little down over his forehead.

There is a line in Tennyson about men rising on stepping stones of their dead selves to higher things: to set forth in one's eighties across the Atlantic, vigorous still in brain, but in body needing constant watching and constant rest, in the cause of international understanding and good will—what word for such an enterprise is there but to call it very noble?

This next head could never be mistaken for an American. Race is not always so sharply defined: Erick Remarque, who has written the most famous novel about the Great War, suggests neither literature, nor that he is a German of French descent; he could easily pass for a base-ball star, or an alert and vigorous cashier from Nebraska; and in Sicily, a blue-eyed, blond, crisp, cynical young chauffeur drove me from Palermo to

Segesta, and, to look at him from twenty yards off, you would have accepted the word of anybody who told you he had been born a farm boy in Vermont.   The wires quite often get mysteriously crossed in national types, but this member of the Roosevelt Familiars has an appearance true to form in every respect.   Shaped by centuries of European civilization; a face modelled by lucid, exact traditions; animate with keen and constant observation; critical and focussed.   He wears a beard; in his shrewd and very kindly glance, there is something at once quizzical and analytic.   A face of much training.   Possibly a scholar of some sort?   Certainly a person of rapid tact, and accustomed to clear thinking; a man of both intellectual and worldly experience.

It is Jules Jusserand, French Ambassador during twenty-odd years; and Meissonier should have painted him.   The delicate complexities of his features all betoken that French quality, which is so indigenous to France and so scarce anywhere else, that all the other nations have had to borrow the French word for it—*esprit*, as well as the adjective *spirituel*: no equivalent words exist in any other language.   This quality, and the gaiety that goes with it, has sometimes misled that particular stamp of English and German that takes none but the dull seriously, to suppose that Frenchman cannot be serious.   This delusion has probably been dispelled by the Great War.

Jusserand came to the White House very often, because he was a member of the Tennis Cabinet.   He illustrated excellently what Roosevelt said of his country in his lecture delivered at the Sorbonne on April 23, 1910, after his return from Africa:

"France has taught many lessons to other nations: surely one of the most important is . . . that a high artistic and literary development is compatible with notable leadership in arms and statecraft."

This French Ambassador made a long and distinguished career in diplomacy compatible with high literary development. Any one who has read his interesting and most agreeably writ-

ten history of Shakespeare in France, knows that he can write
in our language so well as seldom to betray by a turn of phrase
that it is not his own. I transcribe an example of his familiar
English from a letter written in 1929, in which he gives me
directions how to reach him from Vichy.

"The place is called Saint Haon-le-Châtel, an old village
perched on a rock, overlooking the valleys of the Loire, and
having still preserved in a large measure its belt of walls and
towers. The chief arched entrance has still its thick oak gates
with large square nails, which is very rare. . . . We must
spend a fortnight in Paris while you will be visiting red-cathe-
dralled Rodez, and far-famed Rocamadour, far-famed in the
middle ages, a place of pilgrimage abundantly visited by English people and mentioned in Langland's 'Piers Plowman'. . . .
—The nearest city to us is Roanne. . . . Lyons is at a hundred
kilometers to the southeast. North of us, somewhat to the west
is Nevers with its fine cathedral, its fine ducal palace, whose
mediaeval owner pretended to be descended from Elias, le
chevalier au Cygne. . . . The story of the Knight of whom
certain neighbors of ours, ever ready to annex other people's
goods, have made their Lohengrin, is written in stone bas-reliefs
on the façade. . . ."

At the Franklin celebration, of which I have already spoken,
Elihu Root began a formal address to the French Ambassador:

"Excellency: On the 27th of April, 1904, the Congress of the
United States provided by Statute that the Secretary of State
should cause to be struck a medal to commemorate the two-
hundredth anniversary of the birth of Benjamin Franklin, and
that one single impression on gold should be presented, under
the direction of the President of the United States, to the Republic of France. . . ."

During these days of April, 1906, San Francisco, and all direct
news from there, had been cut off by the earthquake and fire.

Toward the close of his reply to the Secretary of State, Jusserand, representing France, said:

"My earnest hope is that one of the next medals to be
struck . . . will be one to commemorate the resurrection of

JULES JUSSERAND, MADAME JUSSERAND, AND OWEN WISTER

that great city which now, at this present hour, agonizes by the shores of the Pacific.   The disaster of San Francisco has awakened a feeling of deepest grief in every French heart, and a feeling of admiration, too, for the manliness displayed by the population during this awful trial.   So that what will be commemorated will be not only the American nation's sorrow, but her unfailing heroism and energy. . . ."

The French Government ratified these unauthorized but happy words of its Ambassador, and three years later the gold medal which he had suggested was formally received by the Mayor of San Francisco.

Two further specimens of Jusserand's use of English will suffice to illustrate this, and also somewhat to illustrate him.

In his address in memory of his friend the great editor of the Variorum Shakespeare, Horace Howard Furness, made in Philadelphia before the American Philosophical Society, he says:

"In the years of early manhood one sees, far ahead on the road, those great thinkers, scientists, master men, tall, powerful, visible from a distance, ready to help the passer by, like great oaks offering their shade.   They seem so strong, so far above the common, that the thought never occurs that we of the frailer sort may see the day when they will be no more.   Who was ever present at the death of an oak? . . ."

And finally this, picked almost at random from the pages of his *Shakespeare in France,* where he touches upon the interesting moment when the path of the drama in England might turn the classic way (as it did in France) while in France it might go in the romantic direction (as it did in England):

" . . . French writers, being still so near mediaeval picturesqueness and unruliness, were very far from adhering to classical dogmas.   We are still in the sixteenth century, an age of wars, duels, rebellion, and debauch, the age of Marignano and of the League, of Catholic and Protestant butcheries, the age of Montuc, Brantôme, and Maugiron; the time when France delighted to follow the rambling thoughts of Montaigne, the 'enormous' inventions of Rabelais, and the audacious soarings of Ronsard.   This prince of poets found room in his verses for all sorts of words, many of which would not be allowed now even in prose; he was afraid of nothing, admitted in his poems low and subtle expressions alike, and coined new words. . . ."

How many signs are there either in his informal letter dashed off at ease to me without any thought of style, or in his more formal addresses, or in his still more carefully meditated prose meant to be read, not heard, that here is a man using a language not his own?   You will find this almost complete mastery of our idiom throughout all that he has written in it; and in everything he has written, be it in English or in French, you will meet an intelligence which drips with erudition, yet never once bristles with pedantry.   Charm and vivacity underlie all his learning, and his books, like his diplomatic life, illustrate another of Roosevelt's contentions.   Roosevelt preached a sermon (although he called it delivering an address) before the American Historical Association, where he protested against that school of students who insist that History which would be serious must be unreadable.   He thought that a book might be truthful, even though it was interesting.

But Jules Jusserand, though so perfectly at home in our alien grammar and our ill-regulated spelling, never got the better of our utterly lawless pronunciation.   Few of us Americans, I imagine, ever reach the point where we can converse in French, and pass for French with a Frenchman; but many of us, I am sure, come nearer to the right accent without knowing the tricks of the language half so well.   Between the Ambassador's control of our words and his utterance of their sounds, a gulf was fixed: his enunciation was as *succlent* as he had comically and justly described Roosevelt's French to be.   When I reminded him of that description in after years, he repeated it, and added how often he had seen Roosevelt stop in the middle of a French sentence, and search, and grope, and stretch, for the exact word he wanted, and finally catch it as you seize at length a slippery piece of soap that has escaped you in the bath: only, Jusserand's vowels and consonants never were captured firmly.   His unexpected version of a word saved the Tennis Cabinet at their last meeting, the dinner where they assembled in March, 1909, to bid each other, and their President, and those years of delightful exercise and fellowship, farewell. The table was decked with emblems—symbols from the years they had played their lively sets on the court behind the White House; "Teddy Bears" were arranged at each place; Roosevelt had already, earlier in the day, presented each member of the Cabinet with his memento—a diploma of appointment, formally phrased and engrossed, and signed, in imitation of a State document. The company was not far from tears. It drew still closer to them when the French Ambassador rose and began an address to Roosevelt. The Cabinet had united in a token, and asked Jusserand to speak for them; and he spoke as always, from the heart, simply and beautifully. Just at the close, as he held out the token, he said:

" . . . And I have the honor to beg your acceptance of this silver bowl" (pronouncing it to rhyme with howl).

They all did immediately howl, and so their sadness did not overcome them.

The vivacity which pervaded the mind of Jules Jusserand animated his body as well, and his muscles were as nimble as his wit. On the tennis court he could judge a ball as accurately as a foot-note in a book of reference; he seemed always to know where the ball was going, and to be there first. I remember my astonishment at his activity one afternoon when Stewart Edward White had arrived for a visit, and was playing as gracefully as a panther would, if a panther could. Garfield was in the game, and Robert Bacon, and the President of course, whose game about matched Jusserand's. Others cut in from time to time when a set was ended. That Tennis Cabinet seems to me as remarkable in American annals as the Roosevelt *salon*.

When Jusserand arrived in our country as successor to Jules Cambon, it was my fortune to make his acquaintance not long after. This must have been in 1904; and from then on to the very last days of his stay with us, when the Great War had come and gone, and the Peace Conference had come and gone, and the world was never going to be the same again for any of us, I saw him often, and in many different circumstances: holding up his witty end among the Familiars at dinner, holding forth in Sanders Theatre, Harvard, as Phi Beta Kappa orator, speaking at meetings of the Alliance Française, in New York, and in Philadelphia during my presidency of our group there, and then most pleasantly and familiarly at the French Embassy and in other houses.

I remember that the last talk I had with him before he departed from our shores, was at the celebration of our 25th anniversary of the Alliance Française in Philadelphia. I told him how sorry I was to see him go, how much I should miss him and Madame Jusserand:

"But," I added, "it's too much to expect that you would never have enough of us."

"Not at all!" he exclaimed with animation. "It's not we who wish to go away. We should like to keep on very much."

"Oh!" I said, comprehending that he was being taken from us by the political hand in Paris.

He gave a short nod.

He was the dean of the Ambassadors by then. He was short in stature, had a way of tilting his head a little to one side, which somehow seemed to add point to his observations; his beard between 1914 and 1918 had grown very grey, but his eye had remained unquenchably bright.

The Flemish poet Maeterlinck has written some strangely imaginative pages, entitled *Les Prévenus*. In certain faces he perceives a look of foreknowledge; they sense their approaching destiny, their eyes almost see it, they are watching for it to appear. None of the other faces—Holmes, Lodge, Adams, none —suggests being set apart from their fellows by this prescience; perhaps I read it into this face because I know of the darkness that fell around the path of the man. The same grain of austerity of which the face of Holmes is made is here, and the same nobility, but none of the latent mischief, or the domination of intellect; resolve, conviction, command, these are present. Not a mind given to subtle formulations; not a reflective, rather a performing nature; fairly simple.

John Sargent was the painter for this man, and did paint him.

Leonard Wood was inclined to be silent, inclined to be grave, I never saw him throw his head back and roar with laughter, as Roosevelt and most of the others did on occasion: but he looked the very thing that President Eliot finely entitled him at Harvard Commencement, when he gave him his honorary degree—Restorer of a Province. In a way, I think there was some sort of latent splendor about him, something massive, and capable, and impressive, that brought such words as Rome, and Proconsul, to mind. I even think that if a stranger had come in and seen all those Familiars, distinguished and interesting, sitting at the table, his glance might have stopped at Leonard Wood, and his first inquiry might have been, Who was that?

Roosevelt was apt to ask if there was any particular person I should like invited to lunch. It was so that I first met Leonard Wood on the day following the Diplomatic Reception which I have described. He asked me to take a walk with him after lunch, and if I minded stopping at his tailor's, where he had an appointment to try on a new suit. So I had a view of him in shirt sleeves, and of his superb chest, and he seemed more impressive than ever.

As we went walking and talking along the pavements of Washington, I grew very curious to know the exact truth about an anecdote I had been told in San Francisco in 1887, something that the more I looked at him the less it seemed to fit the serious man that he so patently was. I had heard it from the most enthralling and fantastic narrator of adventures which he claimed to be personal and actual, that I have ever known. He would begin one of these in a plain simple way, and as he developed it, his picturesque and humorous invention would take wings until his audience grew breathless with laughter and his own intense solemnity would break utterly down, overcome by what he heard himself improvising.   But in this tale he had definitely mentioned Leonard Wood's name, until then quite unknown to me.   So I began.

"Did you ever know Hugh Tevis?"

Wood turned in surprise.

"Why, yes," he said.

"When you were stationed at Huachuca, and he was on a ranch of his father's in that region?"

"Why, yes."

"He went to school with me, and to Harvard for a while, and after that I saw him a great deal in San Francisco.   He was the first person who ever mentioned your name to me.   He told me that you and he took hashish once at Huachuca."

"We did."

"You really did!   Did you suddenly start diving round and round the bed after each other?   Or did he make that up?"

"No, Tevis didn't make it up.   That's exactly what we did."

"Well, well, well.   Some day I'll put that in a story, if you don't mind."

"Tevis was a lovable chap," said Wood, and laughed a little. "Lovable and pretty wild.   Nothing mean about him, though. But he had a rich father."

Forty years after Tevis had told me about the hashish, I put it into a story, with some other actual incidents at our old frontier army posts, to paint the infinite ennui of that life; and Leonard Wood suggested a character in three of my tales as I imagined he might have been in the days when he was a young army surgeon, not yet at the threshold of his splendid career.

Not long after that dangerous accident near Pittsfield, which cost one life, and nearly cost Roosevelt's, I went for a walk with him and Wood in Rock Creek Park.   It was a scrambling walk, up and down steep slippery places; and the watchful care that Wood took of Roosevelt, whose leg had but lately healed of the wound he received in the Pittsfield crash, and the caution which he now and then reminded the President he ought to be

LEONARD WOOD

Photo by Brown Bros.

taking—and was not—illustrated more than one side of Wood's character.

When Leonard Wood addressed an audience, his direct sentences, not long, and very simple, carried all the weight and conviction of which his strong character was so full. No one who heard him at the Harvard Club in New York City, where he came to organize that camp at Plattsburg for training Americans to serve as officers in the war into which he knew we were bound some day to be drawn, will ever forget that meeting; the quiet, eloquent fervor of Francis R. Appleton, President of the Club, in introducing him; and Wood's own words, as he told that hushed and serious crowd of men how utterly unready we were for a day that was surely coming, and how in that day our country would need instantly all the military knowledge and all the devotion they could give her: her present number of commissioned officers was scarce a drop in the bucket to meet the approaching crisis. And none that was there is likely to forget how from that day in 1915, until the day we entered the War in 1917, the administration took no opportunity to encourage Leonard Wood in his patriotic work, and lost no opportunity to discourage and humiliate him: when April, 1917, came, it was glad enough thanklessly to avail itself of the results which his zeal and foresight had accomplished; and so, as Roosevelt said, we drifted stern foremost into the War; but thanks to Leonard Wood, we had the makings of a crew.

The soldiers that he then trained in the Middle West, adored him; he was not permitted to go overseas. In my life I have known nobody, except Roosevelt, who served his country in the grand manner more nobly and effectively than Leonard Wood, whether as "Restorer of a Province" abroad, or as forger of sword and shield at home. His brief candidacy for the White House was a blunder of friends; no more than General Grant, was he the stuff of which Presidents should be made, and in being saved from this ordeal he was more fortunate than Grant. In the performance of his last national service—which killed him— he merely added to the lustre of a life already shining with honor.

I hope that the story of Leonard Wood may be written right, and in full, in American school books, and taught with zest and pride to American souls in the bud.   It is spirits such as his that should people the minds of our youth and point them the true road to noble living.   Our past has dropped some of this gold into our national treasury of inspiration, let us hoard every precious piece we can find.   A captain of industry may set a good example, but no such example as this captain set.   Let it be summed up.

He was just a Yankee boy of the true blood.   He came from New Hampshire to his schooling in Massachusetts, graduated at twenty-four from the Harvard Medical School, got his appointment the next year as assistant surgeon in the United States Army, and reported for duty in the distant Southwest, at Huachuca, below Tucson.   Within twelve months, his conduct while serving in an Apache outbreak, brought his qualities and character immediate recognition from those who knew of it, and twelve years after the event, Congress bestowed upon him its medal of honor.   A greater opportunity came his way upon our going to war with Spain.   He took it, was equal to it, and was seen to be equal to more than Colonelcy of the Rough Riders in Cuba.   To that island he was sent back as its Military Governor. At Harvard Commencement, President Eliot had addressed him as Restorer of a Province; at Havana to-day, a statue of him stands in memory of his cleansing the city, and bringing order out of forlorn and long established confusion.   This task ended in 1903, when Cuba, under his rule, was deemed by the United States ready to rule herself.   After that, he met his successive responsibilities step by step, now in our Pacific island domain, next as a Department Commander at home, again on a mission to South America; and so, one post after another, until the Great War.   He was Chief of Staff 1911–13.   The Plattsburg Camp, instituted in 1915, stands as his own creation, his school of training for officers against the day that he saw was to come. Without this school, we had a few hundred trained officers to count on.   We should need several thousand.   The day came.

How we should have fared then, but for Leonard Wood, it is not worth while to guess.   He next poured his energy into organizing divisions, regiments, and battalions, which fought in France. The Great War over, because he had been right, the Administration punished Leonard Wood by giving him all the obscurity and ingratitude at its command.   In time the tide of politics turned, but not soon enough to head off Congress from a typical piece of mischief.   Under Roosevelt, we had set up and carried on a management of the Philippines, naturally without any ripe experience; yet, new as we were at this game, in the strong and able hands of Governor Cameron Forbes, matters got along. But he was a Republican.   Under the Democratic Administration, he was removed in a manner—and with manners—that would make a good burlesque.   The burlesque was made perfect by the Jones Act in 1916.   Mr. Jones felt that Democrats should always undo what Republicans had done, but he felt more than this.   He carried Jefferson's idea a long way beyond Jefferson: not merely are all men created equal, they are created identical.   Therefore he gave the Filipinos what Washington gave us, a white system for brown men, a Congress, a Court, an Executive; a machinery of government devised by an English speaking and thinking and feeling race, for a tropical race. Now bodies that have worn since the beginning a breech-clout, or feathers, or leaves, or paint, and practised head hunting, can put on the white man's pants any minute they wish: but it takes their minds longer than that to learn to think in the white man's way.   This does not seem to have occurred to Mr. Jones.   A deserving Democrat was sent to govern the islands.   Upon returning, it was his happy boast that he had reduced them to such chaos that the United States would hasten to cut them loose and drop them into space.   This was the state of things offered Leonard Wood in 1921, when he was sent there as Governor. Almost as well put Pershing in command at St. Mihiel with the army free to go or come as it preferred.   Even so, Leonard Wood managed to accomplish something until that point came when the will of the spirit could no longer surmount the body's exhaustion.   On his way home to die, the pictures taken of this great and romantic figure were to those who knew him in the splendor of his grave strength, something to wring the heart. He went to a hospital in Boston.   That was the end.

Duncan is in his grave;
After life's fitful fever he sleeps well.

During the latest years of the eighteenth century, a Frenchman, in whom his first master, Boucher, had found no enthusiasm for his own style and art, developed much for the new classic style, in which modern people were painted to look like Brutus.   Confirmed in this by a sojourn in Rome, he romanized Paris with his brush, beginning as painter to the King, going over to the Revolution, voting to behead the King: and in his portraits of that violent and idealistic generation, all this is reflected.   Louis David is the very man to have painted the next Familiar.

This is the youngest face among them, and one of marked and particular beauty, in which enthusiasm and asceticism seem to mingle about equally.   Give it the classic treatment, and it would serve as a model for Leonidas bidding welcome to his destiny.   There is a suggestion of zeal in excess of restraint, the possibility of following some idea too far.   Neither History nor Letters qualify this countenance, nor the temper of a judge. The eyes do not look as if they read books, but as if they gazed upon a Cause.

Gifford Pinchot was obliged to read books, since he graduated from Yale; but a Cause did enlist and absorb him very early; it led him to do a permanent service to his country.   For this he deserves all the greater credit because he was rich and had no need to work.   There are mystic tales of statues, effigies, talismans, which you had but to touch, and you received virtue from them.   If such miracles could be, I would have set up at Yale an image of Gifford Pinchot for all boys dowered with the gift of wealth to touch and be inspired to serve their country discerningly for the sheer love of serving.

GIFFORD PINCHOT

It was this quality in Pinchot, this dedication of himself to a cause and an unpopular cause at that—which brought him and Roosevelt so close together in those years.  Before they had found each other's quality out—the enthusiasm which was in Pinchot an ardent blaze, and in Roosevelt a fiery furnace— Pinchot had gone of his own accord to Germany that he might study and master the science and the art of Forestry.  Of this Americans knew nothing, and did not know there was anything to know.  The free town of Frankfurt-am-Main, for instance, having been paid for its loan in the fourteenth century to a powerful lord by a forest he owned near by, has used that forest for its lumber from that time to the present day without using it up; while Americans had already used up some of theirs in less than one century, and were using them up faster and faster all the time.  Resolving to stop this if he could, Pinchot equipped himself, and came home.

"I was forced to try a dozen pieces of doubtful and difficult work . . . irrigation and forestry work, etc., etc.  In each case, partly by hard and intelligent work and partly by good fortune, we won out. . . ."

This is Roosevelt, writing to me in a letter which I shall presently quote entire.  Most of it appears in Bishop's book about Roosevelt; yet in that excellent work in two volumes, the name of Pinchot, although in the text, is not to be found in the index, where the names of friends not nearly so close to Roosevelt, and not half such benefactors to the United States, do appear.  I have wondered if this was an inadvertence, or if subsequent events caused it to be intentional.

The "hard and intelligent work" Roosevelt owed to Pinchot; without such an able lieutenant he could not possibly have put his project through—any more than the lieutenant could have carried his point without the backing and the common sense of Roosevelt.  He became the head of the National Conservation Organization.  He was thoroughly hated by free-born American Citizens who didn't see why they "hadn't the right" to cut down just as many trees as they wanted. In a way they cannot be blamed for this notion, inherited straight from the backwoodsman who hewed his way westward through the unfooted wilderness. But Robinson Crusoe can do in a desert island all sorts of things that he would not be allowed to do in Central Park. And this is an idea not easy to bring home to a hundred million people—that there is no such thing as a *natural right,* that a natural right is merely something a man will fight for. If he doesn't win, his natural right is a mere ghost of the imagination.

The "natural right" in this case was merely Roosevelt's farseeing perception that trees and rivers were more important to all of the people than their destruction was to some of the people—and thanks to Pinchot he won.

"The people will take the sticks," I remember a sulky Senator from the West saying, while the fight was on.

To-day "the sticks" are what is left of that part of our capital which we were stopped from eating up: the stuff our homes are made of, our beams, our chairs, our floors; the shelter where rivers are born to flow through the fields of grain that would die but for the forests; the sticks which Germany has known enough to use for seven hundred years without using up.

Gifford Pinchot was tall and spare, and as active on the tennis court as in his forestry work. That service to the nation cannot be wholly obliterated by his subsequent career. This his early career, under the restraining hand of Roosevelt, had prepared few to expect. As I cannot speak well of it, I will not speak of it at all.

More familiar in a way than any of the Familiars, was Winthrop Chanler. He held no office, he was a private friend, no book about him will ever be written; yet Roosevelt's familiar letters not only to me, but to members of his family as well, constantly mention him. If the Civil Service Commissioner Roosevelt is going from Washington to New York for a night, and wants an agreeable dinner and pleasant evening made ready for him, he writes his sister Mrs. Cowles to get it up for him, and be sure to ask Chanler; when Roosevelt, editor of the Boone and Crockett Club's volume, writes me of the best articles for it that he has been promised, Chanler is to contribute one of these; and when Chanler in 1902 asks him to come to Newport on the special errand of standing godfather to his boy, the President goes.

A book should be written about Winthrop Chanler—and had he written such a book himself, as Trelawny did, telling of the distinguished people he had known everywhere in the world, and of his adventures upon land and sea, that book would be one to read, re-read, and to own.   He once told me that he wished his epitaph to be:

"Here lies one who laughed in many lands."

He was not at Harvard with Roosevelt, he graduated five years later.   When a senior, I met him as a freshman; and when he had become a junior, and I a bank clerk, we fell into the friendship that lasted all his life.   Roosevelt could hardly have seen much of him until the Civil Service days in Washington.   In college he had adventures enough, and was worshipped—for instance—by the Irish proprietor of a saloon in Essex Street, who hung upon every word he said, rejoiced in every act he did, would have gone to the world's end for him, and instantly accepted me because I was his friend.   Out of Harvard, his larger adventures were merely the unbroken continuation of his smaller ones in Cambridge and Boston.

With a friend he journeyed in the East, and at Fez, either their Christianity, or something else not pleasing to the prejudices of the local mind, raised a mob.   The two at length fled for refuge to a place of safety, and from this were rescued unharmed by whatever in Fez was equivalent to the police.   They immediately complained to the ruling potentate.   He learned that they were American citizens upon a journey of relaxation, made for the purpose of enlarging their horizon; that they had been favorably impressed with Fez until this inexpressible outrage had dispelled all their illusions; and that if the United States Government got wind of the incident, there was no telling what steps might not be taken.   The ruling potentate was perfectly horrified.   With the rest of the world at that date, he held an as yet undispelled illusion that the United States protected the lives of its citizens abroad as well as at home, and would really hold any power that did them injury to *strict accountability*.   "We want Perdicaris alive or Raizuli dead," was a message to a foreign country about an American kidnapped for ransom by a bandit, to be sent some years subsequent to the experience of Winthrop Chanler; but it represented the attitude of our country at the time.   So the ruling potentate was profuse, and in haste.   He loaded Chanler and his friend with apologies, offered them every civility and comfort at his disposal, music, food, drink, odalisques as many as they wanted, and the decapitated heads of the ring leaders of the mob that afternoon, if they would like to have them.   To accept this crowning atonement seemed to Chanler and his friend unwise: they had to get out of the country, and they wished to get out alive.

Chanler came home, engaged to be married, while I was at the Harvard Law School.   Many of his college friends were in Boston and Cambridge, and he paid us a visit of some days.   One night, long after I had gone to bed, something heavy on my feet awakened me, and there sat Chanler on them.   There was a dim light of dawn in the room, and I could not make out what big object he was holding against his face.

"Merciful heaven," I said, "weren't you going to New York?"

It was a raw beefsteak he was applying to his eye.   He had missed the midnight train on the Shore line, had found a restaurant open near the old Providence Station in Park Square, and had gone in there to have some oysters.   Near him had been sitting a woman with a baby, who howled without interruption, and of which she took no notice, except now and then to give it languidly a mouthful of the strong hot black coffee she was drinking.   Chanler's oysters had not yet been served; and while

WINTHROP CHANLER

he waited, the deafening noise of the baby got on his nerves. He turned to its mother, and said:

"Excuse me, madam, but your child makes me sick."

Immediately upon this, two large figures appeared from nowhere, he was whirled from his table, and found himself in the gutter outside, and the doors shut. Having told me this, he continued to sit on the bed, and sang:

> There's the capting and he's our Commawnder,
> There's the bosum and mate of the crew,
> There's the first and the second class pawssengers
> Knows what we poor conwicks goes through.

It was from a song he had been singing us at the Club during his visit to Cambridge. I do not recall where or how he had procured the beefsteak. No doubt it did something for him, but not enough; he sailed for Italy, where he was married with a black eye.

Wedlock did not fundamentally change him; and his wife, brought up in Rome, a niece of Julia Ward Howe as he was her great-nephew (the two were second cousins) was far too wise to wish him changed as much as that. She had not chosen a sparkling belated Elizabethan in order to iron him into a flat American husband capable of giving her no picturesque surprises.

If, after Winthrop Chanler had grown his rich brown mustache and his pointed Van Dyck beard, you had put a ruff round his neck and clothed him throughout according to the ruff, he could easily have sat for a portrait of Sir Walter Raleigh. And, had he lived in the age to which so much of him belonged, he would have sailed with Raleigh or Drake any day at a moment's notice; and during his intervals in London, he would have sat in the taverns hobnobbing with Shakespeare, and attending every first night of that dramatist's productions. Chanler could have sat for his Mercutio. He would have appealed to Elizabeth to a certainty, and for precisely the same reasons that he appealed to Theodore Roosevelt.

"I expected Winty to be here," I said upon arriving one day to stay at the Chanler house on the Hudson.

"He'll be here to-morrow," said one of his sisters. "At least, if he hasn't gone to Pawtucket, or Portland, or Fitchburg, or Atlanta, to see some Punch and Judy show."

"Whatever Winty does," added another sister, "his conscience sits looking on, beating happy applause."

I was at my law work one day in Francis Rawle's office in Philadelphia, when a vague, well-dressed, pleasant youth entered, inquired for me in a European voice, and handed me a note. It was from Chanler, and it said:

DEAR DAN:

This is my brother-in-law. . . . Do what you can for him for my sake, for his sake, and God's sake.

During those years, New York State had among its various governors one by the name of David B. Hill, a politician of no great credit; and on election day, when he was running for the office again, Chanler was in the smoking car of an afternoon train going up the river. Chanler had gone to sleep. At Poughkeepsie, a mottled faced citizen lurched into the car and stood swaying while he burst into song:

"When love has conquered pride and angwer."

Chanler woke up and saw him.

"Did you vote for Governor Hill?" he asked at once.

"Ye-arh!" shouted the citizen. "Hoo-rawr!"

"You have all the symptoms," said Chanler.

It was not long after this that Roosevelt was made Police Commissioner in New York City, and set about his job in various vigorous ways that severely disturbed some of the politicians: at first some of the police too. One of his novel methods was to follow the example of Haroun Al Raschid in Bagdad, and prowl about the town in the midnight hours to see with his own eyes and not the eyes of others what was happening. He walked in upon many scenes where his presence was not expected, and these raids left their legend in the Department of Public Safety. Winthrop Chanler often went with him. Roosevelt was glad enough to gratify his friend's ceaseless thirst for adventure and his endless curiosity about life. Roosevelt may perhaps have been ready to help Chanler harness his alert and restless mind to some sustained occupation. That was never to be. No doubt Roosevelt saw it was never to be, saw the inveterately mercurial element in Chanler which gave him his sprite-like charm. This, nevertheless, did not save him from periods of deep boredom at the monotony of his own continuous variety. The publication of my short biography of General Grant brought requests from publishers that I write others for this or that series, and among a few that I considered for a while was a book about Benjamin Franklin. Roosevelt was against all these projects; he advised me never to write for a series, because it robbed you somewhat of your own identity. I talked Franklin over with Chanler. I told him that it would demand quite a heavy labor of research in libraries. Grant had demanded six months hard labor, making notes and verifications.

"For goodness sake, let me do some of that for you!" he broke out in quite a gust of earnestness. "You don't know what a boon it would be. Here I sit rotting at Newport. Eating damned Astor and Vanderbilt dinners, and drinking more than's good for me. You could send me headings of what you wanted, and I could easily run up to the Boston Public Library, and we could work together splendidly."

He would have done it excellently, and I should have hugely enjoyed such a collaboration, festooned as it was bound to be with Winthrop Chanler's lively comments upon details of our Colonial history which he would have unearthed. But I took Roosevelt's advice.

Chanler, having gone on raids with Roosevelt, got up a raid of his own soon after that. Attended by a band of fellow conspirators whom he collected, he landed on the shores of Cuba with the purpose of helping to liberate that island from the clutches of Spanish oppression.   Those were the clutches into which he and his band promptly fell.   Their arrival must have been expected.   They found themselves almost immediately hemmed in, and in momentary danger of bullets, without a chance of seeing anybody they could fire at in return.   They spent several tropical days and nights hiding among thorns in some kind of dry ditch.   Food and water grew very hard to find, and the spirits of the band steadily sank.   One morning when they had about touched zero, Chanler rose up somewhere in the cactus, and remarked in a tone of cheery conviction:

"This is no place for a married man."

It restored the conspirators to buoyancy, but the liberation of Cuba was accomplished a little later by others.   I don't recall how Chanler got out with nothing worse than a bullet in his arm. He always got out.   But the arm was still in a sling when he reached Rome, some time later.

His various expeditions after elk in the Rockies, moufflon in Corsica, were followed at length by an undertaking much more formidable, from which some of his intimate friends in vain did their best to restrain him.   Quite in vain.   He was far from strong, undermined by a truly terrific illness when his life hung on a thread for weeks and out of which he came with one kidney to get on with thereafter (he wrote me a letter saying that he had christened this good kidney after me); but when we entered the Great War, nothing could keep his indomitable spirit out of it.   He got an appointment on Pershing's staff on the strength of his fluency in French.   I have a photograph of him in his uniform, standing on the stairs in the headquarters; smiling, it is true, dauntless, alert, but a pale, gaunt ghost of that once ambrosial Elizabethan; cheeks lined, hair receded, body gone elderly, that the years had caught up with at last, and no longer that sparkle of the irresponsible sprite in his eye; in its place, the valiant, sombre reflection of what he was seeing on the Western Front;—and yet a spirit still unscathed.   He waved off the particulars of how he won his decoration, he made light of it when we met again, and assured me that he hadn't known he was doing anything, and couldn't place the precise moment when his behavior rose to the dimensions of the heroic: he had been gratified to discover that he was a hero when they informed him of the fact.

No warnings kept him back from any effort he had made up his mind to make. And so being absolutely unfit for it, being told in fact that he ought to go to bed and take care of himself, he decided to go to Crete, and he went. In Crete, there was but little food or lodging for one in his feeble state; but his spirit carried him through his climbings and expeditions; these accomplished, he came back to Paris, indeed at the end of his tether. He knew it, too, from some words about himself that he dropped to one of his family.

From Paris he reached New York, ill almost to extinction, but quite determined to go right on to the Harvard Commencement, a sustained series of functions academic and convivial, covering several days, and apt to fatigue numbers of even the fairly robust, not in their first youth. Amos French was actually able, by employing every protest, short of physical force, to deter him from this madness, and induce him to go to bed and keep quiet. He remained quiet at the Knickerbocker Club for a day or two, and then left for his home at Geneseo, where he had been master of hounds since the death of Austin Wadsworth. But Crete had finished him, he was over, though he did not accept the fact. He fretted to be on horseback, and to ride a particular horse, an animal that required a vigorous hand. At length, in the face of remonstrance, he carried his point, mounted, and rode out with his wife. The effort to hold the horse in was visibly a tax upon his last drop of determination. After they had ridden a short while, he said:

"Let's have a little canter."

It was the last conscious word that he ever spoke. Almost at once he fell to the ground. Whether from exhaustion or from a stroke, is uncertain and of little consequence; a stroke certainly followed. His magnificently vital heart continued to beat for a few days, and then ceased.

"Let's have a little canter."   The last words of few men have been so fitting: his life had generally been a canter when it was not a gallop.   He lived more lives at once than any other man I have known.

In his letters, Winthrop Chanler used sometimes to break into verse; and in my turn once, in memory of our old mutual taste for Horace, I addressed him these in a Horatian metre, while he was spending a winter in Rome:

> Friend, what spicy vintage of mirth regales you
> Now, while dark is long, and the days end early?
> What sweet bard or bowl do you sit with, burning
> Oil of the midnight?
>
> Wide between us flow unreturning seasons;
> Wide have we two sailed from the shores receding,
> Where our youth stands watching, and waves farewell to
> Us faring outward.
>
> Lo, now on these waters of separation
> Do I pour this oil of the midnight, smoothing
> Tranquil voyage to you, so we two once more shall
> Keep happy vigil.

About those ladies who came to the Roosevelt *salon* I wish that I might speak at length: of Winty Chanler's wife, her music, her many sided cultivation; of Mrs. Wendell Holmes, her quaint and wholly individual raciness, her beautiful embroidery like none other; of Emily Tuckerman, Mrs. Cameron, Mrs. Lodge, Mrs. Grant La Farge, Mrs. Cowles, Mrs. Robinson—each an accomplished woman of the world, her native wits seasoned by experience with many people and familiarity with many books; and every one well able to hold up her end in the talk.

Never in our history, let me repeat, at any other time has such a company as these Familiars gathered in the White House. To the society of the present day, they seem to bear the same relation that Gobelin tapestry bears to linoleum.

After all, good society is the best invention of mankind.

## XIV.

To be our President must have kept all but a few of them extremely busy.   I often saw how busy it kept Roosevelt—yet he never lost track of his friends.   All but one of the following letters are an illustration of this.   The remaining letter is about the things that were keeping him busy

WHITE HOUSE
Washington

March 9, 1904.

DEAR DAN:

I would much like to see you, on general principles.   Can you get down Friday, spend Friday night, Saturday and Saturday night?   I have asked Grant down and you and I and he would take a walk of a slow and decorous character on Saturday afternoon.

Ever yours,

THEODORE ROOSEVELT.

"Grant" in this note is Grant La Farge, one of the special non-political Familiars, and architect of the great room at Sagamore Hill: a great lover of forests and lakes, a great canoeist and woodsman, an energetic officer of the Boone and Crockett Club.

WHITE HOUSE
Washington

March 11, 1904.

DEAR DAN:

I am very sorry to hear that you have been so much under the weather.   Do stop with us on your way back from the Hot Springs.

Always yours,

THEODORE ROOSEVELT.

WHITE HOUSE
Washington

April 10, 1904.

DEAR DAN:

I have your letter of the 9th, and look forward to seeing you on Saturday, to stay as many days as you can at the White

House.   Mrs. Roosevelt may be away at Groton School, but I shall be here.   Will you be alone, or will Mrs. Wister and the various young "Smoots" or "Smootinas" be with you?   We have lots of room.

I am concerned at what you tell me about yourself.

Always yours,

THEODORE ROOSEVELT.

WHITE HOUSE

Washington

November 11, 1904.

DEAR DAN:

Hearty thanks to you and the madam from The Sun of York.

Always yours,

T. R.

A sweeping majority had elected him a few days before, and we had telegraphed him: "Richard Third Act one Scene one Lines one and two."   He knew the rest; hence "The Sun of York." Four years later, when his term was ending, and Congress would do nothing that he recommended, I think he probably had to open his Shakespeare to decipher what we then telegraphed: "Romeo and Juliet Act three scene one line three preceding Mercutio's exit."   The words are: "A plague o'both your houses!"

Personal.

WHITE HOUSE

Washington

November 19, 1904.

DEAR DAN:

Later I do want you and Mrs. Dan to spend a night here at Washington with us if you can.

I value much your letter.   You give expression to exactly what I have felt.   I have been most abundantly rewarded, far beyond my deserts, by the American people; and I say this with all sincerity and not in any spirit of mock humility.   The stars in their courses fought for me.   I was forced to try a dozen pieces of doubtful and difficult work in which it was possible to

"WILL YOU PLEASE HUSH?"

From the New York Herald

deserve success, but in which it would not have been possible even for Lincoln or Washington to be sure of commanding success. I mean the Panama business, the anthracite coal strike, the Northern Securities suit, the Philippine Church question, the whole Cuban business, the Alaska boundary, the Government open shop matter, irrigation and forestry work, etc., etc. In each case, partly by hard and intelligent work and partly by good fortune, we won out. Moreover, Parker, who had been most carefully groomed for some years to bring the democracy back into power by uniting the Bryanites and Clevelandites, and who had very strong political and financial interests behind him, when actually tried in the great strain of a struggle for the Presidency, proved a poor type of candidate; so that many outside circumstances, over which I could have exercised but partial control, favored me. Of course it would be foolish for me to say that I did not think that I myself was responsible for part of the victory. I have done a great deal of substantive work. I have never sought trouble, but I have never feared to take the initiative when, after careful thought, I deemed it necessary. Moreover, in Hay, Taft, Root, Knox and one or two others I have had as staunch and able friends and supporters as ever a President had. My relations with these men have been very close and very, very pleasant. If circumstances had been different I would most gladly have served in the Cabinet of any one of the four men I have named; and we have had the most thorough comradeship of feeling now that circumstances have been such that they have all served in my Cabinet.

Moreover, it is a peculiar gratification to me to have owed my election not to the politicians primarily, although of course I have done my best to get on with them; not to the financiers, although I have staunchly upheld the rights of property; but above all to Abraham Lincoln's "plain people"; to the folk who work hard on farm, in shop, or on the railroads, or who own little stores, little businesses which they manage themselves. I would literally, not figuratively, rather cut off my right hand than forfeit by any improper act of mine the trust and regard of all these people. I may have to do something of which they will disapprove, because I deem it absolutely right and necessary; but most assuredly I shall endeavor not to merit their disapproval by any act inconsistent with the ideal they have formed of me.

But the gentlefolk, the people whom you and I meet at the

houses of our friends and at our clubs; the people who went to
Harvard as we did, or to other colleges more or less like Harvard: these people have contained many of those who have been
most bitter in their opposition to me, and their support on the
whole has been much more lukewarm than the support of those
whom I have called the plain people.   As you say, I do not at all
mind what Mr. Baer, or Mr. J. J. Hill or Mr. Thomas F. Ryan
does in the way of opposing me.   Mr. Baer was doing what I
thought wrong in the coal strike.   Mr. Hill was doing what I
thought wrong in the Northern Securities Company.   Mr. Ryan
was doing what I thought wrong about the franchise tax law in
New York.   And I upset them all.   They are all three big men
and very wealthy.   They are accustomed to being treated with
great consideration, and they have doubtless quite sincerely
come to feel that their own wisdom and right-mindedness are
such that it is improper to oppose them.   I do not wonder that
they are bitter towards me.

But the Evening Post crowd, the Carl Schurz and Charles
Francis Adams crowd, are hypocritical and insincere when they
oppose me.   They have loudly professed to demand just exactly
the kind of government I have given, and yet they have done
their futile best to defeat me.   They have not been able to do
me personally any harm; but they continually do the cause of
good government a certain amount of harm by diverting into
foolish channels of snarling and critical impotence the energies
of fine young fellows who ought to be a power for good.   Take
Carl Schurz's attack upon me for acting as any gentleman would
act with Hanna and Quay when they were on their death beds;
or take his statement that because I had seen Addicks and Lou
Payn I was to be repudiated, as "the friendship of the wicked
has its price."   In the first place, I had seen Lou Payn just once,
at his request.   I have seen Addicks perhaps three times, at his
request, of course.   I have never since I have been President
done for either Addicks or Payn one single act: never made an
appointment for either of them or done anything else for either
of them.   In the next place, I shall continue to see both of them
whenever they choose to call, and to see anybody else who
chooses to call—unless it be some creature who renders it impossible for me to see him.   For instance, if Hearst, while Congressman, calls upon me I shall see him as a matter of course.
I continually see "Dry Dollar" Sullivan.   If my virtue ever becomes so frail that it will not stand meeting men of whom I thor-

oughly disapprove, but who are in active official life and whom I must encounter, why I shall go out of politics and become an anchorite.   Whether I see these men or do not see them, if I do for them anything improper then I am legitimately subject to criticism, but only a fool will criticise me because I see them. Moreover, the hypocrisy of Carl Schurz and the Evening Post crowd is the more evident because they support Parker, who owes his political existence to Hill, and is the intimate social and political friend of Hill, Sheehan and Tom Taggart, and yet attack me for seeing men not one particle worse than these men whom Parker has seen all the time, and with whom he is on terms of hand-in-glove intimacy.   To choose Tom Taggart to run his campaign was precisely as if I had chosen Lou Payn to run mine; and the morality of Hill, his creator, is no more advanced than the morality of Addicks.

Of course in my work I have made certain mistakes, as was inevitable when I had such countless questions to meet all the time.   I do not think that they have been very numerous or very important.   Furthermore, there are some decisions I have made where I think I was right, but where doubtless other people with the same state of facts before them would think I was wrong. But in the great majority of the cases for which I am criticized by the people in question, the fact simply is that they have criticized in ignorance of all the circumstances of the case; in ignorance of the conditions which I, being at the center of affairs, must know better than any one else, and upon which I must act upon my own responsibility.

There—I have written you a long screed!

Good-by and good luck.

Ever yours,<br>THEODORE ROOSEVELT.

P.S.   Take the college bred men of the country on a whole, and I think I have the majority.

WHITE HOUSE<br>Washington

Personal.

December 2, 1904.

DEAR DAN:

Don't you want to come down here and spend a week in the White House, just to rest yourself?   I would see a good deal of you at odd moments, and you would have plenty of chance of resting. You could read, walk about, see the Congressional Library, and know that you were with people who were very glad to have you in the house. The change might really do you a little good.

Always yours,

THEODORE ROOSEVELT.

This solicitude for his friends when they were in trouble and he thought that he could help them, might be termed a habit of mind with him—or rather, perhaps, a habit of his heart; no matter how busy he was, nothing turned him from it. Enough illustrations where I was concerned have been given, and to these I will add but one more, which concerns another of his close friends. This friend arrived, not very well, for a short visit to Sagamore Hill, and fell into a sort of nervous collapse the next day. This compelled a much longer stay than had been expected. Quiet, rest, and a very little gentle exercise in the fresh air were the only medicine prescribed. Each day, at an hour in the afternoon when the sun was favorable, Roosevelt knocked, took the visitor down stairs, and they walked up and down the piazza together for the length of time that was recommended, after which the host conducted his guest back to rest and quiet.

In the preceding pages certain words have recurred more than once, and in Roosevelt's letter from the White House, dated November 19, 1904, which is evidently an answer to whatever I wrote to him after the sweeping victory of his election, some of these words appear again:

" . . . the Panama business, the anthracite coal strike, the Northern Securities suit. . . ."

And farther along in the same letter he says:

" . . . I do not at all mind what Mr. Baer, or Mr. J. J. Hill . . . does in the way of opposing me. Mr. Baer was doing what I thought wrong in the coal strike. Mr. Hill was doing what I thought wrong in the Northern Securities Company. . . .

And I upset them all.  They are accustomed to being treated with great consideration. . . .  I do not wonder that they are bitter towards me.  But the Evening Post crowd . . . are hypocritical and insincere when they oppose me.  They have loudly professed to demand just exactly the kind of government I have given. . . ."

I wonder how much these various sentences, written in a political and social past which the Great War has pushed so far behind us that it seems a century ago—I wonder how much they signify to the reader of to-day, how loud they ring in the ears of a man of thirty, or even of forty?

The air was full of the din which they made during that first decade of our century; you heard *Panama, Coal Commission, Northern Securities,* issue from people's lips as frequently and violently as you are hearing *Prohibition* during these later decades.  This din did not cease with Roosevelt's triumphant election in November, 1904, it grew louder; and it was my lot to be sitting in the middle of it from first to last.  The fact that he had been re-nominated by acclamation, and was the first Vice President in our history to become President and succeed himself, is more than strong evidence, it is absolute proof, of what the American people as a whole thought of this gentleman and Harvard graduate, who had become the storm-centre of our fortunes.  But what Mr. Baer furiously said to me was:

"Does your friend ever *think?*"

That was early in the storm; the storm had begun to rage in February 1902, when the suit against the Northern Securities was started, and the stock market sank like lead.  In the following October, the Coal Strike Commission turned the storm into a hurricane, and Mr. Baer made his remark.  Not the least striking part of it is that he made it in the presence of George Gray, who was chairman of the Commission, and at that time, I suppose, the first citizen of Delaware.

It must have been at the November dinner of the Mahogany Tree Club in Philadelphia that it occurred.  I was the youngest member of this company, a group of agreeable busy men who

met for pleasure and talked well.    All are dead, and none have
filled their place.    They knew that I had been an intimate friend
of Roosevelt's long before he became President.    They were
A. J. Cassatt, president of the Pennsylvania Railroad, George F.
Baer, president of the Reading Railroad, Senator du Pont, from
Wilmington, James Mitchell, Chief Justice of Pennsylvania,
Judge Gray, Weir Mitchell, and others, doctors, lawyers, each
in some way eminent, and none, save Dr. J. William White, with
much admiration for Theodore Roosevelt.    White was a brilliant surgeon, with a rough tongue, and very dear to the students of the University of Pennsylvania on account of his interest and influence in athletics.    He was enthusiastic about Roosevelt, whose out-door pursuits, and out-spoken way of talking,
were the sort of thing that particularly appealed to him.

Some fifteen of us sat dining at that round table, where Roosevelt's latest "outrage" against law, and the vested rights of property, was being forcibly condemned by the lawyers and the railroad magnates; and so George F. Baer, whom I warmly regarded, and saw often, shouted:

"Does your friend ever *think?*"    He almost literally roared
the word think.

"He certainly seems to act," I answered, very mildly.

"Why don't you stand up for him, Owen?" called Dr. White
across the table.    "Why don't you fight 'em?"

"What good would that do?    I couldn't kill 'em!    They
know what I think of him, and it doesn't happen to be what they
think.    But every citizen has a right to discuss the public actions of the President."

At that same Mahogany Tree table, not many years later, but
just how many I can not remember, George F. Baer said to me:

"About the best thing your friend ever did was to appoint the
Coal Strike Commission."

Does this amaze the reader?    It certainly amazed me.    Nobody reminded George Baer of what he had said in November,
1902, when the Coal Strike Commission was Roosevelt's latest
"outrage."    Other outrages had followed—the Railroad Rate

Bill, the Pure Food and Drugs Act, the Anti-rebate law, Employers' Liability. These may have seemed so much worse, that the Coal Strike Commission had become negligible. Or was it that since emotion, and not reason, is always the force which precipitates human affairs and governs the minds of men, Mr. Baer had cooled down?

Beside being good company, he was an unusually powerful and able person. When he took hold of the Reading Railroad, it had come through one re-organization after another, paid no dividends, was a by-word of failure, as the New York, and New Haven became later; and its single previous chance of coming back to life through the imaginative energy of a far-sighted brain, had been snuffed out by Wall Street hostility to that brain. Mr. Baer set the Reading Railroad on its feet. In keeping it on its feet, he thought any interference from people with whom he had no dealings, such as presidents of labor unions, was a wholly unwarrantable act.

His attitude was neither surprising nor exceptional, it was more than natural, at that time it was inevitable; and many a great captain of industry was of precisely the same way of thinking. *Hands off!* was what Big Business felt about itself in relation to the entire outside world; whatever it saw fit to do was, in its own eyes, right. It had come to resemble a good deal what a church was in the Middle Ages, a sanctuary in which you were safe from all hostile assault. Roosevelt, in bringing the Northern Securities suit, had violated the sanctuary, and his Coal Strike Commission was another violation; not even the Government of the United States must dare to call Big Business to order.

The months of the coal controversy had run to years before Roosevelt stepped in. Each time that the miners through their representatives requested a conference with the operators, these declined to deal with any union, or to discuss any question except with their own men. The situation was at a dead lock, the prolonged coal strike was producing a coal famine which grew more serious every day—and the days were growing cold, and winter

was at hand.   Yet George Baer sat immovable in a position
which nothing could better describe than his own words.   In
July of that year, 1902, he had answered a correspondent who
had appealed to him in the name of humanity and religion:

". . . I beg you not to be discouraged.   The rights and interests of the laboring man will be protected and cared for—
not by the labor agitators, but by the Christian men to whom
God in His infinite wisdom has given control of the property
interests of the country. . . ."

Knowing Mr. Baer, I suspect his words were ironic—they
certainly proved untimely.

The day came when coal in New York went to thirty dollars
a ton.   Little flames of violence began to flicker out here and
there, where cars carrying coal were seized and looted as they
trundled past the dwellings of people who had no fires.   Mayors
of many towns began warning Roosevelt of the dangerous temper that was rising in the minds of their communities, he was
flooded with appeals from every sort of person conveying tidings
of alarm.   So far from not thinking, the time came when he
hardly thought of anything else, and sought the wisest council
he could find as to what, as President, it was in his power to do.
And at length, after many consultations and the most careful
pondering, he reached his decision.   The doubtful legality of
any step never hindered Roosevelt from taking it, once he felt
it was imperative.   He acted with that swift finality which always threw those who were hit into the same exasperation as
George Baer's when he shouted:

"Does your friend ever think?"

Soon after the commission had performed its work of solving
the differences between the operators and the miners, and the
Anthracite Board of Conciliation had granted its awards, and
order instead of confusion reigned, Roosevelt took me on a walk
and we talked the whole matter over; what had been hanging
over the country was still present to us.

"I doubt," he concluded, "if we could have gone on as we

were in that deadlock ten days more, without riots and destruction of every kind breaking out in our cities as well as at the mines. We were on the brink of a chaos that might have spread nobody knows how far." And he told me of the plans he had made to send troops to the coal fields.

Mr. Baer, as it seems to me, through long successful practice of the law, followed by the very great responsibility of restoring a dead concern to life and saving hundreds of innocent shareholders from a total loss of their property, had suffered in his brain what the French so admirably describe as *déformation professionelle*. I cannot find for this any English phrase as brief and graphic. All of us have met these over-specialized brains in one walk of life or another. The West Point officer judges any war policy from nothing beyond his technical standpoint; the lawyer looks at, let us say, the constitutional right of the Southern Confederacy to secede, from a purely legal standpoint; the oculist is apt to suspect that your headaches prove that you are in need of glasses, while the dentist attributes the stiffness in your knees to presence of abcesses in the roots of your teeth, and the throat specialist is sure your tonsils should come out. Every one of these people who have trained their intelligence like a gun upon one particular target, may hit the right mark—and likewise they may miss the vital spot altogether. Thomas Jefferson, with that brilliant agility of mind which he not infrequently exercised, told somebody that any state had "the right to secede." And, upon being asked, What then? continued, that the other states then "had the right to stop it by force." His *déformation professionelle,* was that of the typical idealist or doctrinaire; that of George Baer, and many another great captain of industry during Roosevelt's administration (and of a few even to this day) is succintly stated in those famous four words of one of the Vanderbilts; while in conference over the affairs of his railroad:

"The public be damned."

True, the circumstances in which that remark was made quite justified its making, the particular point was the railroad's business only; but the phrase became a slogan for the malcontents.

Probably, no state of things can ever be traced back to its exact origin; but for the Wall Street *versus* Roosevelt state of things, the year 1865 may be set as a sufficiently good starting point. We recovered from the Civil War and began to expand more and more vigorously, with the Government's cordial approval, even with its assistance. Four years after Lee's surrender to Grant at Appomattox, the first railroad linked the Pacific with the Atlantic coast. By the time that six vast systems, from the Great Northern to the Southern Pacific, were in operation, the Sugar Trust had appeared, and Standard Oil, followed quickly by other combinations of powers which had discovered competition to be bad economy for all concerned, even for the person known as the consumer. But the consumer did not believe this, because he had seen, for example, railroad wars, when competing companies had sold him tickets much cheaper than when, say, the New York Central and the Pennsylvania had by agreement fixed the sum they would charge between points which they both touched. The mind of the average consumer could not grasp the fact that if a railroad carried him at a loss to itself long enough, ruin for it, its employees, and its shareholders, would in the end bring ruin upon him also; he could merely grasp the fact that there had been a day when he could have gone from New York to Chicago for five dollars, if he had wanted to go. This was a very attractive idea to him; and so, to hundreds of thousands of American minds, the word "monopoly" came to mean something wicked, dangerous, and oppressive, and the word "competition" something good and wholesome. More and more each year, the trust was breeding distrust; between "Capital" and "Labor" a great gulf had opened, and American sanity was diseased. By the time that Bryan, with good intentions, but an ignorant mind, had offered quack remedies for this real and dangerous disease, and John Jay Chapman, in his book *Causes and Consequences* had put a keen accurate finger upon the core of the trouble, not only the words "competition" and "monopoly," but a group of words had become sacred to one set of people, execrable to another, and vibrating with exaggerated and indiscriminating significance to both.  I remember William Dean Howells, then our leading man of letters, speaking of monopoly as if it were the root of all our ills and of competition as if it were the only cure.

To the champions of commerce, *property* was sacred; to the Samuel Gompers, *labor* was sacred; to the labor leaders, a strike was the road to salvation, to the captains of industry, it was the road to perdition.  When anybody held and expressed an opinion on either side—Capital or Labor—there was rarely any measure in the opinion, rarely any balance or sense of proportion; merely vituperation.  The thunder of a distant war between classes growled in the Homestead riots of 1892.  The storm remained local and passed.  Upon the cheerful and inattentive American mind it left no impression, suggested nothing to think about, was forgotten overnight in the onward sweep of our expansion.  In 1893, Coxey's army of the unemployed marched across the continent to the White House, to appeal to the President.  I saw them out of a Pullman window one evening in New Mexico or Arizona.  So did a lady near me, who was conversing with a clergyman.  She gave an exclamation, and pointed to the army of the unemployed, seated at its camp fires, cooking supper.

"Oh, look!" she said, with a touch of alarm.

"I never can bear the sight of suffering," said the clergyman; and he averted his eyes and changed the subject.

At the White House, Coxey's army was arrested for walking on the grass, and so ended as a joke; and the cheerful American people went on expanding, for there is nothing that they love so much as a joke.

During this period of expansion, unregulated by any restraint, and smiled upon by the Government, blackmail grew into an accepted custom, an established matter of course, merely a part of the machinery of progress.  It wore the disguise of harmless names, such as "contribution to the campaign fund."   When an election, state or national, promised to be very close, a great insurance company, or bank, or railroad, or any corporation having the care and responsibility of millions, and which was either in need of friendly or in fear of hostile legislation, would be likely to contribute to *both* parties: whichever won, Republican or Democratic, the corporation would be "taken care of."   Has the reader ever travelled through the large city of Syracuse in a New York Central train, and watched the sidewalks and houses pass by on the level for block after block as the locomotive slowly puffs along the street?   Why has the track never been elevated in all the years since the beginning?   Some day it is bound to be.   In Pennsylvania, such matters were arranged just as smoothly.   The historic figure of Senator Matthew Stanley Quay is associated with "contributions" in Pennsylvania.   There, even if the legislation which the railroad desired was of unquestionable benefit to the community, the right pockets had to be filled before the matter had a chance of favorable consideration.

John Jay Chapman was the pioneer intellect who perceived, analyzed and pointed out the vicious circle:

> Inferior characters elected to be law makers;
> railroad contributes to elect them;
> railroad asks inferior characters to pass a bill;
> inferior characters reply, Hands up first;
> railroad has to put up its hands;
> and so, round and round.

In Pennsylvania, not seldom during the good old days, a single law maker would demand two thousand free passes.   His pretext was of course that these would be distributed "where they would do good."   His wife, his children, his friends, and his relatives, were thus spared the expense of buying tickets. It grew into a heavy burden for the railroad—for all the railroads.   That is one of the reasons why Roosevelt was able to carry successfully through Congress the measure which put an end to it.   The Dolliver-Hepburn Rate Law had plenty of adroit enemies, but they failed, and the abuse of free passes must be counted as helping in their failure: although the law makers fought to save the restriction of their perquisite, the railroads did not heartily side with them; certain provisions in the law were far from being to their taste, but the limitation of free passes was very much to their taste.   And so the enemy was somewhat divided.

Just after the law was passed, I wished to watch the working of a recent style of express locomotive with the link motion outside; a novelty which the Pennsylvania Railroad had copied from a Belgian model, and was trying out.   I wanted to travel from Philadelphia to New York with the engineer, and permission was granted.

"But you must buy a ticket," said de Witt Cuyler, the director who had got me the favor; "we have to be good now."

"Being good will be good for you," I said; and Cuyler laughed as if he partly agreed with me.

The sight of Coxey's Army from a Pullman sleeping-car on a Southern Pacific train in Arizona, had given me a glimpse of social discontent; but amusement was the chief impression which the incident left with me.   I did not live in coal mines or railroad yards; the talk I commonly heard was the talk of powerful people, well-to-do, sheltered by their own ability and the success which it had brought them—the Alexander Cassatts, the George Baers, the Weir Mitchells, whose early struggles were well behind them.   It was once again on the Southern Pacific that my next glimpse of discontent began, and it was again in Arizona, less than a year after I had seen Coxey's army.

I had been staying with army and ranch friends in the Southwest, scouting with a troop of the First Cavalry wandering about silver mines with a past and no future, and far from the newspapers.   Vaguely I had heard something about a strike at the town of Pullman, where the company had its works; vaguely I had noticed here and there the name of Eugene Debs.   One day I got on the Sunset Express at a junction called Benson, and I expected to get out of that train at Oakland in two days, and cross in the ferry to San Francisco. I heard passengers asking each other and the conductor if the train would be allowed to continue its journey, or if it would be stopped. And then Eugene Debs became a very definite reality. All the way to Los Angeles we discussed him, and the sympathetic strike; at Tucson, at all the stations, we eagerly asked what the latest news was, and never got any news, nothing but rumors. I was absolutely confident that nothing and nobody would interfere with our journey. Why was I so confident? Because my life was chiefly passed among the Cassatts, the Baers, and the Mitchells; and that I should be disturbed in my projects by people I had never seen, never injured, and had no relation with, was an inconceivable notion. At any rate, I assured everybody, although trains that had not yet started might not be allowed to start, certainly a train like ours would be allowed to complete its course. The possibility of trouble gave me a pleasurable excitement, but I disbelieved in trouble.

We reached Los Angeles on the following afternoon. We sat a long while in our seats. A curious silence and inaction pervaded the Arcade Depot, as it was called. We were informed that our Pullman would go no farther, because it was a strike against the Pullman Company; and we were advised to get into the day coaches. We crowded into the day coaches and sat in them till it grew dark. Nobody told us anything. That was because nobody knew anything. Then I got out, left the station, found a hotel close by, a very rough and dubious hotel, passed the night there, saw that long train empty and stationary next morning, exactly where I had left it, noticed a cue of people up the street, joined them, bought a first-class passage on the steamer *San Pedro* for San Francisco—I was in time to get the last one sold—sailed that noon, found my first-class ticket gave me the privilege of sleeping on any portion of the vessel that I could find unoccupied, paid a steward for the use of his bed, found the bed dirtier and smellier than I could endure, went up to the cabin, and on its floor arranged myself among my fellow victims like a domino in sniff, my feet in the hair of one passenger and another passenger's feet in mine, and so we spent two nights, and finally reached San Francisco.

This experience sank rather deeper than seeing Coxey's army out of the car window in the preceding November; and it was not over by any means. I had reached San Francisco, where I wished to be, I could sleep clean and comfortable in a bed at the Palace Hotel, instead of on the floor of a ship's cabin, wedged in among the breathing bodies of a wretched crowd; but if I had wished to leave San Francisco, I could not have done so, except again in some boat; by land, the town was in a state of blockade. As the strikers and their sympathizers put it, "not a wheel was turning" on thousands of miles of railroad. For the first day or two, it seemed, at least it was so declared by hopeful spirits upon I know not what authority, that only the trains which carried Pullmans would be stopped, Mr. Debs and his friends having no grievance except against the Pullman Company. But the sympathetic strike is a phenomenon which can spread like the influenza. Not alone in the midst of Nevada, Utah, in all the wide space across which long trains full of passengers and longer trains full of freight had started toward the Pacific Coast from the centre of the United States, were those trains standing stock still, but next, the short local trains went out of existence. The last one out of Oakland had a dramatic end. As it was passing some point at no high speed, a Debs-minded citizen threw his baby, wrapped in the American flag, in the path of the locomotive. The engineer jerked the train to a stop, the strikers sprang on the locomotive and "killed it," as they say—put it out of business, as they also say. Until it could be repaired in the shops, it could not move.

As we sat, day after day, in San Francisco, we read in the papers each morning of violence on the increase, destruction of property, destruction of life; and of the hand of the Federal Government restraining the strikers for interference with the transmission of the mails; and of more violence in consequence of this restraint, and more sympathy with the strikers from the sort of person who will wrap a baby in the American flag and throw it in front of a locomotive. Soldiers of the regular army next appeared at various points—at Sacramento, for example, where they protected the station and had a cannon or two ready for the mob, and finally escorted the first local which the Southern Pacific attempted to run from Sacramento to Oakland. This train crashed through the trestle-work on which the railroad crosses the marshy tules of that region. Debs-minded sympathizers had sawed through the supporting piles. Almost nobody was killed except those on the engine, because the train was virtually empty. At length, between injunctions of the courts, and the use of the regular army to enforce these injunctions, wheels began to turn again; letters posted in Philadelphia on June 24, 1894, reached me on July 14; trains arrived from where they had been halted in Nevada, or Utah, or elsewhere; and excited passengers, full of anecdotes about their experiences, told us tales of these for several days. Eugene Debs was beaten in this war—for civil war is the only name for it—and went to prison, where he lived for many years, worshipped as a saint and a martyr.

So once, long ago, was John Brown worshipped. Between those two, Debs and Brown, there is unquestionably a spiritual kinship. Those who saw Brown in his prison at Harper's Ferry, even those who were about to hang him, discerned something in him far aloof from the common, something like a prophet in the Old Testament. Debs in his prison made a similar impression. Both men excited violent feelings among adherents and enemies alike. Debs had stood out in his own way, possibly the only way open to him, against a genuine grievance. What set me against him, what lodged this very grave event in my thoughts, was my own inconvenience in the strike, shared by a legion of other absolutely innocent citizens who were in no manner whatever to blame for the grievance of Debs. Just as plainly as Vanderbilt had said it in words, Debs had said by his act:

"The public be damned."

In their battle for self-preservation, Debs and Pullman had

both implicitly said "The public be damned."    This is just what miners and operators implicitly said in the coal strike a few years later, it is just what was invariably said in any of these altercations.    What I said to myself, when the collapse of the Debs strike liberated me from my captivity in San Francisco and I journeyed eastward in a train, was, Where do we come in? These people in their fights are looking out for themselves. Who is there to take care of us?    We outnumber the fighting parties by millions, but they are organized and we are not, and therefore every time this sort of thing happens, we shall be helpless.

I journeyed East, full of all this, and expecting to find people on the Atlantic side of our continent eager to hear what I had to tell them.    It was a very innocent expectation.    They were not in the least eager.    None of them had been obliged to get out of their Pullman and lie packed on the floor of a steamer's cabin for two nights.    They had been placidly passing those June and July days at Bar Harbor, or Newport, or pursuing their holiday or their business as usual.    They had lived in perfectly tame security; who has ever cared for consequences until he has felt them?    They remembered vaguely seeing something or other in the papers.    My story about the baby wrapped in the American flag elicited very much the same sort of interest that some dramatic event in a play provokes in the audience.    At the end of the play the audience goes home and next morning goes to its office or its housekeeping.

But the Debs strike sank into my mind rather deep.    It had been driven home to me not by hearsay, not by reading of it in the morning paper while I went on living in my tame security; if that were all I had known of it, I should have forgotten it too, like my Eastern friends.    But I had felt the consequences, and I did not forget.    When my Eastern friends said, "But the trains are obliged to carry the United States mails," or, "But a court can always enjoin these strikers," or "But a few soldiers can always discourage these strikers very quickly," it seemed to me rather a feeble answer.

It was not merely the strike organizers and leaders, some of them like Debs then, or like the more reasonable and intelligent Mitchell in the coal strike later, perfectly sincere protesters and rebels against corporate arrogance such as George Baer typified, it was not merely certain determined individuals such as these; nor yet was it their followers the workmen with their valid grievances; nor yet the horde of human rats, purely predatory and criminal natures, lurking and waiting in the shadows for their chance to leap out and destroy; something more than all this had to be reckoned with.   Wrapped up in the American flag with that baby was a vast popular and undiscriminating sympathy with the strikers, the sympathy of people whose means were modest, who were no more superior to the vice of envy than most of us are, and who were steadily coming to believe that if you are rich you are wrong.   In short, deep in our vitals we were carrying a huge growth, a perplexing compound of substances good and bad, so intricately mingled that surgery was sure to cut away the good with the bad; and yet, if some remedy for the bad were not found, the consequences would be of the gravest kind:—and these consequences were slowly and undeviatingly approaching straight through the eighties and nineties.

Who was to blame for it?   Nobody.   It was the logic of events.   As a people, we had early declared for the doctrine of *laissez-faire;* the Government was to keep its hands off the energetic man of ability, the creative constructor.   He was to be let alone, not to be hampered by legal restrictions, but to be encouraged to go on and build his railroads and set up his mills. He developed the country, from him came prosperity and power. Results showed no doubt of this.   Prosperity and power did come, and along with them came naturally the attitude of the creative constructor, the unhampered man of ability, such people as Pierpont Morgan, Alexander Cassatt, C. P. Huntington, James J. Hill, Andrew Carnegie, E. H. Harriman, George F. Baer.   Merely the great success of every one of these men made bitter enemies for them; all of them did more good than harm; but all, born in the happy days of *laissez-faire,* and so taking it for granted that they could carry on their vast plans as they saw fit, were used to having their own way. When they were stopped, they were very naturally not pleased. The sensation of having their acts questioned was too novel for their equanimity.

"Mr. Baer was doing what I thought wrong in the coal strike. Mr. Hill was doing what I thought wrong in the Northern Securities Company. . . . I upset them. . . . I do not wonder that they are bitter towards me."

How came Roosevelt to upset them?

I cannot set the date when his mind fixed itself on the dangerous state of things, the threatening growth inside us of which the Debs strike was merely a conspicuous symptom. Was this one of the menaces he had in mind when he wrote me on February 27, 1895, half a year after that strike:

"I recognize that all the time there are numerous evil forces at work. . . . I am not so sure that I can look at the coming years with levity"?

Did it lie behind his thoughts at lunch in 1896, when I asked him and Cabot Lodge how long they gave the Government to live, and one of them answered, "about fifty years," and the other assented to this limit?

If any one knows when Roosevelt's chief purpose became to make such things as the Debs strike and the coal strike impossible, or at any rate less likely, it is not I. Through those decades, he must have watched like many another man, the increasing symptoms of intemperate thought and intemperate emotion on the part of both the creative constructors and the men to whom they paid wages. And he must have seen—it did not need his extraordinary intelligence to see—that to stop a strike by means of an injunction and soldiers to enforce the injunction, was no cure for the deep-seated social disease, to which the strike bore exactly the same relation that the rash of scarlet fever bears to that highly infectious malady. But beyond those sentences of his which I have quoted, I find nothing in his letters, and remember nothing in his conversation, to indicate that the day was coming when he was to direct all his power and all his resourcefulness to establish some sort of methodical equilibrium between the George Baers and the Eugene Debses, some sort of calm which their quarrels should no longer be able to turn into a devastating storm that put everybody's ship in peril.

H. Harmony in the Philadelphia *Public Ledger.*

Of Bryan's "cross of gold" and his crude remedies for the economic evil, Roosevelt held the same opinion that was held by any enlightened mind, aware that such experiments had been tried again and again in history, and had never ended in anything but failure. Yet Bryan's protest was a just one, unquestionably, and his campaign of 1896 may have set Roosevelt to thinking. He couldn't think long or thoroughly just then, for he was at the head of the Police Board of Commissioners in New York, and this was enough to think about at one time. Not much leisure for extra reflection could have been his while he was Assistant Secretary of the Navy, or next, as Lieutenant Colonel of the Rough Riders; but by the time he sat at Albany as Governor of New York State, what Bryan was so constantly saying may very well have afforded him substantial matter for meditation.   At any rate, not so many years later, Bryan jocosely said that every plank but one in the Republican platform had been a plank of his own.   It's not very important to decide how much one man who carries a principle into effect is indebted for suggestions to a man who didn't; and if Roosevelt owed something to Bryan—Shakespeare owed something to Marlowe; Raphael to Perugino; Beethoven to Haydn; Washington to Hamilton: there is no definite moment when any progress begins.

While Roosevelt was Governor of New York, John Jay Chapman's book, *Causes and Consequences* was published.   Few people read it.   Those who did, and spoke to me of it, were all bankers and brokers, their approach to any economic question, or any public question at all, suffered from the *déformation professionelle;* they could see nothing in the book but idealistic extravagance.   But I had seen the Debs strike, and I thought that Chapman had touched us where we lived (and where we might sicken and die) with a much more skilful finger than ever Bryan did, or could.   Did his analysis of Big Business and its evil control of legislation make an impression upon Roosevelt? I never asked him, and I do not know.   One can only feel sure that many things, speeches, books, and occurrences, led Roosevelt to think closely, perhaps for a while almost exclusively, upon the unstable economic and political equilibrium which jeopardized the welfare of the United States.   Perhaps he had seen, as I had seen all over our country, the mere mention of such names as Morgan and Rockefeller, raise a black scowl of hate.   Not six months after he became President, he brought the Northern Securities suit: to be exact, he became President on September 14, 1901, and under his instructions, his Attorney-General, Knox, brought the suit on February 20, 1902.   Though

they had been conferring about this step for weeks, going carefully over every aspect of it, not a word, not a rumor, not a suspicion leaked out: it fell upon the country like a flash of lightning.

I place this act at the top of all Roosevelt's great and cour-
ageous strokes in the domain of domestic statesmanship.  I
think that to make up his mind to take this first step, to declare
this war, on the captains of industry, was a stroke of genius;
and I more than think—I know—that it marked the turn of a
rising tide.   Years before the Debs strike, and for years after
it, I had been rambling in every corner of the country; in big
cities, remote valleys, frontier stores, ranches, and saloons, east,
west, north, south.   Excepting Oklahoma, I had travelled in
every state in the Union, in trains, stage coaches, on horses;
sleeping in important hotels, log cabins, and blankets out in the
open.   I had heard every kind of citizen talk about everything.
Many of them said that the Government of the United States
was situated in Wall Street.   More of them were saying this
each succeeding year.   Their hatred of Wall Street was excessive, but it was perfectly natural.   They detested the arrogance of wealth, and they believed that all wealth was ar-
rogant, and that to be rich was to be dishonest; any captain of
industry was a public enemy.   In fact, that baby, wrapped in
the American flag and thrown in front of the locomotive, was a
vivid symbol of the rising tide.   More and more thousands of
the plain people, inspired by Bryan, inspired by all sorts of in-
fluences and experiences, were coming honestly to believe that
the Government at Washington had taken a back seat and given
the front seats to the Baers, the Morgans, the Rockefellers, the
Hills, the Huntingtons, the Harrimans, and their like.   Moreover, these powerful men were more than ready to occupy the
front seats: "We are the law and the prophets," could have stood
for their motto.

Harriman himself, in 1906, when the battle between Roosevelt
and the captains of industry was at its bitterest, stated his position with what Roosevelt in a letter to Lodge calls "naked
brutality."   Harriman declared that *whenever it was necessary*

*he could buy a sufficient number of Senators and Congressmen or State Legislators to protect his interests, and when necessary he could buy the Judiciary.* Standard Oil and other powers expressed the same view less nakedly.

And so by bringing the Northern Securities suit, Roosevelt served notice on everybody that it was going to be the Government, and not the Harrimans, who governed these United States. It was a tremendous and imperative object lesson to the nation; and, as I have said, it marked the turn of the tide. The heart of the plain people went out to Theodore Roosevelt. Relief and reassurance moderated their angry mood. Babies were less likely to be thrown in front of locomotives. That is one side of the huge historic picture. There is another.

The hearts of E. H. Harriman and his brother magnates did not go out to Roosevelt. The Northern Securities burst among them like a bomb. Stocks fell. People speculating on margins lost their money, their tempers, and their senses. We had a vile demagogue in the White House. In a short time the country would be at the mercy of the proletariat. Even Pierpont Morgan, a far better, broader man than Harriman, could see the Northern Securities suit only from his special angle. "Are you going to attack my other interests?" he asked Roosevelt. A clear case of *déformation professionelle.*

Nearly all of my friends in Boston, New York, and Philadelphia, were on Mr. Morgan's side. But I had been in the Debs strike; and they had not. I had travelled in forty-seven states of the Union and they had not. Most of them had never left the Atlantic seaboard, except for Europe. Their first question when a war, or an earthquake, or a great fire, or a pestilence, or an election occurred, was apt to be:

"How will this affect the stock market?"

There was little good in telling them about the baby in the flag; about the enemies that Standard Oil and such things were making every day; that if it went on like this, something would smash; and that if they should live to see the day, they would wish with a heart-breaking earnestness that the Government was in the front seats.

"And I upset them all," wrote Roosevelt to me that day in 1904, after his election had been a sweeping triumph in the face of all the Harrimans that were banded to beat him.

The upsetting of the Harrimans by no means stopped him; he might have remarked, like Paul Jones of the *Bonhomme Richard*, that he had only just begun to fight.

"They had much better accept me," he said in his characteristic mutter, with his brows knitted and his head bent down, as he always used to do when we were walking, and had got on the subject of his public measures, and the turmoil raging round them. "I am on their side. I believe in wealth. I belong to their class. They had much better accept me, instead of some Bryan who'll come along and ride over them rough shod."

"I think the Government should allow them to protect themselves from themselves," I said.

"Themselves from themselves!" he exclaimed. "Yes. Precisely!" He understood me perfectly. Competition had often worked nothing but evil, combination had often worked nothing but good; a Trust could be the very best arrangement for everybody: let it live: but let it never say:

"The public be damned!"

In fact, as will presently appear, Roosevelt did not intend any one set of people to disregard the whole people, if he could prevent it.

Our conversation during that walk, his part in it at least, was either an echo or a precursor of his words in a speech he made about that time before the Gridiron Club, which had invited him and Pierpont Morgan to the same dinner. Roosevelt, at the dinner, as he had been when I walked with him, was in a towering and concentrated preoccupation over his policies of reform. The Gridiron Club meant him to talk about them, of course. Most probably, it likewise expected Pierpont Morgan to answer Roosevelt and defend his own position. What it hardly could have anticipated was the dramatic climax which Roosevelt brought on, carried utterly out of himself by his own intensity. After referring to the unstable temper which he believed the country at large to be in, he came to the steps which he and his advisers were trying to take in order that confidence might be restored, and general security established. As he went on, advocating and justifying those remedies which he proposed to administer, he suddenly turned, walked along the table to where Pierpont Morgan sat, and shook his fist in Morgan's face, as he concluded:

"And if you don't let us do this, those who will come after us will rise and bring you to ruin."

I cannot vouch for the exactness of every syllable, but that is exactly the import of Roosevelt's words.

"What a shocking thing to do at a dinner party!" was the comment made to me by a friend who disliked him.

Upon a later occasion, equally dramatic, and in the presence of many more witnesses, he shook his fist in the face of another important man; but that time it was in the face of Samuel Gompers. Gompers was attempting to identify our aims and methods with those of Soviet Russia. I make this juxtaposition of fist shakings here, because I doubt if any two simple gestures of Roosevelt could draw more instantly and adequately the outline of Roosevelt's sensible and admirably balanced brain—his hostility to all extremes, whether of capital or of labor, his instinctive repudiation of any sort of extreme whatever.

## XV.

That growth of financial arrogance on the one hand and popular discontent on the other through the eighties and nineties, which Roosevelt set out to remedy by some legislative surgery, had already in 1890 caused Congress to take action. It was an attempt to curb the Morgans and Harrimans in their trust making, and was known as the Sherman Law. It forbade "combinations in restraint of trade." It was aimed at all persons who united under one management their sugar refining, or their steel plants, or their railroad systems, or their coal mines, or anything which competed with any similar thing in selling its

### THE SOAP-AND-WATER CURE.

President Roosevelt: *"As I recently remarked at Nashville, Tenn.: 'During the next sixteen months of my term of office this policy shall be persevered in unswervingly!'"*

American Eagle: *"Je-hoshaphat!"*

[PUNCH: Oct. 30: 1907.]

*Reproduced by permission of the Proprietors of "Punch"*

product to the public. Its far too sweeping scope has made trouble since and brought it into disrepute to-day; but in those days the superstitions of the multitude (including many superior people like William Dean Howells) surrounded it with the same magic halo of unmixed beneficence that surrounded "competition," just as "monopoly" magically meant unmixed evil.

Under the Sherman Law in Cleveland's time, the Government had brought a suit against the Sugar Trust, and lost it. The decision of the Supreme Court in this case was very good news to the captains of industry, and they naturally, in perfectly good faith, went ahead with their vast combinations. One of them was the Northern Securities. By a device, now familiar, known as a Holding Company, Pierpont Morgan and James Hill brought some large railroads, hitherto competitors, under a single harmonious administration. So far as both the railroads and those who used them were concerned, this was really a wise and excellent arrangement, an advantage for everybody. But, it was a defiance of the policy of the Federal Government as expressed in the Sherman Law; to the popular and discontented mind it was one more proof that Big Business was above the Law, and outside Government control. The courage of Roosevelt was not only in calling to order a combination that was on the whole a good thing for the public, but in attacking the great figures who supported his own party.

He won his Northern Securities suit. The Supreme Court distinguished between it and the suit against the Sugar Trust in 1895.

Today, the magic has fallen away from the words "monopoly" and "competition." The popular mind no longer thinks that you can force producers by law to undersell each other to their own ruin if they do not choose to do so. The popular mind— or a very large part of it—realizes that combinations enable producers to reduce their "overhead charges," and to offer their products to the public at a cheaper price in consequence. Mergers are taking place constantly. In a word, the popular mind has been reassured, because it knows that the Government, through its Interstate Commerce Commission and other legal means, has the power to control great combinations in case they undertake to say "the public be damned." And this far more reasonable and stable state of things is directly due to the object lesson which Roosevelt gave to the country when he brought the Northern Securities suit on February 20, 1902.

Many of his historic measures during the succeeding years of his administration merely followed out this early case, were merely further instances of his determination to keep powerful groups in their place below the Government, and not above it; and to remind them that in their quarrels with each other the rights of a third party must be recognized, and that this third party, the public, was the most important of them all.

Under the Sherman Law, some more combinations were attacked and broken up, possibly to drive the object lesson home, and possibly for the sake of consistency. In 1906, the combination of the Union and Southern Pacific (The Harriman lines) was dissolved, as much to my disgust as the Northern Securities had been to my satisfaction. The geography of the two roads bore no analogy whatever to that of the Northern Pacific and the Great Northern, which both started at St. Paul, and terminated in the Puget Sound cities, both passing through Spokane on their way. In their case, competition could reasonably be inferred, reasonably according to a narrow majority of the Supreme Court. The Union Pacific started at Omaha, the Southern at New Orleans, they were never less and sometimes more than five hundred miles apart, they served widely different territories, and when they met it was not at a competing terminal point, but at Ogden. To contend that they competed was to stretch reason to the breaking point—and by that time there had been object lessons enough. So I thought at the time, so I think still. Many years after it was all over, as I have already recorded, I ventured to tell a very liberal-minded member of the Supreme Court that I had never admired the decision in that case. I found quite to my astonishment that he did not admire it either, and did not particularly admire the Sherman

Law.   But he explained, the last thing it was the business of a Supreme Court judge to do, was to allow his opinions to be colored with his own personal approval or disapproval of any particular law involved in the case.   He sat there for one sole purpose, to pronounce upon the constitutionality of whatever law was before the court.

Roosevelt battled on for his chosen aim year after year.   He put the railroads, the Chicago packers, the makers of canned foods, and patent medicines—all who had come to assume themselves above the Law—in their place; and the hue and cry of "demagogue" followed his steps, as well as the gloomy prediction that we should soon be at the mercy of the proletariat.   I doubt if any President since Andrew Jackson, when he declared war on Biddle and the Bank, had raised any turmoil such as that which rose around the Northern Securities and swelled in volume as each new step was taken.   Let the chief of these be recalled: The Rate Bill, the Pure Food and Drugs Act, the Anti-Rebate Law, the Employers' Liability Act.   Each may be described as providing special means to check the abuse of power by an organized minority; and the whole group was generally characterized by the financiers as Roosevelt's assault on property.

But the financial body was not at all the only organized minority which had the *déformation professionelle.*   Labor unions had their own deformity of vision.   This excluded everybody's rights but their own just as blindly and at times far more dangerously.   The average workman hadn't the intelligence or the education of the average financier, and this meant that he had less to restrain him from actions which were bound to recoil and hurt him just as fatally as they damaged his adversary.   And he too, when he was fighting the organized minority that paid him his wages, cared nothing how much anybody else was going to suffer.

A railroad president, when asked once what rates should be charged, had replied:

"All the traffic can bear."

To many ears this sounded abominable.   In its own language,

Labor frequently said exactly the same thing—and on occasions demanded from its employer wages that were so much in excess of what his business could bear, as to put him out of business. In short, when it came to comparing the greed of Labor with the greed of Capital, Labor, being less intelligent, could easily outswine Capital. At times it spoke out and gave itself away, as one of its leaders did at the time of the Adamson Bill, brought by four railroad brotherhoods.

"We are the vultures," said the spokesman Garrettson, "and the public is, perhaps, the carcass."

Roosevelt wanted no carcasses. This famous word of his expressed his balanced view:

"The door of the White House shall swing open just as easily to the poor as to the rich—*and not one bit easier.*"

The Adamson Bill was signed by Woodrow Wilson. Not long after this a leader of one of the railroad brotherhoods was at Sagamore Hill, and the subject came up. Roosevelt, addressing the man, whom he had long known, by his first name, said:

"If I had been in the White House, you wouldn't have had your bill signed."

And the man answered:

"Colonel, if you had been in the White House, we wouldn't have brought in our bill."

If that first step of Roosevelt's, the Northern Securities, had created any illusions in the minds of the organized minorities of Labor, that the door of the White House was henceforth to be shut against the rich, and open exclusively to the poor, this illusion was presently dispelled.

The Miller incident added one more storm to those already raging round Roosevelt. It had immense publicity at the time; it even brought on a symposium in the *Saturday Evening Post;* there I appeared as demonstrating that John D. Rockefeller and Union Labor were merely twins when it came to assuming themselves above the law; and Clarence Darrow, an expert in defending assassins, wrote something or other. Miller had been employed in the Government Printing Office, and lost his job there because he had been expelled from a labor union. Such a reason for dismissing an employee, against whom there was no other ground of complaint, was held a violation of the Civil Service Law, by the Commission who investigated the case, and Roosevelt ordered Miller to be taken back on his job.

Up in the air went the American Federation of Labor, up in the air went Samuel Gompers, up in the air went everybody with the particular *déformation professionelle* of Labor, that saw nothing wrong in putting Morgan and Hill in their place, and nothing but outrage in putting Union Labor in its place—not above, but below the Government of the United States. They passed an angry resolution:

"That the order of the President can not be regarded in anything but an unfriendly light."

And so now the hurricane blew from two quarters at once, and Roosevelt had no chance of being elected in 1904, because the door of the White House swung open alike to John D. Rockefeller and Samuel Gompers, and each demanded that it be shut against the other, and both would therefore vote against him and defeat him.

But somebody did vote for him on November 8, 1904, when he received the greatest popular majority and the greatest electoral majority ever given to a candidate for President.

What has he to say about this in his letter to me, eleven days later?

"Moreover it is a peculiar gratification to me to have owed my election . . . above all to Abraham Lincoln's 'plain people.' . . ."

He never lost their love. He was the sort of man after their own hearts. That word about the door swinging open was the kind of word they wanted to hear, and they understood it particularly well; it spoke their moral language, the core of their faith, the creed handed down to them from the Declaration of Independence, generation after generation.

None that has taken intelligent note—or has attentively read —of the course of events in the United States from the day of the Homestead riots in 1892 to the present time, can doubt for a single moment that the working man could ever have compelled his employers to treat him fairly, had he not used the Union and the strike as weapons of defense an attack: he owes his present favorable state to this: the employer has learned his lesson: the George Baer attitude is obsolete.   But it is just as true—and no one who has taken in the significance of Labor greed and Labor crimes can doubt it—that if Labor were let loose upon us we should indeed be the carcass very soon, and that the span of fifty years which Roosevelt gave our Government to live, would have been cut short already.   When San Francisco was wrecked in 1906 by earthquake and fire, and thus lay at the mercy of Labor let loose, the working man immediately charged a good deal more than all the traffic could bear; the brick layers and their kind exacted twenty dollars a day from the helpless community before they would lift a hand to help rebuild the stricken and fallen city.   I wish that I could feel as sure that the Eugene Debses of the present day had learned their lesson as well as the present George Baers.   In the end, our mainstay and safeguard is not wise and temperate legislation, such as Roosevelt introduced, but the common sense of the "plain people" who so emphatically endorsed that legislation in 1904.   If that common sense ever dies, we shall have either a Mussolini or a Lenin in its stead.

The factional storm of disapproval raised against Roosevelt, when he ordered Miller to be given his job again in the Government Printing Office, I can understand much better than the hostility which my rich friends felt for him, and which his triumphant election by no means silenced.   It might have been supposed that his action in the Miller case would have considerably weakened the accusation that he was a demagogue. It did nothing of the sort.   As one measure followed upon another after the Northern Securities, his political enemies—those, that is, who represented the rich—grew more bitter.   It is remarkable, but very characteristic of him, how little bitterness he felt towards the bitter magnates of finance:

". . . I do not mind at all what Mr. Baer, or Mr. J. J. Hill, or Mr. Thomas F. Ryan does in the way of opposing me. . . . I do not wonder that they are bitter towards me."

It is in the next paragraph of his November 19th letter after the election that he expresses bitterness:

"But the *Evening Post* crowd . . . are hypocritical and insincere when they oppose me.   They have loudly professed to demand just exactly the kind of Government that I have given. . . ."

He is not going to stop giving that kind of government, however:

"I may have to do something of which they will disapprove. . . ."

It is the plain people of whom he is speaking here; he will not shirk offending them any more than offending the Wall Street corporations, or the *Evening Post,* or the Labor Unions, if he deems it "absolutely right and necessary."

From the day in the Harvard Gymnasium, when he deemed it absolutely right and necessary to silence the friendly but mistaken hisses at the man who had given him a bloody nose, to the last day he lived, this essential spirit in him flamed out unquenchable.   He lived to see banded Capital cease to be the menace that he had found it when he entered the White House; but banded labor ran another course.   At Victor, Colorado, twenty murders of non-union men were done at a single blow. The murder of the Governor of Idaho followed—he, too, had upheld the law.   The same two groups—organized destruction and sheltered sentimentalism—were sympathetically clamorous over the persecuted innocence of the brothers McNamara, who were defended by the same Clarence Darrow that defended the murderers of the Governor of Idaho.   It was very embarrassing to their sympathizers when the brothers McNamara con-

fessed to the crime.   To-day, for the present at least, the signs
are healthier than they became during the administration of
Woodrow Wilson and the upheaval caused by the Great War.
American Labor has repudiated the doctrine of the I. W. W.
and of any "religion," native or alien, of which the bomb is the
first article in its creed.   This "religion" is the most virulent
poison ever injected into the veins of any nation, and not merely
an army of the nomadic idle, but a herd of the sheltered sentimentalists are the constant members of its church; it finds de-
fenders in the halls of great Universities as well—sheltered doc-
trinaires.   In 1916 and 1917, it broke out in San Francisco,
and in Arizona; and Woodrow Wilson very materially gave it aid
and comfort by asking three times the Governor of California
to pardon a bomb thrower, a murderer whom the court had
convicted, and whom the I. W. W. was straining every nerve
to save.   It demanded the recall of the District Attorney who
had conducted the prosecution.   Directly after this, the citizens of several towns in Arizona ran the I. W. W. out of the
State, because it had entered the State with the avowed purpose
to help a strike by murder and destruction of property.   Woodrow Wilson sent an Oriental to investigate the rights of the matter, and report.   This report gave the I. W. W. a clean bill of
innocence, and evoked from Roosevelt a letter, which I should
suppose that any man who belonged—if only officially—to the
ranks of self respect, would have either withered under, or have
been stung to energetic vindication of his character.

"The I. W. W.," wrote Roosevelt, ". . . are never concerned
for justice.   They are concerned solely in seeing one kind of
criminal escape from justice, precisely as certain big business
men and certain corporation lawyers have in the past been concerned in seeing another kind of criminal escape from justice
. . . murder is murder, and it is rather more evil when committed in the name of a professed social movement. . . .   I have
just received your report. . . .   No human being in his senses
doubted that the men deported from Bisbee were bent on destruction and murder. . . .   Your report is as thoroughly misleading a document as could be written on the subject. . . ."

The letter is quite long, very well known, and has been often quoted and even printed as a pamphlet.    But you can not easily wither or sting emissaries of that stripe.

But the signs indeed are brighter to-day.    Though Roosevelt did not live to see the healthier era of co-operation between employers and employed which has dawned upon us, to him it is that we owe its existence.    His vigorous hostility to both overweening Capital and overweening Labor, his eloquent and hard hitting words, translated into hard hitting deeds, opened many eyes that prejudice had kept shut; they blazed the trail for the tremendous economic revolution through which we have passed without a national convulsion.

The Panama Canal is of course his greatest visible monument; but to me this other invisible monument is greater, even though possibly less enduring.    Let the reader who is not familiar with the significant proof of our new social and economic stability, ask any great corporation, such as the Pennsylvania Railroad, how many shares of its stock are bought each year by its own employees.    There is small temptation to make war upon a company upon whose welfare your own so directly depends; indeed, in times of stress for which your company is no more to blame than you are, you are more likely to accept a temporary reduction of wages for the sake of your dividends than you are to go on strike which may cut all dividends off.    This desirable state of things may blow up in some fashion or other when all the employees become sole owners of all the corporations—but that time is not yet.

## XVI.

The blazing of the trail during those seven years that Roosevelt was in the White House was attended by increasing hostility from the extremists of the two groups—The Harrimans who boasted they could buy a judge whenever they needed one, and the Haywoods who escaped hanging through the very curious charge to the jury made by the judge in the trial for murder of the Governor of Idaho.    Each group of these enemies was tireless in leaving no stone unturned to trip Roosevelt up. Did he order the discharge of nearly three companies of negro soldiers at Brownsville for shielding those among them who were the murderers of the citizens in that town? One of his pet enemies, Foraker of Ohio, denounces him in the Senate, and a storm of the sentimentalists rages round him. Did he acquiesce in the purchase of the Tennessee Coal and Iron Company by the United States Steel Corporation? An equal storm from another group denounces him for inconsistency in not prosecuting the Steel Company on the same grounds as the Northern Securities. Is Mrs. Minor Morris forcibly put out of the White House because she insists upon seeing the President, and will not leave peaceably when told he is busy? A mob of political enemies and sentimentalists shouts itself hoarse at this insult to our womanhood, and a Congressman loudly tells the United States that—

"When the President stands in the presence of an American mother, he stands in the presence of his superior."

When the panic of 1907 falls upon the Wall Street speculators, it is all Roosevelt's doing. When he speaks of Harriman and Haywood as being *equally undesirable citizens,* the hornets of federated Labor swarm and buzz. One of their leaders writes him a letter with the pointed heading, "Cook County Moyer—Haywood—Pettibone Conference. . . . Death can not—will not—and shall not claim our brothers." In his reply to this, he puts his finger on exactly the same point which his letter to Wilson's emissary to Bisbee emphasized in later years:

". . . You and your associates are not demanding a fair trial, or working for a fair trial, but are announcing in advance that the verdict shall be only one way and that you will not tolerate any other verdict."

My old and warm friend Amos French wrote me a letter during these tempestuous times, which conveys the Wall Street feeling about the fall of prices in the stock market with a touch altogether and incomparably his very own:

March 31, '07.

DEAR UNCLE DAN'L:

You see I miss being an April fool by a day. . . . We in Wall St. are feeling utterly busted at the moment. This is going to be a great and good and pure country when Roosevelt gets the rascals all suppressed—but unfortunately his rat poison has been so widely distributed that he has sickened all the household pets as well as the vermin. Even the most conservative lap-dog, long fed out of the hand on investment bonds, has writhed with prolapsus tickeri. The widowed puss and the orphan canary find vitriol in the milk and bird seed. And Pretty Poll who was bold enough to buy and eat some appetizing Hill food (he alludes to Northern Securities) now hangs inverted from his perch with all his tail feathers missing and a red sore head.

Goodbye Dan'l. Come and see me this summer. You will find me in last year's straw hat and my 1881 duster, shelling acorns in the empty pig sty, and burying them as food for next Winter. But my welcome will be warm, and there is fine fresh water in the lake still—and I'll pick a dandelion or two, and we'll have a feast of reason in the place of those old horrid debauches we used to enjoy under McKinley.

Always affectionately in sun or sorrow,

STOCKINGS.

"Stockings" had been my name for French ever since one early morning in the Cambridge and Boston days when he had removed his shoes and dropped from a second story window in the club to the pavement—a performance others of us were wont to indulge in with our shoes on, considering it the very pink of exploit.

There was never any foretelling what either Amos French or Winthrop Chanler would improvise to do next. My memory sparkles with their inventions. At New London one morning about sun rise of a rare day in June, when Harvard had actually beaten Yale on the afternoon preceding, I watched French, completely dressed, gently lead by the hand a perfectly passive and also completely dressed old gentleman down some stone steps of a wharf into the waters of the river Thames, saying as they descended:

"Let me persuade you to join the American Navy."

No attacks from the Harrimans or the Haywoods, or any hostile group whatever, budged Roosevelt an inch from his fixed and constantly declared intention to allow the United States to be ruled by no organized minority against the interests of the whole people.   And during these days I not infrequently went walking with him.   As we started from the White House door, he would wave the secret service men away.   Whether they really went wholly away, or merely removed themselves from sight and continued their duty of shadowing him, I do not know. They were out of ear shot at any rate, and we were free to talk intimately.   Very intimate those talks sometimes used to be.

"When you turned those niggers out of the army at Brownsville," I asked him, just in the middle of that particular disturbance, "why didn't you order a court of inquiry for the commissioned officers?"

"Because I listened to the War Department, and I shouldn't." And he added presently: "Of course I can't know all about everything.   I don't pretend, for instance, to any technical familiarity with finance.   And I never take any important steps at all without consulting everybody available who I hope will help me by telling me what they think and why they think it."

He then related an extraordinary story (I hope it has been preserved in some of the books about him, for I have forgotten the details) of a great financier whom he had consulted; who had emphatically urged upon him certain measures, giving his reasons; who quite shortly after this, had recommended legislation almost the reverse; and who, when reminded of his earlier advice, had said that the conditions since then had changed. "Now suppose," said Roosevelt, "I had accepted his first opinion and the law he then advised had been passed.   He would have told me it should be repealed.   He sincerely and naïvely expected," continued Roosevelt, "the Government of the United

States to blow hot or cold, just as it happened to suit his own concerns."

"And so," said I, "the best you can do is to stop, look, and listen—and then jump!"

"Yes. And then jump. And hope I've jumped right."

The notion that he did not think before he acted was very wide spread then. This delusion was due to his way of jumping: he always cleared the fence clean, never balked, or knocked the top rail off, once he had decided to take the fence. But no President we have ever had looked the whole ground over with more care and attention first. Every person who had familiar and close sight of him during the days of his Presidency knew this. In certain later days, I am not so sure that he looked the ground over with quite the same thoroughness and caution.

On one of our Washington walks I began like this:

"You know how often, how nearly always, I agree with you."

He looked at me quickly. "What's the matter now?"

There was almost a shade of hostility in his tone—and no wonder. The panic of 1907 was being laid at his door by the enraged people in Wall Street, the walls of Congress were filled with sound and fury, and he was rasped by the ceaseless falsifications and misconstructions not so much of his natural enemies, but of his unnatural enemies; those whom his letter after his election in 1904 alluded to bitterly as:

". . . the gentlefolk, the people whom you and I meet at the houses of our friends and at our clubs; the people who went to Harvard as we did. . . ."

He knew—and knew that they knew—the true cause of the financial crisis we were in. And I think that it was their hostility which had given his face a different look when he left the White House from what it had been when he entered it. Then, it had been already hammered by his experience of life into an expression of pugnacity and determination; and new battles, like the Northern Securities, were to hammer it still more; but when he left the White House, you could see the scars of pain, when his countenance was not animated by what happened to be going on at the moment. And so he was prepared to be formidable when I reminded him how often I had agreed with him; and asked, what was the matter now?

"Well—I can't support your San Francisco earthquake."

For a single second, he stared in perfect blankness at me, and then saw the whole thing, and burst into hilarity.

"Of course you can't! Of course you can't! And I wouldn't ask it of you!" And he went off into more laughter.

"I have just been reading the fourteen volumes of Washington's letters edited by Ford," I explained. "And this panic you've brought on is merely the old, old story. Washington, during his second term, writes to I forget which one of those two or three intimate friends he had, that the crops are going to be poor in consequence of the exceptionally prolonged drought, for which as usual the Administration will be held responsible. It's the *as usual* that's the point, I continued. "Poor Washington had already found out that the President would be blamed for everything, including the weather."

"Including the weather," murmured Roosevelt, in that half whisper he would fall into. And he nodded to himself. "Including the weather."

The true causes of the panic of 1907 are not open to discussion; the final straw was the weakness of great insurance companies the world over, in consequence of the losses that they suffered through the San Francisco fire in 1906, which was started by the earthquake. The earthquake destroyed the water supply, the fire engines had nothing to pump on the flames, and so a huge area of the city went to ashes. I have no doubt there are people still alive, whose *déformation professionelle* places Roosevelt in their limited vision as responsible for that panic.

Once at Oyster Bay, during the Great War, I gave him a prescription to use in times of stress. It was taught me by Dr. Frederick Shattuck of Boston, one of my intimate and wise advisers since I had been a boy of seventeen. I had gone to him for medical and philosophical help.  After hearing my story, and going over me both physically and morally, he said:

"There are two kinds of troubles a man can be in: trouble that he can do something to cure, and trouble that nothing he can do will cure.  If he is in the first kind of trouble, the longer he thinks about it, the worse he'll he: let him start at once, let him get into action and try to remove the trouble.  That will help him to feel better very soon.  But if it's a trouble he can't cure, let him dismiss it from his mind and think of something else."

"That's much easier said than done."

"Of course it is.  But it can be done by resolving hard enough to do it.  And here's what I prescribe when you're in a mess that's none of your making and which it will do you no good to brood over.  Say this little poem to yourself:

> The dog is in the bedstead,
> The cat is in the lake,
> The cow is in the hammock:
> What difference does it make?"

George Washington was the occasion of another discussion during a most extraordinary walk which the President took me; we climbed under and over various things, we went up on the railroad bank as it was then, near the point where the track used to enter the Long Bridge across the Potomac on its way to Alexandria.  Both of us resented equally that inquisitiveness about matters that are none of their business, which Americans have developed, and which is undoubtedly a national characteristic of a peculiarly disagreeable sort, a perfectly unwarrantable invasion of one's privacy.  One is told by the reporter that the public "has the right" to know something which it has no right to know whatever, and which merely serves as trivial gossip to help sell the newspaper.  I remembered Washington and the haughty silence with which he met a deputation of parsons, who had intruded to ask him for his religious views, in fact, to demand them.  Americans certainly began minding their neighbors' business very early. Washington ceased taking the Communion before he became President. On Communion Sundays he used to leave the church, until the clergyman made him feel that, as President, this was not a good example to set. After this, he remained. As President, he was particular about going to church; at home in Virginia not at all so; and on his quiet death bed, the scene of which was carefully recorded by those around him, the conventional words about eternity, and sin, and forgiveness were none of them spoken. It is evident from his own letters that he was what we call a religious man, very deeply so, but also very broadly, and had outgrown formulas.

Walking with Roosevelt that day, and going over with him in a discursive, fragmentary fashion these incidents in the life of our first President, and the hint which they afforded as to his final attitude to the mystery of the Universe, brought my own attitude up to me—and Roosevelt's. Much, very much, had befallen human thought in our civilization since Washington's day; and as we stood looking down the Potomac in the direction where Mount Vernon lay, I quoted those words at the end of the first chapter of Genesis: "And God saw every thing that he had made, and behold, it was very good."

Roosevelt had taught Sunday School for a while at Harvard; to-day, as President, he conformed to the propriety of George Washington. He now stood silent, looking at the river. Our silence was a unison of our thoughts. And again I quoted, this time not from the Bible:

> Oh Thou, who Man of baser Earth didst make,
> And even with Paradise devise the Snake:
> For all the Sin wherewith the Face of Man
> Is blackened—Man's forgiveness give—and take!

"Yes," he said quietly. "Yes. It will trouble a great many people for a long time still."

How much had it troubled him? I did not ask then, I never asked, if he had gone through that struggle to hold his belief in what he had been taught in church and in prayer books, when his maturing reason began to question it. It was a period of disturbance and unhappiness which came to many youths of our generation. The tender-minded suffered most and longest, and came out believers still, some of them, and some of them embittered and hostile. The tough-minded were able to throw it off and put it behind them.

He would have been willing to speak to me about his own experience, I think, had I ever started the subject; but there are doors of sacred seclusion which must be opened from within, bidding one enter; to turn the handle from outside is the grossest liberty one human spirit can take with another; even a parent should not take it with a child. I never took any liberty with Theodore Roosevelt. My surmise is, that although he was very tender hearted, he was in every way very tough minded, robust in spirit as in brain, a man of action throughout, and therefore saw no use in trying to solve the great eternal problem, when he could direct his mind and his energy to the solution of some material problems, whose cause was much more accountable than the cause of the Universe—and very much closer at hand.

I do wish very much that I had remembered and repeated to him that afternoon as we stood by the Potomac for those few minutes, a conversation I had held in the spring of 1896 in Paris, with a French nobleman who was showing more interest in the welfare of that Republic than is apt to be met with in persons of his class.

Huysmans (if I recall the right name) had recently published a novel, in which were described the rites of the Black Mass. These were at once perfectly bestial, and perfectly ridiculous; childish, necromantic; as if a lot of children had broken out of Sunday School in a revolt and gone to a closet and locked themselves in, and celebrated an elaborate worship of the Devil.

"Is it true?" I asked this French gentleman. "Or did he invent it?"

"It is true. He was one of them, but he has left them. The

Black Mass was being held until quite lately. Perhaps they are doing it still."

"But why? But why?"

"It is a gesture of reaction and defiance."

"Defiance? To Christianity, you mean?"

"To God."

"What is the use, what is the point, of taking so much trouble? Here is the situation—yours, mine, the world's: Either God exists, or He does not. If He does not, whom exactly are you defying by these blasphemies and obscenities? You are defying a vacuum. That seems a bit childish for grown up persons. If God exists, then He is so far above and beyond any little foolish antics which we may choose to play, that although they might be visible to Him, they would be utterly negligible and beneath His notice. That is how I look at it."

The Frenchman stared, surprised; more than surprised; a little displeased, I think; or disapproving.

"Your logic is very cold, sir," he said. "A Frenchman could never reason in such a manner."

But I never thought of this while Roosevelt and I were standing by the river, looking down towards Mount Vernon.

His mind was still on Washington; for, as we resumed our walk, he said:

"Washington told Dr. Craik when he had grown so feeble that speaking came hard for him, that he was not afraid to die."

"Well, I suppose one may take that as a possible indication of his attitude towards the question of a future life. If there was a future life, he was not ashamed, on the whole, of the manner in which he had spent this one. If death was the end, that was all right, too. If you cease to be aware of everything, you will miss nothing, and be troubled by nothing.—What a number of attempts they have made," I went on, "to account for the presence of evil! To get away, in fact, from the Creator's finding everything that He had made very good. They invented another woman by whom Adam had children before Eve was created from one of his ribs. That doesn't go very well with Adam's innocence until he and Eve had eaten the apple. And then there's that horrible and grotesque myth of Cain's being only half-brother to Abel, and the child of the Serpent by Eve."

Before the end of that walk, I said to him:

"When one has to do without the old-fashioned incentive of future reward and punishment, what's left is simply to go ahead and try to be decent because it's decent! 'One world at a time', as Emerson said to a friend."

"Precisely!" assented Roosevelt.

And so, although I never trespassed upon his reserve through that walk, and he never broke it, I know that our thoughts were in union; and his assent to my remark at the end indicates sufficiently well his feeling about the eternal mystery. He said once in the presence of Aleck Lambert, his friend and doctor, that no better supernatural hypothesis than the Manichee's had been offered.

It may very well have been the following day that I said to Mrs. Roosevelt:

"If they treated Theodore as they deal with certain composite substances in chemistry, and put him in a crucible, and melted him down and down until nothing of him remained at the bottom of the crucible but his ultimate, central, indestructible stuff, it's not a statesman that they'd find, or a hunter, or a historian, or a naturalist—they'd find a preacher militant."

Mrs. Roosevelt agreed.

More subjects came up between us in our walks that I have forgotten, or can remember; and of course many of these turned upon events of the moment. He referred once to his visit to the dying Quay, which had so scandalized the New York *Evening Post* and its disciples: Quay was so wicked, they said, that a person with Roosevelt's pretensions should be unwilling to have any dealings with him.

"I can't understand a creature who claims to be human not being ashamed of feeling like that," said Roosevelt. "But they're not even ashamed of making an indecent exposure of it to the world.    That old miscreant wanted to see me about a matter that was wholly unpolitical and which I think was closer to his heart than anything else.    He had Delaware Indian blood in his veins, and he was exceedingly proud of it.    During his life, he had always seen to it that these Indians were treated fairly.    No one knew better than he the injustice with which we have treated the Indians in general; and why he had begged me to come, and what he wanted to ask me was, to protect the interests of those Indians after he was gone."

On another occasion, being disgusted with the injurious stupidity that one of his pet creations, the Interstate Commerce Commission, was showing, I said:

"Look here.    I'm not crazy about some of the things they are doing.    I could do better myself!"

"My dear Dan, I'll not say that you couldn't!    But how many successful lawyers would be willing to do it for the salary our penny wise pound foolish Government pays?    Do you suppose any capable man would leave a lucrative business in these times for ten thousand dollars a year?    That's only enough to hire second rate people."

On two occasions, he took my head off.    About something he had done, I said:

"I don't see why on earth you saw fit to do that."

"That's because, my dear Dan, you don't happen to know anything about it!"    And he proceeded to give me the details and steps which led to it.

The other time was when I suggested, in pure mischief, at lunch, that since the law permitted as many successive wives as a man wished, I didn't see, when you remembered Abraham and others in the Bible, why simultaneous wives should not be as respectable now as they had been then.

"No, that's immoral," he said, with great severity.    "I'll not allow any discussion of it."

New fashioned as his public policies were, so abruptly novel as to set our whole generation agog; new and bold as his public utterances continued to be as long as he lived—so arresting in

both their matter and their manner, that when they ceased and
his voice spoke to us no more, it was a silence that could be felt
in the whole country, a dullness, a lost stimulant to the zest and
interest of life—notwithstanding this side of him, on another
side he was, and remained, conventional, old fashioned, just as
easily shocked by certain fundamental inevitabilities, just as
quick to shun a face to face contemplation of their existence, as
if he had sprung from the loins of New England, and was a
brother of the wilfully optimistic Emerson.   Tolstoy abstains
from censure of his characters when they do wrong, presents his
portrait of life to us without personal comment; Roosevelt
shakes his head in disapproval; a novelist should give us a lecture when his men and women misbehave.   Gorky, another
Russian, arrives here and asks to pay Roosevelt a visit.   Roosevelt, who went to the dying Quay, declines peremptorily to receive this writer.   He knew Gorky's fiction.   This would have
been enough for Roosevelt; but this was not all.   Gorky was accompanied by a person not his wife.   His wife had long been
shut up, hopelessly insane.   The companion who came to
America with him was no wanton; she devoted herself singly
to him, she was a superior and very courteous and considerate
person.   They would have been married, but for the Russian
rule which prevented a divorce of the deranged wife; while she
lived, Gorky could not remarry.   About this situation, accepted anywhere but here, Roosevelt felt as sternly as he did
about Gorky's political creed.   As President, with our social
conventions to uphold, and the outcry raised over Gorky and his
mistress, he was bound to decline to receive the Russian.   But it
was personal with him as well.   He considered Gorky "immoral,"
and that was enough for him; he would have declined to receive
Gorky at any time.   Roosevelt did not respect our social conventions when he held them to be wrong; he invited Booker
Washington, an honorable and useful citizen, but a negro, to
lunch at the White House.   Now I had come to dislike Tolstoy as much as he did, and I disliked Gorky as a morbid sen-
timentalist as much as he did: but I never dared to tell him

that I thought Gorky, sensationally ejected from New York hotels because of his not being married to his companion, and made a target for denunciation, had been very cruelly treated. He would have taken my head off: on his public side he could innovate, could disregard a convention which he thought wrong, and have Booker Washington to lunch; but never Gorky. And this rigid conventionalism going along with bold innovations somehow endeared him to me in a special way, for which I cannot account.

I would have dared readily enough to tell him, had I ever happened to think of it when I was with him, that his putting E. H. Harriman with Big Bill Haywood together in the class of undesirable citizens, was a stroke of injustice. Call them both undesirable if you like, but not equally. Harriman's offenses were those of his era; the purchase of political favors by powerful interests was an accepted practice. Harriman left many great railway systems in a better state than he had found them; he built up, he was a constructor. Haywood was by temperament a destroyer, with murder and bombs as his chief instruments; a malignant public enemy. I have seen many miscarriages of justice, but his escape from hanging is the most flagrant of the lot. The one type of citizen more undesirable than Haywood, is his sheltered, drawing-room sympathizer. If ever our Democracy by its excesses brings on itself a Mussolini, I think that it will be these parlor political perverts whom he will order first to be stood up against the wall.

It was on one of our Washington walks that Roosevelt's shy, old-fashioned reluctance to discuss, or even to hear about, a whole set of topics which offended his Puritanic sense of delicacy, showed itself once more. The mystery of the subject had aroused both the biological and artistic interest of my cousin Dr. Weir Mitchell. When I had broached my theory to Remington, he had already felt its truth without formulating it. Weir Mitchell has never looked at it in this way, he said. He thought there was something in it, though it lay not in the grasp of the exacting hands of science, but in the fascinating domain of guesses.   And so Weir Mitchell turned my suggestion over, both as the famous author of *Hugh Wynne* and other novels, and as the far more famous doctor, whose original scientific work had given him an international renown.   I had come to believe that an artist's creative power came not *from* his brain, but *through* it.

The *Faust* which the world knows, originated in a Goethe who was twenty-six; its sequel, the second *Faust*, came from a Goethe who was approaching eighty.   The first *Faust* was flesh and blood; the second mostly intellectual abstraction; thought unclothed with life; the product of a great mind from which the creative force had gone.   The *Romeos,* the *Hamlets,* the *Meistersingers,* the *Carmens,* any works of art, distilled their vitality from a source more elemental than intellect.   Once the generative power in a man had died, his intellect might go on producing brilliant abstractions but it could no longer transmit life to what it made.

All this set Weir Mitchell speculating: instances came to his mind; the span of generative power differed with individuals, like its intensity.   He turned the subject over for perhaps half an hour, talking more than I did.

Roosevelt did not stop me when I opened the theory to him; but if he turned it over, it was in silence.   Now and then he would say in rather a quiet tone: "Really!" or, "That is *very* interesting."   Nothing more.   He might almost have been a refined, nineteenth century lady, to whom I was making risqué remarks.   It ended by embarrassing me, and I was visited with inspiration.   I stopped short in our walk.

"But," I abruptly exclaimed, wheeling to him and pointing my finger at him impressively, "if I'm destined to reach the age of the white-bearded Faust, I trust I'll not summon Satan to rejuvenate me.   And what's more, I—don't—believe—*you* would."   I spaced my words in parody of his own manner when he grew emphatic.

Then I started on.   I think we must have gone fifty yards before he had done laughing.   Then I shifted to the less passionate theme of anthracite coal, and told him how George Baer lately at the Mahogany Tree had utterly reversed himself about the Coal Strike Commission.

## XVII.

Cabot Lodge, it may be recalled, bade me notice the big curly-haired man who stood close behind the President throughout the Diplomatic Reception, with a hand on his revolver ready for any one who might need a bullet. This perpetual hedging round her husband's safety must have put a strain upon Mrs. Roosevelt from which no absence from the White House could relieve her as absence did provide relief from her duties as mistress of the house and mother of her children. If she was away, she knew that her competent and delightful social secretary, Miss Hagner, could carry on as to those matters; as to the other—what wife could drive such a thing out of her thoughts and keep it out? But she gave no more sign of this preoccupation than as if it, too, had no existence for her. Already in our history we count three assassinated Presidents. No doubt Mrs. Roosevelt was visited at times by such reflections, no doubt when the telegram from Milwaukee reached her during that speaking tour in 1912, she thought, So it has come at last! Yet her telegram in answer merely suggested that he come to Sagamore Hill where he always rested well. With a husband who insisted on keeping his engagement, and addressed the audience for an hour and three-quarters with a bullet fresh in his chest, somebody had to be calm! On reaching the Chicago hospital, she ruled that sick room as quietly and absolutely as she had directed the White House.

Roosevelt took all such peril fatalistically—had it been her peril instead of his, it is not likely that he could have done so—and the only sign I ever saw him give that he was aware of its existence, was his impatience with those whose office it was to keep strangers from approaching him—as when, upon our starting for a walk, he would wave the Secret Service man away.

But that was outside the house; inside it was a different situation; both situations had to be watched, and silence had to be kept about incidents which occurred in the waiting room of the Executive Office.    Of course, if even a personal friend had come in there without an appointment, Mr. Loeb, the President's secretary, would have asked him to wait in any case, would never have showed him in during business hours without first finding out if the President could be interrupted; and when it was somebody unknown, the secretary very naturally had to be particularly sure what they wanted before he went any further.

Since those days, Mr. Loeb has told me a good deal about all that.    A number of things that I never imagined then, lay behind those impatient gestures to the Secret Service men.    Roosevelt protested to his secretary, he did not wish the Secret Service men to be dogging his steps.    The protest must have been made with some emphasis, for the secretary—who was officially charged with the protection of the President—was forced at length to declare that the President would have to put up with the Secret Service men, or do without his own services: he was to be sole judge of whatever precautions he thought necessary to the full performance of his duty.    He begged Roosevelt not to ask for any particulars as to why he deemed so much care essential.    And so Roosevelt, after some flouncing (as Washington described his own behavior before sitting for a portrait) gave in.

"Billy, you are perfectly right, and you will not hear another word of complaint from me," he said.

Mr. Loeb has given me two instances of the kind of particulars he begged Roosevelt not to ask him for, and I will quote his own account of them:

"My colored doorman brought in an engraved visiting card, which he said was that of a very high-class lady.    She was shown in, and I asked her what I could do for her.    She said that she must see the President, and only the President.    I told her that I would like to help her, but that she must first tell me the business that she wished to present.    She said that the Post Master at Pittsburgh had been opening her mail and she wished him

MRS. ROOSEVELT

removed.     I then said to her, 'Ah, that is a matter you should take up with the Postmaster General.'   She had been getting more and more excited, and at that point she opened up a large reticule she carried on the top of which reposed a pearl handled revolver which I grabbed before she could reach it. . . .

A Slav tailor turned up at the White House office, but was so incoherent and wild that the officers at once took charge of him. On the way to the police wagon, he whipped from the sleeve of his coat one of the blades of a tailor's shears which had been sharpened to a needle-point and he severely cut up one of the officers. . . ."

The high-class lady and her engraved card arrived with the pearl handled pistol late in 1905, the Slav tailor came with his blade up his sleeve early in 1906.   Between these, appeared Mrs. Minor Morris, January 4, 1906, another link in an endless chain of callers.   She wrote a poem about insomnia, which you may read in the *Congressional Record* covering June of that year; there also to be read are what sundry doctors had to say of her mental state, as well as the impassioned speeches of our statesmen.   The whole business fills a quantity of pages, with other business of really national moment intervening on different days.   It took me a long time to read it.

The affair was made one of national size with that same frenzy into which the chance for an investigation seems invariably to throw out members of Congress.   It was during this excitement that one of our legislators exclaimed so imaginatively that when the President of the United States stood in the presence of an American mother, he stood in the presence of his superior.

No more than when the engraved card lady or the Slav tailor paid their call, did the President stand in the presence of this visitor; he knew nothing about Mrs. Minor Morris until afterward.   It was not in the least to champion a helpless and insulted woman that Congress and certain newspapers raised their preposterous outcry; it was because of their rage over the Rate Bill, the Interstate Commerce Law, the Pure Food and Drugs Act, the Anti-Rebate Law, Employers' Liability, Gifford

Pinchot's very unpopular crusade against the waste of our forests: here was a chance to upset all this treading on toes of powerful profiteers by distorting the truth, and exciting the hasty emotions of the American people.   To turn popular sentiment against Roosevelt was why Congress talked through many large pages of the record.   A few sentences can tell the story.

Mrs. Morris arrived and told Assistant Secretary Barnes that she wished to see the President regarding her husband's dismissal from the army.   He referred her to the War Department; it was not a matter for the President to take up.   Presently she saw that the Secretary was not to be argued out of what he was there to do, namely, to shield the President's valuable hours of work, as well as his person, from importunate visitors.   Excitement gained upon Mrs. Morris, turned to rage; and on that she was asked to go.   She refused, then resisted an attempt to lead her out, and was then half carried out by two officers.   Away off in the house Mrs. Roosevelt heard her screams.   That is all.   It was painted redder and redder while the investigation went on.   As we put it nowadays, Mrs. Minor Morris had "asked for it," by her improper conduct.   The violence of Congress in magnifying so slight an affair is like a straw to show which way the wind was howling round Roosevelt.

When a President sits in political weather like that, is in fact the storm centre, with organized misrepresentation listening at the door and peeping through the key-hole to catch and distort and send flying to the four points of the compass every gesture that he makes and every syllable that he speaks, it behooves him to be circumspect.   And the politician in Roosevelt was remarkably canny, and loved to be, as any man loves to do the things he does well.   But Roosevelt also rejoiced in not being a politician, in throwing it off and dropping all caution, as he did with his Familiars.   And so it happened one day that he nearly put himself into what, but for his cat-like quickness at jumping, might have been a very disastrous hole indeed.

The tempest was raging, and organized misrepresentation on

the alert. Roosevelt was taking an hour off. During this interval of relaxation, the card of Professor Hugo Münsterberg, of Harvard, was brought him. He was glad to see the professor, who was making a tour of lectures upon the German Constitution. The historian in Roosevelt forgot all about the politician, the making of our own Constitution led him into an eager talk; he discussed some of the obstacles which the fathers of our Republic had to overcome, or side-step, and this brought him to Thomas Jefferson. He spoke his mind freely.

"You don't mean to zay so!" exclaimed Professor Hugo Münsterberg. "But after all—there iss the Declaration of Independence."

Roosevelt spoke his mind again freely.

"That is most inter-ez-ting," said the Professor. They talked a while longer, and he bowed himself out.

Presently he was speaking to an audience in a large Western city. During the course of his address, he made some remarks about Thomas Jefferson. These were not heartily received. He followed them with some criticisms on the turgid style of the Declaration of Independence, and these were still less well received.

"Well, anyway, ladies and gentlemen," said Professor Hugo Münsterberg, "those are the very worts of President Roosevelt, spoken by him to me in the White House last week."

Not many hours later, a newspaper correspondent laid a telegraphic report of those remarks before Roosevelt, and asked if he had anything to say.

"It is too ridiculous for comment," said Roosevelt instantly, and turned away to other business.

Less than a second's space had intervened between question and answer; just enough time for Roosevelt's eye to race through that telegraphic dispatch and see in the same flash big black capitals glaring across front pages of hostile newspapers: Roosevelt now assaults the memory of Thomas Jefferson! Spurns the Declaration of Independence! Harvard Professor aghast at display of despotic tendencies in President!

With that amazing indiscretion of Münsterberg's once in the hands of Congress and the enemy press, what would happen to Gifford Pinchot's forests, and the Pure Food and Drugs Act and Employers' Liability, and everything else?

"It is too ridiculous for comment."

Six prompt words, with the matter left there, other business taken up, and the newspaper correspondent free to draw his own conclusions.

"It was one of those quick remarks," wrote Mr. Chief Justice Taft, when I applied to him for verification of the anecdote, and for permission to tell it.   Here is the whole of his answer, of which a sentence to illustrate his generous amiability has already been quoted:

"What Dr. Thayer of Baltimore has said to you is quite true. You are a friend of Roosevelt, I know, and therefore would use the story in a way that would not bring any criticism upon Mr. Roosevelt, for I would not wish to circulate it and have any such result.   It was one of those quick remarks of his to avoid the unjustified curiosity of newspaper men looking for opportunity to criticize, and I am glad to think that it defeated a possible sinister purpose."

Possibly the purpose may have been sinister, but I do not feel as certain of this as I should if I knew which newspaper correspondent it was on that occasion.   Those fellows, no matter which newspaper they represented, had almost to a man been won over to a personal devotion to Roosevelt, merely through seeing him daily at close quarters, and thus coming to know him as he was much better than the politician who distorted him so busily.   Reporters are apt to be more decent than the papers they serve; this one and Roosevelt may have understood each other perfectly; he had his answer in a formula that relieved him of all professional responsibility.   Professor Hugo Münsterberg never rose to the eminence of defeating, even unintentionally, Roosevelt's policies; the story was "killed."

It astonished me that a friend to whom I repeated this, should think it not to Roosevelt's credit.

C. K. Berryman in the Washington *Evening Star*.

"Then," said I, "while Walter Scott was doing his best to keep the authorship of the Waverley novels a secret, and a lady asked him straight out before a lot of people one day if he had written them, you think it was his duty to the truth to say that he had, instead of saying that he hadn't, which is the answer that he gave the indiscreet lady?"

Let us imagine an outsider approaching George Washington on a day in December, 1776, and inquiring if it were true that the General planned to cross the Delaware and attack the Hessians at Trenton on the coming Christmas night. This is conceivable; but it is not conceivable that Washington would have acknowledged the fact. To any young man who should ask my advice as to his proper reply to an improper and impertinent piece of inquisitiveness, when the truth would be disastrous, I should answer:

"Lie at once and invariably."


## XVIII.

Although Roosevelt had not been re-elected to the Presidency in November, 1904, he chose to call it his second term; and on receiving definite news of his election, he gave out immediately, the same night, that statement that in no circumstances would he be a candidate for re-nomination. Looking back across twenty-five years upon all that was to follow, and how those who were waiting till he should be out of their way used that statement in a twisted interpretation against him—made it to seem not only that it was a promise given in *exchange* for his election, instead of a gratuitous outburst after his election, but also that it was a promise *never at any time in the future* to run again—Mrs. Roosevelt's remark that she would not have allowed him to make the statement, had she been at hand, seems like a prophecy.

Between the election and the new year, I have no remembrance of any talk with him, except by correspondence, until a telegram from Mr. Loeb on January 12; "the President says to

come in at six o'clock Friday and if possible stay to dinner at
seven thirty." This visit was made between trains. I was on
my way South, and spent about three hours at the White House,
of which my vivid recollection is Cecil Lyon, the Rough Rider.
I was a dazzled listener. The President and his favorite Rough
Rider, a fast and firm and intimate friend, whom he had often
hoped I would meet, talked Spanish War and Southwestern politics, while my hair stood most agreeably on end until it was
time for me to go. To my joy and pride, Cecil Lyon went with
me, enticed me to some place where I met a Southwestern friend
of his, and hypnotized me into drinking champagne, which I did
willingly, though feebly; and then departed for the sleeping car
to Camden, South Carolina. There the Editor of *The Saturday
Evening Post* once again called upon me for an article about
Roosevelt—This time at the close, instead of on the threshold of
his first administration—and I should have forgotten all about it,
but for a line from the White House on March 6, 1905: "I liked
your article on the Square Deal." Finding this note has touched
my memory up and reminded me that while I was writing that
article at Camden, I asked him to send me the official particulars about the affair at Indianola. This had raised one of
those tempests of the same kind (but in different quarters)
as silly and as violent as the affair of Mrs. Minor Morris—
which it preceded by a year or so. The official particulars arrived at Camden promptly—quite a *dossier* of type-writing,
which I must have destroyed after making whatever use of it
that I did for *The Saturday Evening Post*. But he must have
forgotten that he ever had this sent me, for he goes over
the whole thing again in the longest letter I ever had from
him.

After *The Virginian* had headed the foolish and meaningless
list of "best sellers" long enough to be a source of material
satisfaction to its publisher and its author, George P. Brett,
president of the Macmillan Company, told me that he could
promise me a very remunerative public if I followed that story
by another cow-boy story. I told him this was precisely what

I did not intend to do; I had written four volumes about the West; I expected to write more, but not just then; I wished to turn to other themes for a while, even if the box-office receipts should fall away.   George Brett was splendid.   He said, Write whatever you feel moved to write; as a business matter, I had to say what I did; but your plan is the better one for your own sake in the long run.   So I wrote a novel about Charleston, South Carolina, and followed this by a short biography of George Washington for the sake of adding something in the same line as my short biography of General Grant.   The box-office receipts did fall off, of course; I doubt if George Brett cared very much, and I didn't care at all.   The people whose opinion I valued more than cash, read both books—and I was able to build a house in Rhode Island for Summer weather with the royalties from *Lady Baltimore*.

Our Winter of 1902 in Charleston, where I had completed *The Virginian*, left a wonderful and sad impression, which as time went on aroused a persistent longing.   In my mind I had known well enough since childhood—and my study for General Grant had much deepened this knowledge—that our Civil War was a tragedy which had broken many hearts both North and South; but when I saw Charleston, it seemed to me *the* tragedy of all, except Lincoln.   Whatever these people had done—and my political faith was wholly Union—obliteration was a heavier punishment than they deserved.   They had taken a splendid hand in the first making of our country, and the civilization they had produced was altogether the most civilized in the United States.   A Bostonian who had known it well in its flower, the wife of the great Agassiz, told me while talking to me in her house in Cambridge about *Lady Baltimore,* that she had recognized this upon her first visit as a young woman to South Carolina, which must have been during the fifties, or even earlier. Here it was now, fifty years after, in its dying embers, that civilization, first beaten down by a war that it had undoubtedly precipitated, and then trodden out by the infamy of Reconstruction.   It had been founded, true enough, on the crime of slavery, but this crime was not its own, it was part of its inheritance from England. Moreover, I had found in Charleston, and wherever I had gone in the South, many more people, whether urban or rustic, who were the sort of people I was, with feelings and thoughts and general philosophy and humor and faith and attitude toward life like my own: *Americans;* with whom I felt just as direct a national kinship as I felt with the Western cowpunchers, and which I feel less and less in places like New York, Boston, and Philadelphia, that are affected by too many people of differing traditions.

So I wrote *Lady Baltimore,* not as a tragedy but as a comedy; calling Charleston Kings Port, owing to the suggestion made by Henry James that I invent some slight disguise for the real name; it would help me to move more freely. Into the action of the comedy, I wove the incident of Dr. Crum's appointment as Collector of the Port; and because it was a very delicate matter to write about so small a community, I got two members of that community, survivors of Charleston's great civilization, to read every word of the story before it went to the printer. When the book appeared, I sent the first copy to my cousin, Dr. Weir Mitchell, to whom it was dedicated, and the second to Roosevelt.

The numerous changes and interpolations in his own handwriting through the fifteen type-written pages of his letter, show that he must have gone over it minutely. His indictment against the slave-holding minority who took the Confederacy into the Civil War, cannot be answered; it is borne out to the full in the thorough and dispassionate pages of James Ford Rhodes; but I have never been able to agree with some of his other severities about those unfortunate people. Was he still stirred up about the Indianola affair? Would he reiterate to-day his opinion, unmoderated? Who can tell? But I have accepted the objections to my book that he makes in his postscript. When I came to prepare the novel for the uniform edition of my books in 1928, a good many sentences were changed and quite a number of paragraphs wholly omitted.

THE WHITE HOUSE

Washington

Personal.                                    April 27, 1906.

DEAR DAN:—

That I have read Lady Baltimore with interest and that I think it a very considerable book the length of this letter will show. If my wife were to write the letter it would be one of almost undiluted praise, because she looked at it simply as a work of art, simply as a story, and from either standpoint it is entitled to nothing but admiration. The description of the people and of their surroundings will always live in my memory, and will make me continually turn back to read bits of the book here and there. Moreover, (to a man of my possibly priggish way of looking at novels), the general tone of the book is admirable, and to one who does not look at it in any way as a tract of the times it leaves the right impression of sturdy protest against what is sordid, against what is mere spangle-covered baseness, against brutal greed and sensuality and vacuity; it teaches admiration of manliness and womanliness, as both terms must always be understood by those capable of holding a high ideal.

But I am afraid the book cannot but be considered save as in part a tract of the times, and from this standpoint, in spite of my hearty sympathy with your denunciation of the very things that you denounce and your admiration of the very things that you admire, I cannot but think that at the best you will fail to do good, and that at the worst you may do harm, by overstating your case. The longer I have been in public life, and the more zealous I have grown in movements of true reform, the greater the horror I have come to feel for the exaggeration which so often defeats its own object. It is needless to say to you that the exaggeration can be just as surely shown as in any other way by merely omitting or slurring over certain important facts. In your remarkable little sketch of Grant, by reciting with entire truth certain facts of Grant's life and passing over with insufficient notice the remainder you could have drawn a picture of him as a drunken, brutal and corrupt incapable, a picture in which almost every detail in the framework would have been true in itself, but in which the summing up and general effect would have been quite as false as if the whole had been a mere invention. Now, of course, I don't mean that this is true of Lady Baltimore. You call attention to some mighty ugly facts and tendencies in our modern American civilization, and it is because I so earnestly wish to see the most effective kind of warfare waged against exactly what you denounce that I regret you did not put your denunciation in a way which would accomplish more good. In the first place, though it may have been all right from the standpoint of the story, from the standpoint of the tract it was a capital error to make your swine-devils practically all northerners and your angels practically all southerners. You speak so sweepingly, moreover, that you clearly leave the impression of intending the swine-devils to be representative not of a small section of the well-to-do North, but of the overwhelming majority of the well-to-do North; indeed, of the North which leads. Now, as a matter of fact (remember I am speaking from the standpoint of the tract) the contrast could have been made with much more real truth between northerners and northerners, for then there would not have been a strong tendency to divert the attention from the difference of quality to the difference of locality, and to confound this difference of quality with difference of locality.

In the next place, I do not regard your sweeping indictment of the northern people as warranted. That there is an immense amount of swinish greed in northern business circles and of vulgarity and vice and vacuity and extravagance in the social life of the North, I freely admit. But I am not prepared to say that these are the dominant notes in either the business life or the social life of the North. I know they are not the only notes. I am struck, whenever I visit a college, whenever I have a chance to meet the people of any city or town, with the number of good, straight, decent people with whom I am brought in contact, with the number of earnest young fellows with high purpose whom I meet, with the sweet young girls whom I see. The men I get together to settle the Anthracite Coal Strike, the men I see when there is a scientific gathering in Washington, the artists like Saint Gaudens and French and MacMonnies, the writers like Crowther and Hyde, the men of the army whom I meet, the young fellows with whom I am brought in contact in doing political work, the families with whom I am intimate, yours, the Grant La Farges, the Gilders, my cousins, the Bacons, and so I could go on indefinitely—all these go to show that the outlook is in no shape or way one of unrelieved gloom. There is plenty of gloom in it, but there is plenty of light also, and if it is painted as all gloomy, I am afraid the chief effect will be to tend to make people believe that either it is all black or else it is all white; and in its effect one view is just as bad as the other. Smash vacuous, divorce-ridden Newport; but don't forget Saunderstown and Oyster Bay!

You also continually speak as if we have fallen steadily away from the high standard of our past. Now I am unable to say exactly what the proportion of good and evil are in the present, but I have not the slightest doubt that they are quite as favorable as in the past. I have studied history a good deal and it is a matter of rather grim amusement to me to listen to the praise bestowed on our national past at the expense of our national present. Have you ever read Leckey's account of the Revolutionary war? It is perhaps a trifle too unfavorable to us, but is more nearly accurate than any other I have seen. Beyond all question we ought to have fought that war; and it was very creditable to Washington and some of his followers and to a goodly portion of the Continental troops; but I cannot say that it was very creditable to the nation as a whole. There were two and a half millions of us then, just ten times as many as there were of the Boers in South Africa, and Great Britain was not a fourth as strong as she was in the Boer war, and yet on the whole I think the Boers made a good deal better showing than we did. My forefathers, northerners and southerners alike, fought in the Revolutionary army and served in the Continental Congress, and one of them was the first Revolutionary governor of Georgia, so that I am not prejudiced against our Revolutionary people. But while they had many excellent qualities I think they were lacking as a whole in just the traits in which we are lacking to-day; and I do not think they were as fine, on the whole, as we are now. The second greatest Revolutionary figure, Franklin, to my mind embodied just precisely the faults which are most distrusted in the average American of the North to-day. Coming down to after the Revolution, we have never seen a more pitiful exhibition of weakness at home or a greater mixture of blustering insolence and incapacity in reference to affairs abroad than was shown under Jefferson and Madison. So I could go on indefinitely. But let me take only what I have myself seen; where I can speak as a witness and participator. Thirty years ago politics in this country were distinctly more corrupt than they are now, and I believe that the general tone was a little more sordid and that there was a little less of realizable idealism. The social life in New York was not one bit better than it is now.

Gould, Sage, Daniel Drew, the elder Vanderbilt, Jim Fisk and the other financiers of the day of that type were at the very least as bad as the corresponding men of to-day.  No financier at present would dare perpetrate the outrages that Huntington was perpetrating some thirty years ago.  Nothing so bad has been done in the insurance companies as was done in the "Chapter of Erie."  The Newport set is wealthier and more conspicuous now, and I think the divorce business is more loathsome, but I would certainly hesitate to say that things were worse than then, taking it as a whole.  The Porcellian Club of the last ten years, for instance, averages at least as well as the Porcellian Club for the ten years before I went into it.  Among my own friends and in the little circle in which I live at Oyster Bay I don't see that there is any difference of an essential kind as compared with my father's friends and with the circle in which he lived.  In the Civil War our people—a mere democracy— were better than in the Revolution, when they formed in part a provincial aristocracy.

When you come to the South and imply or express comparison between the South and the North, I again think you have over-stated it.  I am half a southerner myself.  I am as proud of the South as I am of the North.  The South has retained some barbaric virtues which we have tended to lose in the North, partly owning to a mistaken pseudo-humanitarianism among our ethical creatures, partly owning to persistence in and perhaps the development of those business traits which, however, distinguished New York, New England and Pennsylvania a century ago just as they do to-day.  On the other hand the southerners have developed traits of a very unhealthy kind.  They are not as dishonest as, they do not repudiate their debts as frequently, as their predecessors did in the good old times from which you think we have deteriorated; but they do not send as valuable men into the national councils as the northerners.  They are not on the whole as efficient, and they exaggerate the common American tendency of using bombastic language which is not made good by performance.  Your particular heroes, the Charleston aristocrats, offer as melancholy an example as I know of people whose whole life for generations has been warped by their own wilful perversity.  In the early part of South Carolina's history there was a small federalist party and later a small and dwindling union party within the State, of which I cannot speak too highly. But the South Carolina aristocrats, the Charleston aristocrats and their kinsfolk in the up-country (let me repeat that I am of their blood, that my ancestors before they came to Georgia were members of these very South Carolina families of whom you write) have never made good their pretentions.   They were no more to blame than the rest of the country for the slave trade of colonial days, but when the rest of the country woke up they shut their eyes tight to the horrors, they insisted that the slave trade should be kept, and succeeded in keeping it for a quarter of a century after the Revolutionary war closed, they went into secession partly to re-open it.   They drank and dueled and made speeches, but they contributed very, very little toward anything of which we as Americans are now proud.   Their life was not as ignoble as that of the Newport people whom you rightly condemn, yet I think it was in reality an ignoble life. South Carolina and Mississippi were very much alike.   Their two great men of the deified past were Calhoun and Jefferson Davis, and I confess, I am unable to see wherein any conscience-less financier of the present day is worse than these two slave owners who spent their years in trying to feed their thirst for personal power by leading their followers to the destruction of the Union.   Remember that the Charleston aristocrats (under Yancey) wished to reopen the slave trade at the time of the out-break of the Civil War.   Reconstruction was a mistake as it was actually carried out, and there is very much to reprobate in what was done by Sumner and Seward and their followers. But the blame attaching to them is as nothing compared to the blame attaching to the southerners for forty years preceding the war, and for the years immediately succeeding it.   There never was another war, so far as I know, where it can be honestly and truthfully said as of this war that the right was wholly on one side, and the wrong wholly on the other.   Even the courage and prowess of those South Carolina aristocrats were shown only at the expense of their own country, and only in the effort to tear in sunder their country's flag.   In the Revolutionary war, in that remote past which you idealize, as compared to the present, the South Carolinians made as against the British a fight which can only be called respectable.   There was little heroism; and Marion and Sumter, in their fight against Tarleton and the other British commanders, show at a striking disadvan-tage when compared with DeWet and Delarey and the other Boer leaders.   In the war of 1812 South Carolina did nothing. She reserved her strength until she could strike for slavery and against the Union. Her people have good stuff in them, but I do not think they are entitled to over praise as compared to the North. As for the days of reconstruction, they brought their punishment absolutely on themselves, and are, in my judgment, entitled to not one particle of a sympathy. The North blundered, but its blunders were in trying to do right in the impossible circumstances which the South had itself created, and for which the South was solely responsible.

Now as to the negroes! I entirely agree with you that as a race and in the mass they are altogether inferior to the whites. Your small German scientific friend had probably not heard of the latest scientific theory—doubtless itself to be superseded by others—which is that the negro and the white man as shown by their skulls, are closely akin, and taken together, differ widely from the round skulled Mongolian. But admitting all that can be truthfully said against the negro, it also remains true that a great deal that is untrue is said against him; and that much more is untruthfully said in favor of the white man who lives beside and upon him. Your views of the negro are those expressed by all of your type of Charlestonians. You must forgive my saying that they are only expressed in their entirety to those who don't know the facts. Are you aware that these white men of the South who say that the negro is unfit to cast a vote, and who by fraud or force prevent his voting, are equally clamorous in insisting that his votes must be counted as cast when it comes to comparing their own representation with the representation of the white men of the North? The present leader of the Democrats in the House of Representatives is John Sharp Williams, a typical southerner of the type you mention. In his district three out of every four men are negroes; the fourth man, a white man, does not allow any of these negroes to vote, but insists upon counting their votes, so that his one vote offsets the votes of four white men in New York, Massachusetts or Pennsylvania. During my term as President bills have been introduced to cut down the southern representation so as to have it based in effect only on the white vote. With absolute unanimity the southerners have declared that to deprive them of the right of the extra representation, which as white men they get by the fraudulent or violent suppression of the black vote, is an outrage. With their usual absurd misuse of nomenclature they inveigh against the effort to prevent them crediting themselves with the votes of which they deprive others as "waving the bloody shirt," or being a plea for "negro domination." Your Charleston friends lead this outcry and are among the chief beneficiaries, politically, of the fraud and violence which they triumphantly defend. The North takes absolutely no interest in any such measure, and so far from having any feeling against the South or giving any justification for the South's statement that it wants to interfere with the South's concerns, it is really altogether too indifferent to what is done in the South.

Now remember, Dan, what I am saying has nothing to do with the right of the negro to vote, or of his unfitness generally to exercise that right. It has to do simply with the consistent dishonesty championed and gloried in by your special southern friends who will not allow the negro to vote and will not allow the nation to take notice of the fact that he is not voting; and insist upon his vote counted so as to enable them to overcome the honest white northern vote. I may add that my own personal belief is that the talk about the negro having become worse since the Civil war is the veriest nonsense. He has on the whole become better. You say you would not like to take orders from a negro yourself. If you had played football in Harvard at any time during the last fifteen years you would have had to do so, and you would not have minded it in the least; for during that time Lewis has been field captain and a coach. When I was in Charleston at the exposition the very Charlestonians who had hysterics afterwards over Crum's appointment as collector of the port, assured me that Crum was one of the best citizens of Charleston, a very admirable man in every way, and while they protested that negroes ought not to be appointed as postmasters they said there was no such objection to appointing them in other places, and specifically mentioned the then colored collector of customs in Savannah as a case in point. You cannot be more keenly aware than I am of the fact that our effort to deal with the negro has not been successful. Whatever I have done with him I have found has often worked badly; but when I have tried to fall in with the views of the very southern people, which in this volume you seem to be upholding, the results have been worse than in any other way. These very people whose views you endorse are those who have tried to reintroduce slavery by the infamous system of peonage; which, however, I think in the last three years we have pretty well broken up. I am not satisfied that I acted wisely in either the Booker Washington dinner or the Crum appointment, though each was absolutely justified from every proper standpoint save that of expediency. But the anger against me was just as great in the communities where I acted exactly as the Charlestonians said I ought to act. I know no people in the North so slavishly conventional, so slavishly afraid of expressing any opinion hostile to or different from that held by their neighbors, as is true of the southerners, and most especially of the Charleston aristocrats, on all vital questions. They shriek in public about miscegenation, but they leer as they talk to me privately of the colored mistresses and colored children of the white men whom they know. Twice southern senators who in the Senate yell about the purity of the white blood, deceived me into appointing postmasters whom I found had colored mistresses and colored children. Are you acquainted with the case of the Indianola post office in Mississippi? I found in office there a colored woman as postmaster. She and her husband were well-to-do, and were quite heavy tax-payers. She was a very kindly, humble and respectable colored woman. The best people of the town liked her. The two bankers of the town, one of them the Democratic State senator, were on her bond. I reappointed her, and the Senators from Mississippi moved her confirmation. Afterwards the low whites in the town happened to get stirred up by the arrival of an educated colored doctor. His practice was of course exclusively among the negroes. He was one of those men who are painfully educating themselves, and whose cases are more pitiful than the cases of any other people in our country, for they not only find it exceedingly difficult to secure a livelihood but are followed with hatred by the very whites who ought to wish them well. Too many southern people and too many northern people, repeat like parrots the statement that these "educated darkies" are "a deal worse than the old darkies." As a matter of fact almost all the Tuskegee students do well. This particular negro doctor took away the negro patients from the lowest white doctors of the town. They instigated the mob which held the mass meeting and notified the negro doctor to leave town at once; which to save his life he did that very night. Not satisfied with this, the mob then notified the colored postmistress that she must at once resign her office. The "best citizens" of the town did what throughout the South the "best citizens" of the type you praise almost always do in such emergencies; that is they "deprecated" the conduct of the mob and said it was "not representative of the real southern feeling;" and then added that to save trouble the woman must go! She went. The mayor and the sheriff notified her and me that they could not protect her if she came back. . . . I shut up the office for the remainder of her term. It was all I could do and the least I could do. Now, Dan, so far from there being any reprobation of this infamy the entire South screamed for months over the outrage of depriving the citizens of Indianola of their mail simply because they let a mob chase away by threats of murder a worthy, refined, educated and hard working colored woman whom every reputable citizen of that town had endorsed for the position! This is at present the typical southern attitude toward the best type of colored men or colored women; and absolutely all I have been doing is to ask, not that the average negro be allowed to vote, not that ninety-five per cent of the negroes be allowed to vote, not that there be negro domination in any shape or form, but that these occasionally good, well-educated, intelligent and honest colored men and women be given the pitiful chance to have a little reward, a little respect, a little regard, if they can by earnest useful work succeed in winning it. The best people in the south I firmly believe are with me in what I have done. In Trinity College in North Carolina, in Roanoke College, Virginia, here and there elsewhere, they have stood up manfully for *just what I have done*. The bishops of the Episcopal church have for the most part stood up for it. The best southern judges have stood up for it. In so standing up all of these college professors and students, bishops and occasional business men have had to face the violent and angry assaults of the majority; and in Lady Baltimore you give what strength you can to those denouncing and opposing the men who are doing their best to bring a little nearer the era of right conduct in the South.

Now Dan, I have written to you as I should only write to a dear friend whose book is a power, and who has written about things as to which I think I know a good deal, and as to which I hold convictions down to the very bottom of my heart.

Can't you get on here soon and spend a night or two? I will get Root and Bob Bacon and Taft to come to dinner and perhaps Moody, and I will tell you in full detail some of the various facts about the North and South on which I base my beliefs.

With love to Mrs. Wister,

Ever yours,

THEODORE ROOSEVELT.

P.S.  Have you read "Democracy," a novel published nearly
thirty years ago?  Of course you have read "Martin Chuzzlewit," published over sixty years ago.  Each deals mainly with
the society of the North; each makes a number of statements
which are true as isolated facts; and each would go to show
worse conditions than those you set forth.  I think poorly of
the author of "Democracy," whoever he or she may have been;
but Dickens was a great writer, and the American characters in
"Martin Chuzzlewit" are types that are true as well as amusing,
and the book itself is valuable as a tract even to-day; yet as a
picture of the social life of the United States at the time which
you are tempted to idealize, it is false because it suppresses or
slurs over so much of the truth.  Now in each of these books,
as in yours, I eagerly welcome the assault on what is evil; but I
think that it hinders instead of helping the effort to secure something like a moral regeneration if we get the picture completely
out of perspective by slurring over some facts and over-empha-
sizing others.

David Graham Phillips has written a book called "The Plum-
Tree."  I only read the first half.  In it he portrays all politics
as sordid, base and corrupt.  Sinclair, the socialist, has written
a book called "The Jungle," about the labor world in Chicago.
He portrays the results of the present capitalistic system in
Chicago as on one uniform level of hideous horror.  Now there
is very much which needs merciless attack both in our politics
and in our industrial and social life.  There is much need for
reform; but I do not think the two books in question, though
they have been very widely read and are very popular and have
produced a great effect, have really produced a healthy effect,
simply because, while they set forth many facts which are true,
they convey an entirely false impression when they imply that
these are the only facts that are true and that the whole life is
such as they represent it.  Of course "Lady Baltimore" is the
work of a master and so can not be compared with either of these
two books; but as a tract on the social life of the North; as compared with the North's past and the South's present, it really
seems to me to be about as inaccurate as they are; and what is
more, it produces the very feeling which makes men followers
of David Graham Phillips, the Hearst writer, and of Sinclair,
the socialist, and which makes them feel that there is no use of
trying to reform anything because everything is so rotten that
the whole social structure should either be let alone or destroyed.

One may feel pretty sure that many brains have existed along the course of the centuries, equipped with every faculty to accomplish something of mark, except the driving power, just as even the most excellent locomotive can only crawl along unless its steam is kept at a certain pressure.  At the time Roosevelt wrote that letter he was going at top speed with several reform measures, each of which was designed to shear somebody's excess of power, and consequently had its group of determined enemies in Congress.  But he drove so hard that he broke through their opposition and left them uttering various imprecations of defeat—such as these from Senator Tillman, whom it will be remembered that he once invited and then uninvited to dinner.

"If the country wants to go to the dogs or the devil along the lines of changing the form of the Government and surrendering the rights of the people into the keeping of one man, I suppose I will have to stand it."

The rights of the people were being surrendered in the form of thirty-six indictments and nine convictions against railroads under the Anti-Rebate Law, the railroads being the people in this instance; the stopping of several thefts of Government land by large corporations and powerful magnates, who were the people here; and compelling Chicago packers and makers of patent medicine to print truthfully on their labels outside their bottles and cans what was inside: and to see what the newspapers, even democratic newspapers often opposed to Roosevelt on purely party grounds, had to say about these results of his measures, it looks as if the people had very much liked to have their rights surrendered in this manner.  And yet, in some nook of his brains, he was carrying *Lady Baltimore* along, even after he had already unburdened himself at such length on that subject.  He wrote again, May 3, 1906:

May 3, 1906.

DEAR DAN:

Yesterday I received a letter containing the following sentences:

"I suppose you read what Adams said about the negro in the May Century. That question will never be settled, just as conflict between capital and labor will never be settled. They both take on phases acute or mild according to conditions. You have done more than any living man to make the negro question take on a mild aspect."

It is written by J. M. Dickinson, of Tennessee, a Mississippian by birth, an ex-Confederate who was Solicitor General under Cleveland and is now a leading lawyer of Chicago. He is a Democrat who voted for Parker. It is very difficult for a man to be sure that a man who passes judgment on his acts to his face is telling the truth. What Judge Dickinson has said is precisely what Governor Aycock, of North Carolina, has told me; what Governor Montague, of Virginia, has told me; as well as Senator Clay, of Georgia, General Luke Wright, of Tennessee, and the entire Louisiana delegation in Congress, as well as Judge Jones, of Alabama. Personally, I believe that it expresses the very best sentiment, the most intelligent sentiment in the South. The most earnest, intelligent, and honest-minded young men of the South, like those of Trinity College, North Carolina, are if anything inclined to feel that I have been slightly over-cautious. I do not believe that the feeling of those Charlestonians which impressed you so much represents anything substantial save the survival of the old Yancey slave-trade reopening feeling. It is a feeling which, if it had its way, would even now plunge portions of the South down that short and evil path which ends in the Avernus of Haiti.

I know the negro fairly well. I have seen him at close quarters in the Yazoo delta, where he formed ninety per cent of the population, and where universal suffrage in his hand is the veriest criminal farce. I see the hideous difficulties of any solution of the problem. The solution of the impracticable visionaries who adored Sumner and still adore his memory, was perhaps the very worst, save only the solution advocated by the extreme reactionaries of the type of your attractive South Carolinians.

One word more as to what you say of the North. Remember, I agree with you entirely as to the evils you denounce. There are points in which we are worse than we were thirty or sixty or ninety years ago. But there are other points as regards which we are better. My plea is merely for that sense of proportion which can come only if the good and bad are presented as they stand relatively to each other.

Ever yours,
THEODORE ROOSEVELT.

Mr. Owen Wister,
 328 Chestnut St.
  Philadelphia.

I seem to have stayed with him immediately after this; on May 7 he writes my wife:

May 7, 1906.

MY DEAR MRS. WISTER:

That is a nice note of yours and I thank you for it.   It was such a pleasure to have Dan here.

With warm regards,

Sincerely yours,
THEODORE ROOSEVELT.

Mrs. Owen Wister,
 328 Chestnut St.,
  Philadelphia.

Evidently, however, we did not finish *Lady Baltimore* in conversation.   A few weeks later there is more of it:

June 21, 1906.

DEAR DAN:

I have received a letter running as follows, which portrays what has now happened in connection with the Cox family at Indianola:

"It will interest you to know that the Cox family, over whom such a disturbance was made in connection with the Indianola, Miss., post office, have started a bank in that same town which direct and reliable information convinces me is in a prosperous condition.   The bank has the confidence of both races.   It is a curious circumstance that while objection was made to this black family being at the head of the post office, no objection is made to the black man being president of a bank in the same town.

"A letter just received from a reliable banker in Mississippi contains the following sentences:

" 'Now with reference to Mr. W. W. Cox, of Indianola, Miss.,

I beg to advise that no man of color is as highly regarded and
respected by the white people of his town and county as he.    It
is true that he organized and is cashier of the Delta Penny Sav-
ings Bank, domiciled there.    I visited Indianola during the
spring of 1905 and was very much surprised to note the esteem
in which he was held by the bankers and business men (white)
of that place.    He is a good clean man and above average in intelligence, and knows how to handle the typical southern white
man.    In the last statement furnished by his bank to the State
Auditor, his bank showed total resources of $46,000.    He owns
and lives in one of the best resident houses in Indianola, regardless of race, and located in a part of the town where other
colored men seem to be not desired.    The whites adjacent to him
seem to be his friends.    He has a large plantation near the town,
worth $35,000 or $40,000.    He is a director in Mr. Pettiford's
bank at Birmingham, and I think is vice-president of the same.
He also owns stock in the Bank of Mound Bayou.' "

You will remember that in my letter, before the last I furnished you full facts about this case.    The Coxes are the new
Negroes of the generation that has grown up since the war; the
educated Negroes, the very type to which Charleston "aristocrats" have objected and about which they lie so unblushingly.
The Indianola white people are of the stamp of these Charleston people.    Some of them took part in turning out, and the
other acquiesced in turning out, of office this woman.    The
Charleston papers went into hysterics over my actions, portray-
ing it as part of my general plan for "Negro domination", miscegenation", and the like.    Bands of valorous "southrons" from
Arkansas and other seats of culture volunteered to rush to the
defense of the imperiled white race in Indianola, and join in
mobbing or killing the colored postmistress—who had already
served there for six years and who was backed by all their
decent citizens.    I told you what ultimately happened.    This
woman and her husband came to the conclusion that perhaps
their death, certainly the destruction of their property, would
follow any effort of the woman to retain her office; and the
Mayor and Sheriff said they could not protect her.    Out she
went.    Now the fantastic fools and moral cowards who encouraged or permitted the mob to turn her out are depositing their
funds in the husband's bank and have him as a director in a white
bank, and she and her husband own one of the best houses in
Indianola and one of the best plantations in the neighborhood.

Exactly what scheme of morals or intelligence can justify the theory that the Coxes are excellent bankers, should be encouraged as such, and are excellent postmasters up to the time a mob objects, but that if the mob chooses to jeopardize them they are not to be protected, I am really unable to understand.

Ever yours,

T. R.

Does anybody read *Lady Baltimore* to-day? Baedeker's Guide to the United States recommends it, but this is for foreign, not American eyes. A recent critic of my scribblings, who chooses for his praise only my most disagreeable Western stories, which he feels may therefore possibly be true to a life that he never saw, finds the picture of Charleston "a total loss." Besides the letters from Roosevelt, the book brought enough comments, public and private, to fill quite a number of pages in *Babel*. *Babel* is my scrap book. When it had reached volume 6 some twenty years ago, I grew tired of compiling it. I wish I hadn't. Time imbues even trifles with interest. Somebody, who remained anonymous, was moved by *Lady Baltimore* to quote me this from the book:

" 'We were the victors, we the North, and we had gone upon our way with songs and rejoicing—able to forget, because we were the victors. We had our victory: but the vanquished have their memory. But here was the cry of the vanquished coming after forty years. . . . The poetess had come after it was all over. Why should she prolong such memories and feelings!' "

Of this she has to say:

"Not only has the poet come but the historian, and the latter shows how your 'rejoicing' should be turned into mourning, how repentance should follow the most unjust war in modern times. Pause in your complacency and consider the wrongs perpetuated and the evil consequences in destroying the federal character of the U. S. Government and violating the principles of 1776.

*"A Daughter of the Confederacy."*

But this Daughter is not done with me. Her postscript quotes me some more from *Lady Baltimore:*

" 'If my state seceded from the Union to-morrow (state in the book written with a small s and Union with a big U!) I should side with the Union against it.' "

My capital U and small s, indicating my belief that the whole is greater than any part, strikes her as flagrant heresy.   She continues:

"To this utterly ridiculous and plainly unlawful position has the modern Republican come!   See the Ratifications of the Federal Constitution.   This compact had been reached upon the basis (1) That each State was an individual sovereign voluntarily entering the new organization; (2) That as States they each gave—did not receive but gave—existence to and surrendered under certain conditions part of their sovereignty to the Federal Government.   There were two things which the ratifying ordinances emphasized: (1) State sovereignty shall lie dormant; (2) Conditions under which it may be used or recalled.

"Northern Rebellion and Southern Secession" p. 18, 19. By E. W. R. Erving, LL.B. Richmond, Va. J. L. Hill Company, 1904."

I still remain in my "utterly ridiculous and plainly unlawful position": if my state seceded from the Union, I would side with the Union against her.

The question has been purely academic since April 12, 1861, when the Confederacy took its case to the Supreme Court of war by firing on the flag of the Union at Fort Sumter in Charleston harbor, and the Union joined issue.   This Supreme Court handed down its decision on April 9, 1865, when Robert E. Lee surrendered to U. S. Grant at Appomattox.   To keep sacred the memory of all their heroes, is the pious and fitting office of the Daughters of the Confederacy; had they attended with equal piety to the grave counsel of their chief hero, Robert E. Lee, and followed his example of putting sectional rancor behind them, they would not be to-day the only enemies of the South that are left.

The other specimen I select from *Babel* is likewise anonymous:

"Wouldn't (not hadn't—see Ps. 7 and 12 'Lady Baltimore') you better study your grammar rather than indite books to Dr. S. Weir Mitchell?

"I am one who read and enjoyed 'The Virginian'—and who read (half) 'Lady Baltimore.'

"What was it Mark Twain said of Jane Austen's books?

"As to 'Lady Baltimore' the illustrations are good at any rate."

I could make nothing out of the "wouldn't" and "hadn't" until I referred to the book, and found that the "had" complained of was a use of the subjunctive mood which had apparently been omitted from my correspondent's education.

In the *Charleston News and Courier,* the Woman's Exchange advertised presently "The 'Lady Baltimore' cake that made Owen Wister famous;" while about the same time, a confectioner in the North informed the public that he sold " 'Lady Baltimore,' the cake that Owen Wister made famous;" and twenty-two years after, a friend sent me the prices of loaf cakes listed by a Kitchen Company where

| | |
|---|---|
| Cushing Cake . . . . . . . . . . . . | .85 |
| Okemo Lady Baltimore. . . . | 1.75 |
| Round Owen Wister . . . . . . | 1.50 |
| Square Owen Wister . . . . . . | 1.25 |
| Baby Baltimores . . . . dozen | 1.44 |

were sold.   What author would wish to be more numerously read when he circulates so freely as a cake?

November 5, 1906.

DEAR DAN:

I have your letter of the 1st.   You are taking just the right ground.   Of course I can not go into State contests save in some wholly exceptional case like that of Hearst.   I am dealing with national issues.   Do let me see you as soon as possible after I come back from Panama.

No, I haven't the slightest idea about the "passing on the right" horseback business.

Ever yours,

THEODORE ROOSEVELT.

The last sentence is evidently in response to my having asked him what he knew about the rule of the road in the United States.   In England you pass to the left, in France to the right, as we do here.   If we began the English way on the first colonial roads we made, did we repudiate it in assertion of our independence, and adopt the French way as a compliment to our owing that independence so largely to France?   And so on. I thought it the sort of thing he would be likely to know; we discussed this on various occasions.

The second sentence in the letter refers to one of those rare moments in the more recent history of Pennsylvania when virtue rears its head.

## XIX.

I was playing a humble and wholly futile part in the ephemeral outbreak of decency.   We were in the Quay era of our politics. Our politics under Quay had acquired national renown.   Just as students seeking the master of the subject to which they intend to dedicate their lives, be it chemistry or economics or whatever, go to the University where he lectures, so those who desired to perfect their political skill sat at the feet of Quay. Bosses bowed to him, bosses of Chicago, San Francisco, all bosses.   At one of our elections Quay said he could sometimes do without a governor, but that he always needed a treasurer. He referred to our State treasury as "the plum tree," which he was accustomed frequently to "shake" as he expressed it.   He used the fruit as a margin in Wall Street.   It did not always come back.   Quay's friends stepped in and "got behind the treasury and made it look good," as he described these timely rescues.   But sometimes there was no friend at hand to save discovery by supplying plums for the shaken tree.   Nothing ever happened to Quay; but three cashiers of banks where State money should have been and was not, blew their brains out, and other men died, and one ran away into exile, all on account of the plum tree.   Kemble, a stout ally of Quay, described Pennsylvania politics as "addition, division and silence."   How and where the money went when we built our new State Capitol in 1906, closes a chapter twenty years long, which I told in an article called *The Keystone Crime; Philadelphia Corrupt and Contented* was the title of another article by another hand about us. Some good people declared it was time this stopped. For a while we had reform parties and meetings; and were quite excited. To-day in our capitol stands the statue of Quay, which those to whom he handed the torch raised to their patron saint as an inspiration for Pennsylvania boys and girls.

It is seldom printed words that affect the course of politics. The little splash they make vanishes at once in the smooth surface of the current. Every state has its own little Quay. You could not tell Pennsylvania from a monarchy, save that the names of the kings, instead of being Quay the first, Quay the second, and so on, change. It was upon its author alone that his *Keystone Crime* brought consequences.

The party of revolt, in whose ranks I had been fighting, was not yet extinct. Virtue was going to rear its head again, and they came to me early in 1908, a few months after my article about the Capitol had been published. One of their most enterprising spirits paid me a visit in my office, where I was attempting to continue to write fiction.

"The City Party wants you to run for Select Councils in the seventh ward."

My heart chilled at those words. Roosevelt rose in my mind like an accusing shape. "You are taking just the right ground," his letter had said on November 5, 1906. At that moment we revolters had helped to put a little temporary spoke in Quay's wheel. The facts about the plum tree were beginning to come out, thanks to the disclosure of Berry, the treasurer we had selected. I had written Roosevelt all about our struggle, and I was taking the right ground, he said then. But there was another thing that he was saying all the time, not only to me, but to the country: he thought little of the citizen who talked and talked and found fault in his comfortable arm chair, while others got into the fight. I had talked. My *Keystone Crime* was merely talking, even though it had cost me a visit to hear the investigation at Harrisburg, and those weeks of collecting and verifying the facts, and their presentation in a narrative. Mere talk, and my heart grew cold; for if the emissary of reform who now stood in my office was not joking—

"We want you to run for Select Councils in the seventh ward," he remarked when I had asked him to say that again.

"That's perfectly ridiculous. I should make no sort of select councilman. I've no training."

"Don't let that trouble you. There's not the slightest chance of your being elected."

"In that case, I will run!" I exclaimed as cheerfully as I was able.

And so, because I had talked, there was nothing for it but to go on, to "put up or shut up," as they say. Again I dropped my plans and my writing. For the sake of keeping up the organization of the reform party in our ward, I, chosen its candidate because I had talked, led a forlorn hope to predestined defeat. Up and down the seventh ward of Philadelphia, I made speeches in stinking halls amid rank tobacco smoke to dirty niggers and dingy whites. I made a speech for a brother reformer in the twenty-second ward, a cleaner place. It was extraordinarily good fun, once you got going. A little band of reform pilgrims attended me, some neighbors, shop keepers, and others. These disliked the "Corrupt and criminal organization, masquerading as the Republican party," as Elihu Root had styled it. They came to meetings in our small parlor in Pine Street, gave me every good word they could, and assisted with the posters, manifestoes, and other mechanisms of my candidacy. I recall one night as I was walking with my friends from one hall where I had finished a speech, to the next where I was to make one, that a highly soiled and disreputable youth of perhaps twenty-five, slid out of the dark and walked beside me, whispering.

"Say," he began, "if yus want to beat Charley Hall, I can show yus—"

"Speak louder, friend," I said loudly.    "Tell us all about it."

"Say," he complied, drawing away from my ear, "you're wise to it."    He was a simple youth, after all.

I think no other traps were laid.    Traps were quite needless, there was no chance whatever of beating the pocket Quay of our ward, honestly, or by any trick the lad had been sent to tempt me with; but very naturally it would have given great pleasure to him and his chief, a larger model of Quay, if I, an apostle of honesty, could have been reported to them by their henchman as having fallen into whatever trap had been set.    It was freely circulated that the pocket Quay had announced he would move out of the seventh ward if I polled more than the excruciatingly meagre maximum of votes which he set as my limit.    I did poll some two hundred more, but he retained his residence, and it was understood that he had been misquoted.

I cannot imagine what novel I had sent Roosevelt, to which the following letter refers.    The rest of it touches on the suggestion that he made about dropping the religious motto from our coinage, and to my *Seven Ages of Washington,* published a few days after the letter was written; and also to my *Keystone Crime,* at the close of which I had traced the political pacifism of Pennsylvanians to the non-resistant Quaker doctrine and the docility of the Pennsylvania Dutch temperament.

WHITE HOUSE

Washington

November 15, 1907.

DEAR DAN:

I welcome any novel, even one far inferior to "Lady Baltimore," if by any unconscious cerebration it will steer me right in a matter like the "In God We Trust."    I suppose some very good people will regret what I did; but, whether wise or not from the standpoint of politics, I can not help feeling that it was the right action from the standpoint of good taste, and indeed of a little more than good taste.

I look forward to the George Washington.    I do wish you could come down here and let me get a glimpse of you.    I have been immensely amused over the fluttering in the dovecotes over your remarks on non-resistance, whether of German or English stock.

 With warm regards to Mrs. Wister, believe me,

Ever yours,
THEODORE ROOSEVELT.

 He had recommended that the motto "In God We Trust" be dropped from our coins.

 "Founder's Week" is the anniversary celebration to which he refers in the letter following. It was conducted under the administration of Mayor Reyburn, who left our city finances embarrassed. I had written Roosevelt not to let the "corrupt and criminal organization" pull his leg by enticing him to Philadelphia as a drawing feature for the show. Evidently in the same letter I had reproached him with having spoken at Harrisburg when the new Capitol was unveiled. That was a plain pulling of his leg. They were no friends of his. They were only waiting for the happy day when he should leave the White House. His reply neither consoled nor satisfied me in the least. But on the day of the unveiling, the scandal of the Capitol was yet to be brought to light in all its details. My letter was written long after the investigation. He had gone to Harrisburg before it. This letter is one of the very few in which his brief aberration on the subject of simplified spelling appears in the word "thru."

THE WHITE HOUSE<br>Washington
February 24, 1908.

DEAR DAN:

 Until I received your letter I never heard about the anniversary celebration. I have not the slightest thought of accepting. As to keeping silence about the Reyburn election, it was of course the only thing I could do. The alternative is to take part in every municipal contest, and that would represent real usurpation and overstepping of Executive authority. Reyburn seems to be a rather unusually well-developed type of prize hog. A comic feature of the situation is that Mrs. Reyburn, thru General Crozier, just made an earnest request to attend the last reception, which was of course granted.

You speak of my attendance at the Harrisburg celebration. I went there with Knox, on the invitation of the Governor and the Legislature.   My dear Dan, I should have a large order of trouble on hand if I declined to visit State capitals when I did not like their governors or legislatures.   Why, I visited Little Rock, Arkansas, on my southern trip, altho Jefferson Davis was then Governor; and if I had stayed away it would have been ludicrous.   The city celebration, however, stands on an entirely different footing, and I have not the slightest intention of accepting.

Ever yours,<br>
THEODORE ROOSEVELT.

I must immediately have replied to him with some energy— not about his having gone to Harrisburg and made that speech on October 4, 1906—but about the present state of things in Philadelphia, and the forlorn hope that I was leading more or less in consequence of his constant sermons that people who talk and criticize, must back up their words by action.

WHITE HOUSE<br>
Washington

February 26, 1908.

DEAR DAN:

Three cheers!   I am so pleased that you can come down in April or May.   There are one or two expressions in your last letter that I much admire and shall keep for my next disquisition on undesirable citizens—and there are no more undesirable ones than those against whom you are warring.

Ever yours,<br>
T. R.

I wanted to get him on for a very select meeting of the Boone and Crockett Club which I organized, but he was too busy.

WHITE HOUSE
Washington

March 13, 1908.

DEAR DAN:

I have your note of the 12th.  It is a simple impossibility.  I could not come.  When are you coming on here?

Ever yours,

THEODORE ROOSEVELT.

The paper he mentions in the next letter, was an address I had been invited to deliver on honor day in Sanders Theatre, at Harvard, in the preceding December.  It was entitled *Our Country and the Scholar*.

WHITE HOUSE
Washington

April 15, 1908.

DEAR DAN:

Your paper was placed face up on my desk, so I did not see your endorsement on the back of it; but I had not read four lines before I said, "Why, this must be by Dan," and sure enough, it was!  I was delighted with it.

I am sorry that there seems to be no chance of your coming down here, and still more sorry about the illness of your mother. I hope she will soon be well.

Always yours,

THEODORE ROOSEVELT.

The five that follow are the last that he wrote me from the White House; they tell their own story, they reveal Roosevelt in several aspects, official and domestic, and his elation at the election of Taft to succeed him.  The two lines on March 3, mark the very end.  I had written him from bed, where I had been since mid-January, with a temperature that went up every night to 103 for three months and down every morning; I was to be in bed till the middle of August, not at all proud of the glory of having something wrong with my insides that no doctor, including Mitchell and Osler, was able to name.

November 5, 1908.

DEAR DAN:

About the Reverend Mr. Scott, I have sent what you say of him and the letters enclosed to the War Department and asked them to send him the information as to how to file his application for consideration when a vacancy occurs.   I do not understand that there is any at present in the Episcopalian quota of army chaplains.

Will have the case of Princess Kropotkin lookt up by the State Department and then let you know.

Indeed, we *are* heartily to be congratulated on the result of the election!

Ever yours,

THEODORE ROOSEVELT.

November 10, 1908.

DEAR DAN:

I have gone over that Princess Kropotkin matter with the Department of State and the Department of Commerce and Labor.   They are clear that she ought not to come.   If she calls herself an anarchist that would be sufficient reason why she should not be admitted; and I think under the law it would be absolutely conclusive.   Permit me to add that I think it highly undesirable that she should come. . . .   People who call themselves anarchists, no matter how they qualify the word by calling themselves "reformers," by just so much add to the strength of the worst and most vicious elements of our civilization.

Ever yours,

THEODORE ROOSEVELT.

December 29, 1908.

DEAR DAN:

Will Mrs. Wister and you and the children take lunch with us on Tuesday, January 5th, at 1:30 o'clock?   If the children are too young I will arrange to have them take lunch in the adjoining room!

No, Dan, if the epic poem had been by you I *suppose* I should have read it; but it would need strong personal friendship for the author to overcome my volatile mind to such a point.   The praise you give the author—that his intentions are good—somehow does not make the prospect of reading the poem any more attractive.

Ever yours,

T. R.

January 7, 1909.

DEAR DAN:

Fine!   Can you spend Sunday and Monday, the 17th and 18th with us here, or Monday and Tuesday, the 18th and 19th? Tuesday night we have to go out to a Cabinet dinner.   I can not tell you how we all enjoyed seeing Mrs. Wister and yourself and those four blessed children.   It gave me a pang to think that my own children were all grown up beyond the age of real little boy and little girl attractiveness.

Ever yours,

T. R.

March 3, 1909.

DEAR DAN:

It was good of you to write me.   May all good fortune be with you.

Faithfully yours,

THEODORE ROOSEVELT.

The saying that a man is known by his friends, must be rounded out by adding his enemies; without looking at both, you see him in but one dimension; taken together, those for him and those against him make a background against which he stands as a fairly solid figure.   Few decided characters have missed being both liked and disliked, and among our Presidents from Washington down, this is conspicuously true.   There is a vague popular notion that Abraham Lincoln was universally beloved. The fanatics of Reconstruction were so delighted to have his moderate and merciful spirit no longer between them and their ruinously cruel and oppressive designs against the prostrate South, that they could hardly assume a decent solemnity over his assassination: The violent section of Lincoln's own party hated him. Just so, Cleveland was hated by the fanatics of free silver—his own party—because he stood between them and the ruin to the national credit that they would have accomplished.

"I shall miss you very much," said lonely Henry Adams, bidding the Roosevelts farewell.

Who were they that were by no means going to miss Theodore Roosevelt? Who on March 4, 1909, felt that now, with this new man in the White House, and that other one off in Africa, possibly there to be eaten by some providential lion, the good old days were dawning again? The extremists of Big Business, and the extremists of Big Labor, the Harrimans who boasted they could always buy a congressman or a judge when they needed one, and the Haywoods, who could bomb a governor of Idaho and go safe from justice, both these groups hated Roosevelt as bitterly as the fanatics of Reconstruction had hated Lincoln.

"You can never be sure what he'll do next," said the angry bankers, when Roosevelt's Northern Securities, or his Rate Bill, would upset the stock market.

"Resolved, That the order of the President cannot be regarded in any but an unfriendly light," said the Central Labor Bureau, when he upset their dismissal of a Government employee, remarking that no labor union could be permitted to over-ride the laws of the United States.

These were his enemies; who were his friends? Just about the whole American people. They loved his courage, the way he would come out with a thing, and the assurance he had given them that it was neither the labor unions nor the trusts, but the Government who ruled the United States. They would have kept him in the White House for the sake of what he had done and would go on doing, he had to choke off various plans to renominate him—but, had he not dictated the nomination of a successor, a close friend, an able colleague, enthusiastically in sympathy with his policies, bound by his own word, and the platform on which he had been elected, to carry them on?

Never before had such a dictation been stomached in this Democracy.

What had his policies been, and what in the main had he done?

He had sent our battle fleet round the world, able to put shots generally, instead of rarely, where they were aimed; had accomplished the Panama Canal; had brought peace between Russia and Japan; had put the Kaiser in his place regarding Venezuela, and by causing the Algeciras conference; had settled the coal strike; saved the forests; developed irrigation in the West; laid the law's restraining hand upon Corporations and Unions; upon railroad rebates and free passes, and upon the sale of unsanitary food and drugs.   On the day he left the White House for Africa, one of his latest acts bore fruit: the Sugar Trust, against which he had caused Henry L. Stimson to bring suit for tricking the custom house by a secret and clever mechanism in the weighing scales, was found guilty by the jury on March 4, 1909.   The trust had escaped in a previous suit not instituted directly by Roosevelt.   This one resulted in various sugar corporations paying three and a half million dollars into the treasury.

It might be imagined that a President with such a record behind him would sail away to Africa with a light heart.   But his successor, whom he had forced upon the country with a high hand, had expressed his gratitude to him in words that rang over the country:

"I am bound to say that I owe my election more to you than to anybody else, except my brother Charley."

Mr. Charles Taft was the close friend, and ally, and promoter of precisely everything and everybody in Wall Street and in politics that Roosevelt had spent seven years in fighting.   The very most lovable characteristic in Roosevelt, enthusiasm for any friend his heart had wholly adopted, had led him again—and of his several misjudgments this is the most grievous—to think that a man so good in many things must be the right man for this.

He sailed away to Africa with no light heart, he went with a millstone round his hopes.   That word about "my brother

Charley" had flashed upon his vision what was going to happen as clearly as if it had been on a screen. Just ten days after his inauguration, Mr. Taft was supporting Cannon, the enemy of all Roosevelt's progressive policies, in his election as Speaker of the House. In that moment, the Republican party began to commit the suicide which it completed at its convention in 1912 —and Mr. Taft helped it at every stage. He had not a sus- picion of what he was doing; he supposed that he was support- ing the Roosevelt policies.

## XX.

### THE OUTLOOK
287 Fourth Avenue
New York

Office of
Theodore Roosevelt.

July 22, 1910.

DEAR DAN:

Can you not come down and see me for a night sometime? I have so many things I would like to tell you.

Faithfully yours,

THEODORE ROOSEVELT.

So many things! He had been at home just five weeks from Africa, from the crowned heads of Europe, from a greeting and an attention such as no American had ever received before. He had ridden about with the Kaiser while the German army was manoeuvering, he had played a miraculously clever part in a diplomatic comedy at Rome, he had lectured to the French at the Sorbonne, walked with Sir Edward Grey in the woods, and told the somewhat surprised English at Guildhall that they had better rule Egypt, or get out of it. I should have liked to hear about all this while he was still fresh from it; but matters at home were more engrossing still.

We had not met since January 5, 1909, and a new President was in the White House, running true to those odd words about "my brother Charley," and further and further away from conservation of natural resources, or any other conservation, except of what had come to be known as the Stand-pat group in the Republican party.

The country, after a brief moment of bewilderment, had found out that the new President was as wax in the hands of Big Business, and that his sincere belief in the Roosevelt policies had been—without his ever growing clearly aware of the process— changed to implicit faith in all the people who had been so eagerly waiting for Roosevelt to be out of their way. Cartoons had appeared in all the progressive papers, the group of Roosevelt's supporters in the Senate were no longer known as the Progressive, but as the Insurgents; and Dolliver, one of these Insurgents, had described the new President as, "an amiable gentleman, entirely surrounded by men who know exactly what they want."

The first thing they wanted was a new tariff bill—that is, certain people wanted it. It was heralded as a reduced tariff. Five months to a day after the inauguration of Roosevelt's successor, they passed it. It proved to be a reduction upside down. This was the Republican party's next step in suicide, speeded still further onward when Mr. Taft exasperated the country in a speech delivered at Winona, made expressly with the idea of soothing the country. He declared that such a good tariff bill never had been seen. It sent a tidal wave of anger from the Mississippi to the Pacific. Mr. Taft said that he had "dashed off the Winona speech hastily between stations" in the train on his way to make it.

Close upon the new tariff, a scandal about some coal lands in Alaska followed, not so bad as at first reported by Gifford Pinchot, head of the National Conservation Organization established by Roosevelt. Pinchot accused Ballinger, Secretary of the Interior, of so arranging matters as to turn the coal lands over to the control of a monopoly for private benefit. During the controversy which this precipitated, the President denied all knowledge of a certain memorandum sent by him to Ballinger.

He had sent it—but had completely forgotten it; his denial was absolutely honest, his acknowledgment of it when he remembered, restored confidence in his word, but none in his administration.

The country had ceased to rub its eyes over his cordial acquiescence at what was being done by Congress in the way of uprooting everything that Roosevelt had done—and this is what I certainly should have got Roosevelt to talk about, had I been able to go to Sagamore Hill when he asked me on July 22, 1910. But I never went until 1912, when I was at last able to cut loose from medical care, and the tiresome business of convalescence. Instead, I had to go to Wyoming by easy stages, one of which was Winona; and I stared with fascination at the place where Taft had driven a new nail into the coffin of his own party.

Would Mr. Hughes have done better as President during those darkening years? He had been thought of, but he had made it impossible by sticking firmly to the principle that the office should seek the man. He refused to fall in with the essential preliminaries for getting in line as a candidate. Elihu Root, the man of all men that Roosevelt would have chosen to succeed him, had no chance with the American people. It was not enough for them that he had made an illustrious Secretary of State. In their minds he was associated with the corporations that they had come so deeply to distrust; and Roosevelt's conviction that Root would serve to the full any cause to which he had avowedly dedicated his service, would not have changed their minds. Scene by scene, the tragedy proceeded.

To be President was not at all what Taft had wished. By predilection, by temperament, by every quality of character and mind, he was best fitted to be a judge. He had declared once that it would be a "cold day" when he went to the White House, and this perfectly expressed his disinclination. But—had he not been good in the Philippines? Had he not been good as Secretary of War? This, with Roosevelt's faith and affection, moved the tragedy on. The very reluctant Taft, under pressure from his friend and other pressure which may have proved the last straw, yielded; instead of to the bench, he went to the White House.

When Roosevelt landed in New York on June 18, 1910, already disenchanted by what had been going on during the year of his absence, which I have summarized above, and about which Gifford Pinchot had rushed over to Europe to tell him in a somewhat high key, he nevertheless gave out in the first words that he uttered, that he meant thenceforth to be nothing more than a citizen.   He said, in his reply to Mayor Gaynor's speech of welcome, that it was peculiarly the duty of one who had been President of the United States to help to solve our problems "in private life as much as in public life."

Just nine days afterwards, he said: "I had intended to keep absolutely clear from any kind of public or political question after coming home—until I met the Governor this morning—and after a very brief conversation, I put up my hands and agreed to help him."

A very brief conversation—and the Rubicon crossed!   Not at all in his own interest; wholly against it.   For Roosevelt's Rubicon flowed between the territory of his privacy at Sagamore Hill; his ease, his liberty to go and come as he wished, to do what he liked, to hunt game, to write books, to see his friends; to be domestic and at his own disposal—it flowed between this and more controversy, more campaigns, more speeches, more miles of travel in sleeping cars, more of everything he had told himself he was going to drop.   In all his life, I see no decision more crucial than this one.   And he crossed the Rubicon.   He had told himself that he was henceforth to be a private citizen, and this he sincerely meant.   Then, "after a very brief conversation," to reverse himself like that!   In a character of such determination as Roosevelt's, to change a meditated plan of life so utterly in a few minutes' talk, is a very striking act.   This, with all the events which flowed from it inevitably as fate, has been accounted for differently by friends and enemies.   I am at variance with both.

Many a man has told himself something that he thought he

meant, and when the time came has found that he did not mean it.   I do not agree with Roosevelt's enemies that ambition had anything to do with his sudden change of plan—then or thereafter; nobody can read his letters and hold such an opinion; nor do I think with his friends that the choice he made that morning after his brief conversation with the Governor, was a sacrifice to obvious duty, the performance of a plain obligation —though he put it that way to himself and believed it just as sincerely as he had believed until that moment that he had done with politics.   My explanation of it is, that below every motive attributed by him, or by friend or enemy, to his action, lay the strongest element in his character.

Pierpont Morgan once said: "A man always has two reasons for what he does—a good one, and the real one."

The lynx eyed Winty Chanler saw that brief conversation taking place, though he could not hear a word of it.   He was with Dr. William S. Thayer, in the back of Sanders Theatre, at Harvard.   It was June 29, Commencement Day, and they were attending the exercises.   On the platform with other personages, sat Roosevelt, then President of the Alumni, and Hughes, then Governor of New York.   This was the first time Hughes had seen Roosevelt since his home coming.   He turned to Roosevelt and spoke to him with great earnestness, beating one hand into the other to emphasize his words; and Roosevelt listened with increasing attention and animation.

"Look at them!" said Chanler to Thayer.   "Do you know what Hughes is saying?   He's telling Roosevelt that the Republican party is in a bad way in New York, and that Roosevelt's duty is to jump in and back the direct primary bill.   And Theodore is going to do it."

The exercises took place, and the company went to lunch.   At that lunch, Roosevelt made his announcement that he had "put up his hands," and agreed to help Hughes in New York.   He telegraphed that day to Senator Davenport, Progressive leader for the bill against William Barnes, head of the Stand-pat Republicans in New York, that he would support the bill.

I would not go so far as to argue that a generous impulse to stand by those now who had stood by him in other days, did not count with Roosevelt in making this decision.   Of course it did. Always—until the day when the lunatic fringe of his followers became too much for him.   But what had Hughes told him that

**MAYBE MR. TAFT'S EARS DIDN'T TINGLE!**
From the Baltimore Sun

he did not know already?   Before he sailed home, he had learned from Pinchot how ill his friends, the Progressives, were faring; he knew that the Administration had fallen into the hands of his opponents, that Cannon, and Aldrich, and Payne, and all their friends, were having their way, and that his way had been abandoned wherever it could be.   Yet with this knowledge, his first word to the country on landing at New York had been that he was out of politics.   He had refused to listen to the appeals that he resume his leadership of the Progressive party which various people had made to him during the nine days before the Harvard Commencement.   I think that the "real reason" for his change of mind on the platform of Sanders Theatre, was the same reason that a duck takes to the water.   Among all his bents, historical, zoölogical, whatever, he was the preacher militant perpetual, and to be in a fight for his beliefs was his true native element.   In the appeals made to him before he met Hughes, the water had not come quite so close to the duck. Hughes had dragged him to the edge of a definite pond, and into the pond he plumped.   What a small pond after all—one bill in one State—for an ex-President to notice!   And then, the pond flowed speedily into a brook, and the brook speedily into a river, and down the river he went toward a sea that neither he nor friend nor enemy dreamed of.

All this is perfectly clear now, as simple as a detective story —when you have finished it.   Some shake their heads over it to-day, as if they had foreseen it from the beginning.   Could they have told you on June 29, 1910, that in consequence of Roosevelt's promising Hughes on the platform of Sanders Theatre, that he would come out in favor of a direct primary bill in New York State, that we should have three candidates dividing our votes in 1912, and an enigma as inscrutable as Louis Napoleon in the White House, telling the warring world that there is such a thing as being too proud to fight, two days after Germany had sent the *Lusitania* to the bottom of the sea?

I certainly foresaw not even the near future, I was very glad that Roosevelt was going to take a hand in public affairs again; public affairs, ever since his back had been turned on them, had begun by bewildering me, and ended by filling me with much stronger emotions.

I was not alone in my joy.   By August, some two thousand requests had come that he made a speech in some two thousand places.   Did this sign of discontent convey no warning to Senator Aldrich, and Payne, and Crane and Speaker Cannon, and the Administration in general?   Did the fact that their unquestionably excellent and desirable bill, providing for what we know now as the Federal Reserve Bank, was rejected because they had so disgusted public opinion in general that nothing they proposed was acceptable any longer—did this signify nothing to them?   Apparently everything outside their own designs was insignificant to them; and so they too went sailing down the river to the sea.

The point as to what Roosevelt's real reason was for the step he had taken, must not be labored too far.   I think the preacher militant in him drove him to leap before he looked into the New York fight; after he had leaped, he saw what was ahead without a particle of illusion, he even saw obscurely what his mind by no means yet accepted, the inevitable break with the friend he had left behind him in the White House.   His letters show this unanswerably, and they also dispose of the idea that personal ambition had anything whatever to do with his course. No honest minds could read the letters and retain such a notion.

"The fight is very disagreeable," he writes Cabot Lodge, September 21, 1910.   "Twenty years ago I should not have minded it in the least . . . but it is not the kind of fight into which an ex-President should be required to go.   I could not help myself. . . ."

". . . We shall in all probability be beaten at the polls," he had written Lodge ten days earlier, referring to the election in New York.   He was temporary chairman of the Republican convention.

"I have been cordially helping the election of a Republican Congress," he writes Root a little later, "having definitely split with the Insurgents on this point . . . though I am bitterly disappointed with Taft . . . very possibly circumstances will be such that I shall support Taft for the Presidency next time. . . ."

In those words, one sees the coming events casting their shadow before.   They cast a much sharper shadow a month later, when the Democrats carried any number of other States, as well as New York. But Speaker Cannon, and Senators Aldrich, Payne, and Crane, and the rest of that company in Washington, seemed to discern nothing ominous in this.

I have often come from a long American journey to Washington, to find how little my impressions of the general popular feeling in the country corresponded with the notions of it which even the political leaders entertained. Can it be that in Washington some special atmosphere prevails, which blinds office-holders to the true state of things? Half-way to the end of Taft's administration, the country was already in a temper to vote any Republican candidate for the Presidency down, excepting Roosevelt. But of Roosevelt they were afraid, those people in Washington—afraid instantly. His announcement at Harvard that he would support Governor Hughes and his direct primary bill, may be likened to the dropping of a hat which starts a race. Although they were blind enough to what the increasing discontent with the Administration portended, their sensitive, but purely political nerves, had received a shock. They started running their race at the dropping of that hat. They began the race in their newspapers. Attacks upon Roosevelt were appearing in a very few weeks. Two hypnotic suggestions were either crudely or ingeniously imbedded in every specimen of this propaganda that I saw for the next two years; one was, that Roosevelt was a dangerous and ambitious demagogue, and the other was, that he had solemnly promised the American people never again to run for President. He had promised nobody anything. After his election he had made a voluntary statement. Had he dotted his i's and crossed his t's on that November night of 1904, this statement of his complete adherence to the unwritten doctrine that no President shall have three continuous terms, and that he considered his stepping into McKinley's second term as his own first term, could never have been distorted to mean that a President can never hold office again at any time. It was so distorted by the propaganda which also represented it as a promise. Plenty of active minds in Wall Street and elsewhere required no hypnotizing; but upon passive minds it stamped the grotesque myth: that the American people had said to Roosevelt, "we'll vote for you this once if you'll promise never to do it again." That is the English of the myth; but passive minds don't reason things out. So, through hearing about the broken promise every day for many days, simple citizens lost touch with the fact, and grew to thinking of a voluntary statement made after election as if it had been an exacted promise given before election. A man of honor keeps a promise; but what law binds him never to change his mind? Today when I hear the old song sung that when Roosevelt returned from Africa, his personal ambition led him to break his promise to the American people, I am apt to say: "how very odd! Because in order to nominate Taft in 1912 they had to steal 72 delegates instructed for Roosevelt by the American people, and people as a rule don't enjoy being lied to."

Let us look a little more at his own mind during that period.

"As for the nomination, I should regard it from my personal standpoint as little short of a calamity." This is from a letter to his friend Joseph Bucklin Bishop in 1911, when discontent with the Administration was deep and wide.

To Frank Munsey, who had asked him to say he would run: "I am not and shall not be a candidate. . . . If my position were only a pose, I should certainly act differently . . . the way I am acting is not the way in which to act if I desire to be made President. . . ."

Somewhat earlier, to William Allen White: ". . . I think the American people feel a little tired of me, a feeling with which I cordially sympathize. . . . I feel most strongly that I never again should take any public position unless it could be made perfectly clear that I was taking it not for my own sake, but because the people thought it would be to their advantage to have me do so."

He was not at all deceived by the situation he had created for himself by his capitulation to Governor Hughes. Oscar King Davis, to whom I think he gave his intimate and hearty trust, reports in his admirable and graphic book a talk held with Roosevelt in his office at the *Outlook*, about the propaganda that was being so busily manufactured, even by August, 1910.

"There are only two elevators in this building," said Roosevelt, "and I must use one or other of them.    If I go down by the side elevator, that is evidence of furtiveness.    If I go down in front, that is proof of ostentation."

And it is in his letter to William Allen White, in December, when the campaign was over with the Democrats victorious in many places, and he could rest from his speech making, that he says:

"I have been almost ashamed of the fact that in spite of my concern and indignation over Stimson's defeat, I have been unable to keep from being thoroughly happy since election." Henry L. Stimson had run for Governor of New York on the Republican ticket.    The letter continues; he is writing from Sagamore Hill:
"Mrs. Roosevelt and I have been out here in our own home, with our books and pictures and bronzes, and big wood fires and horses to ride, and the knowledge that our children are doing well.    I do not think that I have had such a pleasant five weeks for a great many years.    In fact I know I have not."

Mrs. Roosevelt had married the whirlwind, and for a while it was not blowing!
Is it not plain, what he wanted to do?    Is it not plain that his mind during the recent campaign had not been at ease over the position into which he had got himself?    Just after the campaign was over, he wrote in a letter to Bishop:

"They have no business to expect me to take command of a ship simply because the ship is sinking."

Does not that sound like a cry from the heart?

"Nor did I believe until lately . . . that . . . every act of my administration would be tortured . . . in such exaggerated and indecent terms as could scarcely be applied to . . . a common pickpocket."

This will not be found among the letters in Bishop's book. Roosevelt did not write this to William Allen White, or Oscar King Davis, or to any of his friends: Washington wrote it to Jefferson. And Washington, twice President, weary to the bone, not far from his end, desirous of nothing but to be let alone "beneath his vine and fig-tree," was ready nevertheless to leave Mount Vernon and lead our army, in case we went to war with France.

I suppose that the people who had used the terms which could scarcely be applied to a common pickpocket, called that ambition, just as Roosevelt's rush to command the sinking ship in 1910 was (and is still) attributed to ambition. Neither man could help that sort of ambition, it was his driving force, the mainspring of his existence.

"God knows when we shall be able to do anything for to deserve better of our country."

That is young Colonel Washington, writing to Governor Dinwiddie after a frozen expedition in the backwoods.

"My anxieties are in this order . . . not to be nominated if it can be honorably avoided . . . and . . . if nominated, to have it . . . clear that it is because . . . the public wishes me to serve them for their purpose. . . ."

That is elderly Colonel Roosevelt at the end of 1911, writing to Bishop.

Ambition!

And all the while, a college president was making quite a stir at Princeton.

## XXI.

It was here that a letter properly belongs, written by Roosevelt in reply to one I had sent him, after reading what is still known as his Osawatomie speech. This letter is unluckily missing. It was not long; the wonder is, that he found time in

the rush of that 1910 campaign to write at all.  He told me that
he was glad I liked that speech, because it was a statement of his
"American creed"—those two are the only words I can recall
from the letter.  The greater wonder is, that he could go through
those weeks, and many worse weeks that were to come, and
speak so vigorously when his heart was but half in it.  Three
weeks after the address at Osawatomie, he writes Lodge in a way
that makes the mood he was in even plainer than what I have
already quoted from his letters.  He says:

"This whole political business now is bitterly distasteful
to me."

I fancy that Cabot Lodge, for reasons quite different, enjoyed
this fight Roosevelt was making even less than Roosevelt did.
Lodge, whose personal sympathies were with Roosevelt, was
politically with the Administration, and he could not possibly
have failed to see that his friend was helping the popular mind
to turn more and more against the Administration.  Did Roosevelt see it as clearly?  Did he see as early as 1910, that he was
heading straight for the worst hole he had ever got into, or was
ever going to get into?  That remark in his letter to Root, written about the same time, that he might, "very possibly" support
Taft at the next election, looks as if his mind was refusing to
acknowledge to itself what was quite certainly bound to happen.  I suppose that he was keeping out of his thoughts as hard
as he could the idea of a personal break with the friend he had
chosen and persuaded to be his successor in the White House.
I only imagine this; but I more than imagine how he looked back
upon that time of distress, and the error of his choice, and its
consequences.  It was at lunch one day long after, at Sagamore
Hill, and talk had touched upon those years.  I spoke out my
undisguised feeling about the unfitness of the successor he had
given us.  To say that Roosevelt winced is a little too strong;
but his face filled with that look of pain that I knew so well.
He did not take my head off for my bluntness; he was silent a
moment, before he leaned forward and said, almost as if in
apology for his choice:

"He was such a good lieutenant!"

Some things he was perfectly clear about.   He knew that too many of his enthusiastic followers now belonged to that element which he had years earlier described as the "lunatic fringe;" that he was powerless to disavow these ragged thinkers who were enlisting in his army; and that, worse still, some of those temperate citizens who had been his cordial adherents hitherto, were falling out of his ranks.   He had no faith in the Democrats, he believed that the welfare of the country was much safer in Republican hands; yet he saw in the Republican ranks men so extreme and inflexible in their narrowness, as to constitute another lunatic fringe, exactly as blind in its demands as were the star gazers who had tagged on to him.   In short, he forced himself onward, unhappy, haunted by doubts as to the validity of his own position, yet able to keep up his momentum because all the combative elements in him, the preacher militant, the canny political strategist, were aroused; and they saw him through.

One symptom of his disturbed state is the phraseology which began to appear in his addresses.   Their most salient characteristic had always been the balance of their statements; such as, that the door of the White House should swing open as easily to the poor as to the rich, and not one bit easier.   A masterly power of proportion, of stating the common sense in any controversy where something was to be said on both sides, this, with his buoyant and fearless outspokenness, had won him the hearts and the heads of all sorts and conditions of men.   He now at times misrepresented himself, made use of phrases that overstated what he really meant.   This gave his enemies the best chance they ever had.   They could quote, without always distorting, utterances of his which injured his standing seriously, and made it seem as if he were waging war upon all economic, social, and legal stability.   Distortion, of course, was not lacking; in Denver, for example, they left out the beginning and the end of his address, which perverted its application into an unqualified assault upon the Supreme Court.   To go into this, and the details of the famous Bake Shop case, would lead me too far: all I wish is to give the reader some general impression of the hurricane that was blowing. I am borne out by his own remarks in my notion that the hurricane put him into mental haste, deprived him not only of the leisure, but of the critical detachment with which he was in the habit of going over a public address beforehand, pruning down over-emphatic statements, and balancing one statement against another.

". . . I had no business to take that position in the fashion that I did. A public man is to be condemned if he fails to make his point clear . . . and it was a blunder of some gravity not to do it."

That is what he wrote Lodge. He had never had to make such an admission as this before. Often enough, he had hammered his thoughts hard to drive them home, but now he was hitting them out of shape. Acerbity on the part of everybody grew worse and worse, past matters were raked up and flung at him, incidents about which the general mind had forgotten the details—if it had ever known them. He had caused the panic of 1907, and would cause another. Nobody remembered that deflation, following inevitably upon ten years of inflation, of piling up on the part of certain powerful interests, and the troubles of the Equitable Life, and the failure of the Knickerbocker Trust Company, these and similar reverses were the causes of that panic, as any business man who knew about it will tell you. He had been false to his own doctrine about the trusts, when he allowed the Steel Trust to purchase the Tennessee Coal and Iron Company, and so permitted a "combination in restraint of trade" just like the Northern Securities, which he had stopped. Nobody remembered the truth. Two courts later sustained his action as perfectly consistent. One declared that the transaction was as he had stated it, "made in fair business course"; the Supreme Court laid additional emphasis, on this, adding: "The law does not make mere size an offense." Nobody does remember in such times of excitement.

They create mob thought.    A phrase, a fact, is wrenched from
its context, caught up and hurled about, and regardless of its
being utterly senseless, does just as much damage as if it were
pregnant with significance.    To use a misused term, politics
create a *complex* in human beings which delivers them to the
mercy of prejudices more blind and violent than any, save those
which are created by the religious *complex*.

It is later in the progress of this acerbity and tumult, that
Roosevelt again failed through haste to make his point clear.
It was so little clear that I fancy he never recovered from the
political injury that it did him; and if one thing more than any
other startled his friends and lost him adherents, it was this particular phrase that he used.    Two other novelties had raised
considerable outcry—the "initiative" and the "referendum."
Does the reader understand these methods of reaching what
was called " social justice"?    You hardly ever hear them mentioned any more, and they are very rarely put into use.    They
were short cuts by which popular will or popular discontent could
override the established forms of legislation or redress, and get
something or stop something that it wanted without delay.    To
put it baldly and briefly, they express American impatience.    It
was a kick at the legal thwarting of what might be very desirable, but was far more likely to be an ephemeral whim.    It was
ephemeral whims that the makers of the Constitution had clearly
foreseen, wisely dreaded, and carefully provided against.
Roosevelt would have said that the initiative and referendum
were engines of popular power to be used only on very special
occasions.    He did say so; but not often or emphatically enough
to reassure his friends and confute his enemies.    But the "recall of judicial decisions" was a phrase which struck at the very
root of our system.    It was the climax.    People said that Roosevelt was simply running amuck.    In this case, too, he had misrepresented himself, and according to his own confession in the
letter to Lodge, "a public man is to be condemned if he fails to
make his meaning clear."

And so he thought, and so he said in another way, to his

friend Thomas Robins, five years later. He had come to Philadelphia to address the Railroad Trainmen's Union in June, 1917. After the speech, when he and Robins were alone, Robins said:

"What you proposed in 1912, I believe, lost you the Republican nomination for the Presidency. It was really Constitutional revision by popular vote in the states: in other words, revision by the same power that approved the Constitution. Who gave it the name of 'Recall of Judicial Decisions?' "

"I did, for my sins!" exclaimed Roosevelt. "The label did not describe the commodity; it was inaccurate and unlucky."

Yet in the heat of all this battle, he was not in too much of a hurry to step out of politics and talk morals. There is something comic as well as endearing in the preacher militant and the old fashioned mid-Victorian emerging suddenly in Roosevelt the Progressive, when he spoke at Reno.

"I don't care what you do with those of your own State who seek divorces, but keep citizens out of other states who want divorces out of Nevada. Don't allow yourselves to be deceived by the argument that such a colony brings money to your city. You can't afford to have that kind of money brought here."

Equally endearing and comic is his astonishment on the first election day after women had obtained the vote. His conventions had finally come round to female suffrage, bowing to the course of human events. The November day arrived, and he entered his car to go to the polls at Oyster Bay. Mrs. Roosevelt got into the car with him.

"Why Ee-die, why are you coming?"

"I'm going to vote, of course, Theodore."

"Going to *vote!*". . .

He sat back in the car, silent for some time. Female suffrage as a just principle, as a Constitutional Amendment, was one thing; the sight of his own wife casting a ballot took his breath away. This old-fashioned, conventional streak in him lived in a compartment shut entirely off from initiative, referendum, recall, and from his whole progressive political make-up; and so it remained as long as he lived.

## XXII.

THE OUTLOOK
287 Fourth Avenue
New York.

May 23rd, 1911.

Office of
THEODORE ROOSEVELT.

DEAR DAN:—

Mrs. Roosevelt loved "The Members of the Family," and so did I.   I think I especially liked "Timberline," "The Gift Horse," and "Extra Dry;" and I don't know but that I like the preface even more than anything else.

I must see you soon.   I want to tell you that I felt just as you felt when I passed through my own old country this year; except that I am not quite as certain as you are that the change is subjective as well as objective.   I enjoyed my African trip when I was fifty as much as I enjoyed the West when I was twenty-five; but in the west the old country that I knew so well has absolutely vanished.   I realized this more fully than at any other time when we stopped at what used to be a homeless siding—near which I had spent thirty-six hours fighting fire, with a wild set of cow punchers, a quarter of a century ago, and which I had once passed leading a lost horse through a snow-storm when I got turned round and had to camp out—and found a thriving little prairie town with a Chamber of Commerce and a "boosters' society," of which the mayor was president.

Give my love to Mrs. Wister.   Cannot you come out and see us soon?   We so long to see you.

Faithfully yours,
THEODORE ROOSEVELT.

Heavens!   Think of your daring to wish Henry James to write of the west!

No wonder he said Heavens!   In the eighties, I had begged Henry James to drop Europe and do this.   My preface mentioned it, and caused Roosevelt's postscript.   This, as well as two or three phrases in the above letter, is added in his own hand writing—and not a line in the whole of it suggests the political storm in which he was passing most of his time, both in thought and action!    But no storm ever hindered Roosevelt from remembering a friend.

I had not seen him yet; and during his tempestuous weeks before the recent November election, my own weeks had been among the quiet mountains.    Out in Wyoming, I had not only got as far as riding a horse again, and fishing; I had attained enough energy to write a short story.    It was entitled *The Drake who had Means of his own,* and was inspired by the interesting behavior of some ducks that I used to watch several times a day from my cabin window.    This tale, with others, scattered over ten years, made the volume I had sent him, and which his letter acknowledged.    If he liked the preface best of all, it was not merely because it was full of "Insurgent" political sentiments about the initiative, referendum, and recall, as to which I had hinted some discreet doubts, but because of a home-sick sigh which expressed a recent experience, and ran all through that preface.    It was the sigh which caused him to tell me of his own similar experience on revisiting the scene of old associations.

The last time I had ridden and fished among the beloved mountains of Wyoming, I had been what is called "still young," had climbed among the Tetons above Jackson's Lake, carried a rifle all day, shot mountain sheep.    But now. . . .

This was my recent experience, before I reached the mountains:—

My train was trundling over the plains, a branch train, one like the trains of other days; half passenger, half freight, no Pullman, ancient coaches, ancient locomotive with a big wide smoke-tack, stops for meals, the regular original pattern of newsboy with bad novels, bad candy, bad bananas.    It was like a dream.    But I was awake.    Suddenly through the open window there floated in upon the sun-filled air the first whiff of the sage-brush—and then the dream grew magical, and the past became visible. I saw them once more, standing there out in the alkali by scores and hundreds; the antelope; only a little way off; a sort of cinnamon and amber color in the clear Wyoming light; transparent and phantom-like, with pale legs; only a little way off. Now they were running. They bobbed away into the distance, white, receding dots of motion, out of my rifle's range; and between them and me trembled the heated air over the sage-brush and the prickly-pear, the alkali, the dry gullies, the mounds, the flats, the enormous sun light. The dream broke. No antelope were there. But everything else was—alkali, sage-brush, and all, so natural, so natural!—surely those antelope would be just over the next rise? or the next? The sage-brush smelled very strong, the dream descended on me again. I looked out the window and saw thousands of cattle, and horsemen galloping around and among them. But they vanished. Alkali, gullies, were there, but no cattle, nor riders. Over the next rise? No. Only a little way off, but gone for evermore. And hour after hour, the smell of the sage-brush floated in at the window, conjuring old sights before me; and at length the desert spoke to me, and said:

"No more than the cattle, no more than the horsemen and the antelope, are you here to-day, it is only your ghost. I was once the cattle range, and I am a ghost, too. And what you seek, what your eyes have been straining to see, is yourself at twenty, your youth before you ever thought that it—like me—would pass."

This was my sigh. Very gently, in his sentence about Africa, Roosevelt deprecates any admission that youth will pass.

THE OUTLOOK

287 Fourth Avenue
New York.

Office of
THEODORE ROOSEVELT.

DEAR DAN:—

May 26th, 1911.

After writing my few lines the other day, I was quite amused to find that Ethel was also writing you. Mrs. Roosevelt has been bemoaning the fact that you seem for the time being to have passed out of our lives. Cannot you come here soon? We will promise that you shall be left absolutely alone. You shall talk to us when you want to, and you shall not talk to anyone you don't want to, and you shall stay in your room or do anything else that you wish.

Ever yours,
T. R.

But I could pay no visits yet. I went back to Wyoming, where I lived a highly tame existence in Jackson's Hole. Very quiet; but less so than it was represented by the Associated Press, which announced my death on September 11. It was run off on the ticker of the Wall Street stock exchange, right in the midst of Steel Common, Union Pacific, and all. This is our equivalent to burial in Westminister Abbey. It did not affect the market, but it turned me loose without my identity. Quite unaware of my loss, I travelled for several days as I don't know who, vaguely puzzled by the atmosphere that my arrival anywhere created; until the hotel clerk at Ogden refused to give me a parcel addressed to me and left there by my own order. He explained to me that I was no more. He called witnesses to prove it. They had all read it last week. A strange experience; stranger still, to be reading presently some twenty obituaries. These were kindly, and couched in that faintly patronizing tone into which the living unconsciously fall when they speak of the dead.

Tame does not describe the life that Roosevelt was living in those days which brought 1911 to an end. The hurricane was blowing ever and ever more fiercely. He was exaggerated alike by the lunatic fringe of friends and enemies, whose language did not fall far short of making him out in their papers every morning both the savior of the nation and the enemy of mankind. The lunatic fringe of his enemies was by now in hysterical alarm lest he break into the White House again, and interrupt, as he had already interrupted during seven years there, the oligarchy of wealth in its program to govern the United States

solely in the interest of its own greed.    Hence their violent language.    Behind them, silently, were the masters of that party,
Aldrich, Payne, Boies Penrose, and the rest, with their eyes upon
the Republican convention, less than a year ahead.    They were
going to see to it that Taft was re-nominated.    It may be that
they had already picked on Elihu Root as chairman of the
convention.

No skill equal to theirs was to be found in the camp of their
opponents.    The Progressives were counting simply on the
preponderating will of the people.    The people wanted no more
of the oligarchy of wealth; they wanted the thing called "social
justice," a fairer distribution of the dollars earned by and ordered
and harmonious collaboration of brains and hands, and laws to
alleviate hardship which the courts should not declare unconstitutional.    Roosevelt would do this for them.    The lunatic
fringe on their side promised he would shower blessings upon
the country in such quantity and of such a kind as truly none
but a supernatural power could have wrought.    That was the
trouble; a great deal too much was promised in his name.    He
was not a magician; he was merely a man whose extraordinary
gifts made him seem able to work miracles.    And he still battled on through that Autumn, preaching his doctrines, overstating himself in the exasperation of the effort he was making,
affording his enemies grounds for their denunciations that
were only too plausible, and worst of all, steadily estranging
many good people who had until now, given him their confidence and sympathy.

If only he had kept silent during those years!    But the duck
had taken to the water, and it had carried him from the original
pond down into a raging river.    Even now he did not see what
was coming, though it lay right ahead.

None of this gave much comfort to me, watching it after my
death in Jackson's Hole.    I made him as public a gesture of
affection and faith as I was able, in a second and much longer
dedication to him of *The Virginian*, handsomely re-published
just then, with a quantity of new illustrations.    He was passing

into an eclipse with many of my own friends, people of his kind and mine, not because of his politics, not because they were afraid of their pockets; he had done something which they felt "isn't done."

How was it possible to go on opposing the course of the Administration without the thing becoming eventually personal? You can easily differ politically with a man you have never known, and make no enemy of him; you can differ with a friend as Roosevelt constantly did with Lodge, without any hurt to friendship; but with the very friend whom you put in your own place against his inclination—how can you attack his official acts while he still holds the office which you persuaded him to accept?

"It isn't done."

This is what I felt even in the silence of friends who abstained from saying it, and it was what I had to answer and defend when it was said.

Matters quickly came to a head in the new year. The President's cronic and unsuspecting amiability had been surprised in the early days of Roosevelt's public divergence; as this continued and grew more outspoken and more unmeasured in its expression, the President grew ruffled, then at length outraged. But the worst had not come yet. The two were at swords' points, but they were not actual competitors for the next Presidential nomination by the Republican party. Roosevelt was far from any wish to enter those lists. Senator La Follette had been the possible candidate for the Progressive element in the party. That Roosevelt himself should be, was no new suggestion; it had been often made to him during the recent months, and he invariably repelled it. It was as late as December 13, 1911, that he had written Bishop he would regard his nomination, from a personal standpoint as "little short of a calamity." Later still, January 29, 1912, he writes:

"Very possibly I will have to speak at the open primaries. I hope not, however. . . . If I speak it looks as if I were making myself a candidate. . . ."

Just four days later, Senator La Follette laid to rest his own
chances for ever.   What he did makes one of those spectacular
and supreme dramatic moments that set in with the assassination of McKinley, and became, before they stopped, momentous
not merely for the United States, but the world.

On February 2, 1912, the Periodical Publishers gave a great
dinner in Philadelphia.   I was a guest of *The Saturday Evening Post*.   I listened to speeches by Weir Mitchell, and by
Woodrow Wilson, no longer a college president, but now Governor of New Jersey, and whispered about as destined to fill
a greater office.   He spoke with flawless art; his dignity and
upstanding presence commanded attention, while his voice
made every symmetrical sentence melodious.   The whole company, easily eight hundred men, sat under the spell.

Then the turn was La Follette's.   I had admired him from
a distance so heartily that I had gone once to the Senate and
begged for a word with him.   When he came, I said that it was
merely to shake his hand, that in spite of being a Philadelphian
I was a Progressive, merely a private citizen, who desired to
express my admiration of his course.   His face as I was speaking
was not what I had expected.   I had looked for rugged, belligerent candor.   Craft was what I saw, and coldness, not
warmth.   It was an instantaneous disillusion, much more effective than some previous words of Roosevelt's one day at
Sagamore Hill.   Roosevelt had said that La Follette had never
been of real support in his Progressive measures at the Senate.
La Follette thanked me, and said we should win out.   After
that, his paper with his biography in it, came to me regularly.
Looking back, I see the explanation of his coldness: I had told
him of my admiration for Roosevelt.

And now La Follette rose to address those eight hundred
men.   Before he began, he made Woodrow Wilson a bow.   I
have never seen such a performance on such an occasion.   The
sentence of salute with which he accompanied it was spoken
in a tone just like the bow; the two together were a mocking
defiance.

I wondered in stupefaction.   I didn't discern then that it was La Follette's political instinct, scenting a competitor.   My stupefaction did not end with that.   With manuscript in hand, he began to speak.   He was going to tell, he said, the true story of money in the United States; by whom it was actually earned, into whose hands it had invariably gone, by what means it had been stolen from those to whom it rightfully belonged.   He prefaced this with an attack on journalism and journalists.   As he was the guest of journalists, this was an unusual beginning.

Presently everybody at our table had begun to look at each other.   Next, I saw the faces at neighboring tables staring in the same surprise.   We were soon listening to not even a pretence of accurate financial history, but a harangue of distorted denunciation, aimed apparently at us all.   The speaker's voice grew acid and raucous, his statements had ceased to be even caricatures of reality.   I could not understand why he should take the trouble to utter such absurdities before an audience that he must be aware knew better, until it was explained to me that this speech was made for home consumption, where it would appear in all the papers, and save his paying for publicity.

But he had not counted on what was rapidly overtaking him. He was not worth listening to, even as a curiosity, and people began to leave the room by the glass doors at the end opposite him.   He shook his fist at them and said:

"There go some of the fellows I'm hitting.   They don't want to hear about themselves."

The chairman called him to order, and told him that personal abuse would not be permitted.

He continued his speech, and a new astonishment came over us; whole passages were being repeated.   At first one was not sure, then it was obvious.   And the repetitions made havoc with his coherence.   In fact, all consecutive meaning departed. It was noticed by those sitting closer to the speaker's table, that La Follette was not laying the finished pages of his address down but shuffling them among what were still to be delivered.   At half-past eleven I went home. He had been speaking since ten. The hall was half empty.

Next day, I learned that he had spoken until half-past twelve, and then sank forward on the table. He had been under a great strain of suspense owing to a domestic anxiety, a surgical operation on one of his family, as I recollect, and had taken a stimulant to help him get through the effort of his speech. A nervous collapse followed. La Follette dropped from the list of possible Progressive candidates.

Eight days after that, the Republican Governors of seven states wrote Roosevelt, asking him to be their man. They put it on the ground of duty to the American people, thwarted in all their hopes by the Administration.

This brought out the not unnaturally indignant Taft in a speech at New York. He alluded to extremists; such persons were not progressives; such people were "political emotionalists or neurotics."

Just as what he had said at Winona could not have been more damaging to himself if an enemy had said it, so now. Who was the neurotic? If, after the letter of the seven governors, any desire to keep out of it still held Roosevelt back, neurotic settled him.

So did these two old friends reach the personal break which was bound to come, once Roosevelt had stepped out of private life to champion, no matter how impersonally at first, the cause he had confided to Taft's inappropriate hands, which Aldrich and the others had taken good care should slide out of those hands to the ground.

Roosevelt put "his hat in the ring." Within nine days, he made a speech at Columbus that drove more of his former friends away from him. Next, he sent his acceptance to the seven Governors. It is strange to note how temperate, how reasonable, many passages in his speeches at that time seem to-day. For example, he said in New York, shortly after his Columbus speech:

"If on this new continent we merely build another country of great but unjustly divided material prosperity, we shall have done nothing; and we shall do as little if we merely *set the greed of envy against the greed of arrogance, and thereby destroy the material well-being of all of us.*"

Not many would disagree with that to-day. Many italics emphasize his unchanged hostility to the extremes of Labor and of Capital, the balanced measured attitude which had always brought him the emnity of the Gompers and the Haywoods, alike with that of the Harrimans and the Aldriches, and the love and confidence of the people at large. He did not lose the people at large in 1912. Enough of them all over the country wished him enthusiastically to be the next President; but he had alarmed too many trained and thoughtful minds, who saw our institutions steadily and saw them whole. To these minds, Roosevelt's utterances during this tempestuous period sounded constantly as if his intention was to wade to "social justice" through the wreck of every Constitutional barrier that stood in the way of his impatience. His phrase, the "recall of judicial decisions" sounded his final knell as definitely, I think, as Mr. Taft's fatal simile. Hurt, aroused and outraged by Roosevelt's attacks, he entered the lists to defend his own cause. "Even a rat will fight when cornered!" he exclaimed in a speech. It raised the deadly laugh of ridicule. He hadn't a chance of election, even if the machinery of conventions, as worked by Penrose and Aldrich, should force upon the will of the majority his nomination by a skilful, unscrupulous, and determined few. And this machinery was going to be worked by Penrose and Aldrich, with the last turn of its wheels engineered by Elihu Root.

Let me do those men justice. In their place, with their perfectly wise and well-founded value for the system of government so slowly and thoroughly forged for us at the beginning, and quite aside from their determination to uphold a vicious and dangerous oligarchy, I should have been so concerned at the intemperance with which Roosevelt only too often defined

his aims, that I should have been afraid of him.  I was not in
their place, I was not afraid of him; I had heard him run away
with himself in private; and now the roughness of his public
phrases in my opinion correspond as little with what his deliberate acts were likely to be, as it always had.  I was not much
enamoured with the initiative and referendum, still less with
the recall; I classed them with those quack medicines of which
Americans are so fond, but I doubted their being administered
in the prodigal doses that Roosevelt sounded as if he were
prescribing.  I am certain that in the intensity of that campaign, and the exasperation at finding himself enmeshed in it
against his inclinition, though absolutely in consequence of
every step he had taken, he lost his sense of proportion, and
had no idea how much further his words went than his intentions.  Once in the White House he invited me to look on
while a Japanese expert taught him the tricks of jiu-jitzu.  Did
I catch the way one of them was done? he inquired.  I hadn't,
the motions of the wrestling had been too quick.  He would
show me, he said.  He took hold of me, told me how to put my
arms in defense, and then he showed me.  It may have taken
thirty seconds.  After that illustration, my Adam's apple was
sore for three days.  Swallowing hurt.  Of course he never
knew it, and of course I never told him.  In 1912 he had no
notion of how it hurt to swallow some of the things he was
saying.

But more than his political doctrines, his break with Taft
damaged him with many friends of mine.  To hear him called
ambitious, which I knew very well that he was not, save in the
same sense that Washington was ambitious, could only be met by
amicable contradiction.  None of us ever quarrelled about it;
appearances seemed to favor it; and until his letter after his
death proved how little it was true, there could be no proof.  It
was more difficult to answer the charge of disloyalty to an old
friend for whose predicament he was responsible.  He owed
it to the friend to keep silence and stand off, no matter what his
thoughts were.

In my secret heart I wished that he had never spoken, but I went about maintaining that it was the only thing he could possibly do: what was friendship when the welfare of the nation, as he saw it, was being betrayed?   Could he allow that to go on, and not speak?   So I contended, so I replied to letters.   Worse, however, than what I had to hear, was what I sometimes overheard.   Not aware I was within earshot, an old and dear friend said:

"If I met Roosevelt in the street I would not speak to him. I would not permit him inside my house."

This was the eclipse into which Roosevelt passed in 1912, and out of which by 1917 he was destined so wholly and splendidly to emerge.

"During the days of The Bull Moose aberration," said Dr. Fred Shattuck as I was driving in Boston with him in 1916, "I considered Roosevelt the most dangerous influence in the country.   And I would vote for him as President to-morrow." Shattuck was not hasty minded; his wisdom is remembered in Boston.   His remark expresses the opinion of many thousands.

It was an exciting, but not a happy time, for any one who had taken part in the White House years and remembered the Familiars, their laughter, their good will, and the mutual regard between Roosevelt the President and Taft his secretary. This conflict of 1912 is dimly reflected in some, but not all, of the letters which Roosevelt wrote me as it proceeded.   The first of them happens to be dated on the very day that La Follette was to destroy whatever prospects he had as Presidential nominee.

THE OUTLOOK
287 Fourth Avenue
New York.

Office of
THEODORE ROOSEVELT.

February 2nd, 1912.

DEAR DAN:—

Cannot you come and see me for a night or two soon?   There is so much that I wish to talk over with you.   As you know,

ever since the publication of your last book, I have been wanting
to talk over the preface.

Love to Mrs. Wister.

Ever yours,

T. R.

The conflict, with his private feelings about it, is quite visible
in the following:

THE OUTLOOK

287 Fourth Avenue
New York.

Office of
Theodore Roosevelt.

February 9th, 1912.

DEAR DAN:—

By George!   That is firstrate.   You shall be absolutely
alone, and if any beast of a politician turns up, I will slaughter
him quietly and unostentatiously in another room, and you will
not even know that he is there until he is a corpse!

But most unfortunately the dates you mention are not possible for me.   On the 21st I go to Ohio to speak at the Constitutional Convention, returning on Thursday the 22nd, and
from the 24th to the 29th I shall be in Boston.   March, however, at any time suits me down to the ground; but Mrs. Roosevelt and Ethel on receiving your letter put in a most vigorous
plea that you should not come until after March 15th.   They
are going down to Panama on the 24th of this month, and will
return on the 14 or 15th of March.   Now if it is more convenient for you to come out say on Friday or Saturday March
1st or 2nd, for Sunday, and as much longer as you wish, come.
If, however, you will yield to the clamors of Mrs. Roosevelt and
Ethel, then put it off for two weeks or three weeks, whichever
is convenient for you.   Come any day in March; but let me
know as far in advance as is convenient.

With love to Mrs. Wister,

Ever yours,

T. R.

The next is evidently in reply to my suggesting that we should
meet in New York at the Harvard Club, and lunch there; this

we sometimes used to do.   What or who I was to bring over
on Friday, has dropped into oblivion.

THE OUTLOOK

287 Fourth Avenue
New York.

Office of
Theodore Roosevelt.

February 20th, 1912.

DEAR DAN:

Don't ask me to come in on Saturday.   It is the day I am
always in the country.   Could you not bring them over on
Friday?   But, my dear Dan, I could not possibly make such
a speech as you request.   I have had to quit all speech making
for the past nine months, and from now on I shall make only
the two or three speeches that I cannot possibly get out of.

Your proposal for Thursday, March 21st to stay until Saturday 22nd is splendid.   If it is absolutely convenient to you I
would suggest that you come on Wednesday and stay until Friday, simply because on Fridays I am in town.   But Mrs. Roosevelt and Ethel will be out on Friday anyhow, and I would be
back in the evening.

Give my warmest regards to Mrs. Wister, and wish her all
good luck with her Civic Club.

Always yours,

T. R.

His letter of April 11 partly indicates the situation.   It is
dictated on a train.   He is in the whirl of his battle.   He writes
to Doctor J. William White, that belligerent member of the
Mahogany Tree Club who in the days of the Coal Strike Commission had assailed me for not defending Roosevelt more
vigorously against the denunciations which George Baer was
hurling at him while the Club dined.   White and van Valkenburg were now the leaders of our small, ardent, and widely
frowned-on Roosevelt group in Philadelphia.   White had come
to me and said that I must introduce Roosevelt when he made
his speech at our Metropolitan Opera House.   I was very glad
of this chance to show my allegiance by something more conspicuous than the re-dedication of *The Virginian*.

It was to come in some seven days.   I set to work to think up something with a point and short, that I could say in three minutes or so to very much the largest crowd I had ever faced. On the day itself, a day of heavy clouds, a devoted three of us met.   Roosevelt at Coatesville on his way East through the State in his special train.   He was indeed the buzz saw that Winty Chanler had called him at the White House table.   His greeting was enough to reward one double for the small part I was playing.   I went through a whirling introduction to people I had never heard of, who had never heard of me, and whose names I totally failed to grasp and retain.

We moved eastward out of Coatesville.   Roosevelt shut himself in with papers and secretaries.   I had my little speech with me, ready for criticism.   White and Robins pronounced it too short.   So we worked together to add a couple of minutes to it, while the train rolled on and at the stations along its course crowds to the right of us, crowds to the left of us volleyed and thundered.   They demanded the buzz saw—a look at him, a word from him.   He gave it: often bursting out of his busy seclusion and back into it again, all in a breath.   The energy, the action, the hammered words, the blaze of genial, jocund power, the prompt and marvelous application of some special sentence to some special place,—I can call it nothing but gigantic.

One lull in this tempest came with dinner in a small room, high up in the hotel at Philadelphia.   It was at the meal that Roosevelt's manner of drinking was illustrated as well and typically as ever I saw it.   The rest of us had something before sitting down, and at table some champagne.   Roosevelt took none of it.   He asked if he might have some white wine. A bottle of sauterne was brought him.   "Thank you!" he interrupted his stream of talk to say to the waiter, and resumed his talk instantly.   Throughout the meal he discoursed to us steadily—I don't remember any words from any of us but a syllable of assent to something now and then—and so to the coffee. We got up to start for the Metropolitan Opera House.   There near his plate on the table was the bottle with its cork half-drawn. The bottle was full. His glass was dry. He had forgotten all about the white wine he had asked for.

Up the street to the Opera House, more crowds volleyed and thundered and outside the place itself was a swimming sea of people who could not get in. Inside, back of the stage, music started, I marched forward in a sort of daze, was aware of palms and flags and chairs and a table, and a white welter of faces gazing and hands clapping from floor to roof; then a wilder crash of applause as Roosevelt pranced into full sight—for he did literally spring and step to the music—then silence, and my turn.

An inspiration flashed on me.

"The weather was dark this morning," I began, "but to-night the sun is shining."

It went off well. They were with me, and I gave them no time to become impatient. When I turned to Roosevelt, he was not prepared for the gesture I made. Being an amateur at this game, I walked to him and shook hands; he looked at me a little at a loss; I sat down at once. I had wanted to emphasize in the sight of that crowd what my feeling was for him.

He made one happy improvisation during his speech. A voice from the gallery called out something indistinguishable.

"What was that?" asked Roosevelt, looking up.

No reply.

"What did you say?" Roosevelt repeated.

Again silence.

"Well," said Roosevelt, "a Bull Moose can make various sounds."

It was in Milwaukee a few months later that he made another happy improvisation. He had just been shot in the street by an assassin on his way to make an address; but he would not stop. On the platform he drew his manuscript from his pocket and found the hole made by the bullet which it had deflected from his heart. He held up the perforated wad of manuscript.

"It takes more than that to kill a Bull Moose!" he told them —and spoke to the finish.

The bullet put an end to his speaking tour, but not to any inch of Roosevelt.   In bed at the hospital in Chicago next day, he dictated to Beveridge a message to his party:

"It matters little about me," it began.   "Always the cause is there," it ended.

This is his letter to us in Philadelphia, written the day after our meeting at the Metropolitan Opera House:

> En Route
> Pullman Private Car "CONVOY"
>
> April 11, 1912.
>
> My dear Doctor:—
> I wish you would show this letter to Messrs. Wister, Robins and Morris.
> In the first place, I wish you to understand that I appreciate all that you four men have done for me and all that your support has meant to me.
> In the next place, I feel I ought to tell you that Mr. van Valkenburg informs me that it is your four men to whom most is owing for the success of the great meeting last night, and indeed for the success of the whole movement here in Philadelphia. As Mr. van Valkenburg says, it needed genuine courage to take the stand that you did at the time that you did.   Believe me, my dear fellow, I appreciate it and I want you four men to know that I understand very clearly and value very, very highly what all of you did.
> Give my love to Mrs. White,
>
> Always yours,
>
> THEODORE ROOSEVELT
>
> Dr. J. William White,
> 1810 S. Rittenhouse Square,
> Philadelphia, Pa.

The others, not I, had done all the heavy work—but who would object to being included in such a letter?

## XXIII.

Two days before his letter to us, the voters in Illinois had fired the first shot of popular opinion.   They elected at their primaries fifty-eight delegates to the convention. Fifty-six were for Roosevelt. Thirteen states had presently chosen two hundren and seventy-eight delegates instructed for Roosevelt against sixty-eight for Taft. Great excitement prevailed at all the primaries, the count of the votes was challenged in many districts and a storm of discontent rolled up, ready to break at Chicago. It did break there against Taft bulwarks that were storm proof.

Ten hundred and seventy-eight delegates came to Chicago in advance of the convention, Roosevelt's outnumbering Taft's by more than a dozen, and over two hundred seats contested. Five hundred and forty votes were necessary for a choice of Presidential candidate.

The adventure of a delegate between his primaries and his seating in the Republican convention with full right to vote somewhat resembles that of a coin in the mint. The coin as stamped with its image and value may be what it looks, but before it becomes true money its weight is tested. It is sent through machinery so delicately adjusted that if it falls short by even a feather, it is automatically flung out and along comes the next. A delegate with his credentials of election may look like a delegate, but between him and his seat is the National Committee. He and his credentials must pass through that machinery.

The powers behind Taft were ready for all cases of contested seats. The machinery of the National Committee had been carefully adjusted. Coins were to be flung out not according to weight, but according to how they were stamped. A coin might be full weight, but if it were stamped with Roosevelt's image, it might be rejected in favor of a short weight coin bearing Taft's image. With two hundred seats contested by rival delegates, the way was open to validate the credentials of whichever claimant suited the machinery, and report him to the convention as rightfully seated there.

The membership of the National Commission in 1912 was fifty-three, controlled by Senator Boies Penrose of Pennsylvania and Senator Murray Crane of Massachusetts. Both had been defeated at their primaries as delegates, neither therefore, represented the will of the voters; but they held over their term on the Committee from 1908.  In addition to them were twenty-nine others representing the will of no voters; some fifteen had been defeated in their States like Penrose and Crane, about ten were from Southern States where the electoral vote would be democratic, and Alaska with other territories having no electoral vote contributed four.  This band with eight other adherents making thirty-seven in all, stood ready to take whatever orders Penrose gave them.

The machinery being adjusted to this point, one part still required attention.  To have a roll-call in case of doubt as to votes cast, a request by one fifth was necessary in the Senate and the House under the Constitution, and the Committee had hitherto followed this precedent.  A request by ten out of fifty-three would suffice here.  It was too few for present purposes. Ten were there who might demand a roll-call or the votes as to the weight of Roosevelt coins, and a roll-call might prove awkward.  They raised it to twenty by a special rule.  With this adjusted, the machinery could declare counterfeit as many coins as needed for the emergency, and substitute as many others. Five hundred and forty being necessary to nominate, they shut their doors to the world and settled to their jobs in safe seclusion. It was thoroughly done.  Of the contested seats, two hundred and thirty-three were given to Taft delegates, six to Roosevelt, and in *seventy-four decisions no roll was called*.

This was not accomplished in peace.  Some noise of protest came through the closed doors; but it was when the convention began on June 18 that the storm broke out wild and deafening before the roll was called there.  The Governor of Missouri appealed from the decisions of the National Committee, where Penrose with his thirty-seven followers had unseated seventy-four Roosevelt delegates.  He was ruled out of order by the acting chairman.  The business of electing a temporary chairman proceeded amid a chaos of vituperation.  The victory for the powers was fairly close, but enough.  It shut off all chance of reversing the Penrose decisions. It insured a committee on credentials that would undo nothing that had been done behind the closed doors of the National Committee. It cleared the way for the seventy-four contested delegates to be their own umpire. As each case came up, that delegate did not vote, but the seventy-three others voted for him. In other words the counterfeit Taft coins were allowed to decide that they were genuine, and that the genuine Roosevelt coins were counterfeit.

No need to go into details. During five days, mostly of tempest, under the rulings of Elihu Root, first temporary and then permanent chairman of the convention, the storm beat against the Taft bulwarks in vain. The work of Penrose and his thirty-seven was ratified, and jammed through to the end. And so on that occasion thirty-seven men, twenty-nine of them repudiated as delegates, virtually nominated a President of the United States behind closed doors in defiance of the expressed will of a large majority.

The battle wavered once or twice. Offers of compromise, possibly genuine, were made to Roosevelt. He met these by announcing his readiness to support any candidate but Taft— if the roll of delegates was first purged of fraud. He rejected one offer that came from another quarter and was certainly genuine. On the fourth night of the convention, word was brought him that some thirty delegates were tired of this. They had been instructed for Taft, but not to assist at the dissolution of the Republican party. They had no wish to witness this any longer. They would cast their votes for any new nominee, if the Roosevelt men would also throw him some of theirs. This would lose Taft the nomination in the first ballot. If he failed then he would drop out. It was known that a stampede to Roosevelt would follow; no Penrose or Root could stem the tide with the wind blowing as it was. Roosevelt would not hear of it. He would listen to nothing and he would accept nothing from a convention that was crooked. With these well authenticated and recorded facts, those who still repeat that he wanted that nomination have not a toe, much less a leg, to stand on.

The mood of the powers behind Taft was implacable to the point that so long as Taft was nominated in June, his defeat in November was of less importance. What their eyes were fixed on was the present moment alone. Let the Democrats win and have the next four years. In 1916 the Republicans would come back. Roosevelt must be choked off now at any cost. Some of them foresaw well enough by then that it would cost them the election.

This was manifest to other observers also. Among the newspaper men reporting the convention was Bryan. They liked him so well, that upon his appearance among them day after day they would drop their own quarrels to unite in applauding him. This was so invariable that one of them said to him that if he would prove as popular as this at the approaching convention of his own party to be held in Baltimore, he would find himself nominated to run against Taft. But Bryan had already been a defeated candidate three times, beginning in 1896 when he lost to McKinley. He had no thought of bringing bad luck to the Democrats again. He replied:

"My boy, do you think I'm going to run for President just to get the Republican party out of a hole?"

And there sat Mrs. Roosevelt watching Elihu Root ruling out her husband, his old associate and friend, throwing in some extra Taft coins from Massachusetts and Louisiana for good measure, and carefully avoiding her eyes; delivering the goods as faithfully and capably as he always delivered the goods to those who had engaged his services, whether it was Croker the boss of Tammany, or Penrose the stand-pat Republican, or Roosevelt the Progressive.

In breaking with Taft, Roosevelt allowed sincere political convictions to outweigh friendship. In breaking with Roosevelt, Root (I will assume) allowed sincere political convictions to outweigh friendship. Is there much difference between these cases? I see little. Yet never once have I heard a critic of Roosevelt's act apply the same reasoning to Root's. Is it that they avoid a parallel which fails so strikingly at one point?

Roosevelt would take nothing from that convention because it was crooked; upon this crookedness Root had deliberately set his seal.

Perhaps some others are of my mind and wish that both Roosevelt and Root for the sake of the days of auld lang syne had held back. Lodge did. Though the recall of judicial decisions was to him just the reckless slashing of a rift in the great levee which had been raised to fend the nation from the floods of mob rule, altogether the worst heresy yet, nevertheless Lodge took no active hand in defeating his friend. He held aloof. I know that those days were deeply painful both to him and to Mrs. Lodge; and I know also that Roosevelt at this time as at all times felt no personal resentment against any whose honest political convictions differed from his own. But I doubt if he ever wished to see Root again.

How can a preacher militant see eye to eye with legal minds? As Tweed, another legal mind, and chief counsel for the Southern Pacific System, summed the preacher up to me during an ocean voyage in 1906:

"He is very lawless."

"He is," I admitted.

For Tweed, for Lodge, for Root, quite aside from Roosevelt's brusque foreshortening phrase for the process, it was intellectually impossible not to recoil from the slashing of the levee; intellectually impossible not to think that some other—if slower —road to social justice should be surveyed according to law, and that meanwhile it was better for the future of all the people that some of the people should suffer injustice for the present. I am sure this was their view, and I know that it is mine. Time may show that the Constitution can be improved; never that it must be undermined.

It was in a quiet valley of New York State that I read day by day of the very unquiet scenes at Chicago; and of how, when the powers behind Taft had consummated their work and put the Republican party in a hole, Roosevelt with his Bull Moose followers had walked out of the convention and started their own campaign amid the singing of hymns.

I was not enthusiastic about this singing of hymns. Had such psalmody broken out over the emancipation of slaves, well and good. But heartily as I hated the undoing of Roosevelt's progressive work under the Taft Administration, equally in my heart I did not think initiative, referendum, and recall, quite sacred enough for hymns. This singing did not cease with its first spontaneous outburst. The Bull Moose kept it up at later meetings, when it was high time that they cooled off and settled down to work that was more practical, if less inspirational. Moreover, there was nothing inspired in the manner of their falling out with each other over the Sherman Anti-Trust Law, which they proceeded promptly to do. Some wished it amended thus, and some thus; and this early mess came all too soon upon what I had written Roosevelt from my valley. I had bidden him god-speed, but to beware of his own lunatic fringe. Of course my allusion to it was more cautious than that. He replied:

THE OUTLOOK

287 Fourth Avenue
New York

Office of
Theodore Roosevelt

June 28th, 1912.

DEAR DAN:

You are absolutely right. But, my dear Dan, that danger is only one of a multitude of dangers ahead of me! I have had to do a good many difficult and perplexing jobs in my time, but never one as perplexing and difficult as that on which I am now engaged.

With love to Mrs. Dan.

Sincerely yours,

T. R.

This followed me from my valley and found me in Santa Barbara. The Democrats had held their convention and nominated Woodrow Wilson at Baltimore. Bryan went there to head off the nomination of Champ Clark, which would have put the

Democrats in the same sort of hole that the Republicans were in. To Bryan's own surprise, he succeeded not only in keeping them out, but in deepening the hole for the Republicans. The political creed of Wilson was progressive like Roosevelt's; if elected, he was certain to push liberal measures and oppose such measures as would have been urged by Champ Clark and the Tammany powers behind him. The fact is, that if Roosevelt had not been running, I should have voted for Wilson, and so would many like me all over the country. So far from killing Taft's chances—which had already ceased to exist—Roosevelt's candidacy took more votes from Wilson than it took from Taft.

Henry S. Pritchett was in Santa Barbara, and we discussed the highly dramatic situation. I confessed to him that although I should vote for Roosevelt naturally, he had been committed by some of his followers to so many and such extreme promises of reform that he could not possibly fulfill all of them, and that his prestige would in consequence inevitably suffer. I almost hoped that Wilson would win. Pritchett could not hope such a thing. His personal acquaintance with Wilson had convinced him that Wilson had a curiously inflexible mind. Once he had made it up, neither reasoning nor facts could alter it. This, Pritchett feared, might prove dangerous for the country should some crisis arise where the President must follow events with an open and ready mind.

Although this did not affect my opinion at the time, in after days it came back to me with great force. I suppose that all prophecy since prophesying began, no matter how sound, has had the fate of falling in vain upon unwilling ears.

I went from Santa Barbara back to Jackson's Hole, and on the way there did my little bit, a very little bit, for the cause of the Bull Moose party. At the Idaho town of St. Anthony I made a speech. I told them about that sparring match in the old Harvard Gymnasium. I told them that we had the same Roosevelt now, and I developed the theme of his magnanimity and fair mindedness by sundry illustrations. I should doubt having won many votes.   Borah was in command of Idaho; and though Borah had been ardent for Roosevelt at the start in Chicago, he found himself at the finish in a position so delicate that nothing but the nicest skill could adequately deal with it.   The only other bit I did was to write an article for the San Francisco *Chronicle,* making more elaborately the same points of my St. Anthony speech.

But all those months of 1912 were bitter ones to live, in spite of their excitement; and not a word that Roosevelt wrote or said that I know of, gives the slightest notion that he took any joy in them.   He had not wished to be nominated at the beginning, he would not accept nomination from a crooked convention at the end, he had little belief that he could be elected by the Bull Moose party, and little in common with their lunatic fringe.   I believe that the only thing which kept him going at all was the zest of action in battle which came from the preacher militant.

I went from Jackson's Hole to Boston to attend the first meeting of the Harvard Overseers in late September.   There I fell into talk with President Eliot about the three candidates for the Presidency.

"For whom do you intend to vote?" he asked.

"I always voted for Cleveland," I answered, "though I'm a Republican I suppose.   But I'll never vote for Taft again."

"You're for Roosevelt, then?"

"Oh, yes."

"I could not support him.   He is too headlong," said President Eliot, without harshness, with a sort of almost indulgent disapproval.   I had heard him express great admiration for Roosevelt.

"Well, Mr. Eliot, I should be for Wilson—but how can I vote against my friend?"

"No, you can't do that!" he assented, with his quiet, wise, and magnanimous smile.

What History will say about the bitter days of 1912 when three ran for President and the Democrat won, who can tell?

History often misses the truth, or we should not have contradictions about past events.    Two opinions, both cock-sure, prevail to-day, according to which camp you are in: that Roosevelt lost Taft the election by running independent, and that the Republican managers killed the party by forcing Taft upon an angry people.    I am convinced that no Republican but Roosevelt had a chance in 1912, just as no Democrat at all had a chance in 1920. That I am in the Roosevelt camp hinders neither my regret that he did not keep out of it on returning from Africa, nor my opinion that Taft had a right to feel hurt.    He had not wished to be President.    He was the victim of Roosevelt's honest enthusiasm for him.    The whole story would be irredeemably painful, had not these old friends come together before the end, and had not Taft come to his own as Chief Justice of our Supreme Court.

How bright he shines in his generosity when he writes me in 1929—"You are a friend of Roosevelt, I know, and therefore would use the story in a way that would not bring any criticism upon Mr. Roosevelt, for I would not wish to circulate it and have any such result. . . ."

When news came of Wilson's election, it was a positive relief! My faith and hope were fixed upon him, in spite of Henry Pritchett.

## XXIV.

Whether or not I told Roosevelt this at Sagamore Hill that Autumn, I cannot remember.    The very fact that no recollection of our touching upon politics at all remains with me, is good evidence that if we did, it must have been very slight.    The only talk we had which is still vivid was quite wide of politics.    We were in the great back room that Grant La Farge had built for him.

"Listen and attend with care," I began.    "I want your advice.    Which of these books shall I write?"

Then I sketched the plan of each.    One was to be the story

WILLIAM HOWARD TAFT

of a young actor and his wife.   The young actor makes a great hit, which casts his wife and her acting wholly into the shade. He becomes an idol, she remains nobody.   But after his first success he meets failure after failure.   His hit was the accident of his part calling merely for a playing of his own personality. He goes steadily into the shade, while she emerges steadily into the light because she has genuine talent and works very hard. Develop this situation.   Title: *The Fixed Star*.

Roosevelt had listened in silence.   "Now for the next," was all he said.

I sketched it.   A picture of Philadelphia, and its passing from the old to the new order; the hero of no social position, married to a wife of good social position elsewhere, and turning out superior to his wife.   Possible title: *Dividends in Democracy*.

"Now for the third," said Roosevelt.

"That is to be called *The Marriages of Scipio*," I said. "Scipio Le Moyne, a character in The Virginian, will be the central figure.   It is to be the tragedy of the cowpuncher who survives his own era and cannot adjust himself to the more civilized era which succeeds it."   And I told him some of the chief incidents and the conclusion.

"Why, my dear Dan," he exclaimed, "you must write all three!   And you must begin with your Philadelphia story. And when you come to your cowboy tragedy, why—don't leave it in such unrelieved blackness.   Let in some sunlight, somehow.   Leave your reader with the feeling that life, after all, does—go—on."

While he was saying this—in fact his tone was one of urging —that look of wistfulness which I had come to know so well clouded his face and eyes.

In 1913 I saw him but once.   Ethel was married to Richard Derby at Oyster Bay.   The day was beautiful and warm with the airs of Spring and the approach of Summer.   Its brightness came in through the open windows among the flowers and the friends that filled the little church.   As one looked about, familiar faces were smiling everywhere. After the quiet and solemn service, in whose sweetness the whole congregation shared, the same feeling went with us all to Sagamore Hill. That concourse of men and women, so many of whom knew each other so well, had a quality that was like the flowers and the day. Most of us had been at the White House when Alice was married in the East Room. In that stately atmosphere, beneath the inevitable spell, we could not be quite as we were in that country house. The cordiality, the welcome, were alike beneath either roof—but here at Sagamore Hill, the host was not our President, Mrs. Roosevelt and he were free from every obligation but their own natural hospitality and the pleasure they always took in showing it.

One intimate moment was the same in both houses. The bridegroom at each wedding was a member of that club at Harvard where I the sophomore had first talked with Roosevelt the Senior, thirty-three years ago now. As the years had fallen away from us in the White House, they fell away at Sagamore Hill when we members of that club, young and old, gathered by ourselves for a little while in a room apart, and in the name of our dearest undergraduate memories became one in age and in spirit. . . .

Ethel's father and mother created a chance for certain friends to see a little more of them on that day of many guests. They summoned us at the propitious time to a corner of the drawing room where a small table had been laid by the window. There we few sat and lunched and talked with them at leisure. That is a precious memory: the beautiful day, the concourse of old friends, friends from youth, the host and hostess; it was the last radiant excursion that my wife and I were destined to share.

In October Roosevelt went to South America. He wrote me one letter at that time from certain depths of heart and spirit that he seldom opened. I had gone to Nauheim in Germany before his return. He was presently in Spain to be at Kermit's wedding. At Nauheim I debated writing him to give me a letter which might serve to procure me an audience with the Kaiser.

I did not; too many Americans must have plagued him for passports to crowned heads.

One afternoon at Nauheim, in late May or early June, a zeppelin floated quietly above us, while in the neighborhood some military manoeuvers were going on.

"These people are so thorough," I said to my companion, "that I shouldn't wonder if the Berlin war office had blue prints tucked away of every bridge, signal tower, and tunnel of the Pennsylvania Railroad."

Some months later I mentioned that random guess to the president of the road. It was virtually right. Such details had been more than once furnished on request. When engineers of the road had once asked similar courtesies at Berlin, they had been bowed politely from door to door, and so—out!

On June 28 I walked into our hotel at Triberg in the Black Forest. Some six or seven clustered by the bulletin board. This announced the assassination of a couple I had never heard of in a place with a strange name that I could not pronounce. And a voice at the edge of our group spoke:

"That is the match which will set all Europe in flames."

He was a tall lean grey man, pale, and of great distinction. I had noticed him at meals. It was the first word I ever heard from him, and the last. It made no impression on me at the time. I did not think of it again until August, in mid-ocean.

About July 25, an old English lady asked me if I believed that Austria would actually declare war on Serbia. I didn't know what she meant. Trouble between England and Ulster was all that the London papers seemed to be talking about.

On August 1 I laid some sovereigns down to pay my London hotel bill. Did I not need gold for myself? the landlady asked. No, I was sailing. Why did she ask? Because gold had been stopped at her bank. She was very grateful to receive my sovereigns.

I drove through restless streets to St. Pancras. There I got into a train amid unrest. In two hours I was steaming down the Thames from Tilbury docks. At the mouth of the river, battleships searched us with their shifting glare.  We reached the open sea.  Each morning wireless told of new fires leaping out in Europe.  By the fourth, England was at war with Germany.  On the seventh day, most of the lights on our ship were put out, blankets were stuffed in all the port holes, the vessel trembled as she suddenly sprang to her utmost speed, and we rushed for two days through a thick fog in silence, never a whistle sounding.  I slept in my clothes, but could not understand the agitation of a stewardess about our German pursuers —they were said to be two.  What could they do to a passenger ship but take us to the nearest German port?

"Oh, sir, you don't know them.  They'd send us to the bottom of the sea."

I didn't believe a word of it.  In two days we reached the Nantucket light ship, and slowed down, and so docked at New York.

Our ship now lies at the bottom of the Mediterranean with a hole from a submarine in her.

## XXV.

All Europe was indeed in flames; flames which Roosevelt saw very early in that appalling conflagration—saw and proclaimed —would end by setting us afire if we did not make ready against them.  Important bankers told the world that these flames would die down in three months.  The Kaiser told the world that he would eat his Christmas dinner in Paris.  Kitchener told the world that it would be thirty-six months before the fire was extinguished.  Fifty months after these predictions, the flames were put out.

And in the White House sat a man who had taught school too much.  He never shook it off.  He instructed men from behind a perpetual desk.  When they dared to instruct him, he expelled them.  He appointed inferiors to be his official advisers, and never consulted them.  Did he listen to Colonel House because Colonel House was not an official adviser?  Finally, he expelled him too.    Does the habit of teaching exclude the power to be taught?    Does it treat contradiction as if it were a crime?    What continually defeated the true greatness that was in Woodrow Wilson, what made him only the fragment of a great man?    Too much of self?    Too much rigidity?    Through him, tragedy fell upon great multitudes, and in the end upon himself.    Wilson might have steered us well enough in smooth weather, but storms found him unequal to his task.    His course in the Mexican storm showed this.    And in 1914, none save a leader quick to see, ready to learn, and of prompt and firm decision, could have struck and held the true course in this monstrous roar of events novel and incessant, this world of another dimension that had cracked off from all life we had known, and had become such a place that one was glad some old people one had loved were no longer on earth to know what earth could be.    And henceforth for many a day, two voices were destined to speak to the American people, who would learn, very slowly, to listen less and less to the voice from the White House, and more and more to the voice from Sagamore Hill.

Flames!    They became the background of existence.    Whatever one might be doing or thinking, in moments of pleasure or laughter, or of brief forgetting, the lurid glow was there day and night.    In sleep one got away from it, as one does in times of a supreme sorrow, waking at morning unhaunted by it for a few seconds, only a few—and then it rushes back.

I landed with my mind still in a fog as thick as that our ship had rushed through.    Ten days of wireless had brought more news than ever ten days before—but who was the original incendiary?    I knew that England and France could not be.    Germany had violated the neutrality of Belgium.    That looked bad for Berlin.    Yet in the second week of August I was groping for the true incendiary.

That tall grey gentleman at Triberg: who could he have been? Had he guessed, or had he known?    But who, on the very day a fanatic youth named Princip had shot the heir of Austria in a corner of nowhere in particular, was in a position to say that this would start a war from Petersburg through Berlin to Brussels, London, Paris, Vienna, Belgrade, Constantinople, and much between, and a great deal beyond—and have his prediction come true in about nine weeks?

He could not have known. Nobody had planned such a thing. Even the original incendiary recoiled nervously from the fire he had lighted, when he saw on July 30 and 31 how it was going to spread. After it had been raging two years, he shrank peevishly from having it referred to in his presence. It never touched a hair of his head. He is the most contemptible figure in the whole story. How contemptible none of us had means of knowing for several years, when diplomacy had divulged more of its secrets. We laid the whole blame at the door of the German Emperor. But he had not lighted the fire; his guilt lies in fanning it one day and trying to blow it out the next. He may be said to have spoken his own doom on July 5, 1914. His habit of fanning and blowing, of pulling his sword half way out and pushing it back, had already earned him the name of the *four-flusher* in poker circles. His ambition zig-zagged between the rôles of Europe's Peace-warden and Europe's War-lord; he tried to assume both parts. Fate finished with him in November 9, 1918, when he abdicated. Long before that, more ruthless hands than his had grasped the guidance of the Empire and were conducting it to ruin. It was his misfortune—had he stayed and faced death one would call it his tragedy—to have a brilliant clear-sighted mind across which the clouds of his vanity constantly swept. Many good people were warmly attached to him. Had he kept silence in his Holland exile, a few rags of dignity might clothe him still.

That two murders at Serajevo would plunge a dozen nations into war, was that Triberg gentleman's shrewd deduction, based upon the omens of many years. He put a number of manifestations together: The Algeciras conference, The Agadir incident, the demoting of Delcassé by France at the order of Berlin, German-Austrian alliance, English-French-Russian pact, the periodic rattle of the sword, that toast of the German navy,

*der Tag!* the prosperous industry of Krupp, the race in dread-
noughts, the deserters of Casa Blanca, the Treaty of Bucharest,
Russia's Balkan pets, always snarling—he put these and other
portents together.   He knew how unstable was the equilibrium
of Europe.   And so he was able to tell us immediately and cor-
rectly in front of that hotel bulletin board what we were going
to witness.   It was a daring mental jump into space on June 28,
1914.   Memoirs, histories, state papers, have disclosed so far
no other jump like that.

Sometime in December, Roosevelt made an uncanny suggestion to me, suddenly.   We were discussing the War.   We discussed little else any more.   He twisted his face up, and said:

"How many lies do you suppose that Viennese Christmas-tree
jumping-jack told that male prima donna at Potsdam?"

He had put his finger on the original incendiary.   This was
also a remarkable jump to make, though not equal to the one at
Triberg.   We had learned a great deal by December, 1914; but
everything we knew pointed to Berlin as the main culprit.
Berlin was by no means innocent, but the basest guilt was not
there.

The prime instigators of what had come upon the world could
have sat without crowding in a room of ordinary size; these
with their collateral abettors in Vienna, Belgrade, Berlin, and
Petersburg, could be lodged easily in an Atlantic City hotel,
every man with a bed to himself, and a number of rooms unoccupied.   This collection of ministers, ambassadors, and generals, sent some ten million perfectly innocent men to die of
shells or gas or disease on land and sea, without one of themselves getting a scratch.

The more we learn about the court of the Czar, the less we
grieve over its obliteration.   The Kaiser, too, was surrounded
by persons of such a character that to read of them is to wonder
how his Empire kept going, and going so strong; it is an immense testimony to the stable worth and to the docility of that
people.   The court of Francis Joseph was also honeycombed
by mental and moral decadence, his dual Empire was groggy

with its racial jealousies.    Paris was no equal in putrescence to
the others; merely a crook or two, merely a personage here and
there who looked toward getting Alsace and Lorraine back some
day.    Bismarck had exerted all his influence to prevent Germany from taking them in 1871.    London was a clean and decent oasis; sincerity, and aversion to all war, characterized those
at the head of the British government.    Nobody there was sus-
picious enough.    Lord Roberts had been warning them against
Germany and *der Tag* for seven years.    Nobody listened.    Admiral Lord Fisher had said war would be due on the completion
of the Kiel canal.    It was completed in 1913.    Lord Haldane
had gone to Germany with hopes of international friendship—
and returned without them.    He feared trouble some day and
made ready for it as far as he could in his incredulous country.
But Petersburg, Berlin, Vienna, and Paris in a less degree, lived
in eternal suspicion of a few things in particular and of everything in general.

Out of this welter emerge two figures, one the most ignoble
and the other the most noble in the diplomatic drama which the
youthful Princip started by his crime.    Berchtold, Austrian
Secretary of State, the original incendiary, and Sir Edward
Grey, Secretary of State for Great Britain.

When Berchtold, smarting under diplomatic defeat in recent
wars, heard that the heir of Austria had been shot in the street
at Serajevo, he resolved in his heart that here was Austria's
great moment and his own as well, which was more precious to
him: Serbia should pay for that murder.    Never mind if she
were not responsible.    But unless Germany backed him he was
nowhere.    On July 5, the Kaiser, playing the War-lord, backed
him at that conference of bankers and generals.    Through the
next twenty-five days he backed and unbacked, according to
which rôle he was playing.    The pitiful Czar wobbled at Petersburg in the same way, depending on who talked to him last.
Berchtold was equal to them and their advisers.    He got his
old Emperor aroused, though sluggishly.    It did not embarrass

him to have the people he sent to investigate Serbia's alleged connivance at the assassination come back with a report showing that Serbia had not connived. It would never do for the Kaiser to see this. Berchtold suppressed it. A great many lies began to be necessary. This original incendiary lied right and left: he suppressed, or denied, or asserted, gained time by delay in forwarding or in answering important messages; he lied to his friends, he lied to his enemies; the sum of his falsifications in thirty-two days may possibly be computed by a careful reading of his Red Book of sixty-nine documents, issued in 1915 for home consumption, and the collection of three hundred and eighty-two documents published by others, four years later. These, coming to light at last, may be said to reveal Berchtold as a contemptible figure.

He managed to create and maintain the atmosphere of Serbia's guilt, and he contrived to lull almost to slumber whatever apprehensions Serbia may have entertained; Berlin and Petersburg were much wider awake to the blow that he was getting ready to deal. He nearly had a fall when London thoroughly waked up on July 24. On that day his ultimatum to Serbia reached the capitals of Europe. Sir Edward Grey styled it to the Austrian minister in London the most formidable document he had ever seen one independent State address another. A few Berlin lies at this point were inadvertently exposed by the Berlin Ambassador to the United States. He told us on September 7, 1914, in *The Independent,* that Berlin had seen and backed that ultimatum before it went. It is here that Berlin's guilt is nailed to her hard and fast, and for ever.

But whatever surprise the ultimatum gave to Serbia and to Sir Edward Grey, it was nothing to the surprise which Serbia gave Berchtold in the forty-eight hours he allowed her for her answer. They were all sure Serbia would reject it; they supposed in Vienna that they had made it so "formidable" that no self-respecting nation could do anything else. Sir Edward Grey in the name of peace urged Serbia to accept as much of it as she was able to swallow.   She swallowed the whole thing, except a little piece which she promised to swallow also, if The Hague Tribunal told her she must.   Good! said the Kaiser, when he saw that; we are saved from a European war.   He was playing his rôle of Peace-warden on that day.   But he did not play it to a finish.   Had he remained in it, there would have been no war. One single word from him was enough to call it off.   Instead, he passed to his War-lord rôle, and said that big Germany could not desert her little friend Austria.

Meanwhile, Berchtold who had come so near a fall, hastily told Europe that Serbia's acceptance of the ultimatum was a tissue of deceit, and hurried on to his climax.   The successive requests for discussion between the powers which Sir Edward Grey made more and more urgent, were met with smiling evasion, until Berlin was able to regret that it was too late.   Had Sir Edward Grey been willing to answer one burning question asked him by Paris and Petersburg—Would England come in for them if Germany attacked France? this too would have stopped the war.   He did not.   He was under the great embarrassment of having carried through the step taken by Edward VII, and given France to understand that she could rely upon England. Now, he could not be sure what England would say if he spoke for her and pledged her support.   He could touch no autocrat's button and start cannon firing.   The common sense of the English people was the only button which would start that.   What were young Princip and his two murders at Serajevo to them?

And so neutral Belgium was invaded according to a Prussian plan worked out twenty years before; and the noblest words spoken in Europe then or since were Albert's to the Kaiser— you ask me to go back on my word for the sake of saving my skin.   No.

England came in, the Great War was on, and Woodrow Wilson asked us to be neutral even in thought.   At that moment neutrality was exactly right.

## XXVI.

Very slowly did I come to know all this; very quickly did I emerge from my fog of ignorance as to the rights and the wrongs of it, and side with England and France with my head as well as with my heart.   News of the Prussian methods of war began to come.   To most Americans they were incredible at first.   Nobody remembered that the Teutonic brutality of the Hessians had made them especially hated in our Revolution.   Untruths were circulated in 1914 and disproved later, such as the cutting off the hands of Belgian children.   These are no warrant for the use that some American books have since made of them with the purpose of suggesting to a mass of happy-go-lucky minds that there never were any Prussian "atrocities," that war is always brutal, that all peoples make it in the same way, and that the Allies were just as bad as the Prussians.   The "atrocities," these books suggest, were made up by England to excite Americans against Prussia.   But where did the Allies commit brutalities?   They never entered Germany.   Nevertheless, happy-go-lucky minds have comfortably adopted the suggestion.   They have also comfortably adopted books which suppress facts, documents, and conversations that would embarrass any demonstration of the innocence of Berlin during July, 1914.   Prussian barbarity has been historic for centuries.   Before the doctrines of Bernhardi and the codified decisions of the Military Staff at Berlin had made "frightfulness" part of its deliberated manual and plan of warfare, Prussian barbarity had stood out amid the violence of all wars.   Prussian looting was conspicuous in France at the time they were there as allies of the English.   In 1914 it was of the same pattern, but dyed a deeper red.   The crop of American white-washers of Prussia which has sprouted since the war is as skilful in its suppressions as Berchtold was in Vienna and Jagow was in Berlin.

Before the end of August a book came into my hands, a Prussian book.

"Our aim is to be just," I read.   "The future which Providence has set before the German people as the greatest civilized people known to history." "I must try to prove that war is an indispensable factor of culture." "New territory must as a rule be obtained at the cost of its possessors." This was Bernhardi, a general. In another Prussian book I read: "War is in itself a good thing." "Courts of arbitration are pernicious delusions." And a great deal more of the sort. This was the German historian Treitschke. Prussian sympathizers, upon finding that these doctrines offended Americans, began to say that they had been repudiated in Germany. It was a little late to say that. Sir Edward Grey presently published the English White Book. This contained all dispatches and conversations that he had exchanged with Berlin and Vienna, as well as with the Allies. If anything could have settled my opinion more than this as to the guilt and perfidy of Vienna and Berlin, it was what they themselves published in the same form. Neither one of their books contained a word which had passed directly between them. Such a suppression was louder than any lies they could have shouted.

Neutral in thought after that?

By October we had full knowledge of the doctrine of "Frightfulness," and how this doctrine had been translated into action by the Kaiser's soldiers in Belgium. Before Christmas, a deputation of Belgians came to tell our Government officially what had been done in their country. Woodrow Wilson received them, heard them, and they departed. From them he learned how the Library at Louvain had been burned, how citizens, old men, women, children, had been slaughtered on a deliberately forged pretext, some of their dwellings set on fire in which they were trapped and consumed; and how in the public square at Louvain and Malines, Belgian women had been raped by Prussian officers. Wilson listened to this with polite expressions. He was not obliged to believe what he heard, he was not obliged to disbelieve it—and he never felt obliged to send over an American deputation to report to him on its truth.

Why?

Later, in the midst of it, when the flames were raging and a
piece of France proportionately equal to Maine, New Hampshire, Vermont, Massachusetts, Rhode Island, Connecticut,
New York, New Jersey, Pennsylvania, Delaware, Maryland,
and part of Ohio, had been battered to a blind and quivering
pulp, he announced to the world that the United States was not
concerned with the aims of the contending parties.

## XXVII.

The voices of Woodrow Wilson and Theodore Roosevelt
spoke to the American people during those four tremendous
years.   These two figures rise above the crowd as champions
of irreconcilable doctrines.   In one thing their very dissimilar
characters are alike—unflinching purpose.   Their methods of
achieving it were diametrically opposed.   One locked his intentions inside him and acted in isolation, the other called in ex-
perts and sometimes the whole country to his counsels.

Theodore Roosevelt offers us no riddle.   The man is clear and
accounted for.   People may like or dislike that kind of man,
they may disagree over this that and the other of his actions—
such as his declining to lead his Progressives in 1914, which I
ascribe mostly to sheer fatigue—but as to what manner of man
he was, they are pretty well agreed.   In truth, his character is
not at all complicated: always impulsive, hearty, generous, vigorous in many intellectual directions, aware of the past and
alive to the present, sometimes thinking better of his friends
and worse of his enemies than they deserved, Roosevelt is always
the out-door man and the preacher militant; never old in
soul; young to the end.   When Robins asked him why he
had gone to South America for the sake of a doubtful river,
he exclaimed:

"I had just one more chance to be a boy, and I took it!"

Look at Roosevelt's face: it is all there, even that wistful conflict between his brain and his temperament over what he knew
but did not wish to know: an optimist who saw things as they

ought to be, wrestling with a realist who knew things as they were.

Now look at the face of Woodrow Wilson.   Who should have painted that enigma?   Intellect is there, fathomless intensity, what we call vision, purpose, a noble and beautiful brow, a mouth inferior to all this, and a chin more obstinate than powerful. Many years after our day, posterity will not have done wondering about Woodrow Wilson.   In his life he created violent worship and violent hate, just as Roosevelt did; but Roosevelt seems to shine more brightly in our sky.

As I cannot explain Woodrow Wilson to myself, let the reader do it for himself, if he is able.   If an obscure teacher of history, with no backing but his own gifts, becomes President of Princeton, and leaves behind him storm, schism, and fury; becomes Governor of New Jersey, and leaves behind him storm, schism, and fury; goes to the White House and creates storm, schism, and fury; arrives in Paris the hope of the world, and leaves Paris amid storm, schism, fury and disillusion, you will admit that he is a very extraordinary person.

During his early days in the White House, he braved unpopularity in the matter of the Panama Canal tolls, carried his point, and retrieved the honor of the United States in the sight of all nations.   We had given our word and tried to dodge it.   Popular morality was for continuing to dodge, just as it had been for repudiation of lawful debts by some nine states of our Union in earlier times.   Woodrow Wilson forced the nation, much against its will, to be honest about the Panama Canal tolls, and wiped out that disgrace.   He followed this by another excellent measure, long needed, and highly useful ever since.   He pushed through the Federal Reserve Bank.   This had languished for twenty years in Republican hands.   Debate on this bill brought a curious personal gesture from the President.   A Senator opposed the bill because he thought it could be made better.   Members of Wilson's family had accepted an invitation from the senator's wife.   Wilson happened to learn this some days later. He ordered the acceptance withdrawn; no member of his household should be the guest of a man who was opposing him in Congress.    And in the end, the senator voted for the bill because it was better than nothing.

During the disorder in Mexico, American citizens were imprisoned in Chihuahua.    Wilson held a small conference, Lodge being present, and said that an American force must be sent to release the prisoners, but that there must be no act of war. When it was pointed out to him that this would be an act of war in itself, he replied that the Attorney General must find some way to make it not one; and he repeated that the Americans must be rescued, but there must be no act of war.    Lodge read me the account of this conference from his diary, and described Wilson as sitting in a sort of physical collapse.

When Wilson was about to send a special envoy to investigate American interests in Mexico, his Princeton classmate Daniel Moreau Barringer, a mining engineer, took it for granted that the envoy would be a man of experience in mines.    Wilson replied that a mining expert would be the very last kind of person he would choose; and he chose Lind, who knew nothing about mines, or the Mexican language, or any part of the subject, and had never conducted any negotiation with another country.

"When your eyes troubled you at Princeton," said Barringer to Wilson, "whom did you send for?"

"Doctor de Schweinitz," replied Wilson.

"A distinguished oculist," said Barringer.    "Why didn't you send for a plumber?"

Barringer told me that when Wilson had his classmates to dine with him at the White House in November, 1916, he said:

"Moreau, why do you keep writing me letters about preparedness?"

"Because I'm scared, Tommy.    Things are looking worse and worse."

"Take it from me, Moreau, there is not the slightest chance of our getting into this war."

In London, two years after, he said to an English lady, whose sister repeated it to me:

"Oh, Lady S——, you have no idea what a distress it was not to be able to get into the war sooner."

And yet, during the days when Roosevelt had urged preparedness, and Leonard Wood was doing what he could for it at Plattsburg, it certainly looked as if Wilson had set his face rigidly against it.

What was known as "Schedule K" in the Administration's new tariff bill evoked a protest from wool merchants. To their thinking this change of duties would operate the reverse of what was intended, and they requested an interview with the President. The hour and day were set. A group of them went to Washington, carefully prepared to present their case. Wilson received them and said:

"Gentlemen, whatever your arguments may be, you need not offer them. I have made up my mind about Schedule K, and shall not change it."

After the war had been going some two years, a friend who was sitting with the President asked:

"What have you heard recently from Walter Page?"

"I don't know what he's saying," replied the President, and pointed to a pile of letters on a table. "There are his letters. I haven't opened them."

He declined to hear what his two ambassadors from London and Brussels came over to report to him about the war. Brand Whitlock has related his experience to me. After he reached Paris, the French who had waited and hailed his coming with a sort of religious fervor, expected him to visit the devastated regions at once. Day after day passed, and each morning they asked, would he go to-day? He never saw them. He made one journey as far as Reims, and remained most of the time indoors at lunch, conversing about other subjects. He gave as a reason for not visiting the devastated regions, that he feared the sight would prejudice him too unfavorably to the Germans.

Strikingly like this is his deportment at Buckingham Palace. The English had awaited and welcomed him in much the same spirit as the French. Wounded soldiers craved a sight of him.

These bandaged cripples were brought on stretchers or crowded on their crutches to the palace gates.   The King walked among them, saying a word to each man, shaking hands often.   Wilson went with him in silence and without a gesture.

Is it that his nerves shrank from the sight of ruin or suffering, as the young medical student is apt to be shocked by the sight of his first operation?   If so, is such physical aversion, akin to the mental aversion for all unwelcome news and facts, such as leaving Page's letters unopened because he knew they would tell him what he did not wish to be told?   And are these instances somehow connected with his declining to hear the wool merchants after setting an hour for them to see him?   Does this come in in some mysterious way from the same quality in him which made him leave those officially entitled to be informed of an important step he contemplated, entirely ignorant of it?   On December 24, none of those directly concerned knew his intention regarding the railroads.   On December 26 they learned accidentally that he had taken the railroads over.   It was the same when he declared war.

Or, are some of these manifestations to be explained as the acts of a man of reflection and theory, not a man of action?   Partly, perhaps, but not wholly.   Did he decline to hear the wool merchants, and did he send Lind to Mexico from congenital hostility to all trained minds?   But he sent for an expert when his own eyesight was the point.   Why did he interfere with the decision of the courts of California to save a murderer, a bomb thrower, duly found guilty?   Why did he not keep a sane balance between Labor and Capital?   He leaned so far from the idle rich that he fell into the arms of the idle poor.   The I. W. W.'s were his chosen protégés when the citizens of Douglas expelled them.

His monument will be The League of Nations.   He opposed the plan in the days when Taft, Root, Lawrence Lowell, and many other eminent men were advocating it.   The idea was then known as a League for International World Peace.   Comments by Roosevelt upon the plan are to be found in print.   It was he, I think, who pointed out that the crux of the matter lay in how to establish an international sheriff's posse.   He wrote Van Valkenburg on June 29, 1915, after the sinking of the Lusitania:

"There is one point . . . worth-while considering. . . . I very emphatically stated that it was a program for the future. . . . These gentlemen declined to say a word in favor of our fitting ourselves to go into defensive war . . . and yet they actually wish to make us at this time promise to undertake *offensive* war in the interests of other people. . . .   They propose that we shall pledge ourselves in the future to coerce Germany if it acts, say toward Switzerland, or Holland or Denmark, as it has acted toward Belgium.   These same individuals praise Wilson for shirking his duty under the moderate Hague conventions we have already signed and for failure to prepare either to protect our own citizens when murdered on the high seas or . . . murdered in Mexico. . . ."

I had always supposed until very lately that Woodrow Wilson had pondered that League for International World Peace, had perceived some chance in it for a better world, had changed his mind about this as he changed it about keeping us out of war, and had ended by adopting it and going to Europe as its champion.

This is not what happened.   Others persuaded him to change his mind.   It was not done easily.   The others were many, but chiefly Colonel House when Wilson stayed with him in 1918 at Magnolia.   There, at Wilson's request, Colonel House drafted a rough plan of the Covenant.   This Wilson took, meditated upon, and re-wrote.   A letter from Mr. Root arrived at this time and added its word to the previous arguments of Colonel House. This is, perhaps, the greatest occasion on which the teacher's mind opened to receive instruction; but the process took some three years.   If The League of Nations works out according to Wilson's hopes, he will indeed be a very great figure in history.

During the Peace Conference in Paris, I lunched with Lord Balfour, Mr. Arthur Balfour, as he was then.   It was Wednesday, May 7, 1919.   The Treaty of Versailles had been handed to Count Brockdorff-Rantzau that day.   He was head of the

German delegation. He had received the treaty with a long speech, in which he said that to confess Germany to be the only guilty one would be in his mouth a lie. Woodrow Wilson had pledged himself to propose to the Senate of the United States an engagement to go immediately to the assistance of France in the case of an unprovoked attack by Germany.

Naturally we spoke of Woodrow Wilson at lunch. Naturally I did not express the bitter feelings which I had for him at that time.

"Your President," said Mr. Balfour, "has too honest a mind. He is no match for some of the men he believes to be dealing with him in his own spirit. He cannot grow used to their ways. They take him unawares again and again."

"I suppose," I said, "we Americans should keep out of Continental diplomacy until our minds are *Mediterraneanized*."

"Mediterraneanized!" exclaimed Mr. Balfour. "Just that. —Do you think they will sign?" he continued.

"The Germans sign the treaty? How can I possibly form any opinion about that?"

"I assure you, you are in just as good a position to form an opinion as I am."

"Well then, to use an Americanism, I've a *hunch* that they will."

"I never heard that expression before. Won't you explain it?"

"Well, roughly, I think it means something that you feel pretty sure of without being able to formulate your reasons very exactly."

"In that case, I have the same hunch," said Mr. Balfour.

People to-day still ask why, when Woodrow Wilson went to Paris, did he not take Elihu Root with him? I do not know. Had he done so, the Mediterranean mind would have surprised him less often. Root had met this mind before. When Wilson gave Europe to understand that help from the United States would come if France were attacked, what was there in his thought? Did he expect to cow the Senate? Why, his own party did not stand behind him, let alone Cabot Lodge.   Did he reflect on the portent of our elections in November, 1918? Upon the popular dissent which they expressed?   On the antagonism instantly aroused by his requesting the voters of the United States to vote for Democrats only, if his policies were to be carried out?

Two days after that significant rebuke which he received at the polls, I was in an electric car on its way to West Chester, and a countryman got in.

"Well," said he, sitting down by me, "we've got the Kaiser beat."

"Yes.   It looks as if the war would end very soon," said I.

"I don't mean the Kaiser over *there,*" said the hearty countryman, "I mean the Kaiser *here.*"

It was most fortunate that Hughes was defeated as Republican candidate in 1916.   No Republican, no one else except Woodrow Wilson could have carried through his conscription bill in 1917.   It was a splendid achievement.   And to this must be added his wise view and wise act concerning another very important question.   Wilson vetoed once, if not twice, the fanatical Prohibition Law, and recommended light wines and beer.   Intemperance, assisted by hypocrisy, triumphed over his moderation.

Wilson was charming socially, interesting in talk, he left friends behind him who will hear nothing against him.   Why did he part so invariably with any friend who differed from him? He will be a riddle for a long while.

The figure of Roosevelt is not a tragic one to think about, now that everything is over; the figure of Woodrow Wilson seems to me the most tragic in our history: assuredly the fragment of a great man, whose deeds too often fell below the level of his words.

## XXVIII.

The great darkness and the great enlightenment proceeded. Four years of it drew a line between all we had known and what

we had come to know.   Our new selves could never return to
our old selves; not because we had lost a brother, a husband, a
son, an irreparable friend; some of us had lost no one very near
or dear.   It was not grief that taught us anything unknown, it
was having myths about blood and fire and mutilation and blindness come true.   We had read the words in histories, poems,
plays; we did not doubt that Joan of Arc had been burned, and
that Attila had been known as the Scourge of God.   Books,
nothing but books, romance, far away and long ago, that is all it
meant to us.   It never can mean that any more, unless to those
whose lack of imagination insulates them from emotional cur-
rents.

Turn back to the newspapers.   Look at their front pages.
The spy is no longer Cooper's hero, no longer Mr. Gillette thrilling us agreeably on the stage in his *Secret Service*.   Secret Service, enemy secret service, is in our streets and homes, opening
our trunks and letters, listening to our table talk.   Secret service is blowing up du Pont powder mills; attempting to wreck
communication between Canada and the United States.   I am
watching the Missouri from the rear platform as my Burlington
train crosses the river at Plattsmouth.   A train man tells me to
come inside; no one allowed out there; secret agents drop
bombs on bridges.   Boys you last saw in tennis flannels or dinner jackets are in the Foreign Legion, or with the English, en-
listed by way of Canada.   You hear of their deaths.   You hear
a new word, shell-shock.   You hear of London houses wrecked
by zeppelin raids.   You hear of gas at Ypres.   You hear of
submarines.

THEODORE ROOSEVELT
30 East Forty Second Street
New York City

September 16th, 1914.

DEAR DAN:

I have just read with the greatest enjoyment your article upon
me as President. . . .

Now I do hope that I shall soon be able to see you, so that I may talk over with you many things that I would like to.

Always yours,

THEODORE ROOSEVELT.

December 16, 1914.

DEAR DAN:

Surely you must be in New York some time now! It is pretty dreary coming out to the country at this season but I need hardly say how we would like to have you for a night or a week-end or for lunch, just as suited your convenience. Only do come out when you can stay two or three hours at least so that we can have a talk with you. If you do not want to come into the country now, then I will wait until the spring; and meanwhile, let me know when you are to be in New York and if I possibly can I will get in.

Always yours,

THEODORE ROOSEVELT.

It was during the same talk in which he had given his concise description of the Kaiser and of Berchtold, that I told him of two rumors which had not happened to reach him.

Berchtold, of whom we had no worse opinion in those early days than that he had been the Kaiser's very active Austrian cat's-paw, was reported to have hastened to his own Emperor at Ischl with the glad tidings that war had been declared. It was after lunch. The aged Francis Joseph was dozing in a summer-house. Berchtold frisked across the garden with his glad tidings, and spoke them with respectful eagerness.

"Sire, I have the honor to inform your Majesty that war is declared."

"Good!" said old Francis Joseph drowsily, and pounded his fist. "Now we shall go after those damned Prussian swine."

"Sire! Sire! Majesty!" gasped the alarmed Berchtold, and waked Francis Joseph from the dream to the reality.

"Now, that's too good to be true," I said to Roosevelt. "The next one is too bad to be true." And I told it.

Once embarked in his war, Francis Joseph had sent word to the Vatican and begged the Pope for his blessing.

"Non possumus," was the Latin in which that sad and true Saint refused. He was too honest and too good to bless Austria for what she was doing.

"But," I said, "you'll hear it whispered rather freely that the Pope's end was not hastened by a heart broken over the vast misery he foresaw was coming, his end was hastened by poison. They wanted a Pope who would side with the Central Powers."

"I don't believe either of those stories," said Roosevelt. "But I understand why they got to you."

"Well, of course gossip has gone entirely off its head."

"Yes. It has gone entirely off its head, but that's not why. Those two lies were *appropriate*. The *inappropriate* lie never has any circulation. It expires in the wrong atmosphere. If I heard you had burglarized somebody's jewels, it wouldn't worry me at all. But—if I heard that you had written a story deficient in morals, I should simply"—and here his voice went up into its highest falsetto—"*hope* my best—that—you hadn't!"

At this we both lay back and laughed for a scandalously long time.

THEODORE ROOSEVELT

30 East Forty Second Street
New York City

March 2, 1915.

DEAR DAN:

Langdon Mitchell was here the other night and said that your play was a great success. Now, as soon as the weather grows decent, can't you come out to Oyster Bay for a night or a week-end? But if you prefer not, then let me know some time you are to be in New York and I will come in and we will have lunch together.

Faithfully yours,

THEODORE ROOSEVELT.

I could do neither just then. The war had set aside all plans of fiction, and I was hard at work preparing to write *The Pente-*

*cost of Calamity* by reading entirely or in part more books than I can remember now.    What play my cousin Langdon Mitchell meant I cannot imagine.    There was none.    *The Virginian* had left the New York stage years ago and had taken to the movies.

Oyster Bay, New York.<br>March 13, 1915.

DEAR DAN:

My libel suit begins on April 20th, so I should have to leave here on the 19th.    Any day before that or any day after the suit gets through we should love to have you.

Faithfully yours,<br>THEODORE ROOSEVELT.

That libel suit was famous.    Roosevelt was defendant; the plaintiff was William Barnes, political boss at Albany.    He lost. The dramatic point of the trial was Roosevelt on the witness stand.    His marvellously accurate memory met and rebutted the successive items of evidence produced in passages from even old letters he had written.    They never caught him in a mistake and his explanations hit so true that day by day his cross examiners drooped with exhaustion.    These attorneys begged the court to rule that the witness must confine himself to words, and must not answer with his whole body; this method made an unfairly favorable impression on the jury.    But Judge Andrews ruled that it was beyond the province of the court to regulate the ordinary manner of the witness!

Full reports of this historic trial were cut short by a more historic event; on May 7 the *Lusitania* was sunk by a submarine. I possess a medal struck off in Germany in anticipation of this sinking.    Death stands at a ticket window and receives the tickets of the passengers.    Before the *Lusitania* sailed, the most famous advertisement in the world appeared in the paper.    It warned Americans to keep off that boat.    The German ambassador had inserted it.    Roosevelt said that he would have sent for the Ambassador, handed him his papers and requested him to get aboard the *Lusitania* and go.    Since then the Ambassador has let the world know that by May, 1915, he understood Woodrow Wilson.   A few of the thousand and odd passengers were saved.

"This represents," said Roosevelt next day in the papers, "not merely piracy, but piracy on a vaster scale of murder than old-time pirates ever practised.   This is the warfare which destroyed Louvain and hundreds of men, women and children in Belgium. . . ."

He knew that there were two German-American jurors in the box.   He told his counsel that he was afraid his public statement had made their winning of his case impossible.

"But I cannot help it. . . .   There is a principle here at stake . . . far more vital to the American people than my personal welfare is to me."

Two days later in Philadelphia Wilson addressed fifteen thousand naturalized citizens:

"There is such a thing," he said, "as a man being too proud to fight.   There is such a thing as a nation being so right that it does not need to convince others by force that it is right."

It is at this point that Roosevelt, for what he said at his trial, began to emerge brightly from the eclipse into which he had gone in 1912, and that Wilson, for what he said in Philadelphia, began slowly to enter an eclipse from which he never emerged.

Oyster Bay,<br>Long Island, N. Y.<br>June 23rd, 1915.

DEAR DAN:

Your friend, the English pacificist, turned up.   He seems an amiable, fuzzy-brained creature; but I could not resist telling him that I thought that in the first place Englishmen were better at home doing their duty just at present and in the next place as regards both Englishmen and Americans that the prime duty now was not to talk about dim and rosy Utopias but, as regards both of them, to make up their minds to prepare against disaster and, as regards our nation, to quit making promises which we do not keep.

I was immensely pleased and amused with your last Atlantic article, "Quack novels and Democracy"; and I think it will do good. I wish you had included Wilson when you spoke of Bryan, and Pulitzer when you spoke of Hearst. Pulitzer and his successors have been on the whole an even greater detriment than Hearst, and Wilson is considerably more dangerous to the American people than Bryan. I was very glad to see you treat Thomas Jefferson as you did. Wilson is in his class. Bryan is not attractive to the average college bred man; but the Evening Post, Springfield Republican, and Atlantic Monthly creatures, who claim to represent all that is highest and most cultivated and to give the tone to the best college thought, are all ultra-supporters of Wilson, are all much damaged by him, and join with him to inculcate flabbiness of moral fibre among the very men, and especially the young men, who should stand for what is best in American life. Therefore to the men who read your writings Wilson is more dangerous than Bryan. Nothing is more sickening than the continual praise of Wilson's English, of Wilson's style. He is a true logothete, a real sophist; and he firmly believes, and has had no inconsiderable effect in making our people believe, that elocution is an admirable substitute for and improvement on action. I feel particularly bitter toward him at the moment because when Bryan left I supposed that meant that Wilson really had decided to be a man and I prepared myself to stand whole-heartedly by him. But in reality the point at issue between them was merely one as to the proper point of dilution of tepid milk and water.

Ever yours,<br>THEODORE ROOSEVELT.

The President's first note to Berlin about the sinking of the *Lusitania*, the "strict accountability" note, was followed by a second in a tone so different that it drew from Elihu Root the memorable observation:

"You shouldn't shake your fist at a man and then shake your finger at him."

Taft had humorously described Bryan's statesmanship as:

"Chautauquan diplomacy."

AMERICAN PREPAREDNESS

WILSON'S ARMY

From the London Bystander

Roosevelt had described the President's foreign attitude as: "Waging peace."

During July, he sent me the following letter from the Washington correspondent of an important paper. Its great interest lies in its contemporary record of the moment in which we were living, and the shrewd forecast of how several situations were likely to develop.

Washington, D. C.

July 1, 1915.

DEAR COLONEL:

I have been away a great deal which accounts for my failure to write to you in regard to the Bryan episode and other developments.

It is the impression of all the officials of the Administration that Bryan resigned with the deliberate purpose of advancing his own ambition. He did not entirely favor the protest against the war zone, the "strict accountability" note, but was induced to sign it because he believed that the President did not mean what the note said. That this belief was well founded is shown by the assurance given by Bryan to the Austrian Ambassador that "the note was not to be taken seriously." You will recall that Bryan deemed it expedient to give out a statement in reference to this matter. In his statement Bryan said that he repeated his conversation with Dumba to the President who approved it, and that there was no misunderstanding is shown by the certificate given him by Mr. Dumba. In other words the note was sent for the purpose of placating American public opinion and Germany and Austro-Hungary so accepted it. Could there have been any worse example of hypocrisy and treachery than this! Swept along by public opinion the President realized that he would have to stand by the declaration in the note. Nothing was done about the drowning of Thresher on the Falaba and nothing would have been done had it not been for the Lusitania outrage. How the President induced Bryan to sign the note containing the Lusitania demands I do not understand. In any event he induced the Secretary to take this action. Apparently however, Bryan appreciated that he was hogtied and he came to the conclusion that it would be better for him to leave the Administration. He kept his proposed action entirely to himself but finally called on the President and told him of his decision. Undoubtedly Wilson has played a very astute game with Bryan. He has sought to carry him along as far as possible and to place him in a difficult position in case of a break. I think he has succeeded. The Administration realizes that in spite of what Bryan has done he has a large following and it is apprehensive that Wilson will be beaten for re-election. Whether Bryan will be a candidate or not I do not know. It is assumed he will support the single term plank in the Baltimore platform in which case he will hold if Wilson seeks renomination that the latter is "a criminal worse than an embezzler," a declaration made by Bryan in a Harrisburg speech with reference to the platform. After making this speech Bryan assured Tumulty that he did not have the single term plank in mind but the Administration believes he did and that he will go after Wilson next spring.

The formal break between Bryan and the President will take place undoubtedly in December. It is the intention of the President to recommend an increase in the army and the navy for the purpose of "drawing your tooth" to quote what an official said to me. This will give Bryan his chance to rap the President basing his attitude on his remarkable theory that the war in Europe was caused by preparedness. The President being between Scylla and Charybdis intends to recommend a very moderate increase. It does not make any difference, however, how moderate he may be for Bryan will go after him in order to advance his personal ambition.

The German note will be here in the course of a few days and, of course, it will not concede anything substantial. There will be proposals with strings tied to them to which we will respond. So the negotiations will go on as I told you they would go on, without any real results being achieved. The situation is somewhat complicated by the sinking of the Armenian but the Administration is endeavoring to control the public mind in connection with this catastrophe. If there is any possible excuse for keeping quiet it will be taken advantage of.

You know Lansing. He will make an excellent Secretary of State for Wilson. Lansing is not a captain by any means but he is a first class lieutenant. Wilson himself desires to be Secretary of State. That is to say he will determine the policies and Lansing will see that they are in accord with international law and do everything he can to sustain them.

The Mexican situation is frightfully muddled. There is no

intention on the part of the President to intervene by force.   He is carrying out his plan of giving the leaders of the Mexican factions an opportunity to get together failing which, and of course they will fail, it is his purpose to back Iturbide, who was Chief of Police in Mexico City at the time of Madero's assassination. Judging the future by the past I am confident that Iturbide will not be able to establish peace.   In other words the situation with all its horrors will continue.

There is no chance of European peace and no chance of Wilson's service as mediator.   He is hoping that in the German reply to the Lusitania demands there will be an acceptance of his suggestion that his good offices are at the disposal of the German government.   This suggestion was contained in the last note on the Lusitania.   Germany may express its desire or its willingness to terminate the war but even if it does so it is certain that the Allies will decline to consider any step in that direction. Their prestige is at such a low ebb that it is not possible for them to consider peace at this time.

That Roumania and Bulgaria apparently have reached an agreement is shown by the fact that Roumania has demanded the cession of the Hungarian province of Transylvania.   Austro-Hungary unquestionably will reject this demand in such fashion as to prolong negotiations.   The situation will resemble that which existed for months between Italy and Austro-Hungary. In the end Roumania will go into the war.   Bulgaria and Greece are in negotiation for the cession of certain Grecian territory to Bulgaria.   When this matter is adjusted then these two states will act.   I cannot see any end to the war for a long time. What I am afraid of is that we are being drawn nearer and nearer and nearer to the edge of the maelstrom.   The responsibility, of course, for such danger rests with the supine Administration. . . .

Here is a sentiment from the evidently Teutonic cook of a country club in New York to Daisy, Princess of Pless:

. . . The American people tont understand anything but Grape *Jucie* Politik.

WILLIAM GOETZ, Chef.

Black River Valley Club,
Watertown, N. Y.
Amerika, Feb. 1, '15.

Not many weeks later I listened to Bryan making a speech at the San Diego Exposition. He entitled this speech "The Causeless War," and from time to time he recurred to a sentence something after the manner of a ballad with a refrain:

"If they would only tell us what they are fighting about," went the burden, "we might know what to think."

I was very much struck with coldness of his audience. I noticed men grinning at their neighbors and sticking their elbows in each other's sides.

*The Saturday Evening Post* had by this time published *The Pentecost of Calamity*. Roosevelt wrote me the following immediately:

> Oyster Bay, Long Island, N. Y.
> July 7th, 1915.

Private.

DEAR DAN:—

All the earlier part of your article on The Pentecost of Calamity is so admirable and I feel so very strongly the service you have rendered that I cannot help feeling regret that you fail to draw the conclusion that in my view is the only conclusion to be drawn. You first of all show how dreadfully Germany has behaved, how incumbent it is upon the civilized world that she should not be allowed to succeed, that action should be taken upon her. You then say with equal truth that you "want no better photograph of any individual than his opinion on this war."

But America as a whole could speak only through the Administration at Washington; and the real test, the real photograph, of any individual is whether he does or does not keep neutral about the action of the Administration in itself preserving a thoroughly base neutrality. You praise the New York Times for its stand. The New York Times has consistently supported Wilson and is supporting him now; and that makes all that it says on behalf of the Allies and against Germany mere beating of wind, a mere added discredit. When President Eliot denounces Germany and also upholds President Wilson and says that we must not prepare against war, President Eliot is occupying the very worst position that can be occupied.

To denounce Germany in words and not prepare to make our words good is merely to add to our offense.

You say that it would have been an act of "unprecedented folly" if we had not been politically neutral.   On the contrary, in my view, the really unprecedented folly was in exercising our loose tongues in a way thoroughly to irritate Germany and yet to do nothing whatever to back these aforesaid tongues by governmental action.   If it was our duty to remain neutral politically, it was emphatically our duty to remain morally neutral. Any political neutrality not based on moral reasons is no more and no less admirable than the neutrality of Pontius Pilate or of the backwoodsman who saw his wife fighting the bear.   Either The Hague Conventions meant something or they did not mean something.   Either they can be constructed according to their spirit, or by legalistic device the letter can be twisted so as to give a faint shadow of justification for violating the spirit.   If they meant nothing, then it was idiocy for us to have gone into them. If they meant anything, Wilson and Bryan are not to be excused for failure to try to make them good by whatever action was necessary; and political neutrality when they were violated was a crime against the world and a thoroughly base and dishonourable thing on our part.   As for the Lusitania matter, failure to act within twenty-four hours following her sinking was an offense that is literally inexcusable and inexpiable.   Of course, our people are now all confused and weakened and incapable of giving any coherent support to our own rights or the rights of others in the teeth of Germany's ruthless and cruel efficiency.   This is directly due to the action of Wilson—and he has been able to do this because papers like the Times have shown such ambidextrous morality in cordially supporting him while at the same time taking positions that were justifiable only on the theory that he had acted outrageously and should be denounced.

This people is no worse than it was in the days of Washington and Lincoln.   We were still in the gristle; and, thanks largely to the immense immigration, we have continued to be in the gristle. When we had them as Presidents or as national leaders, the people would follow them.   But if, after the firing on Sumter, Lincoln had made a speech in which he said that the North was "too proud to fight", and if he had then spent sixty days in writing polished epistles to Jefferson Davis, and if Seward had resigned because these utterly futile epistles were not even more futile, why, by July the whole heart would have been out of the Union party and most people in the North would have been following Horace Greeley in saying that the erring sisters should be permitted to depart in peace!  Wilson has not had to face anything like as great a crisis; but he has faced it exactly as Buchanan faced *his* crisis; in exactly the spirit that Lincoln would have shown if Lincoln had acted in such fashion.

I have a perfect horror of words that are not backed up by deeds.  I have a perfect horror of denunciation that ends in froth.  All denunciations of Germany, all ardent expressions of sympathy for the Allies amount to precisely and exactly nothing if we are right in preserving a complete political neutrality between right and wrong.  If Wilson is not wrong in his action, or rather inaction, about the Lusitania and Belgium, then the wise and proper thing for our people is to keep their mouths shut about both deeds.  The loose tongue and the unready hand make a poor combination.  We are justified in denouncing the action of Germany only if we make it clearly evident that Wilson has shamelessly and scandalously misrepresented us.  I don't think that the American people believe that he has misrepresented us!  I think they are behind him.  I think they are behind him largely because their leaders have felt that in this crisis the easy thing to do was to minister to our angered souls by words of frothy denunciation and minister to our soft bodies by taking precious good care that there was no chance of our having to turn these words into deeds.

Faithfully yours,
THEODORE ROOSEVELT.

This reached me in San Francisco, where I also found the book proofs of *The Pentecost of Calamity*.  After thinking over Roosevelt's letter very carefully, I made several additions to these proofs and returned them to the printer.  The book appeared late in August.  I sent the first copy to Roosevelt, and he wrote:

Oyster Bay,
Long Island, N. Y.
Sept. 1st, 1915.

DEAR DAN:—

The book has come.  I prize the inscription.  As for the book itself I believe that from the spiritual side it represents the loftiest expression of the true American feeling that there is—

just as Oliver's book draws for us the practical application of the lesson to be learned.   As an American, none too proud of his country's attitude for the last thirteen months, I am grateful to you, for the sake of my own self respect, because you have written so burningly and so nobly.

Faithfully yours,

THEODORE ROOSEVELT.

I found the quotation to which his next note refers in *Cymbeline*, Act IV, Scene 2:

> Prythee, have done;
> And do not play in wench-like words with that
> Which is so serious.

Oyster Bay,
Long Island, N. Y.
December 29th, 1915.

DEAR DAN:—

Bully for you!   That is the quotation of all others; and I will use it about Wilson the first chance I get.   Can't you manage to let me see you soon?

Ever yours,
T. R.

## XXIX.

The darkness grew more dark.   Within two months of Roosevelt's note about the wench-like words, the siege of Verdun began, February 21, 1916, and lasted into November.   Upon the forts of Vaux and Douaumont alone, merely a fraction of this beleaguered area, ten thousand shells of eight inches and larger fell every day for one hundred and twenty days.   Four hundred thousand French were killed there.   Eighty thousand of these bodies were still bodies, forty thousand with enough faces left to be recognized by those who had known them in life.   The rest, three hundred and forty thousand, were nameless shreds of flesh, splashed over many miles.   I saw Vaux and Douaumont in April, 1919.   The work of lifting what of this could

Sept 1st 1915

Dear Dan,

The book has come. I prize the inscription. As for the book itself I believe that from its spiritual side it represents the loftiest expression of true American feeling that there is — just as Oliver's book draws for us the practical application of the lesson to be learned. As an American, none too proud of his country's attitude for the last thirteen months, I am grateful to you, for the sake of my own self respect, because you have written so burningly and so nobly.

Faithfully yours
Theodore Roosevelt

MR. ROOSEVELT'S ACKNOWLEDGMENT OF "THE PENTECOST OF CALAMITY"

be collected where it lay and giving it burial, had not as yet gone far. Standing on the spot, I wrote in my diary:

Douaumont. Pools, humps, stones, corrugated fragments, dead distance, dead nearby, stumps, steel rail, rusted bits, whiffs from the dead, human bones (a German grave, his shoes, his bones, a cross of twigs unnamed), a pool with thirty dead in it, and larks in the sky.

Speaking for a Liberty Loan in Baltimore, April 6, 1918, Wilson had said:—

"I do not wish, even at this moment of utter disillusionment, to judge harshly."

To the roar of Verdun during the summer of 1916, the roar of the Battle of the Somme was added. We in the East heard nothing else any more. The destruction of Europe confined all our thoughts as if we were shut up in a mental prison. Concentration upon one's daily work was broken increasingly month after month. During the morning and afternoon hours, there was never a minute when the bulletin boards were deserted. Men stepped out of their offices for a glance to see what later news might have been posted since their last look at them.

In the centre of the country this was not the case. The great banks, the great headquarters of corporations in the great cities of the great Mississippi Valley, had printed placards reading:

"Talk business, don't talk war."

The Progressive party had wished to nominate Roosevelt again this year, or to force his nomination by the Republicans. He would consider neither. His reply was that he had no interest in his own or any man's political fortunes, and cared only to awaken the country; and in a speech at St. Louis, he not only challenged the talk-business spirit of that region, he also pierced that joint in Wilson's verbal armor which rhetoric, no matter how skilful, could not hide from him. He borrowed the happy expression "weasel words" and the interpretation of them from a magazine story published sixteen years earlier. This, too, had lived in the grasp of his extraordinary memory ready for instant use. A weasel word is one whose meaning is sucked dry by the word next it, as a weasel sucks an egg; so that it still looks as if it had meat inside. Wilson had said he favored universal voluntary training but that America did not wish anything but the "compulsion of the spirit of Americanism." It was one of his phrases which the more you think of it the less it means; Roosevelt put it into his own English. He said that you might as well favor a truant law for school boys by expressing your belief in obligatory attendance for all who did not wish to stay away.

When Cabot Lodge told me one evening at his house that Hughes was the man the party had decided to nominate, I did not reveal the sinking of my heart until I got home and wrote him my bread-and-butter letter. I told him that I thought the country was now ready to swarm to Roosevelt. His reply was long. It seemed to me another case of Washington blindness to realities outside of it. It is interesting to know that Boise Penrose, who had so ably defeated his nomination in 1912, now wanted him.

Roosevelt said of Penrose to me in earlier days:

"There's a crude power in him that anybody must feel. What a pity he chooses to hamstring his national usefulness by his local machine politics!"

And to Robins he had said of Penrose:

"I like that big buccaneer!"

He gave Hughes his support during the campaign, and some of his letters refer to speeches that he made. The next is in his own hand.

SAGAMORE HILL

Feb. 5th, 1916.

DEAR DAN:—

In a few days we sail for the West Indies, returning about March 20th. Remember that when spring really comes, you are to spend a week or so here, doing absolutely nothing unless the whim prompts you.

I wish you would write a sequel to the Pentecost of Calamity;

the country is now ripe for a stronger lesson; and, as Wilson used to love to say, "guilt is personal"—and he is guilty.   It is Wilson, not Bryan, who is the real enemy; the demagogue, adroit, tricky, false, without one spark of loftiness in him, without a touch of the heroic in his cold, selfish and timid soul.

Our people need to be roused from their lethargy.   Some are silly and sentimental; some are steeped in the base materialism of mere money-getting or the even baser materialism of soft and vapid or vicious pleasure; some are influenced by sheer downright cowardice.

Ever yours,

T. R.

METROPOLITAN

432 Fourth Avenue, New York.

Office of
Theodore Roosevelt

April 11th, 1916.

DEAR DAN:—

I opposed Hicks at the election but I have forwarded the letters to his half-brother Billy Cocks to see whether Hicks can do anything for Skirdin.

Let me say I entirely approved your poem on Wilson.   Do not mind at all what the mushy brotherhood say of it; it's going to last.   The people will in the end be glad that the foremost American man of letters speaks of the Buchanan of our day as it is right to speak.

Always yours,

T. R.

When will you visit us?

Skirdin was an ex-cavalry soldier, a friend made at Fort Bowie, Arizona, in 1893.   I had a deep regard for him.   Much of him went into the Virginian, about whom I had written *Emily* and *Balaam and Pedro* before I met Skirdin, who reminded me of my own creation.

The sonnet to which he refers was written the day Verdun began, and directly upon Wilson's revocation of the promises to push preparedness which he had made to Garrison, his Secretary of War.  Garrison resigned.  With Lane, of the Interior, he was far above the level of that cabinet.  His place was filled by a pacifist.  The sonnet expressed what I felt then, and what I should always feel in like circumstances.  But may we be preserved from living any more in times like those!  Times when our attitude had brought upon us the derision of Germany and the scorn of the Allies, while Europe rocked to its foundations.

Oyster Bay,<br>Long Island, N. Y.<br>June 29th, 1916.

DEAR DAN:—

Who is Gustavus Ohlinger?  That's a powerful little book! I hope he is a real person, but I am just as much content if he is you under another name.  By the way, was not the original Wister a German?

I am inclined to assume that you liked my letter to the Progressive National Committee.

Faithfully yours,<br>THEODORE ROOSEVELT.

P. S.:  Since writing the above your letter of the 27th has come —and my assumption was correct!  I *very* much like your letter, naturally.  I expect the Evening Post to play the cur's part; but I have been disappointed in the New Republic.

Gustavus Ohlinger's book, *Their True Faith and Allegiance,* is a carefully documented and compact exposure of Berlin's intentions toward the United States, and of "hyphenated Americans" living here, ostensibly naturalized, but with their hearts back in Berlin, ready at its beck and call.  It is a very awkward little book for the various white-washers of Berlin, who have been writing their big books to deceive happy-go-lucky readers.  These white-washers must hope fervently that the little book is buried and forgotten.  I cannot let it pass without two or three quotations from it.

During our Spanish War: "American policy in Cuba has been characterized by violence and hypocrisy, and has not a single redeeming feature." *Vossische Zeitung.*  April 22, 1898.

"To expel Satan by Beelzebub can hardly be described as a result of genuine philanthropy." *Kolnische Zeitung.*   April 23.

"You will desire to know how the hostilities will be brought about.   My army of spies scattered over Great Britain and France, as it is over North and South America as well as all parts of the world where German interests may come into clash with a foreign power, will take good care of that. . . .

"Even now I rule supreme in the United States, where almost one half of the population is either German or of German descent, and where three million voters do my bidding at the Presidential elections. . . ."   The Kaiser to his people.   Potsdam, June, 1908.

"War is the most august and sacred of human activities . . . Still and deep in the German heart must the joy in war and the longing for war endure."   *The Youth of Germany,* January 25, 1913.

"Whoever cannot prevail upon himself to approve from the bottom of his heart the sinking of the *Lusitania*—whoever cannot conquer his sense of the gigantic cruelty to unnumbered perfectly innocent victims . . . and give himself up to honest delight at this victorious exploit of German power—him we judge to be no true German."   Pastor Baumgarten in an address on The Sermon on the Mount, *German Talks in Time of Stress,* No. 24, page 7, 1914–15.

Does the reader find it as hard to understand as I do that when you met a pacifist in those years he was almost invariably pro-German?

That is enough, I think.   I could give much more like it. What the Kaiser has said since he descended from his throne so speedily is of no importance.   What he could have said while on the throne, would have held up Austria and prevented the war; and the flesh of those three hundred and forty thousand would not have been spattered over the hills and valleys of Verdun; nor would Berlin since that time have felt obliged so adroitly and successfully to dodge the debt which it promised at Versailles to pay.   That no one could pay the whole of so monstrous a reparation is neither here nor there; nor that the Berlin of to-day seems to be a better disposed Berlin.   My point is, to put on their guard, so far as I can by these reminders, the American readers for whose eyes certain American writers are attempting to exculpate Prussia through distortions and suppressions of the facts as they were in July, 1914.   These facts, officially authentic and now accessible to any reader, lay the guilt heavily on Berchtold, with Berlin second, and Petersburg last.   Were there an eternal fitness of things, save in the minds of just men, Berchtold should have received an international hanging.   Eternal fitness has descended insufficiently on the Kaiser, and on the hapless Czar more than enough; though Russia is well rid of the Romanoffs.

Roosevelt writes the next letter in his own hand:

SAGAMORE HILL

Aug. 24th, 1916.

Dear Dan:—

My Maine speech has been sent out; it's a fighting speech; I hope you'll like it.   I don't make another speech for a month; then I'll try to work in your trilogy, especially no. 3.

Can't you sometime get down here for a night?

Have just been re-reading Philosophy 4.   *You* may think it a skit.   *I* regard it as containing a deep and subtle moral.

Ever yours,

T. R.

The speech to which he refers in the next letter bore the title, "Words and Deeds," and was delivered September 30, at a place with a most appropriate name for such a speech—Battle Creek. I choose a passage or two from it:

"The supporters of Mr. Wilson say that the American people should vote for him because he has kept us out of war. . . . Neither Washington nor Lincoln kept us out of war. . . .   They abhorred war. . . .   But they possessed the stern valor of patriotism which bade them put duty first; not safety first. . . .

"President Wilson . . . had spoken much of the 'New Freedom.' . . .   This has meant freedom for the representatives of any foreign power to murder American men, and outrage American women unchecked by the President. . . .

"The other day, discussing his refusal to recognize Huerta, President Wilson said . . . he would refuse to recognize any— 'title based upon intrigue and assassination.' . . . In February, 1914, at the very time he was refusing to recognize Huerta in Mexico, President Wilson recognized Colonel Benavides in Peru. . . . The Government of Benavides was founded on assassination. . . . Benavides led the garrison troops against the President's palace, imprisoned the President and assassinated the Minister of War. . . ."

It was words like these which brought back to Roosevelt whatever of the American heart he had lost in 1912, and caused citizens of eminence like Dr. Shattuck to say they had considered him then the most dangerous influence in the country but that now they were ready to vote for him to-morrow.

METROPOLITAN
432 Fourth Avenue, New York.

Office of
Theodore Roosevelt

September 28, 1916.

DEAR DAN:—

I do wish I could see you. I am sending you a badly printed little book containing my speeches prior to the Convention; in it I have pasted my Lewiston and Battle Creek speeches. I just wish you to see that I have kept the faith.

Are you never coming out here to Sagamore Hill to spend a night or a week-end with us? There are so many things I would like to talk over with you. Your attitude during the last few years, both to me personally and especially as regards the politics of this country, has been a very great comfort. This is especially so in view of the complete breakdown of the men who ought to be our intellectual leaders. As you said in your last letter to me, not only the Evening Post but the New Republic has played a cur's part. In the case of the New Republic, I feel a genuine indignation, for Herbert Croly is sinning against the light like Walter Weil and Lippman, who know me well and who know the facts well; and when they deliberately misrepresent the facts, they are guilty of grave misconduct.

Always yours,
THEODORE ROOSEVELT.

The poem to which he refers below, was written as a contribution to a Boston war-time periodical, edited by Arlo Bates in connection with a war-time bazaar.   In my letter I had told him—giving examples by way of evidence—that the great American mass doesn't know a good thing from a bad one.

METROPOLITAN

432 Fourth Avenue, New York.

Office of
Theodore Roosevelt

October 30th, 1916.

DEAR DAN:—

Naturally I liked your letter.   That's a capital poem, "Decoration Day"!   When is it to be published?

I am sorry to say that I entirely agree with you as to the fact that America tends to accept indiscriminately dross and gold in every department of existence.   Think of the fact that respectable men are absolutely indifferent to Wilson's lying on every subject, and contradicting himself on every issue!   The worse feature of it is that the so-called intellectuals—such as President Eliot, the editors of the New Republic, the Springfield Republican, the Atlantic Monthly, and The Evening Post, are the men who have given Wilson his strength, and are largely responsible for those weaknesses in Hughes which make us support him, not as the proper President for this crisis, but as infinitely better than Wilson.

I am supporting Hughes with all my heart.   I hope he will be elected.   If he is not, it will be because under some malign inspiration or advice, he tried to shirk the big issues, and paid too much consideration to the support of the Ridders, Brands and Jeremiah O'Learys.   I am sure he will do nothing improper for them; but how I wish he would openly state the things which he assures me that he feels!

I still think we shall elect Hughes, because I believe that the American people are waking up to Wilson; and if we can concentrate their attention on Wilson, we can beat him.

By the way, the British brother is a pretty woodenheaded personage; thank the Lord he is not my brother!   The French thoroughly understood my book, "Fear God and Take Your

Own Part." The British, with acute perception, stated it was an electioneering document!

With the heartiest good wishes, I am,

Faithfully yours,

THEODORE ROOSEVELT.

METROPOLITAN
432 Fourth Avenue, New York.

Office of
Theodore Roosevelt

Nov. 3rd, 1916.

DEAR DAN:—

I am very sorry that I have to refuse the requst of Mrs. Rostand; but it is out of the question for me to go to any of these bazaars. If I went to one I would have to go to hundreds. The only exception that I ever made was in the case of my own daughter Ethel who had herself served at the front with Dick.

With real regret, I am,

Always yours,

THEODORE ROOSEVELT.

P. S. Your Colliers' article is by all odds the best thing written or spoken in this campaign.

But my wise old friend Dr. Fred Shattuck would not have agreed with the over-enthusiastic postscript which Roosevelt added in his own hand. I had spent part of the summer in gathering my facts for that article. These covered the chief steps in both domestic and foreign policy which Wilson had taken during his first term. They were all facts, and they made a pattern. The pattern showed that the President's steps continually cancelled each other, like plus and minus quantities in equations, now a step north, now a step south, now a step forward, now a step back; and that this process, whether you called it "watchful waiting" or "too proud to fight," had accomplished little but clipping the American eagle's wings and causing disagreeable eggs to be thrown at Old Glory. And that if you always dropped any friend who differed from you, you should not talk so much about being humane and just.

Dr. Shattuck said: "That's all true.   But it's too venomous. That tone never persuades anybody."

He was right enough.   We were all venomous by then.   We had winced too long at what other nations were saying of us. And our feelings in the President's favor and against him can be measured by a single illustration.

"I consider Wilson next to Christ," said one Bostonian to another.

"So was Judas Iscariot," said the other.

During those days of 1916 and 1917, I saw Roosevelt, now in New York, again at Sagamore Hill.   The War made the theme to which we perpetually came back—as did every one else.   Many themes, hundreds of topics, come up for talk or reference in usual times, whether in the street, the office, or at the dinner table.   It is a strange experience at the moment and a strange one upon which to look back—a deep breath in human history—when millions meet in the world every day, and have one single thought in common, one mental and emotional tie, that draws them from thinking or speaking much about anything else.

At Sagamore Hill we did get away from it for a little while sometimes.   I remember our disgust when the policy of the Philippines and all the good done there by Cameron Forbes was uprooted by Wilson, and the Jones act, and a deserving Democrat sent to undo the work of Forbes.   It was founded on that Wilsonic doctrine that self government is what every race on earth is bound to reach in the end, and that therefore you should set it up everywhere as a goal at the start.

"My dear Dan," said Roosevelt, "we are all unquestionably members of the human race, just as much at the North Pole as at the Equator.   And trees are all trees, wherever they grow.   But I am prepared to assert that you can give an apple-tree all the time you want and it wants, and it will not produce oranges."

They were punctual almost to the minute at Sagamore Hill, and I don't believe I was two minutes late one morning when

I came down to breakfast, and found them already at table. Something that Congress had proposed, or had done the day before had put me in a rage, because it betokened perfect disregard or perfect ignorance of invariable previous experience everywhere. And so, immediately upon bidding them good morning, and before I was in my chair, I said:

"Every age-old world-old truth which has been as thoroughly established for centuries as the multiplication table, should be proclaimed aloud over the whole United States once every day!"

Roosevelt clashed his teeth. "Once every hour!" was all he said. And we left it at that, and went on with breakfast. But later I made some remarks of a flavor that he never liked. You could always tell when his optimism was feeling uncomfortable.

"Of course," I said, "in a Democracy, a man can do nothing unless the people are behind him."

I saw his eye-glasses fixed on me.

"Equally," I continued, "the people can do nothing unless they've a man to get behind."

"Yesss." It was very short. And rather dangerous—

"And just now they've got behind a dictionary."

This pleased him very much for a moment.

"You know," I went on, "what they say the chaplain of our United States Senate has taken to praying every morning? 'God bless the Senate. God save the people.'"

"My dear Dan, that is very funny, of course. And I will admit that in a country as big as ours it takes a long while for the people to find out anything. But once they do find it out, they act right because their emotions are right, and because self government will educate them much quicker than it's likely to educate the Filipinos."

"Yes,—and meanwhile, before they find a thing out, all sorts of damage can be done. Also, it takes a great deal longer to educate a voter than to beget one."

"This is a Democracy," he repeated, "and you mustn't be of those who always see the worst of it, instead of trying to make the best of it. It's a Democracy, it can't be anything else, and we wouldn't have it anything else. That's all very well about your chaplain and the Senate, but the people we elect are merely a piece of ourselves who elect them. You can't expect them to be superior to the average. A stream cannot rise higher than its source."

"No. But it can sink a great deal lower," is what I lacked the wit to reply. That remark about the stream seemed to me unanswerable at the time, and I shall never know what he would have said to the retort I missed making.

The President's declaration of war on April 6, 1917, was an example of the fine eloquence to which he could rise—the same to which he rose in his Liberty Loan speech in the Armory at Baltimore, April 6, 1918:

> Germany has once more said that force, and force alone, shall decide. . . . There is, therefore, but one response possible from us: Force, force to the utmost, force without stint or limit, the righteous and triumphant force which shall make right the law of the world and cast every selfish dominion down in the dust.

It reads better than Roosevelt's less polished rhetoric, but it reads cold; Roosevelt's reads hot, even to-day. And, if the reader can reconcile it with the remark that the United States was not concerned with the aims of those fighting in Europe, and with his remark that there must be "peace without victory"— I am as unable to do this, as to ascribe Wilson's course to patience. He remains inexplicable.

METROPOLITAN
432 Fourth Avenue, New York.

Office of
Theodore Roosevelt

April 29th, 1917.

DEAR DAN:—

I've put down Captain Terrell's name and I will use him, if I possibly can. Lord, how I wish the Administration would let me raise that division!

Faithfully yours,
T. R.

The letter upon which he comments below, came from this San Antonio friend of mine, who had begged me for a word to Roosevelt in his favor. He was the father of grown sons who fought as Roosevelt's four sons fought, and he wished to fight along with them, like Roosevelt.

METROPOLITAN<br>432 Fourth Avenue, New York.

Office of
Theodore Roosevelt

May 10th, 1917.

DEAR DAN:—

That's really a touching letter. I wish there was a chance of my going with a division, but this Administration is playing the dirtiest and smallest politics, and I don't think they have the slightest intention of letting me go. Wilson feels tepidly hostile to Germany, but he feels a far more active hostility toward Wood and myself. His sole purpose is to serve his own selfish ends. No doubt he would do something that was useful to the country, if he were *sure* it would help him; but his inveterate habit is not to *do* the thing that is useful, but by lofty phrases and sentences to make believe that he is doing it, so as to persuade good puzzle-headed people that he *is* doing it.

Faithfully yours,<br>THEODORE ROOSEVELT.

That year of 1917 and the next, afford a reassuring illustration of Roosevelt's faith in the people acting right once they find out. When the United States were buying horses in the Middle West in 1917, some of the owners directly they learned who the would-be purchaser was, decided to sell them, sometimes with language of violent hostility. In Wyoming that summer, there were mothers declaring that they would hide their sons in the rocks and caves of the mountains, so that the draft could never find them. The Secret Service rounded up fifty sellers of draft exemptions in New York to men endeavoring to escape the draft. Five thousand dollars was sometimes paid for these exemptions. That was 1917.

In this perfectly natural and perfectly discreditable exhibition of human nature, neither the Mississippi Valley nor any other part of our country was in spirit better or worse than could be seen in France and in England.   The peasants of Provence were more than indifferent, they were hostile, to serving their country, and if you look at *Punch* during the early time of the war, you will find satiric allusions to *slackers,* and pictures representing sturdy young men watching and playing football, instead of going to the defense of England.   And so, when our British friends would say at times, very lightly, in their admirable manner of making themselves detestable, "You were a bit late in coming into the war, weren't you?" it was my way always to acknowledge and never to defend it; I thought it, then and now, indefensible. But I was apt to add, "We were a bit further off, you know, than your football slackers, weren't we?" hoping that they found me as unpleasant as I found them.

A friend of mine, an American lady, was in London during those times.   She had taken a house, and through this she made a discovery which accounts for a number of things.   Remarks that her servants dropped now and then, left her at a loss.   It was everybody's duty to help England.   Had not Canada and Australia and all the other colonies helped England?   Of course they had, said the lady.   But her assent seemed to leave something in the air, until one day this materialized.   It was hoped that America would come in soon.   Why was she so long? Canada had been in ever so long now.   Then at last it dawned on her.

"Do you think we're a part of the British Empire?"

"Why yes, madam.   Are you not?"

These were unlettered British.

How may it be among the British lettered?   Behind the fact of our Independence does our having belonged to them in 1775 still stalk in their minds invisible, and affect to some extent their special attitude toward us?   The ghost of Bonaparte unquestionably haunts their objection to a Channel tunnel, just as the Ghost of George III, harmless, dull old king, still

walks in the American mind.    That poor ghost is the best stage
property which our school histories trot out, even to-day, to
scare the young and teach them hate of England.    This persistent infantility delays our growing up.

I had seen the tide which had been so strong against Roosevelt among so many of my acquaintances in Philadelphia sweep
back to him in 1916.    At a dinner given by Robins at the
Philadelphia club, Roosevelt had been welcomed and surrounded.    The very men who had preserved silence about him
when I was present, or whose denunciations of him I had overheard, now grasped his hand, leaned towards him at table to
catch every word that he said.    This tide was flowing stronger
than ever by 1918.    His gallant, ceaseless call to the honor and
faith of the nation in spoken and printed word, a voice lifted at
the very first and unchanged to the very last, was contrasted
with the voice from the White House.    No matter what tonic
syllables about "force, force to the utmost" this voice was now
dropping into the people's mind, how could they undo the enerva-
tion of the past, the "watchful waiting" dose by which the nation's conscience and manhood had been chloroformed?    And
so Roosevelt, whatever his failings might have been, towered
above Wilson, whatever his virtues might be.    In 1918, Roosevelt was the moral leader of the United States.

But in that frozen Winter, when coal was doled out only where
need was desperate, and pipes burst, and people were driven
from their houses to wherever they could find warmth and lodging, the shadow that Brazil had left upon the strength of Roosevelt deepened.    It is present in a few lines that he wrote me on
January 23 in answer to some suggestion I had made:

"I agree with that letter but I think I have got on hand at present all that I can take charge of.    I believe that Wilson is even
more vulnerable at other points . . . is now appearing to the
American people much more nearly as he is, than heretofore has
been the case."

Again the shadow darkens his reply to a Philadelphian who had asked him to come over and assist in the organization of a regiment composed of Philadelphians without distinction as to religious belief, but to be known to the world at large as the Fighting Quakers. It recalled the Rough Riders. Nothing would have brought him more enthusiastically once; but no longer.

"The demands upon me," he writes January 30, "for speeches have become so numerous, and indeed the demands upon me for every kind of service and action have become so heavy that it is a physical impossibility for me to undertake another engagement at this time. . . ."

In five days he was in a hospital. Then in three days we heard that he had died. Early in March he came out. But illness had not stopped him. He came out with a speech written and ready to deliver in Portland.

I soon asked if I might come to see him, and I went. The weather was dull, the air penetrating, the ground half white, half mud, and entirely soft and cold. I do not recall any reference to his illness or any change in his cheerfulness; I do recall his appearance, especially when he was not animated by what you were saying or what he was saying. Before my visit was over, he had to start for Portland. I remember the open hall door, the car at the steps, the hearty hand shake with the bidding to come soon again. He was all bundled up in an ulster, wore his wide soft black hat; and there stood Mrs. Roosevelt, quietly watching to see that he did not go away insufficiently prepared against the northern climate. I think that he may have hoped to escape her vigilance. He failed to do so.

"This is the people's war," he told them at Portland, "if we are men and not children . . . we will look facts in the face, however ugly they may be . . . we must face the fact of our shameful unpreparedness . . . we drifted into war unarmed and helpless. . . . Although over a year has passed, we are still in a military sense impotent to render real aid. . . ."

In the energy of all that speech, and in much else of his patri-

otic service then, even after the hospital, there is no shadow.
It falls in one single word across a few lines he wrote in reply to
some request of mine on April 26.

"I will make the effort at once.   Now for Heaven's sake do
give me the chance of seeing you. . . ."

Effort.   He never used to talk about effort.   More ominous
was a sign I saw in Philadelphia.   He had come to lunch with
Robins.   William Sproul, Governor of the State, was there.
After lunch, several of us went to Chester in the governor's car.
On the way, we were talking about matters wholly interesting
to Roosevelt.   As the conversation went on, we noticed his
head bent forward, and his eyes closed.   He was asleep.

On June 26th, the little note is in his own hand, written at
Sagamore Hill:

When your telegram came we were leaving for the west; and
we couldn't find out where your "office" was.

Now; we are very anxious to see you; we will be home every
*night;* on the 4th of July I shall be away for the *day,* and also
for one *day* the following week.

Come down for a night or a week; we'll hold a commination
service over Wilson, and curse him out of the book of Ernulphus
and with the Greater and the Lesser anathema.

Ever,

T. R.

No sign of effort there.   He thought himself better.   And all
people were feeling better on June 26.   The sky had changed.
Faint light came across the water to us from Château-Thierry
on June 4, and from Bouresches; and from Belleau Wood that
very day the 26.   Soon, as I travelled across Montana in the
North Coast Limited, the light from across the water was growing; but with it, as the train stopped somewhere, came the news
that Quentin was dead.   The day after that, the sun began to
rise at Villers-Cotterêts, where Americans were pressing forward in a tempest of rain.

When the Middle West, when America, came wholly out of
the chloroform, Europe found that we knew how to be awake,

although we have helped her to forget this by being too business-like since that heroic day.  But the debts are a pretext.  No generosity from us could change the fact that the future is giving our civilization the floor.  How should a speaker who has had the floor for a thousand years keep silent gracefully?  The turn is ours, and it, too, will end.


## XXX.

In October I went to Sagamore Hill.  During that stay no other visitor was there, not many came to call, and I had my hosts to myself more than ever before.  Autumn had come to one of those pauses when few leaves are yet fallen and woods still glow with their colors.  Over their tops the bay beyond was as quiet as the trees, a pale level of blue.  Outside this serenity the war was rushing to its close; Theodore, Kermit, and Archie were with their soldiers, Quentin lay in the earth of Tardenois.

Our talks in the house often turned upon the memories that we shared, and always came back to the latest news from the Somme, the Aisne, and the Meuse.  There the Allies were driving the Germans eastward.  Roosevelt would work at a speech part of the time, and stop for a holiday with Mrs. Roosevelt and me.  This was the life indoors.

Outdoors, we three took leisurely walks over the fields and through the woods.  Once or twice we went down a path to the shore.  There the two would get into a boat and row off together, after telling me how to find a new way, or a shorter way, back to Sagamore Hill.  I remember watching the small boat moving outward with them into the placid bay, shining in warm sunlight.  I followed it for a little while, and an overmastering sadness rose suddenly in me.  I turned and took the path away from the water.

At table sometimes, and often in the great room, he would fall from animation into silence.  Once he came out of his silence and said:

THE LONG, LONG TRAIL.   BY J. N. DARLING

"When I went to South America, I had one Captain's job left in me.   Now I am good only for a Major's."

And upon another occasion, without reference to what we had been saying:

"It doesn't matter what the rest is going to be.   I have had fun the whole time."

Once, when the latest news had set us discussing the possible end of the war any day, as well the chance of its lasting into the next spring, and the parleyings between the President and Max of Baden, now at the head of the German Government, this step on Wilson's part aroused us both.   He was ignoring the Allies and speaking to Germany over their heads.   Suddenly Roosevelt's entire vivacity, the old fire, returned.   He sprang to his feet like a boy, stood with his arm flung out, and exclaimed:

"Oh—don't—let's—talk about him—anymore to-day—at all!"

While we were talking another time about our own politics after the war, Mrs. Roosevelt said:

"If we should ever go back to the White House—which heaven forbid! . . ."

One evening he brought in his speech finished.   He was to deliver it in a few days, and now proposed that we go over it. As was his way always, he weighed each comment quickly, and either accepted it with the directness of a young beginner, or gave his reasons for rejecting it.   While we discussed this last speech that he was ever to make, his face, buoyant no longer, battered with conflict, brave to the end, grew eager over the cause he had always served, the cause of his country, the land of his faith and his passion.   I listened as he dwelt upon the points he intended to drive home in Carnegie Hall.   That evening remains with me; he talking, Mrs. Roosevelt sitting near us with her work.   Never again were we to pass an evening together.   The next day my visit was over.

During some hours preceding my departure, he was occupied, and so was she.   Left to myself, I walked up and down outside the windows of the great room where he was sitting, and made up some verses about him.   Then I went in, wrote out a fair copy on note-paper, sealed it, gave it to her, and asked her to let him find it on the morning when he should be sixty.   This was two days off.   I have his letter about these verses; short, in his own hand, and of great sadness.

They stood at their hall door as I drove off, stood watching, after their words bidding me to come again soon, she quiet beside him, he waving his hand; Quentin's father and mother, carrying on.   The car moved from the steps; they passed from sight.   At the turn of the drive they came into view again for a final moment.   There the two stood, still watching, as I went away.

When I came next to Sagamore Hill, she was carrying on alone.

## EPILOGUE: TO EDITH KAROW ROOSEVELT

Always in the days when he was here and the world at so high a pitch that each morning's news, whether of ourselves or of other nations, touched the limits of significance, my first thought would be, What will he say about this? Twelve years are gone since his voice ceased, yet so deep in me had this looking to him rooted itself, that still upon some sudden news of moment the thought springs out, What will he say? before I can remember that he is silent. More than once while these pages beneath which *finis* is now to stand were being written, this old question flashed within me. I shall not try to guess what he would say of them. But you? Should you find this portrait of him worthy a place upon the walls of your memory, I shall count that enough.

### FINIS